HOLDING THE FORT

BOOK TWO

THE INFILTRATION

HOLDING THE FORT

BOOK TWO

THE
INFILTRATION

RYAN PEEK

This is a work of fiction. Names, characters, places, and incidents either are the product of the author's imagination or are used fictitiously. Any resemblance to actual persons, living or dead, events, or locales is entirely coincidental.

Copyright © 2022 by Ryan Peek

All rights reserved. No part of this book may be reproduced or used in any manner without written permission of the copyright owner except for the use of quotations in a book review. For more information, address: ryan@ryanpeek.com

Published by Pebbyville Press

First Edition

Book cover and interior design by Damonza

Blackwoods map art by Bogart Strawn

ISBN 978-1-7357060-3-0 (hardcover)

ISBN 978-1-7357060-4-7 (paperback)

ISBN 978-1-7357060-5-4 (ebook)

Library of Congress Control Number: 2022916127

www.ryanpeek.com

In the final analysis, the machines had learned too much from us.

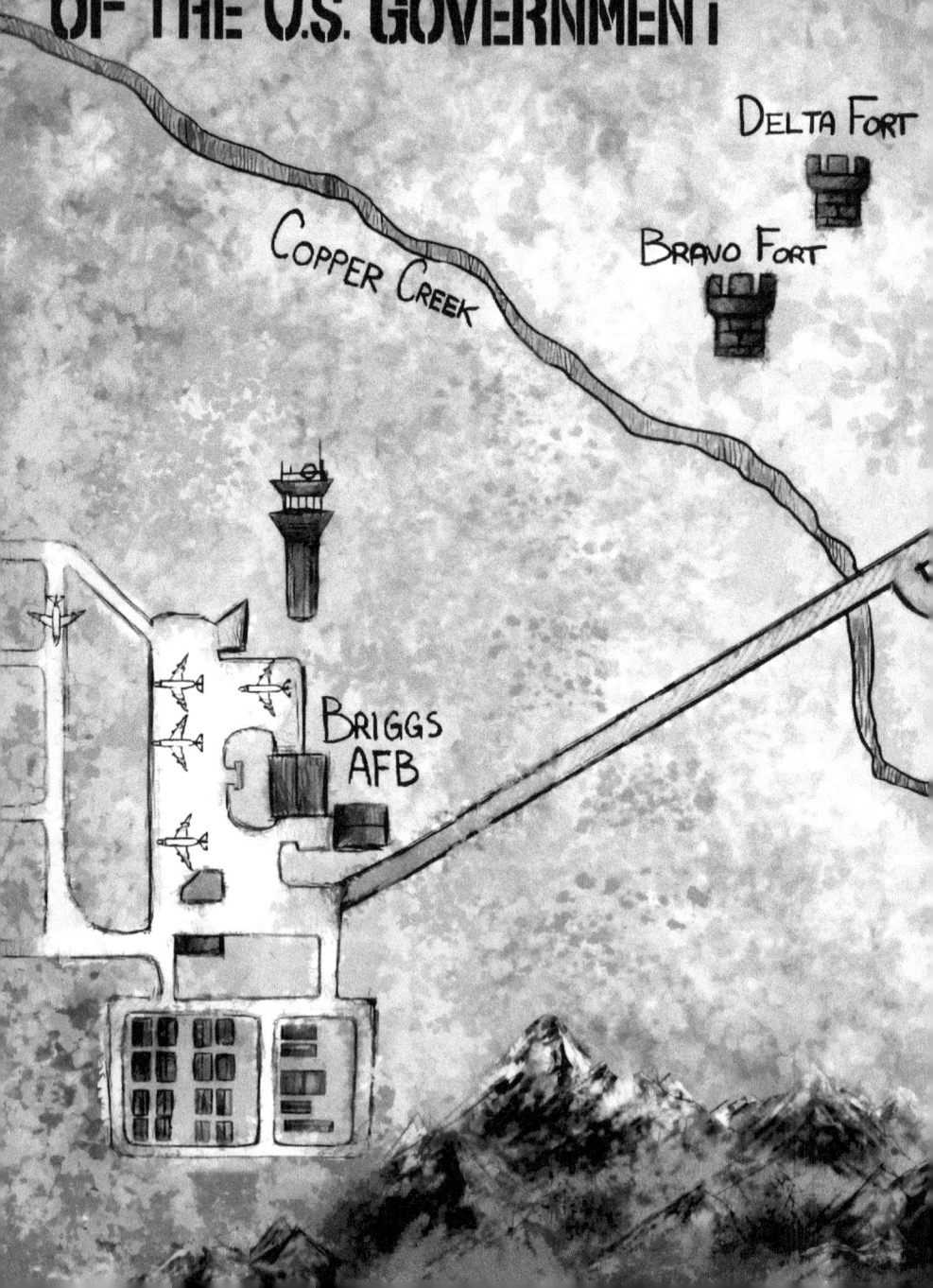

CHAPTER 1

THE MEETING

ETHAN ENTERED JUDY'S Diner a few minutes before two o'clock. The lunch crowd was long gone, and the dinner crowd wouldn't be due for several hours. He had picked that time for a reason. What he needed to talk about with the rest of Team Blackwoods demanded absolute secrecy.

Ethan took a seat in the far corner of the restaurant and waited. Soon enough, Annika, Caleb, Austin, and Glenn arrived and made their way to the table in the back. Everyone sat down and huddled up. They had just saved Blackwoods, and maybe the entire world, but they somehow felt like outlaws. The things they knew were so Top-Secret, if anyone found out, nothing would ever be the same. Their eyes darted around the room anxiously, looking for anyone, paranoid that someone might overhear them.

"We're alone," Ethan said, trying to reassure the group, and himself.

Just then, seemingly out of nowhere, Judy swooped in carrying a tray of ice waters. Everyone flinched in surprise. She began dishing out the glasses of water quickly, like a poker dealer tossing cards. "Sorry to sneak up on you," she said. "You got my undivided attention. You guys are my only table."

"No, no…We weren't s-s-surprised," Caleb said with a nervous stutter.

"So, what can I get you folks?" Judy asked.

"Just five Cherry Cokes," Austin said.

"You guys must've won your game. Congratulations. Five Cherry Cokes it is." Then Judy paused and took a closer look at each member of the group. "Hmm…Now you guys don't *normally* play together, do you?" she asked with an eyebrow raised curiously.

There was no way in the world Judy could've possibly known about the circumstances that'd brought their team together, but, as anxious as they were now, her tone seemed strangely accusing. It was enough to put them on edge.

"Right. This is a new team," Ethan admitted quickly.

"Yep…New day, new team, new friends," Caleb sputtered, then put his arms around Glenn and Austin next to him and squeezed them in a hug.

"Well, change is good," Judy said. "Not fair for the others, though…No team's ever gonna beat the five of you," she said with a smile.

"Thanks," Ethan said, returning her smile. Then his smile evaporated and a more serious look overcame him. "We can't afford to ever lose again."

Judy winked playfully. "With soldiers like you guys around, I feel safer already. Be back with those Cherry Cokes."

Ethan and the others exchanged awkward glances, feeling the irony of the moment. Judy soon came back with the carbonated refreshments. She plopped them down in front of the group.

"You folks wanna run a tab?"

"Sure," Ethan said. "We might be here a while."

"No problem, sweetie."

Just then, a group of Air Force captains in full uniform entered the diner and made their way to a table beside them. One of them caught Ethan's eye and nodded at him. Ethan nodded back politely, but let out a frustrated sigh as soon it was safe to do so.

"Judy, is the arcade busy?" Ethan asked.

"Nope. Not a soul in there."

"Great," Ethan said, then turned to the group. "Feel like video games?" he asked while pointing with his eyes to the captains at the adjacent table.

"Absolutely," Annika said.

Ethan and the group took their drinks to the back room of the diner that served as a video arcade. The peppy noises of video games in demonstration mode filled the air. They sat at the only table in the room. Finally, they were alone.

"It's June fourth." Glenn checked his wristwatch. "We have eight days, three hours, and about forty-five minutes before the fatal error…whatever that is."

"We have to warn them, the generals at the base," Annika said with urgency in her voice. "We have to warn them now."

"No, we have to figure out what the fatal error is first," Caleb said. "If we warn them now, what good will that do? They don't know what their error is because it hasn't happened yet."

"Yeah, they could make the error all over again," Austin said. "Only this time it'd be worse. They'd keep us out of the loop. Treat us like kids. Shut down that access elevator to the research facility. They'd give us no chance to ever execute Project Mulligan again."

"Right. They'd tighten security like a vise," Glenn agreed.

"So, we don't warn them?" Annika asked, annoyed.

"Of course we warn them," Ethan said, reassuring Annika. "But it would help if we knew a few things about what we're up against first, just in case."

"Yeah, but how?" Annika asked.

"That Skulley in the fort," Caleb said with an eager smile.

"No, no, no," Annika raised her voice. "Playing God with that awful machine can't be our first choice. You'd be more likely to speed up the fatal error."

"I could figure it out," Caleb said. "I wouldn't do anything until I was sure."

"*Really?* How could you possibly be sure about technology from another planet?"

"Computers are computers…And I can figure out computers."

"So help me, Caleb, I will call the base myself and tell them everything if you go anywhere near that Skulley," Annika snapped. "There's gotta be a better way."

"There is a better way," Ethan said.

Caleb stared curiously at Ethan. "Like what?"

Ethan took a deep breath and paused for a moment. "We don't have a basement in our house, at least we're not supposed to…yet I found a keypad under the thermostat, just like the one in your house, the one that gets you into your sub-basement."

"Seriously?" Caleb asked in awe. "But I guess that makes sense now, since your dad is a chief engineer like mine." He paused in thought. "So how does that help us?"

"*Your* dad told you about his sub-basement office, even gave you the password. *My* dad didn't…never even told me his real job at the base."

"Yeah, but how does that help us now?" Glenn asked.

"Because I know he's gotta be hiding some pretty important stuff down there."

Caleb cracked a mischievous smile. "Are you thinking what I'm thinking?"

Ethan nodded. "Yeah…You can break that password, right?"

"You bet I can."

"Well, it's crazy…but it's better than reviving that Skulley," Annika said.

"Hey, take a look," Glenn whispered, nodding at the entrance to the arcade room.

It was Zeke and Jeremiah. The brothers nodded, smiled, and uttered a casual, "What's up, guys?" to the group as they walked past them and made their way to their favorite arcade game.

Everyone stared at the Mitchell brothers in stunned silence. It was a very strange experience for Ethan and the others to be watching them. The brothers were alive thanks to the efforts of the group, but they would never know that. Not that anyone especially craved the credit, but it sure made them feel more isolated from the rest of the town. They desperately wanted to tell Zeke and Jeremiah what had happened, though they knew they couldn't. Crazy as their story was, the Mitchell brothers would inform their brigadier general father, if for nothing else but a good laugh. But General Mitchell wouldn't find it funny, and security would be tightened before Ethan and the others could even figure out their next move.

There was no way they could tell them, or anybody, anything. That group of five, it seemed, would be the only ones in the world to know the amazing and frightening truth. It was a lonely feeling. And the video game the Mitchell brothers had decided to play certainly didn't help matters. It was a stand-up shooting game, where two guns are mounted on a platform facing a video screen. The enemy they were fighting…*robots*. The irony almost made them sick.

The Mitchell brothers' taut biceps flexed in their T-shirts as they fired their machine guns at the screen, destroying hordes of oncoming robots. "Get 'em, Zeke!" Jeremiah yelled. "Get the ones on the right!"

"I am!" Zeke shouted back. "You just take care of that left side!"

The blaring sounds of gunfire from the video game filled the room. It also filled the group's stomachs with an intense uneasiness. It was a visceral reaction to the sounds of combat that soldiers returning home from war experience. It was post-traumatic stress. Everyone's hands were sweaty, and their throats were tightly worked into knots.

"They're coming, they're coming!" Zeke shouted with such intensity it was like he was actually trapped inside the video game. "I'm going down!" he said, firing his weapon madly.

"Me too!" Jeremiah yelled back. "There's too many of them!"

Annika couldn't take the tension any longer. She dealt with the mounting stress the best way she knew how: She jumped up from the table and dashed over to the video game.

"Just get out of the way!" Annika shouted in frustration as she nudged Zeke aside and grabbed his gun. "Ethan, get over here!"

Ethan hustled over to the game. "Sorry," he said to Jeremiah before taking his gun.

The Mitchell brothers were stunned and could only watch

as Ethan and Annika began blasting away at the machines on the screen.

"You just let him take your gun?" Zeke asked Jeremiah in surprise.

"Well, you just let *her* take *yours*," Jeremiah snapped back.

The Mitchell brothers' eyes slowly widened in astonishment as they witnessed Ethan and Annika's incredible performance. Animated robots were being blown to bits before they could even get close to them. The scout and the sniper's tactics looked choreographed and expertly planned, though neither spoke a word to the other. It was as if they were reading each other's minds. A perfect combat unit, the deadliest of duos.

"They're doing pretty good, though," Zeke said, cracking a big smile.

"Better than we were," Jeremiah laughed.

"The trick is to spot them from long distance, pick them off before they get too close," Annika said. "Look for the light shining off their metal heads, gives 'em away…find those red eyes and put a laser right between them."

The Mitchell brothers looked confused. "But those robots' eyes are blue," Zeke said. "And you're not shooting a laser gun."

Annika shook her head, shrugged. "Red, blue. Laser gun, machine gun…whatever."

After a few more seconds of intense fighting, an automated voice in the video game made the announcement: "Level Cleared." Ethan and Annika stepped back from the video game and high-fived each other. Then they gave the controls back to Jeremiah and Zeke.

"You two were amazing," Zeke said, mouth agape in shock.

"That was unreal. You totally saved our lives," Jeremiah added.

Annika flashed a wry smile. "Oh, yeah…You guys have *no* idea."

Ethan shot Annika a warning look. "Thanks for letting us play," he said humbly. Then he ushered Annika away from the Mitchell brothers and back to their table before she could say anything else.

"Tomorrow, after class," Ethan said quietly to the others. "Meet at Bravo Fort…No one will bother us there."

CHAPTER 2

AN EVENING OF CURIOSITIES

ETHAN HAD BARELY stuck the fork into his first bite of meat loaf when his mom asked the dreaded question to her husband: "How was your day, honey?" Ethan slowly set his fork down and awaited the reply with the enthusiasm of a dental patient awaiting the drill.

"Pretty good. I'm almost finished fixing the vacuums," Ethan's father responded with a smile, though his smile seemed more shifty than sincere to Ethan upon witnessing it this time around.

It was hard for Ethan to sit there and listen to the lies again, even if his dad thought he was doing it for his son's safety. The last time the fibs flew, it did no good. The fatal error was still committed, and the machines were unleashed. Ethan had a hunch it was going to happen all over again. Annika was right; the generals needed to be warned before it was too late. But Ethan also knew there was a chance they could do everything in their power, warn all the right people as quickly as possible, and still be doomed to repeat the past. If that happened, they had to be ready. They desperately needed to figure out what the fatal error was. Ethan's appetite vanished completely as he thought about the secret room that lay hidden in his house, and what that room might contain. He laid his fork across the remainder of his meat loaf in surrender.

"I'm not hungry," Ethan said. "I'm gonna go to my room."

"Are you feeling okay?" his mom asked.

"Yeah, just a headache."

"Let us know if you need anything, Ethan," his father said.

"Sure, Dad," Ethan responded in a tone that was bordering on sarcastic, though he was trying with everything in his power to hide that feeling.

Ethan lay on his bed, deep in thought for the rest of the evening, until he heard his parents' door close. He gave them a few minutes, so he could be sure they had retired for the night, then he got up and made his way to the computer. He typed in *"37-Geminorum"* and hit the search button. Ethan scrolled through the results with the same sense of awe he had the first time he'd inquired about it. Thirty-seven Geminorum was a yellow-orange star a lot like our own sun. It was just a tiny bit bigger and brighter but was somewhat older—about a billion years the sun's elder. It resided in the northwest part of the constellation Gemini and was fifty-six light-years away. That amounted to over three-hundred trillion miles, but in astronomical terms, it was only about a block away. Scientists had speculated about it being a good place to harbor life, and Ethan knew they'd found the proof. He was sure the military had to have recovered those blue energy rods from something alien. And there was no way teleporters and time machines could've come from humans in this century or the next.

Ethan pulled up a photograph of the star, magnified greatly, shining majestically, sitting front and center against the deep black backdrop of space. He leaned in toward the computer screen. At that moment, an army of questions hijacked his mind:

What planet are they from? What do they want? What do they look like? How exactly did the military make contact? Was it a crashed spacecraft or a planned meeting? If so, where were the aliens? All I saw was a machine that looked like an alien when I was trapped in that janitor's closet. Where were the flesh and blood versions, or whatever they're made of? Or did they evolve beyond flesh and blood? Are they an entire race of machines?

The questions were driving Ethan to madness, especially when he knew his dad probably had the answers to most of them. Not that he figured he'd ever have a chance of getting the truth out of him, but there was a way to get the information that didn't require a father-son chat. There was an entire room hidden in the house, begging to be explored. The secret goodies it might contain overwhelmed him.

Ethan listened intently for any noise in the house until his ears tingled from the silence. He grabbed a flashlight but kept it off, opened his door, and slinked out into the darkened hallway. Like the seasoned scout he was, he moved silently, ever aware of every loose, creaky floorboard that might give him away. Soon enough, he was downstairs and eye-to-eye with the thermostat that hid the keypad underneath. The plan *was* going to be to wait until his parents were out of the house, then have Caleb come in and break the code. But Ethan couldn't wait. There was a large bookshelf next to the thermostat that looked especially suspicious, like a secret door just had to be behind there. It taunted and teased him. Even though his parents were directly above him, and he had no idea what the password might be, Ethan was determined to give it a shot.

He lifted the cover of the thermostat slowly, flicked his flashlight on, and trained it on the keypad underneath. Pausing for a moment, he closed his eyes and listened with every bit of his eardrums for any noise upstairs. Dead silence. Just as he was about to start guessing passwords, finger on a button, he heard quick, heavy footsteps on the stairs. Ethan barely had enough time to close the cover of the thermostat when his father entered the room.

"Ethan?" his father said, surprised.

"Hi, Dad," Ethan replied quickly, trying to hide his nerves.

"Hi. What are you doing down here?"

Ethan swallowed hard. He felt like he was being interrogated. "Oh, uh…just looking for a book. Couldn't sleep."

"Things on your mind?" his father asked.

"Yeah."

"I see. You wanna talk about it?"

Ethan quickly shook his head. "No, that's okay."

"So, which one?"

"What?" Ethan asked, confused.

"Which one…which book?" his father asked, pointing to the bookshelf.

"Oh, right," Ethan said, then spun around and shined his light randomly on a book on the shelf. He couldn't believe where that random beam of light fell.

Ethan's dad spotted the book. "*War of the Worlds*," he said. "H.G. Wells…classic."

"Sure is," Ethan said, still stunned by the irony of picking a book where Earthlings are being attacked by aliens. He clambered up to the top of the bookshelf and snatched the novel.

"Why are you in the dark?"

"Oh, uh…just saving energy," Ethan responded. "We're learning about energy conservation in school…Did you know enough sunlight reaches the earth's surface every minute to satisfy the world's energy needs for an entire year?" Ethan was glad to have remembered that disarming tidbit of knowledge from the fourth grade.

Ethan's dad flashed a smile. "Good to hear. Okay, then." He went over to a drawer and pulled out some matches. He lit a candle and made his way over to Ethan. "Have a seat," he said, motioning to the couch. "You can shut off that flashlight."

Ethan turned off his flashlight, then took a seat beside him on the couch. The candle his father had set on the coffee table in front of them danced around as if it were listening to music. It cast shadows on the walls that seemed to change constantly. Ethan sat in silence with his dad for a long minute, both staring at the flame, neither initiating a conversation. Finally, Mr. Tate looked at his son and smiled. Ethan squirmed a bit, uncomfortable.

"Do you have something you want to talk to me about?"

Something about the way his dad smiled as he asked that question made Ethan nervous. The candle in the room didn't help. The light emitted from the flame reflected a very unwelcome sight. For a brief time, it made his father's eyes glow crimson. The red tint went away, but Ethan's unease did not. He took a deep breath and swallowed hard, trying to forget what he just saw.

"No, not really," Ethan finally replied, lying through his teeth.

"Are you sure?"

"Yep, positive."

"Okay, then," his father said, then paused for a long moment, holding his son's eyes the entire time. "I have a question for you, though."

Ethan instantly felt a tight cramp in his stomach. A couple nervous beads of sweat joined together on his forehead and trickled down to his eyebrow. *He caught me red-handed. The thermostat cover must've had some alarm that alerted him upstairs. I should have waited. How could I have been so impatient and stupid?*

"What's the question, Dad?" Ethan asked softly, then held his breath for the answer.

His father stared at him for a while, then cracked a guarded smile. "Ethan…How would you feel about having a brother?"

"Whaaaat?" Ethan said, totally dumbfounded. That was definitely not the question he was expecting. That was, in fact, *the last* question he was expecting.

"How would you feel about having a brother?" his dad repeated.

"Is Mom, uhh…you know?"

"Pregnant? No. This would be more like an adoption. He's about your age. So…how would you feel about having a brother?"

"I'm not sure," Ethan said. "I had no idea you two were even interested in more kids."

"We didn't either, but something came up. Someone, a wonderful boy. Would you like to meet him sometime?"

"I need to think about it," Ethan said. "Are you and Mom for sure going to do this?"

"Not for sure, but leaning toward it. We'd like your thoughts before we do anything."

Really? Ethan thought sarcastically. *You'd like my thoughts? Okay, here goes: I wonder if you'd tell this new son of yours all your secrets. If you'd let him in on your real life. I wonder if you think he's good enough to know those things.*

But all Ethan could say was: "I'm gonna need more time to think about that."

"Sure, son. Take all the time you need. I love you, you know that?"

"Yeah, I know," Ethan said, but the words sounded hollow.

Ethan's dad leaned over, hugged his son, then got up. "Goodnight, Ethan."

"Goodnight, Dad."

His dad left the room. Ethan stayed for a moment, watching the candle flame dance back and forth in the darkness. He had a queasiness in his stomach, a malady that was equal parts anxiety and frustration. Ethan tried to focus on the positive. At least his father hadn't caught him in the act of trying to figure out the password. That would've been the only thing in the world that could've made the conversation he had with his dad any more awkward.

CHAPTER 3
AN OPPORTUNITY ARISES

ETHAN WATCHED DISTRACTEDLY as Ms. Goodfoot milled about the classroom, passing out a list of possible topics to the class for their upcoming research project. Caleb scooted his desk next to Ethan's to work together, but the class project was nowhere on their agenda. When Ms. Goodfoot finally handed a list to Ethan, he and Caleb perused it for all of two seconds.

"Anything but 'The Role of Artificial Intelligence in the Future,'" Ethan said bluntly.

"Right. *Anything* but that," Caleb agreed.

Ethan decided not to tell anyone about the bizarre talk he'd had with his dad the night before. That even included Caleb. Ethan figured that topic should be the least of their concerns and tried as best he could to push it to the back of his mind.

Another thing that should've been the least of their worries was relationship drama. But no luck there. Bradley Wuddle and Kevin Kim, former members of the Bravo Team, constantly stared enviously at the new team of five, wondering why they had been replaced by Annika and Glenn. And on the flip side, Tristan and the others on Delta Team wondered why Annika and Glenn jumped ship to be with Austin, Ethan, and Caleb. It made no sense to any of them, but they never got much of an answer. Bradley inquired about it once, but Austin gave only a terse reply. He simply said: "It's time to switch up the teams. Got it?" Bradley couldn't do anything but bite his tongue.

Ethan and the others, Annika and Glenn in particular, wished they could let Tristan know the truth. They felt they owed him that. After all, he was the only student they knew who had been impersonated by a robot. Still, there was no way the group could divulge any of their secrets now. It was a risk they couldn't take.

Ethan felt a buzzing sensation in his pocket. He pulled out his cell phone, angling it away from Ms. Goodfoot's line of sight. He smiled big when he saw the text message.

"What is it?" Caleb asked.

"A golden opportunity."

The group gathered on the far end of the courtyard to eat their lunches. Now and again, former teammates would glance at them in confusion, wondering how they had become so close-knit. The tone of the glances seemed to take turns, sometimes angry and irritated, other times just intensely curious. Ethan and the others tried not to pay attention to their prying eyes, but it wasn't the easiest thing to do. Bradley and the rest generally kept a far enough distance away, though. Austin's occasional scowl was as good as any warning shot across the bow.

"My parents are having a date night tonight," Ethan said with a mischievous smile sneaking over his face. "That's our chance to break the password, get a look at what's down there in that secret basement."

"Great," Caleb said. "I'll get my gear first thing after school."

"Good. And we're gonna need some lookouts," Ethan said.

"I'm in," Annika said. "What time will your parents be gone?"

"Dinner's at six. Movie's at seven-thirty."

"Okay, see you at six," Annika said.

Ethan looked awkwardly at Austin and Glenn. "One lookout here at the house is enough." Ethan paused and drew a deep breath before continuing, "But I'll need someone to follow my parents, out of sight, on their date. If they come back early for any reason, you gotta warn us."

"Looks like we're going on a date, Glenn," Austin said.

"Fine, but don't get cheap on me," Glenn replied. "Which restaurant?"

"Angelino's," Ethan answered.

"Mmm, I love that place," Glenn blurted.

"Yeah, the breadsticks are fantastic," Austin said.

Annika chuckled. "See, you guys make the perfect couple."

Austin and Glenn couldn't help but laugh. "So what's the movie?" Austin asked. There's a great movie about a World War Two tank battalion playing."

"Yeah, that's *real* romantic," Annika wisecracked.

"So it's not the war movie…Okay, what is it?" Austin asked.

Ethan paused for a few torturous seconds. He racked his brain to think of the best way to say the title of the movie, but there was no point. The name said it all. Finally, he grimaced and said, "It's called *True Love's Kiss*."

Annika and Caleb snickered. Austin and Glenn exhaled gigantic, pathetic sighs of defeat.

"We're sneaking in *after* the show starts, under the cover of darkness," Austin said.

"Right, right...under the cover of darkness," Glenn repeated.

"That's fine," Ethan said. "Just make sure you keep an eye on them. And if they leave, you gotta follow them."

"Unless you're really into the movie," Annika said, still giggling.

Austin and Glenn rolled their eyes. "She's such a funny girl," Glenn said with a smirk.

"Thanks, guys." Ethan smiled excitedly. "Tonight, we're finally gonna get some answers to our questions."

CHAPTER 4
CRACKING THE CODE

Ethan's parents left for the Italian restaurant ten minutes before six o'clock. Ethan watched them from his bedroom window until they drove to the end of the street, took the left turn, and disappeared out of sight. Soon he heard a few soft raps on the front door. Ethan dashed downstairs. He flung open the door. Annika was on the porch scanning the street up and down, already assuming her sentry duty. Caleb carried a backpack that contained his laptop and some sophisticated software that Ethan dearly hoped could crack the password for the secret door and get them into the basement.

"They're gone, right?" Caleb asked.

"Yeah, they're gone," Ethan answered. "Come on in."

∽

Caleb positioned a TV tray beside the keypad on the wall. He set his laptop on top of it, linked it to the keypad, and began to load the password-cracking software. His fingers flew furiously as he typed commands.

"How long do you think this is gonna take?" Ethan asked.

"Not sure. Depends on the number of digits in the code and the quality of the security program. Guessing it's got twelve digits like my dad's keypad, probably similar security features... How long until your folks get home?"

"Not until nine-twenty, at least."

"I think that'll be enough time to give us a decent peek down there."

Ethan's eyes were eager. "Good. I can't wait."

"All right then," Annika said. "I'm going upstairs to set up a lookout. You need anything, just yell. You crack that code, yell even louder."

"Will do," Ethan said.

Annika ran upstairs and took a surveillance position in Ethan's room. From his bedroom window, she had a good view of the entire street. But Annika was the lookout of last resort. At best, she could only provide Ethan with about a minute's worth of warning. The real surveillance work was being done by Ethan's parents' undercover chaperones.

◈

Austin and Glenn sat behind a frosted glass partition at Angelino's Italian Restaurant. On the other side of the partition, two tables away, were Ethan's parents. There was a small gap in the glass that allowed Austin an unobstructed view of their targets.

"What are they doing now?" Glenn mumbled with a mouthful of breadstick.

Austin rolled his eyes. "They're standing up on their table, throwing food around everywhere," he said sarcastically. "What do you think they're doing? Same thing they were doing last time you asked me... two minutes ago."

"Very funny, Austin...Now really, what are they doing?"

Austin sighed, then took a sip of his Coke. He looked once again at Ethan's parents' table. His eyes widened a bit. "Wait...They're getting their check."

Glenn poked one last bite of breadstick into his mouth, then quickly raised his hand, trying to flag down their waitress. The waitress made her way over to their table.

"More soda or breadsticks, perhaps?" the waitress said wryly.

"No thanks," Glenn said. "We'll take our check now."

The waitress flashed a sarcastic, perky smile, then peeled off their bill from a stack of others. "Let's see," she said. "Two unlimited Cokes and free breadsticks...That'll be four dollars and fourteen cents, you big spenders."

Glenn paid the waitress while Austin pulled out his cell phone and pressed it to his ear. "Ethan," Austin said quietly. "They're leaving the restaurant now. It's movie time. We'll be in touch."

Austin and Glenn darted out of the restaurant to follow their targets. They stood on the street corner opposite the theater while Ethan's parents walked inside. After a few minutes, when they were sure the movie had started, they went inside themselves. It was all they could muster to fork over ten bucks each for a movie called *True Love's Kiss*. They told the cashier they were there to see the World War II tank battalion movie but slinked away into the romantic film when no one was looking. They slouched down and took a seat in the very back of the theater, but still had a good view of Mr. and Mrs. Tate. They were desperately hoping for two things at that moment: One, that Caleb would figure out the password on the keypad. And two, that Ethan's parents wouldn't start making out.

Caleb's password-hacking software was blazing away at a solution. Numbers and letters scrolled rapidly on his laptop screen like reels on a slot machine. At first, there had been twelve reels spinning, but now there were only two. Ethan's parents had just gotten to the movie theater, and they had already figured out the first ten digits of the password. Despite their success so far, Ethan's breaths were tense and shallow as he watched the two remaining reels on the laptop scroll madly. Then another reel came to a stop.

"We just got the eleventh digit!" Caleb blurted.

Ethan flashed a nervous grin and began pacing around a coffee table, wringing his hands like he was angry at them. When another ten minutes transpired, the computer made a pinging sound. Caleb checked the screen. Ethan stopped pacing and unclenched his tortured hands.

Caleb smiled and nodded. "We got it…the final digit."

"We got it," Ethan repeated with a relieved grin. "Annika, we got it!" he yelled at the ceiling.

Annika quickly dashed down the stairs, jumped from the fourth one, stuck the landing, then sprinted into the living room. "Wait for me! Wait for me!" she said breathlessly.

"Of course, I'm going to wait for you," Ethan said. "Everyone ready?"

Annika and Caleb nodded like turbocharged bobblehead dolls. "Yes, yes, yes, we're ready," Annika exclaimed with the cadence of a machine gun.

"All right," Ethan said, taking a deep breath. "Here we go."

Ethan punched in the password from the laptop into the

keypad. After an agonizing three seconds, a small green light lit up on the keypad. Then a *click* issued from behind the bookshelf. The shelf cracked open a couple of inches.

Ethan smiled victoriously. "We're in." He stuck his hands inside the gap and proceeded to pull the bookshelf away from the wall. Then he caught his first glimpse of what was lying behind it. Ethan's smile vanished instantly. There was a bulky metal door made of titanium, just like the door to Caleb's dad's sub-basement. To the side of the door was another keypad, yet another password to crack.

"Noooo!" Ethan yelled in frustration. "Wait, maybe the password's the same." He punched in the code from the first keypad, but there was no green-light greeting. The door remained locked. Ethan pounded his fist several times on the door, then sat dejectedly on the end of the couch rubbing his sore hand.

"How long will it take to crack *this* one?" Annika asked. "We got about an hour before their movie ends."

"Not sure," Caleb said. "Probably the same as the first. Never know, though. We could get lucky."

Ethan stood up, forced a deep breath, and rubbed his hands down his cheeks, trying to compose himself. "Go ahead, Caleb. Try it. It's all we can do."

"I'm on it." Caleb quickly switched his laptop from the first keypad to the second one.

Ethan knocked on the metal door. It was thick. At least as thick as the one at Caleb's house. Ethan shook his head in utter awe. "What could possibly be down there that needs two security codes, a secret bookshelf, and a massive titanium door?"

"I have no idea," Caleb answered, frantically typing on his laptop. "But, God, I wanna find out."

❧

Nine o'clock was fast approaching and only seven of the twelve digits had been discovered. Ethan tried to remain hopeful, but it was slowly becoming apparent that they were going to fall short. When Austin called in a little after nine-fifteen, that last bit of hope slipped away.

"Ethan, the movie's over," Austin said. "They just left the lobby and are heading to the parking lot now...How's it going over there?"

"Not good," Ethan said. "Turns out there are *two* keypads to crack."

"Want me to try and stall them?"

"No, thanks...We're not even close."

"Okay. Whatever you think. Your parents just got in their car. They'll be there soon."

"Thanks, Austin." Ethan tucked his phone back into his pocket. He turned dejectedly to Caleb. "Okay, pack it up. They're on their way home...We're done."

Annika quickly bounded down the stairs. "How many now?" she asked.

"We just got the eighth one," Ethan answered. "Too late, though. They're coming home."

Annika's face dropped. "I just can't believe there were two keypads."

"Well we have the first keypad solved and eight digits of the other one," Caleb said, trying to stay positive. "We should try again next time your parents are out."

"No, absolutely not," Annika snapped. "We need to warn the generals, Caleb. That's the next thing we do."

Caleb sighed deeply. His face wilted in frustration, but

then he perked up with an idea. "We could still try the Skulley in the fort for information on the fatal error, just real quick, see if its hard drive is—"

"No, Caleb," Ethan interrupted. "Annika's right. We have to warn them tomorrow…This was our only shot."

Ethan paused for a long moment. His eyes were fixated on the keypad beside the titanium door, then they drifted to the ceiling, right under his parents' room. In a flash, he felt his head become light, his body tingle, and his chest tighten into a nerve-racked lump. There was one thing they still needed to do before they warned the generals at the base and security clamped down like a vise. Ethan had been too obsessed with the basement to realize it before, but the idea hit him like a train now. His face was pale. There was hardly any time.

"We still need to get the metal briefcase from under my parents' bed," Ethan blurted out desperately. "After we warn them, they'll move it, they'll have to…And we'll never have a chance at fixing things if everything goes bad again."

"Oh yeah, that's right," Caleb said, his face turning as pale as Ethan's.

Annika looked at Ethan, doubtful. "Do you still remember the combination?"

Ethan nodded. "I will never forget those numbers as long as I live."

"Then go. Go now," Annika insisted. "And if your parents get here before you get that briefcase, whatever you do, don't stop. Just get that case. I'll stall them."

"How?" Ethan asked.

"I'll think of something…Now go!"

Ethan and Caleb dashed upstairs as fast as they could. Annika waited by the front door in the foyer. She maintained a lookout through a column of vertical windows that lined the wall beside the door, all the while thinking about what she could do to stall Ethan's parents once they got there.

※

Ethan and Caleb quickly lifted his parents' bed away from the rectangular cutout in the wood floor underneath. Caleb shined a flashlight on the floor, while Ethan pulled out his Swiss Army knife and flipped open the screwdriver. He jammed it into the crevice, pried it open until he was able to get his fingers inside. Then he pulled away the three-foot by two-foot slab of wood and laid it aside. The light from Caleb's flashlight shined brightly off the silvery metallic safe. Ethan leaned down and began with the combination. The numbers "12-32-18-26-8" were ingrained into his memory.

Suddenly, Ethan heard a car pull into the driveway. His reflex was to stop and put everything back like it was, leaving the briefcase in the safe, but then he remembered what Annika had said. Her words still rang in his ears: "Whatever you do, don't stop. Just get that case. I'll stall them." He ignored his instincts and continued working on the combination.

God, I hope she knows what she's doing.

※

Ethan's parents got out of their car. Annika walked out to the driveway to meet them, still not sure what she was going to do or say. Her first reaction was to try to tackle them, then she thought there had to be a better way. Ideas were swirling in her mind, but she didn't like any of them.

"Annika, hello," Ethan's dad said, sounding surprised to see her there.

"Hi, Mr. Tate," Annika answered. She knew she had to make up a reason fast about why she was standing in their driveway at nine-thirty at night. "We were studying...me, Caleb, and Ethan. You know Caleb...nose-to-the-grindstone kinda guy."

"I see," Ethan's father answered.

"It's nice to see you studying so hard...and so early in the summer session, too," Ethan's mom added.

"Yeah, again, that's Caleb's influence," Annika said with a nervous chuckle.

"Well, it's always nice to see you, Annika. Tell your folks we said hello," Ethan's dad said. "Goodnight."

"You, too. I will. Goodnight," Annika replied. Then she glanced sneakily at Ethan's parents' bedroom window and saw some faint shadows still moving around. She quickly stepped in front of Mr. and Mrs. Tate, blocking them from getting to the porch. "Wait, can I ask you something?"

Ethan's parents looked a bit confused, but they smiled cordially at her. "Sure, let's go inside and we can talk," his father said, getting his house key out and aiming for the door.

"No, not inside," Annika uttered and put her hand up to block the key from the lock. She sighed deeply. "I don't want Ethan to hear this. Come back to the driveway," she said, luring them to a spot where she had a decent view of their bedroom window.

Ethan's parents were really confused and concerned now, but they did as Annika requested. "What is it, sweetie?" Ethan's mom asked softly.

Annika took a deep breath and stared at both of Ethan's parents with a very solemn expression. "You see, there's a dance coming up in a couple months," Annika swallowed so hard she could hear the gulping sound in her throat, then continued, "and I was wondering if I could have your permission, your blessing, to ask Ethan to go with me."

Ethan's mom and dad smiled, a sense of relief on their faces now. "Sure, you have our permission," Ethan's mom said.

"Of course. You're a wonderful girl, Annika. I know Ethan would love to go with you," Ethan's dad said.

"Thanks, that means a lot." Annika kept a sneaky eye on their bedroom window. She still saw shadows in there.

"Goodnight, Annika," Ethan's dad said, then made another move toward the porch.

"Wait," Annika said again. Ethan's parents once more stopped in their tracks. "Since I will be asking him to the dance, do *I* have to give *him* a flower, or does *he*, uh, you know?"

Ethan's dad stifled a laugh. "That's a good question, but I'm pretty sure Ethan will be giving you the flower."

"Great," Annika said with a smile. "I was kinda hoping it went like that." Her smile got even bigger, and more natural, when she saw that the shadows in the bedroom window were gone. "Well, I'll let you two get inside now. Thanks…And, please, don't tell Ethan about this."

"You're welcome, Annika. Your secret's safe with us," Ethan's dad said with a grin.

Just as Ethan's parents were about to go inside, the door opened and Caleb walked out onto the porch. "Oh, hi… Didn't know you were out here," Caleb lied convincingly.

"Did you have a good study session?" Ethan's mom asked.

"Oh, yeah," Caleb said. "We were working on the—"

"Well, we better be getting home now," Annika quickly interrupted, jabbing Caleb subtly in the ribs with her elbow.

"Yeah, it is pretty late," Caleb said. "Goodnight."

"Goodnight, guys," Ethan's dad said.

Annika and Caleb turned and walked away. Ethan's parents smiled at each other, shared a laugh, then went inside.

As soon as Annika heard the door close at Ethan's house, she turned sharply toward Caleb. "What took you guys so long in there?" she asked, annoyed.

"The floorboard wouldn't go back in straight. Took forever to get it in so it looked right."

"Well, it seemed like you were in there for days."

"Sorry," Caleb said. "By the way, how'd you stall them for so long? What did you say?"

Thankfully for Annika, the darkness of night hid the fact that her face was blushing three shades of red. "Never mind what I said. I'm just glad we made it."

"Me too. And thanks, again…for whatever you said."

"You're welcome," she blurted. "Now let's just get home."

⁜

In the wee hours that night, Ethan lay in bed with a nervous flutter in his chest. Tucked behind various items of everyday clutter underneath his bed was a briefcase that most countries would eagerly go to war over. It was a briefcase surely worth any amount of money. In fact, there was no more valuable object on the face of the earth. The more Ethan thought about it, the more the responsibility of possessing that briefcase weighed on him. He wished he could get it to a secure location—like the Bravo Fort—immediately. But there was no way he could cross the Dark Highway in the middle of the night without being hounded by security. Moving the briefcase would have to wait until after school tomorrow, almost ten hours from now.

That seemed like an eternity.

CHAPTER 5

SECURING THE BOX

Ethan sat at the kitchen table and watched as his parents dug into a steaming, scrumptious stack of blueberry waffles. They were his favorite breakfast food, but his stomach was queasy this morning. All he could think about was that briefcase under his bed. He had sat up all night guarding it, like a mother bird sitting on her clutch of eggs. Fortunately, Ethan wouldn't be needing to play mother bird to that metallic briefcase for the entire day. Soon his mom and dad would leave for work, and he would have an opportunity to come home after school, grab the briefcase, and get it back to the Bravo Fort without being hassled. Or so he hoped.

"Dig in," Ethan's mom said.

"Mmm, I will," Ethan said, not wanting to give any impression that something wasn't right. He grabbed two waffles and quickly began eating, though his stomach was fighting him tooth and nail all the way.

Ethan was glad there wasn't much in the way of table talk this morning. His dad, normally at work by now, was running late, so his mouth at any given point was mostly filled with waffle or coffee, unable to ask any questions. Ethan didn't need any questions. Not today. He just watched his father in a quiet moment, thinking about all the secrets the supposed maintenance man had kept from him. Then Ethan realized that he was building up a pretty impressive pile of his own. *Maybe I'm more of a chip off the old block than I thought.*

Ethan's dad took one more quick gulp of coffee, rubbed the hair on Ethan's head playfully, then stood up. "Gotta go, kiddo," he said. "Have a great day." Then he kissed his wife, told her goodbye, and left the house.

All Ethan thought in that moment was: *You have no idea what I've seen, where I've been, or what I've done...DO NOT call me kiddo.*

"Are you okay, honey?" Ethan's mom asked.

Ethan sighed. He realized his frustration must've breached the fake smile he had tried to put on. "Yeah, I'm fine," he said quickly, then paused and changed his tune. He couldn't help it. At least this question could come out safely. "Mom, the other day Dad mentioned something about you guys wanting to adopt a kid my age. What's that about?"

His mom's face softened instantly. "He told me he told you, but I didn't want to say anything because he said you needed time to think...Ethan, honey, we're not sure. It's kinda complicated."

"How's it complicated?" Ethan asked.

"It's just something all three of us would have to talk about. There's a lot to consider."

"Like what?" Ethan pressed.

"Well, he's a very special boy. Different. It might take a while to get to know him, see if you want him to be a part of the family."

"Is he nice?" Ethan asked. "How is he different?"

"He's very nice," his mom answered. "It's just...He's never had a family before. And he's got nowhere else to go. He really wants to meet you."

Ethan nodded sympathetically but furrowed his eyes. "I'm still gonna need time to think. This week's going to be stressful enough, anyway." Ethan bit his lip. He wished he hadn't said that.

"Why is this week going to be so stressful?" she asked, concerned.

"Oh, you know...the school project *and* new Laser Wars teams."

His mom smiled warmly. "Sure, take your time...I love you, Ethan."

"Love you too."

"Race you to school today?" his mom said, her smile turning playful.

Ethan flashed a sarcastic grin. "Don't think so, Mom."

That morning the half-day of summer school seemed like it went on for an entire semester. Ethan's nervous leg was tapping up and down like a furiously pumping piston. He couldn't get his mind off that briefcase just sitting under his bed, completely unguarded. Instead of focusing on the current lesson of factoring polynomials, his mind wandered to think about what would happen if his parents came home for lunch that day and decided to do some house cleaning. He imagined them poking around under his bed and finding the secret case. Even though the odds of that happening were remote, it didn't stop him from breaking into a cold sweat. School couldn't end fast enough.

When the bell finally rang, Ethan and the rest of Team Blackwoods sprang up from their seats and dashed as fast as they could out of the room. Before Ms. Goodfoot could flash a reproving look, they were already gone.

⚜

The group walked single file, double-time and with purpose, down the sidewalk of Kingsbury Avenue. They moved like a squad of Marines on a mission. Soon they arrived on Ethan's porch. No one was home. Without a word, Ethan darted inside his house. Sixty seconds later, he returned outside to the group with a large duffel bag slung over his shoulder. Only five people on earth knew the world-changing potential contained inside that plain-looking bag.

The wait at the guard checkpoint for permission to cross the Dark Highway seemed longer than usual today. As the two guards in camouflage approached them, Ethan began to feel lightheaded. *They never checked our bags before, but what if today was the first time?* Ethan tried to put on a normal, relaxed face when he met the guards' eyes, though he was afraid he looked like he was up to something.

"Be just a minute," one guard said. "Got a quick convoy comin' through."

A half-dozen large green military cargo trucks emerged from the west—the direction of Briggs Air Force Base—and rumbled down the Dark Highway. As they waited for them to pass, the guards turned their attention to the group.

"Going out for a Laser Wars game?" one guard asked.

"Yep," Caleb said quickly.

"Forgot your camouflage," the other pointed out.

"Uh, well, um…" Caleb fumbled awkwardly. "It's more of a strategy session, really."

"I see," the guard said. Then he looked at the large duffel bag that was draped across Ethan's back. "So, what's in the bag?"

The soldier asked that question with a strangely serious look on his face. Ethan was about to make up an answer when Annika stepped up.

"The bag is full of Top-Secret stuff," Annika said with a straight face. "But we can't show you because you don't have the required security clearance."

The group uttered a faint, anxious gasp at Annika's bold response. Everyone held their breath. After an unbearably long pause, the guards cracked a smile and laughed at her answer.

"You may go now," the guard said, still chuckling. He motioned to the other guards across the highway that they would be crossing.

They began to walk across the ten lanes of highway. Ethan shook his head and smiled at Annika. "That was a good one back there."

Annika grinned. "Yeah…I thought you'd like that."

⚜

It wasn't until everyone was in the basement of the Bravo Fort, about to stash the duffel bag in a footlocker alongside the dead, crumpled-up Skulley, that they realized there was a problem.

"When we warn the generals, *they will* check every structure in Blackwoods to make sure it's secure," Ethan said. "We can't hide this here."

"Yeah," Caleb replied glumly. "They'll probably even secure the doghouses."

"So we can't keep it here," Glenn said. "Where then?"

"Wolf Cave," Annika said. "They probably won't be snooping around in there. Even so, we could hide it well enough."

Ethan nodded. "Good idea. Let's grab anything we don't want found."

⚜

The group arrived at Wolf Cave with everything they had planned to bury—the duffel bag with the metallic briefcase inside, another duffel full of laser rifles, and a dead Skulley strapped to a dolly cart wrapped in a blanket like a mummy. They entered the cave and crawled through the leftmost tunnel, pulling the Skulley all the way through and into a larger chamber—the same one they had spent about thirty minutes inside before the machines found them in another timeline. A creepy, tingling sense of déjà vu hit them all. They remembered vividly the machines' crimson, glowing eyes in the pitch blackness, and the sounds of metal appendages clanking and scraping across the cave floor.

"Let's find a good place to stash this stuff," Ethan said, shaking off the willies. "And I vote we bury the Skulley first."

"I second that," Austin said quickly.

The group fanned out and searched the area with their flashlights.

"I think I found a place," Annika said, shining her light on a cavity in the floor of the cave, alongside the wall in the back of the chamber. The depression in the ground was about seven feet wide and sloped to a maximum depth of five feet. It was a tucked-away, inconspicuous spot.

"It's perfect," Ethan said.

Ethan and Austin pulled the blanket off the Skulley and rolled the skeletal monster into its grave, then they laid the two duffel bags on top of it. The group smoothed the blanket over their stash and filled the hole with rocks until they had a couple feet worth of coverage. Even flashing their lights directly on the spot, no one would notice a thing.

"Looks good," Glenn said, wiping some sweat from his forehead.

"Great, now we can finally warn the generals," Annika said.

"Right," Ethan agreed, then looked pensive. "We just need to figure out the best way to do that."

CHAPTER 6

THE LETTER

Dinner had just ended at the Tate household when the doorbell rang. Ethan was on dishwashing duty, so his mom answered the door. She found the rest of Team Blackwoods waiting on the porch.

Annika flashed a charming, innocent smile to Ethan's mom. "Hi, Mrs. Tate. We're here for the group project." Annika didn't say it was for school, so it wasn't entirely a lie.

"Wow…and on a Friday night," Ethan's mom said, equal parts impressed and skeptical.

Ethan quickly slung the last of the plates into the dishwasher, then ran into the foyer to meet the group. "I got it, Mom. Thanks," he said as he whisked his friends upstairs.

"Good luck on the project," his mom shouted after them.

"Thanks, Mrs. Tate," Annika shouted back in a perky tone.

"Yeah," Glenn said, grumbling under his breath. "We're gonna need it."

The group had thought long and hard about the best way to warn the officers at the base. They knew, whatever they did, that they had to remain anonymous. No one could know they were the ones who successfully executed Project Mulligan, no matter how strong the temptation was to tell the world. In the end, they decided to write a letter. A plain and simple letter. Sort of.

The group sat around Ethan at his computer. He pulled up a blank page and took a deep, anxiety-cleansing breath.

"We should take turns writing the sentences," Caleb said before Ethan could lay his hands on the keyboard. "When the military gets this letter, they will analyze everything. Even writing style. We need to take turns so it doesn't sound like any one person. And keep it simple, boring…just like you'd imagine a robot would write."

Ethan turned around and shot Caleb a sarcastic grimace just about the same time everyone else did. "Nice one, Caleb," Ethan said, shaking his head.

Caleb chuckled a little. "Sorry, bad example."

"Okay, then," Ethan said. "So I guess we begin with the day everyone disappeared."

"Yeah…June fourteenth," Annika replied, recalling it vividly.

"Well, here goes…"

Over the next hour, everyone took turns typing the events of the robot revolution, beginning with the disappearance of the residents of Blackwoods and ending with the successful completion of Project Mulligan. They were careful not to go into any great detail about Project Mulligan, never mentioned anything about the secret tunnel, just simply said that they had completed the operation. The last thing they wanted was to broadcast that vital information should the wrong people—or things—be reading. They also never mentioned the laser gun chargers themselves, for the obvious reason that it would blow their cover, but they did make sure to include the special frequency that had managed to jam the teleporters. Caleb had figured out the exact frequency by taking one of the chargers apart and studying it, and he was sure the military, knowing that number precisely, would be able to thwart any teleportation attempts by the machines. Throughout the letter, the fatal error was mentioned urgently and repeatedly—that fateful day and time of June twelfth, five fifty-seven in the late afternoon. They just prayed the military could find out what the fatal error was and fix it before it was too late.

When the letter was finished, the group read it over and over again, making sure it included all the necessary information and that it was free of errors. They were satisfied with the finished product, but everyone knew they couldn't just send the letter like it was. In the letter, they referred to themselves as a nameless, super-secret military special forces unit. But no one from the military would ever send a document of this Top-Secret magnitude anywhere without encrypting it first. Fortunately, Caleb had some software that was up to the task. Finally at the bottom of the note, in thick red lettering, they typed: "DESTROY AFTER READING."

After their message had been encoded, Ethan printed out the two-page document. He put on some latex gloves, so as not to leave any fingerprints on the paper, and pulled the letter out of the printer. He carefully folded it and stuck it inside an envelope that they had addressed to "General Carl Vaden."

Glenn wasn't terribly happy that his father would be the

first one to receive the letter, but at least he knew his dad wouldn't take his frustrations out on him. If Austin's dad got the letter first, God knows how he would react. No matter which top general received the news first, though, the result for the town would be the same. Severe security protocols would take over, and life at Blackwoods would be drastically different for everyone.

◈

That night the five of them decided to catch a late movie. Before going inside, they mingled around the far corner of the theater marquee, where a post office mailbox stood. The group formed a discreet blockade in front of the mailbox, and Ethan quickly dropped two letters inside the narrow opening at the same time, making it look like he was sending a single letter. The first letter was for General Vaden. The second was written to Ethan's grandmother, the purpose of which was twofold. One, Ethan wanted to wish her well after her wrist surgery. And two, if security cameras had spotted him placing anything in the mailbox, he wanted to be able to tell the authorities that he was just checking up on Grandma. He was careful to use different paper from the kind they used on the letter to General Vaden. Same thing for the envelope. The ink wasn't an issue, as he had hand-written the letter to Grandma Tate. Also, before leaving the house, he had covered the tips of his fingers with transparent Scotch Tape, so that he would leave no fingerprints on the envelope as he handled it.

When they heard the letters plunk down into the mailbox bottom, it felt as if they had swallowed the letters themselves. Their stomachs were tight and their heads were light. Everyone knew the military would move heaven and earth to find the origin of that letter, to determine who had completed Project Mulligan.

Ethan shook his head dejectedly. "God, I wish we could've gotten into that basement."

"We tried our best," Annika said. "It's too late for that now. This was the right move."

"It was the only move," Austin added.

"Yeah, I know," Ethan said softly.

"Everything's going to be different now," Caleb said.

Glenn nodded solemnly. "Yes it will…So, anyone up for a comedy?"

With the thinnest of smiles, the answer was yes. Then they went inside the theater to try to enjoy one last movie before their world changed forever.

CHAPTER 7

THE RESPONSE

THE NEXT DAY the hours passed torturously. Other than venturing downstairs to grab quick bites to eat, Ethan spent most of his Saturday in his room, avoiding contact with his parents and waiting for the inevitable. He kept thinking about how the situation was going to play out as he peeked through his window, looking for signs of distress from anyone. But everything appeared normal so far. Until 1:15 p.m. Then the blare of emergency sirens ripped through the town like a sonic tornado. The harshness and sheer volume of the sound startled him. He knew it wouldn't be long until his parents came in. Ethan hoped he could pull off the appropriate level of surprise. The anxiety he didn't have to fake.

Ethan's door flew open quickly, and his dad and mom rushed inside. His father tried to hide it, but there was intense panic and dread in his eyes. At that moment, looking into those tortured eyes, Ethan knew his dad had been briefed on the letter. His mom was worried about what was going on too, but her eyes didn't have the same look as his dad's. Ethan figured his father hadn't told his mother yet what exactly was going on. Maybe he never would. It was certainly a town of secrets.

"We're on lockdown, starting right now," Ethan's father said in a commanding voice, sounding nothing like the modest maintenance man he was masquerading as. "Don't go outside, don't even *look* outside until we hear further instructions. Just stay in your room until I tell you it's okay to come out…I love you, Ethan."

Mrs. Tate put a soft hand on her son's shoulder and said, "Don't worry, sweetie. Everything's going to be all right."

Mr. Tate flashed the fleetest of looks that suggested otherwise, then forced a smile on his incredibly tense face. "Your mom's right. There's nothing to worry about."

Lies, Ethan thought. "What's going on, Dad?" he probed, hoping to get a shred of honesty about something.

His father paused, then answered, "I don't know. You know as much as we do."

More lies. Ethan knew it was true that he knew as much as they did, much more in some ways, but his dad didn't know that.

"I'm sure this will all blow over soon," his mom said in a soothing voice. Then his parents left the room.

Ethan slipped out of his room and ran to his parents' bedroom door. The door was closed, but he could hear the clatter of items being moved around and the voices of his parents speaking in low but tense tones. Ethan opened the door just a sliver, barely enough to see inside. He knew what he was going to see, but seeing it still made him sick to his stomach. His father was standing over the open secret compartment under his bed where the metallic briefcase used to be hidden. Of course, the compartment was empty now. Ethan closed the bedroom door gently, but only after he saw the expression on his father's face first. He wished he hadn't. His livid, blood-red face and bulging eyes were a sight he'd never come close to witnessing before.

Ethan ran back to his room and closed the door. His father hardly ever cussed, but now a stream of obscenities penetrated every nook and niche of the house. Ethan's dad was lost in a full-throated scream and sounded like he was losing his mind. Chilled by his father's words, Ethan began to doubt the wisdom of snatching that briefcase. He picked up his cell phone to call Caleb, but then he realized that every incoming and outgoing call would be monitored by the military. Same thing for the walkie-talkie. He was sure all channels would be tapped. So Ethan sat on his bed and tried to calm himself down by rationalizing. *If the military figures out the fatal error and fixes it, then it doesn't matter that we took the briefcase… And if they can't fix it, the case is in a safe location and one that Team Blackwoods can get to. Besides, we could always secretly bring the briefcase back if it was safe to do so.*

The alarm sirens finally stopped. Ethan's dad was silent now, and the house was perfectly quiet. Ethan's rabbit-like heart rate began to settle ever so slightly. But a rumbling noise soon interrupted the peace. Ethan peered out of his window and saw a convoy of camouflaged military vehicles rolling down the street. Troops in transport trucks and Humvees with fifty-caliber machine guns mounted on top led the way. Bringing up the rear were two massive Abrams tanks, with their seventeen-foot-long cannons pointed straight ahead. And high above it all, Black Hawk helicopters circled the town like birds of prey. Ethan watched in amazement and horror. It appeared as if the military was preparing for war.

After the column of camouflaged vehicles passed by, three military buses pulled up to the side of the street. They looked like school buses, except they were all army-green in color. The passenger doors opened, and the drivers got out. But these bus drivers looked nothing like school bus drivers. Wearing head-to-toe military-issue camouflage, pistols on their sides, and faces devoid of emotion, they stood as still as statues beside the open doors. Their rigid torsos, black sunglasses, and firm jaws made them seem almost robotic. Ethan's skin prickled at that. He scanned over the buses and wondered who they were for. Then his parents entered the room and quickly answered that question for him.

"Ethan, honey," his mom said in the most composed voice she could muster, "we need you to pack a suitcase. You're going to be spending a few days in the dorm at Briggs Air Force Base. There's been a threat to the town, you'll be safe there. I know you must have a ton of questions, but you have to hurry now."

"Are you leaving too?" Ethan asked.

Before she could answer, his father turned dazedly from the window and said, "No, Ethan…The adults stay. Kids eighteen and under go." Ethan's dad looked completely distracted as he spoke, never laying his eyes squarely on his son. "You have to pack now."

"It's probably for just a couple days," Ethan's mom said, trying to force a positive tone. "Hey, it'll be kinda like summer camp. And when you come back, everything will be back to normal."

Ethan's dad flashed a dour, doubtful look at his wife. He made no attempt at hiding his expression. "Get packed, Ethan…now," he said much more sternly than the first time. "You have five minutes."

His dad pivoted quickly and left the room. Ethan's mom lingered. "We love you, Ethan," she said as a tear streaked down her cheek. "I'll help you pack."

※

Five minutes later, every person in Blackwoods eighteen and under was standing on the sidewalk in front of their house with a duffel bag at their feet. Children eight years old and under were allowed to leave with relatives of their families, instead of going to the dorm on the base, but none of the adults in Blackwoods were permitted to leave with their children. There was going to be a massive investigation into what had happened at the research facility. Every adult was going to be interrogated. The letter that came out of nowhere about the robot mutiny and Project Mulligan vexed the generals into madness. They were sure someone had to know something. But as security cracked down and armed vehicles flooded the streets, military officials watched cluelessly as Ethan and the rest of Team Blackwoods assembled on the sidewalk.

Ethan's mom and dad gave their son one last hug, then they watched him board the bus. "You'll be back before you know it," his mom said, wiping away a tear. Mr. Tate was more reserved with his emotions. For a fleeting moment, it appeared as if he wanted to say something. His lips pursed, then relaxed, but he walked away without a word.

Ethan made his way past an entire busload of frightened and confused kids to take a seat with the rest of his team in the back. They were the calmest-looking people on the bus, though calm was far from how they felt.

"Any chance of us getting off this bus?" Glenn asked, surveying the surroundings.

"No. Guards are everywhere," Ethan said. "Besides, they're bound to take a—"

"Megan Ambrose?" the leafy-green-clad, gun-toting driver asked in a gruff voice from the front of the bus.

"A head count," Ethan continued.

"Well, we can't just be holed up in Briggs Base if the fatal error happens," Annika said.

Ethan looked through the windows of the bus and saw the six Humvees that would be escorting them out of town. He eyed one of the soldiers manning the fifty-caliber machine gun mounted on top of the nearest Humvee. The soldier was tall, strong, and had a square jaw that looked like a slab of brick. He gave a quick nod to Ethan with no emotion in his eyes. Then he went back to scanning the perimeter.

"I don't think we have a choice," Ethan said.

As the driver continued the head count, Ethan's dad stepped inside the bus. He motioned for Ethan to come forward. "I need to talk to my son," he told the driver. "Just give me two minutes."

The driver grimaced. "You got two minutes, then I got my orders to pull outta here."

Ethan's dad led his son off the bus and back to the driveway of their house. Ethan's mom watched. She knew what was coming. He looked Ethan dead in the eyes and said, "I've lied to you for a very long time…I'm not a maintenance man at the research facility. I'm an advanced projects engineer."

Ethan just stood there, speechless and mouth agape, astonished that his father had finally come clean with him.

"I'm sorry I lied, but I had my reasons," his father continued. "It was to protect you…but I guess I wasn't able to do that."

"I need Ethan Tate on board, now!" the driver barked.

Mr. Tate hugged his son and spoke into his ear. "There's no time now, but we'll talk when you get back. The world we live in is so much more complicated than you can imagine. And it's about time you know the truth."

There were tears in Ethan's eyes. How quickly things had changed. Now *he* was the one holding most of the secrets. Ethan opened his mouth with intentions to tell his father that he and his friends were the ones who'd completed Project Mulligan, and that he had taken the briefcase, but the bus driver began shouting wildly.

"Get on the bus, now!" the driver screamed. He glanced at a few nearby guards. "Grab that kid!"

Several soldiers began to march toward Ethan.

"Go ahead, son," Ethan's dad said. "We'll talk later…I love you."

Ethan's mouth slowly closed, and the soldiers escorted him onto the bus. The diesel engines rumbled to a start, then the buses pulled away. He watched his mother and father through the window until the bus turned off the street. There was so much left unsaid. So many secrets, but now they were *his*. Ethan's dad said he'd had his reasons for lying to him all those years. And Ethan knew he had his own reasons for not telling his dad the truth now. Though, in the moment, that knowledge was a bitter pill to swallow.

Ethan turned to the rest of the group with a dazed look on his face. He spoke quietly. "He told me the truth…My dad finally told me the truth."

CHAPTER 8

LIFE AT BRIGGS AFB

A MASSIVE FOUR-STORY dormitory at Briggs Air Force Base provided the accommodations for the young refugees from Blackwoods. The building was entirely gray and lacked any splashes of color, except for an open courtyard with a well-manicured, lush green lawn that sat in the middle of the structure. The first two floors were reserved for the girls; the top two floors were inhabited by the boys. Each floor was supervised by two pairs of soldiers—basic airmen who lived in the dorm along with them. The military officials in charge tried to cluster the areas as best they could according to age, with the youngest kids closer to the soldiers in charge. It was two people to a room, a small room at that, and every two rooms shared an adjoining bathroom. The setup was a lot like a college dorm, though everyone was pretty sure there wouldn't be any crazy parties going on here.

Ethan and Caleb shared a room, as did Austin and Glenn, on the third floor. Annika bunked with her friend Holly Myers on the second floor. Holly had been a good friend of Annika's for a long time and, except for Holly not being interested in

Laser Wars games, they had quite a bit in common. They both enjoyed reading, movies, zombie-fighting video games, soccer, and perusing videos on the internet of cats in compromising positions. Despite their friendship and varied mutual interests, Annika was going crazy from not being with the rest of her Team Blackwoods squad. They had only been in the dorm for two hours, and she was already feeling out of the loop. Dinnertime couldn't come fast enough.

※

The dormitory cafeteria sat on the ground floor. It was at least three times the size of the school cafeteria the kids were used to. A sixty-foot-long food line stretched in front of the kitchen, with vague aromas of Salisbury steak, mashed potatoes, and peas lingering in the air. The place was bustling with the activity and chatter of everyone from nine to eighteen-years-old eating dinner at the same time. The jam-packed line moved quickly, though. Servers armed with ladles and hairy forearms slopped a mishmash of food onto the kids' plates with the efficiency of an automated assembly line.

Annika got her tray of food and weaved her way through the crowd. She finally spotted Ethan and the group waving at her from a table in the far corner. She took a seat with them and exhaled an exasperated sigh. "Anyone hear anything about when they'll let us out of here?" she asked.

"No," Ethan said. "But from the looks of it, we may be here a while. They just posted an activity schedule for the week on the wall outside our room."

Annika shook her head sharply in protest. "They can't keep us here for *a week*. It's June seventh. Fatal error in five days. Then two days after that the whole town—"

"Psssst," Ethan hissed, interrupting her. He nodded to a table next to them where four young airmen had just sat down. Annika swallowed her frustration and became quiet.

"There's also a rumor going around," Caleb added, leaning into the group, whispering. "Overheard the Mitchell brothers talking about some bigwigs from the Air Force coming in to interview the kids."

"About what?" Annika asked.

"Don't know exactly," Caleb said. "But I don't think it'll be about the food."

At that moment, Annika's roommate, Holly, and three other girlfriends of hers from class sat down at a nearby table. Holly and the girls waved at Annika and motioned for her to come over. Annika smiled at them, then turned and shot a frustrated look at the rest of her team.

"This is awkward," Annika said, speaking quietly and covering her mouth. "Be there in a minute," she said to the girls, forcing a smile.

Then Bradley Wuddle and Kevin Kim sat at a table cattycorner from them. Shortly after that, Tristan Fox, Garret Murphy, and Jason Monroe—former Delta Team members—sat at the table as well. The five of them eyeballed Team Blackwoods for an agonizingly long and uncomfortable moment. The expression on Tristan's face was just one of confusion. He simply didn't understand how the five members of Team Blackwoods had become such good friends, and so fast. But Bradley Wuddle had an especially nasty glint in his eyes. Though he could never in a million years muster the courage to say anything spiteful to Austin, his eyes said it all. They were full of malice.

"Yeah, very awkward," Austin said under his breath.

Finally, the tense moment was interrupted by a broad-shouldered colonel in a sharp blue Air Force service coat. He was tapping on a microphone at the front of the cafeteria. The amplified thumps resonated throughout the spacious room. When everyone saw that a colonel was about to speak, an immediate hush overcame the cafeteria. There was not the slightest whisper or peep. The colonel stood atop one of the tables and stared with ice-cold blue eyes into the sea of students. He held their gaze for quite a long while.

"Ladies and gentlemen, my name is Colonel Grissom," he said at last in a deep, even voice touched with a hint of Southern drawl. "I hope your stay here has been pleasant so far, and that you're enjoying the food and accommodations." The words the colonel used were friendly, but the way he spoke them suggested this wasn't just a social call. The officer's jaw tightened, then he got down to business. "We're investigating a security incident that occurred in Blackwoods yesterday. While we can't divulge the exact nature of the issue, we would like anyone who has witnessed any strange or unusual behavior to come forward, privately of course, and tell a ranking officer right away. We will also set up a secure phone line where you can call in and anonymously report anything suspicious."

Zeke and Jeremiah Mitchell were sitting with some friends at a table nearby the colonel. They both looked confused. Zeke raised his hand with a question.

"What is it, son?" the colonel asked.

"What exactly do you mean by *anything suspicious*, sir?" Zeke asked.

The colonel sighed deeply. "Son, I wish I could tell you

more. I really do. But right now, just be on the lookout for anything at all out of the ordinary."

Zeke and his brother still looked perplexed, but they nodded their heads dutifully. "Yes, sir," Zeke said.

"All right then," the colonel said, his voice stern. "If anyone here has seen anything, we expect to hear from you. Understand?" Everyone in the cafeteria nodded nervously. "Good. We'll be in touch with some of you, I'm sure."

The colonel got down from the table, pivoted quickly on his heels, and left the cafeteria flanked by two of his lieutenants. All the kids breathed a sigh of relief, even though no one, save for Team Blackwoods, had any idea what they had to be nervous about in the first place.

Later that evening, the team met in Ethan and Caleb's room to discuss matters in a more private setting. But they didn't have that much privacy. The soldiers in charge insisted that the doors to the rooms remain open at all times, except during bedtime, and regular guard patrols circled the floor at fifteen-minute intervals. Then there was the annoyance of Bradley Wuddle, who would pretend to just be walking by their room innocently, only to sneak glances inside when he thought no one was looking. So the group still had to be quiet when they spoke, but it sure beat trying to talk about sensitive information in the crowded and boisterous cafeteria.

Ethan gazed outside the window of the room for a long moment, then he turned to the rest of the team with a glum look on his face. "Three sets of fences, guard houses on each side, cameras everywhere, probably guards on the rooftops…

might as well be a maximum-security prison. We're not getting outta here until they let us out."

Annika sighed disgustedly. "So all we can do is sit around, stare out the window, and just *hope* we don't see that blue dome go over the town?"

"I don't see another move here," Ethan said. "Trying to escape would only blow our cover. If the fatal error happens, we gotta have the element of surprise."

"Yeah, Ethan's right," Caleb added.

"And what if the force field dome comes down before we can get inside?" Glenn asked. "Then what?"

"Then we tell the military where we stashed the metal briefcase," Austin said. Then he took a tense, deep breath. "But if that dome comes down again, God help us all."

Ethan stared out the window again, eyes distant, deep in thought. "If the fatal error does happen again, I don't think the attack will be the same as the first time around." Ethan turned to face the group. "The last time they abducted the entire town with the teleporters. But we gave the military the electromagnetic frequency that jams them, so if they listen to what we wrote in that letter, the teleporters won't work. The machines will have to find another way to take control of the town."

"Any guesses on how they do that?" Glenn asked.

"I have no idea," Ethan responded. "But just like we want the element of surprise, they would too. My bet is—" Ethan stopped quickly as he heard some approaching footsteps. Two airmen on guard patrol walked past their room and quickly looked inside. Everyone became silent until they had passed and were a safe distance away. "Like I was saying, whatever the machines do, my bet is they'll do it sneaky."

"Right," Caleb said with a grim face. "And there are much worse things than having that force field come down over the town, locking the robots in...Just think if those things got out?"

A moment of somber silence overcame everyone.

"At least the briefcase is safe," Ethan said, trying to salvage some optimism.

"Yeah, and all this talk might be for nothing anyway," Glenn said, riding the wave of hopefulness. "The officers and scientists at the research facility might've already figured out and fixed the fatal error."

The rest of the group nodded, happy to end the evening on an up note, even if they knew better than to believe it.

CHAPTER 9

THE RAT

Even though the military was on high alert, summer school managed to continue right on schedule in the dormitory at Briggs Air Force Base. With one exception—the school day was now eight hours long instead of four. The officers must've thought the best way to keep the kids out of the way was to saddle them with schoolwork. No one was allowed out of Blackwoods during the lockdown except for a select few teachers. Ms. Goodfoot was one of them. This morning she was picked up by an Air Force staff sergeant in a plain white sedan and punctually delivered to the dormitory at 7:50 a.m. sharp. She was to do her educational duty, then be returned home in the same car driven by the same staff sergeant at exactly 4:30 p.m.

No one on Team Blackwoods felt like sitting through eight hours of instruction, knowing full well that an extraterrestrial-related robot rebellion could happen at any time just a few miles away. But skipping class was not an option. The place was flooded with soldiers making sure the kids were in the right places at the right times. Even if they could break away, the five of them being absent together would look suspicious. And Colonel Grissom was on the lookout for anything suspicious.

Time crawled slowly and tensely for the group. It wasn't even lunchtime yet, but the day seemed like it should've been over already. At any given time, one or more of them was peering outside the classroom window that faced the town of Blackwoods to the east. They were searching for that distinct cobalt shade of blue that had covered the town before. Thoughts of seeing that force field dome again made their stomachs churn. Ethan had to pry his gaze from the window to look at the clock. The only consolation was that, in less than ten minutes, Ms. Goodfoot would dismiss them for lunch. Then he could get together with his team and talk about the things that mattered, though he had no idea how to better their situation.

The mercy of lunchtime was nearly upon them when a hard knock on the classroom door changed everything. Ms. Goodfoot stopped talking about geometry and opened the door. Colonel Grissom stood in the doorway, taking up all the space with his tall, muscular frame. The colonel completely eclipsed his two lieutenant assistants who were standing behind him.

Grissom scanned across the classroom of students with a stern, forbidding face. His jaw was taut and clenched, looking like it was carved from a block of granite. His intense, striking blue eyes were devoid of emotion and seemed to have the ability to stare at everyone in the room at the same time. He looked away from the class for a moment and turned his attention to Ms. Goodfoot.

"Sorry to interrupt your class, ma'am," Colonel Grissom said. Then he handed her a note and resumed eyeballing the students.

Ms. Goodfoot read the note, nodded to the colonel, then looked up at her class and announced: "Colonel Grissom needs to talk to the following students…Caleb, Annika, Glenn, Austin, and Ethan."

Everyone stared at the five of them. A gossipy murmur quickly engulfed the class. As the members of Team Blackwoods filed out behind Colonel Grissom, Austin glanced back into the classroom. He found Bradley Wuddle's beady eyes. Bradley's face flushed a bright red, and he quickly looked away. Austin shook his head in disgust as he left.

※

Colonel Grissom and the two lieutenants who were accompanying him ushered the group into a waiting room. The room was about the size of a small bedroom but lacked any of the comforts of home. The walls were entirely made up of gray cinder blocks, and the only decoration on them was a single Air Force recruitment poster. The poster depicted a formation of F-35 jet fighters streaking across a beautiful blue sky, with the words *"Aim High-Air Force"* in blue and silver lettering below. Two wooden bench seats were the only furniture. Other than the vibrant poster on the wall, which seemed almost sarcastically placed, the room looked every bit like a holding cell.

A place the Air Force put people who were in trouble for something.

"Wait here. Give me a minute," the colonel said as he left, closing the door behind him.

As soon as Colonel Grissom was gone, Austin turned to the group and scowled. "It was Bradley Wuddle, I know it. Did you see his guilty face? The rat didn't even have the guts to look me in the eye."

"Pssssst!" Caleb hissed urgently, then whispered, "Don't say another word. They could be listening to us. This place could be bugged."

"Good point," Ethan said.

The group scoured the room looking for any hidden listening devices. The walls were bare concrete, but they checked behind the poster on the wall, under the wood benches, the light fixtures, and even the door hinges.

"All-clear," Caleb said. "Go ahead."

"Look, I agree Bradley's a rat," Glenn said. "But what could he possibly know to tell Colonel Grissom?"

"He could mention that the five of us never used to hang out together. Then after graduation, we mysteriously became a band of brothers…and a sister," Annika said. "Wuddle wouldn't have to know anything, just pass it along to Grissom as something suspicious."

"Yeah," Ethan agreed. "Bradley Wuddle knows nothing, yet he still knows enough to make Grissom a pain in our butts."

"That stinkin', rat-faced, son-of-a—!" Austin yelled and pounded his fist on the bench.

"Rest assured, the military's going to dig up all the surveillance video they can find on us in the last five days," Caleb said.

"Yeah, but we kept this quiet," Ethan said. "We were careful…Plus, the security cameras around town have great video but no audio. They couldn't hear a thing."

"Well, you can count on them listening to everything we say from now on," Caleb said.

"We gotta stick to the original story," Ethan said. "The one we told when we skipped the last day of school—that

Austin challenged the rest of us at Laser Wars, and we accepted the challenge. After the battle, we settled our differences and became friends."

"Yeah, military officers will buy that," Austin added. "They study history. Lots of countries have gone to war with each other and ended up allies."

"We can even mention that to them," Ethan said. "Say we were like countries going to war and ending up allies. It'll help us keep our stories straight."

"Sounds like a plan," Glenn said.

At that moment, the clip and clop of military-issue dress shoes echoed outside the door. The sounds of footsteps closing in fast. The group silenced themselves and braced for visitors.

Colonel Grissom opened the door. His two lieutenant assistants were no longer with him. Instead, he was accompanied by Generals Turnbull and Vaden. Glenn's father looked concerned. Austin's father was fuming, his face already an unhealthy shade of red.

Colonel Grissom looked at Austin and Glenn with cold, uncaring eyes. "Austin and Glenn, your fathers would like a word with you," he said, then held the door open and nodded politely to General Turnbull and General Vaden.

Austin and Glenn exchanged quick, nervous glances with each other, then looked back at the other members of Team Blackwoods. Glenn left first. Austin lingered for a moment, reluctant to face what he knew was coming.

"Now, dammit!" Austin's father roared at his son.

Austin walked out of the room looking as dejected as an inmate on death row trudging toward the electric chair. His shoulders were slumped, and his head hung so low he was scarcely taller than Ethan.

"We'll be talking to the rest of you later," Colonel Grissom said in a threatening tone. He walked out of the room and slammed the door behind him.

Ethan wasn't surprised that Austin's and Glenn's parents were called first. Colonel Grissom wasn't about to interrogate the top two generals' sons without getting their fathers' consent. Questioning Austin and Glenn using intimidation tactics would be awkward enough with full parental permission. Going forward without it would be career suicide. The permission of the other parents was far less important. Ethan's and Caleb's fathers were military scientists, not ranking officers. And Annika's mother and father were captains, a rank too low for Colonel Grissom to worry about considering the dire circumstances the military now found themselves in.

Five long minutes passed, then Glenn returned to the waiting room first. His face was stoic, and he sat down without saying a word.

"So what happened?" Annika asked straightaway.

"Grissom told my dad he could take me home, ask me some questions in a more relaxed setting," Glenn answered, then shook his head firmly. "But I told my dad I wouldn't leave you guys...I think, in a strange way, he respected that."

"*We* respect that," Annika said.

Ethan and Caleb nodded and patted Glenn on the back.

"Thanks," Glenn said. "Anyone hear from Austin?"

Just then, thundering footsteps approached the room. The door swung open violently. A furious General Turnbull threw his son into the room by the scruff of his neck. Austin's dad's face was beet red, and a vein in his muscular neck was bulging out the size of a garden hose. He huffed and puffed in angry snorting sounds, trying to catch his breath. Sweat beaded up on his forehead like boiling liquid. He turned sharply to Colonel Grissom, who was standing safely a few paces behind him.

"I know when my own son's lying to me!" General Turnbull screamed at the top of his lungs, spit flying from his mouth. "Colonel Grissom, I give you permission to do whatever, and I mean *whatever* it takes to get the truth outta that lying sack of puke!"

Grissom nodded without batting an eye. "Yes, sir."

General Turnbull turned sharply and stormed out of the room. Colonel Grissom made sure to give him a wide berth and stepped out of his way. The colonel peeked back into the room and flashed a sadistic smile at Austin.

"And I thought *my* dad rode my ass," Grissom said. "Boy if I were you, I'd be the first one talkin'. If he wants to come back in here, tan your hide, I ain't stoppin' him." The colonel belted out a hearty laugh, then spoke sarcastically. "Hey, now. Cheer up, kids…it's lunchtime."

Colonel Grissom left and his two lieutenant minions entered carrying a sack lunch for each member of the group. They passed out the meals, then left without a word. Austin took a seat on the wooden bench. He dropped his sack lunch on the floor and slouched forward, elbows on his knees, hands covering his head.

Ethan scooted over and placed a comforting hand on Austin's shoulder. "I'm sorry, Austin. Are you all right?"

Austin slid away from Ethan and wriggled his shoulder free of his hand. "Leave me alone. I don't wanna talk about it," he snapped, reminding Ethan a lot of the Austin of old.

Ethan decided to give Austin some space and bothered him no more. The others followed his lead, leaving Austin to himself. The group eventually dug into their lunch sacks and pulled out a carton of milk, an overripe banana, and a peanut butter and jelly sandwich with razor-thin portions of each. Glenn was about to take his first bite of the malnourished sandwich when he stopped and looked over at Austin.

"Austin," Glenn said. He paused for an uneasy moment before continuing. "I'm sorry, but I don't understand...Why don't you just go live with your mom?"

Austin stared intensely at Glenn, boring a hole right through him. Tears welled up in his eyes, but he willed them not to fall. He clenched his jaw tightly, muscles twitching in his cheeks.

Then he finally spoke. "Because my mom is dead. Almost two years." Austin fixed his eyes down at the concrete floor and said, "You wanna do me a favor?...*Never, ever* mention that again." A single tear dropped and plunked against the concrete. Austin quickly covered it with his foot.

It felt as if the air had been sucked out of the room. Everyone was stunned. No one had had any idea. Austin turned away from the group. The team ate their lunches; there were no more words.

As Ethan gnawed on a rubbery peanut butter sandwich, he figured that Austin's mother must have died right before Austin started sixth grade—around the same time his father enrolled him for that partial semester at Schrodinger's Military Academy. The same time Austin had gone from a good friend and teammate to a constant thorn in his side.

Now it all made sense.

Ethan watched Austin in sympathy. He wanted to say something, but Austin had made his feelings on it very clear. He needed more time. Silence was best for now.

CHAPTER 10

SOME FRIENDLY QUESTIONS

An awkward hour passed before the group saw Colonel Grissom again. Everyone figured he was stalling, hoping that one or more of them would crack under the pressure and come forward with some information, to make his job easier. No one cracked, though. At one o'clock, Grissom opened the waiting room door and motioned with a sharp flick of his hand for Austin to come with him. Austin complied without so much as a word or a glance to the others. He left the room with the colonel and closed the door behind him without a sound.

In thirty minutes precisely, Colonel Grissom opened the waiting room door again. Austin was not with him. Grissom flicked his hand at the next in line to be interrogated. This time he was summoning Glenn.

Glenn stood up straight and proud. He met Colonel Grissom's gaze with sharp, defiant eyes. "Before I go, I wanna know what you did with Austin."

Colonel Grissom clenched his jaw like a high-tension bear trap, then he spoke through gnashed teeth. "Son, you are not the one asking questions here…And if you ever, *ever* look at me like that again, you'll wish you hadn't."

The colonel stared at Glenn with icy blue eyes that looked like death rays. Glenn held his gaze and ground for as long as he could, but eventually looked away and lowered his head as a sign of submission.

"That's better," Colonel Grissom said, flashing a victorious smile. "Now follow me. You can apologize to me properly on the way."

Glenn left the room with Colonel Grissom without another word.

Another thirty minutes had passed before Colonel Grissom came back to take Caleb. Thirty minutes after that he plucked Annika from the room. Ethan was left all alone with the patriotic poster on the wall and his frayed nerves. He wondered what questions Colonel Grissom was asking the others. He wondered if anyone had cracked yet under the pressure. Ethan was pretty sure his friends would stand their ground and keep their stories straight, but he also knew the military had ways of getting answers from people reluctant to give them. As the seconds and minutes ticked away on Ethan's watch, his stomach grew increasingly queasy. Like clockwork, as soon as the thirtieth minute passed since Annika had left the room, he heard footsteps, then a heavy hand on the doorknob. He stood up, eyed the door tensely, and took a deep breath.

Ethan hoped dearly that *he* wouldn't be the one to crack under the pressure.

※

Everything about the interrogation room was designed to produce an intimidated and uncomfortable guest. The room was sweltering, at least twenty degrees hotter than the waiting area, with an oversized incandescent light bulb hanging from the ceiling that bombarded the area with heat like a miniature sun. The room was also much smaller than the previous one. There was barely enough room for the large oak table that sat in the middle, adorned with a simple folding chair on each side.

Colonel Grissom led Ethan to his chair, walking uncomfortably close to him the entire way. Ethan sat down and looked up, craning his neck skyward until it hurt to make eye contact with the colonel, who appeared ten feet tall from the extreme angle. Ethan felt lightheaded and claustrophobic from the heat and lack of personal space. His eyes faded in and out of focus, and a reservoir of sweat dammed up above his eyebrows. Then, out of nowhere, Colonel Grissom's familiar scowl disappeared, and he flashed a toothy smile.

"Relax, kid," Grissom said. "I'd just like to ask you some friendly questions." The colonel's fleeting smile vanished and his hardnosed, dour face returned. The mind games had officially begun.

Colonel Grissom took a seat on the opposite side of the table as his lanky lieutenant assistants walked in and stood at attention behind him. The lieutenants' eyes were dark and their faces lacked any emotion as they stared intensely at the wall behind Ethan, like a couple of highly programmed, flesh-and-blood robots. Grissom opened a file folder and pulled out a notepad, then retrieved a shiny gold pen from his jacket pocket and clicked it open, closed, open. He stared at Ethan the entire time with his uninviting blue eyes. The eyeballing continued for over a minute without a single question. Ethan tried to maintain eye contact and show no fear, but those were impossible feats. He finally broke down and looked away from the colonel.

Colonel Grissom smiled and nodded smugly. Then he began his inquisition.

"I see you've made some new friends recently, Mr. Tate," Colonel Grissom said accusingly. "Tell me, what brought the five of you together so close, so fast…especially you and Austin Turnbull, the boy who used to bully you till you cried to your momma?"

Ethan clenched his jaw and grimaced. "You tell Bradley Wuddle I never cried….I know that's who talked to you. He's just trying to get us in trouble because he's—"

"Never mind who I talked to!" Colonel Grissom roared. "Answer the question!"

Ethan took a calming breath, though it didn't do much to calm him. He had to focus on keeping his story straight. He knew Grissom was just trying to frustrate him, to get him to break from the script, in case there was a script.

Ethan looked squarely at Colonel Grissom and explained plainly and clearly: "Austin challenged the four of us to a Laser Wars game. He thought he could beat all of us. So we skipped school to play. We felt like we had to for our honor. It was a tough battle, but we beat him. In the process, I guess we came to respect each other. No more bullying. Austin and I even became friends."

Colonel Grissom smiled sarcastically. "So you became friends…just like that?"

"Yeah," Ethan responded. "You know, it's like when two countries fight a war and end up becoming allies."

"Funny you should say that...'cause every one of your friends did too," Colonel Grissom said with a *gotcha* smile on his face. "Rehearse that 'countries fight a war and end up allies' bit, did ya?"

"Not really," Ethan responded coolly, gaining more composure the longer he talked. "We just kinda thought of that after we had our laser battle and ended up getting along. Like fighting countries becoming allies. Austin mentioned it first, I think." Ethan paused and stared at the colonel with the endearing eyes of a puppy. "You *are* glad that Austin doesn't bully me anymore and that we became allies, right?"

Colonel Grissom clenched his jaw and fists, frustrated, yet not exactly sure how to respond. "Overjoyed," the colonel uttered through teeth that could be heard grinding.

"Me too," Ethan said with a smile, bordering dangerously on sarcastic. Then he forced his smile away. "So, what exactly do you think we've done?"

The colonel rubbed his chin hard, stared at Ethan through squinty eyes. "There's been a major security breach at the research facility. A breach so severe, I can't even put into words. Our national security...no, the *world's* security is at stake here."

"And you think *we* were involved in the breach?" Ethan asked incredulously.

"Get real," Colonel Grissom snapped. "You brats couldn't take a leak without wettin' yer pants. So no, I do not think *you guys* breached security." Grissom paused and smiled wickedly. "But I think you mighta done something else." He pulled a white envelope out of the file folder and flipped it at Ethan. "*This* look familiar?"

Ethan examined the empty envelope and tried to keep a

good poker face. It was addressed to General Carl Vaden—the same envelope they had used to send the warning letter.

"I don't know," Ethan said. "General Vaden's mail, I guess...What was in it?"

"That's none of your business." Colonel Grissom snatched back the envelope. "All I want to know is...who paid you to send this letter?"

"Who paid us?" Ethan repeated, sounding as confused as possible. "Nobody paid us for anything. I don't even know what you're talking about."

"Is that so?" Colonel Grissom asked with a sneering grin. "This letter was mailed from *inside* Blackwoods," he said, raising his voice with each sentence he spoke. "Specifically, from the mailbox outside the movie theater...We have video surveillance footage that shows you and your buddies conveniently hanging around that mailbox, just the night before the mail was picked up with this letter in it...and, and I haven't told any of your friends this yet, if you look real close, I can even make out *your* hand dropping something into the box." Colonel Grissom took a deep breath and spoke more calmly. "Now...do you want to change your story? All I want to know is who gave you this letter to put in the mail?"

"I haven't seen that letter before in my life," Ethan said as convincingly as he could.

"I think you're a liar," Colonel Grissom said with an eerily calm smile. "And you wanna know what else I think?...I think the five of you took money from someone here in Blackwoods to deliver that letter. And I also think it was the money that turned you and Austin into friends, or at least partners in crime, and not some stupid Laser Wars game."

"That's not true."

"Really?" Colonel Grissom said. "Well, we'll find out. You all will be fingerprinted, the letter checked for prints, and, as we speak, that fort of yours is being searched for evidence... If you got any more money than a kid has a right to, we will find it. Anything else out of the ordinary, we will find it...And if you're lying to me, God help you, son."

Ethan nodded, then he coolly and calmly played his ace-in-the-hole. "I'm sorry, Colonel Grissom, I forgot. I did drop a letter in the mailbox that night...I sent a letter to my grandma. She just had wrist surgery, and I wanted to send her a get-well card. That must've been what you saw on the video footage."

Colonel Grissom's face went from smug to dumbfounded in a nanosecond. He mouthed a couple of words, but no sound came out. He shook his head in frustration and ran his fingers tightly through his short-cropped blond hair. "Why would you wait till now to tell me that?" he said through clenched teeth.

"I was so nervous, I just forgot...Sorry."

"You can't cover up that lie, son. We will check in with Granny. If she doesn't get a letter with yesterday's postmark, I will personally rain hell on you. You understand that?"

"Got it," Ethan said, swallowing hard, dearly hoping that his grandmother's letter wouldn't get lost in the mail.

Just then, the colonel's cell phone vibrated. Grissom picked it up and listened. A smile crept on his face that widened the longer he listened. By the time he set his phone back on the table, he wore the broad, sneaky smile of the Cheshire Cat.

"In the meantime, I gotta little surprise for you and your friends," Grissom said. "Something that might make y'all come clean without even having to bother old granny."

Colonel Grissom led Ethan into a large conference room, where the rest of Team Blackwoods was waiting. Ethan was happy to see his friends, even though they looked like a miserable bunch that had been put through the wringer with the colonel's questioning.

"Be back in a jiffy," Colonel Grissom said with a self-satisfied smile as he left and closed the door behind him.

"So…How'd it go?" Ethan asked.

"Grissom told us not to talk," Caleb said. "And I'm sure this place is bugged, but…" He gave a thumbs up, then everyone else followed suit. Ethan smiled and nodded proudly.

"Grissom forgot to tell me not to talk," Ethan said. "Guess he was too excited about the surprise and forgot."

"What surprise?" Annika asked.

"Grissom told me he's got some sort of surprise for us," Ethan said. "I have no idea what it is, but it's probably not on our Christmas list."

At that moment, the door swung open. Colonel Grissom entered with Annika's and Caleb's dads in tow. Grissom's lieutenant assistants walked in behind them and shut the door.

"Dad!" Annika and Caleb shouted simultaneously. They ran and hugged their fathers.

"What are you doing here?" Annika asked.

"Sit down, all of you," Colonel Grissom interrupted. "I'll tell you why they're here."

Everyone sat down around the conference table. Colonel Grissom paced around the room, intensely eyeing everyone as he passed by. "Annika, Caleb…we have reason to believe that your fathers were involved in the security breach at the research facility."

Annika and Caleb looked completely sucker-punched by the colonel's words. Annika's father, Captain Scott Pepper, stood up and glared defiantly at Colonel Grissom.

"This is insane!" Captain Pepper shouted. "You bring me in front of *my* daughter and accuse me of *that*!"

"You remember that you are speaking to a superior officer, Captain!" Colonel Grissom managed to shout louder. "Now sit down!"

Captain Pepper stood his ground. He was every bit as tall as Colonel Grissom, so he could look him squarely in the eyes, on his level. He fired back, "I was at that security briefing, Colonel. I read the letter sent to General Vaden. Those people are heroes! You should be proud of whatever team pulled off that miracle instead of rounding them up and treating them like traitors. They saved your life, Colonel. They saved all our lives! I wish I was one of them, but believe me, I'm not."

"Well, I'm just tickled pink that they saved the day," Colonel Grissom said sarcastically. "But that group constitutes a major security threat now...And, no, I'm not just going to *believe you*." Grissom turned to his lieutenants and said, "Please escort the captain out of the room."

The lieutenants flanked Captain Pepper and grabbed him firmly by each arm. "Let's go," one of the lieutenants said.

"Get off me!" Captain Pepper yelled and jerked himself free. He turned sharply to Colonel Grissom. "Why is Annika here? What do you want with my daughter?!"

"Get him outta here...Now!" Colonel Grissom ordered.

The lieutenants struggled to restrain Captain Pepper, who was furiously thrashing around and more than a handful for the two young lieutenants to corral.

"Dad!" Annika cried out. She rushed in and jumped on

one lieutenant's back. She began punching wildly at him. The lieutenant wheeled around and slung Annika off, sending her tumbling over a chair. An incensed Ethan led the charge with Austin and Glenn and tackled the lieutenant to the ground. It was total chaos in the room until a half-dozen airmen entered and broke up the brawl. Eventually, it took four men to drag Annika's father out of the conference room and another four to hold back the members of Team Blackwoods. Annika's eyes were brimming with angry tears.

Caleb's dad, Dr. Warren, who had been whisked away from his research before he could even take off his white lab coat, glared at Colonel Grissom. "This is absolute madness. And I'm taking my son home…C'mon, Caleb, let's go."

"I can't let you do that, Doctor," Colonel Grissom said calmly.

"I am his father, and this is not a jail," Dr. Warren snapped. "I'm taking my son home." Dr. Warren marched over to Caleb. "Caleb, we're leaving."

The lieutenants flanked Caleb's dad. "Now, Dr. Warren… We don't want another ugly scene, do we?" Colonel Grissom asked with condescension in his voice.

Caleb's dad backed off. "Unbelievable," he said bitterly. "So when do you plan on letting these innocent kids go?"

"Why the very moment we know they're innocent, of course," Colonel Grissom said in a mocking tone. "But I suspect there's more here than meets the eye…just not quite sure what that is yet."

"You're wrong," Dr. Warren fired back. "Wrong about them, whatever you think they did, and wrong about Captain Pepper and me."

"Time will tell," Colonel Grissom said with a cocky smile.

Then his smile vanished in an instant. "You need to leave now, Dr. Warren…and I'm not gonna ask you twice."

"It's okay, Dad," Caleb said, even though his lips quivered. "We'll be okay."

Dr. Warren hugged his son, then looked at everyone. "Don't worry, we will get you out of here. I'll go directly to General Turnbull if I have to."

Colonel Grissom belted out a hearty laugh. "General Turnbull?" he said, continuing to chuckle. "General Turnbull is the one who put them here. He just entrusted me with this job because I'm *sooooo* good with kids." The colonel finally stopped his belly-laughing. "Now goodbye, Doctor. You and I will have a nice little chat later."

The lieutenants ushered Dr. Warren out of the room. Colonel Grissom eyed the members of Team Blackwoods with a severely stern face that radiated aggravation. "Now you know exactly what the stakes are," he said. "So…does anyone have something to say that might help out Annika's and Caleb's poor, poor fathers? Tell me who gave you that letter to put in the mail. Do it for them."

The temptation for Annika and Caleb to come clean and tell the truth was almost unbearable. The accusation that their fathers were involved in the security breach made the issue unsettlingly personal. But the group knew exactly why General Turnbull and the other top brass had chosen Captain Pepper and Dr. Warren as two who might've possibly been in on Project Mulligan. Captain Pepper was a master marksman and had once been the best sniper in the Marine Corps; Dr. Warren was a chief engineer at the most advanced research facility in the world and was a certified super genius. Someone great with a gun and someone great with technology—crucial ingredients for any crack team that would've stood a chance at pulling off such an amazing operation. The officers investigating the breach were on the right track. They understood the skills the perfect team would've needed. But they had no clue that that team was in the room with them right now, apples that hadn't fallen too far from their trees, hiding in plain sight under the cover of youth.

Ethan stared Colonel Grissom dead in the eyes and said, "No one gave us that letter to put in the mail…and that's the God's honest truth."

Colonel Grissom put his hands on the table and leaned forward into Ethan's face. He exhaled an angry, scorching hot breath. "You just made things a whole lot worse. When we find out you're lying to us, and we will, you'll—"

Just then, the door swung open and one of Grissom's young lieutenants darted inside, a look of urgency straining his face. "Colonel Grissom, sir, I need to talk to you," he said, short of breath as if he had just been sprinting.

"Lieutenant Mackey, not now!" Colonel Grissom roared. "Can't you see I'm in the middle of something?"

"Yes, sir. Sorry, sir," the lieutenant apologized delicately. "But this is important."

Colonel Grissom shot a severely annoyed look at the lieutenant. "What is it? And this better be good."

"Sir, General Turnbull just announced an emergency meeting at the research facility," the lieutenant said. "All officers are ordered to go immediately."

"The research facility?…*Now?*" Grissom asked, face scrunched in confusion.

"Yes, sir. General Turnbull's orders."

Colonel Grissom eyed the members of Team Blackwoods

and scowled. "This is not even close to being over, you hear me? Go back to your rooms and enjoy your free time now… 'Cause when I get back, the party's over." Grissom turned to Lieutenant Mackey. "Lieutenant, escort these little liars back to their rooms."

"Yes, sir," the lieutenant said.

Colonel Grissom left the room. He slammed the door behind him so hard it made their ears ring.

CHAPTER 11

WAITING AND WORRYING

THE GROUP SPENT that evening in Ethan and Caleb's room waiting anxiously for Colonel Grissom to return. It was almost bedtime, and no one had seen the colonel or any other officers in the dormitory since the emergency meeting had been called. The only Air Force members around were low-ranking airmen who were still doing their regular patrols on the dorm floors. The young airmen tried to remain professional, but there was a nervous chatter among them. They were wondering why their superior officers hadn't returned yet, wondering what the security breach was in the first place, and wondering if they, and the kids in their charge, were in any sort of imminent danger.

Annika stared intently through the window blinds, into the darkness outside. She turned to the group, biting her lip. "I know something's wrong...I can just feel it."

"Yeah," Ethan said. "They should've been back by now."

Then a young airman stopped at the doorway and peeked inside. "Lights out in twenty minutes. Everyone get back to your rooms."

"Have you heard anything yet?" Austin asked the airman.

"No," the airman answered. "But that's a good thing. We would've heard something for sure if anything was wrong," he concluded, sounding like he was trying to convince himself.

"How many airmen are in the dorm now?" Annika asked.

The airman looked confused by Annika's question, but he answered: "About twenty."

"That's not many," Annika said. "You should set up a perimeter outside. And if you don't already, get some lookouts on the roof who know how to shoot. Give them night-vision goggles if you got them…in case they might be coming in dark."

Annika's suggestions were creeping out the young soldier. His eyes were wide and his voice jittery as he asked, "What do you mean?…*Who* might be coming in dark?"

Ethan and the others flashed Annika a warning look. She shrugged her shoulders. "Whatever bad guys are out there, of course," she explained vaguely.

The airman exhaled a relieved breath. "Sheesh…for a minute you had me worried you saw something. You're Captain Pepper's daughter, aren't you?"

"The one and only," Annika said with a smile.

"Heck, I've heard about you…the way you shoot, maybe we should put *you* on the roof," the airman quipped.

Annika's smile disappeared in an instant. "Maybe you should."

The airman looked taken aback. "I was just joking."

Annika shot him a hard stare. "I wasn't."

The airman nodded, smiled uneasily, and checked his wristwatch. "Lights out in fifteen minutes. If y'all could go back to your assigned rooms, I'd really appreciate it."

"No problem," Annika said. "But, seriously, get some guards on that roof."

The airman nodded again, looking even more unsettled. "Goodnight, now."

"Goodnight," Annika chirped with a sarcastic perkiness.

The bemused airman left the room and continued his patrol down the hallway. Ethan watched him until he disappeared around the corner, then said, "We should stay alert tonight, try to sleep in shifts in our rooms."

"What about Holly?" Annika wondered with a wry grin. "Not sure she's gonna understand why I'm on guard duty."

"Of course not," Ethan said. "I'll take your shift. If I see or hear anything unusual, I'll come get you."

"What about the airmen?"

Ethan cracked a mischievous grin. "You don't think I can sneak by them?"

"I believe you could," Annika said, smiling back.

Ethan beamed like a proud fool for a moment, then his face slowly turned serious as he addressed Annika and Caleb. "Your dads are going to be fine. As soon as we're sure the fatal error isn't gonna happen again, we come clean, tell Colonel Grissom we did it and where the briefcase is, and explain why we waited to tell them…It's going to be okay."

Annika and Caleb nodded and willed the tears away. Then Annika, Austin, and Glenn left for their rooms. Ethan watched Annika walk down the hall until she disappeared into the stairwell. He desperately wished that everything he'd said to her would come true. But the longer he thought about it, the more he felt like a liar.

⁂

Ethan and Caleb alternated guard shifts for the rest of the night. It was a pointless exercise, though. Neither one of them saw anything out of the ordinary from the vantage point of their room window. They didn't hear anything either. Not a peep. The night passed as smoothly and uneventfully as any other. That made them feel more at ease, until they remembered the last time the fatal error happened—that night had passed routinely as well.

At six o'clock in the morning, a loud knock on the door startled Ethan and Caleb, who were both staring out of their window in the direction of Blackwoods and not expecting visitors so early.

"Rise and shine! Reveille!" an airman's loud voice permeated the door. "Get up, get ready, and get to the mess hall in twenty minutes. Colonel Grissom has an announcement to make."

The airman continued down the hall, knocking on doors and yelling the same bit of news. Caleb looked at Ethan with nervous eyes. "Wonder what that's about."

"I have no idea," Ethan replied. "But, strange as it sounds, I'm kinda glad to hear Colonel Grissom is back."

"Yeah, at least we know the fatal error hasn't happened yet. But I don't think I'll ever say I'm *glad* to see Colonel Grissom."

Ethan smiled. "Let's hurry and get downstairs. Can't wait to hear what he's got to say."

※

The cafeteria was packed with kids waiting surprisingly patiently. They sat upright at their tables with unusually good posture and were eerily quiet. The food line was open for business with steam rising from the hot bins of scrumptious breakfast items laid out buffet-style. The heavenly aromas of biscuits and gravy, scrambled eggs, pancakes, and bacon filled the air, but that wasn't temptation enough to lose focus on the main entryway to the cafeteria. It was there that Colonel Grissom was due to enter anytime and make his announcement. Hungry as the young refugees were, they craved going home and seeing their families more. Many hoped that somehow displaying their best behavior might make that decision come faster, as if they had some control over the matter.

All eyes were on that entryway now. It was so quiet, and with everyone's minds focused on the same thing, you could almost hear the singular, resonant thought seeping through their heads: *When can we go home?*

It was always awkward for Team Blackwoods to go into the cafeteria for meals. They felt like animals at the zoo being observed by a curious public. The former members of Bravo and Delta teams seemed to always surround them, sitting close but not too close. Staring at them constantly, only to jerk their heads away and innocently look at the wall when one of them looked back. Trying to listen in on their conversations, but pretending like they weren't. The only difference for this occasion was Bradley Wuddle. He sat conspicuously as far away as possible, giving further proof to Austin's theory that his former sergeant was the rat. Wuddle was surely afraid that sitting any closer to Austin might result in his breakfast sandwich coming with a fist full of knuckles.

Finally, a hulking shadow on the hallway wall heralded the arrival of Colonel Grissom. His faithful lieutenants were with him again, one on each side, as he made his way to the front of the cafeteria. Grissom stood atop one of the tables and ran his cold blue eyes over seemingly everyone in the cafeteria in one pass. His eyes spent no more time on the members of Team Blackwoods than on anyone else. But no one in the group breathed any easier yet. His face was tight, revealing nothing about his mood or the state of affairs at the research facility. He held the room's attention with those eyes of his until he allowed a faint, upward crook of his mouth. It was a smile, or at least as close to one as he had under the circumstances.

The colonel drew a tight breath through that upward crook. In a hospitable, Southern accent, he said, "Ladies and gentlemen…I'd like to thank you for your patience during what has been a very trying time for you, I'm sure. It's been a trying time for us all, I can assure you that."

Grissom paused for a long moment. Again, he scanned across the assembled students, devoting no more time to one than the other. The fact that he didn't spend at least a few extra seconds glaring at Team Blackwoods brought the group a measure of relief. The colonel's weak smile brought another. Then they got around to wishful thinking: *Maybe Colonel Grissom already verified that Ethan had sent the letter to his grandma. Maybe he realized that Annika's and Caleb's fathers were completely innocent. Or, better yet, maybe the officers and scientists at the research facility had solved the problem of the fatal error.*

The colonel had the same strange, subdued smile on his face when he began again, "Now when you go home…"

The word *home* instantly spawned excited whispers and murmurs among the crowd of kids. The chatter got louder and louder until the colonel silenced the room by simply removing the upward crook on his mouth. His face and affect became flat again, and the kids hoped dearly that they didn't just jinx what they thought he was about to say.

"Now when you go home," the colonel continued, "you will notice the extra security measures we've taken. Some of these may seem odd to you, but they will remain in effect until we are satisfied that the security threat is truly over." Colonel Grissom filled his lungs with air, making him look even more barrel-chested. His face became very stern as he added, "I strongly suggest you respect and obey all newly added security measures. Failure to do so would bring about…a most unpleasant situation."

The team was wary of the colonel's remarks. *Failure to respect and obey…Odd security measures…Would bring about a most unpleasant situation.* It all sounded pretty ominous. The group began thinking again. But this time, it wasn't as wishful. *Maybe the officers and scientists hadn't gotten a grip on the fatal error. Maybe they still didn't even know what it was.*

The upward crook of a smile returned to Colonel Grissom's face when he spoke again. "Folks, you enjoy this fantastic breakfast. After that, get packed up and be on the curb outside by zero nine-hundred hours…You're going home."

Everyone in the cafeteria cheered. Team Blackwoods was glad to be going home too, but they refrained from any celebration. There was a gigantic loose end to tie up with Colonel Grissom, though he appeared to be leaving without so much as looking at them. The group got up from their table and rushed to intercept the colonel as he was walking out of the cafeteria.

"Sir, what about us?" Ethan asked.

Colonel Grissom stared at the five of them for a quick moment, then said, "We're done here. You may go home."

"So you checked and found out I sent that letter to my grandma?" Ethan asked.

"That's right," Colonel Grissom said matter-of-factly.

"What about my dad? And Annika's dad?" Caleb asked. "They go home too?"

"Everyone goes home," the colonel said. "Now, if you'll excuse me, I must be going." Grissom left quickly with his lieutenants in tow.

"Well, that's good news, right?" Glenn asked hesitantly.

Ethan looked pensive. "Maybe."

Annika's face furrowed. "What are you thinking, Ethan?"

"I'm thinking either everything went really great at that emergency meeting, or that everything went really wrong… I'm just not sure which one."

As the rest of the kids in the cafeteria ate their breakfasts and rejoiced in the fact that they would soon be going home, Team Blackwoods did neither. They knew there was much more to the story, much more to consider. They didn't feel like eating, and they certainly didn't feel like celebrating. A vague sense of dread hung over them like a dark thundercloud. The hair on their necks tingled, and they felt a chill in the air.

They sensed a storm coming.

CHAPTER 12

A STRANGE REUNION

THE ATMOSPHERE ON the bus ride back to Blackwoods resembled a party, like a bus ride for the fans of a football team who had just smashed their opponent. Except for the five kids in the back. Team Blackwoods mostly sat in silence during the fifteen-minute trip. All they could think about was the fatal error, and what exactly Colonel Grissom was talking about when he'd mentioned that the security measures they put in place might seem odd.

The bus pulled onto Kingsbury Avenue and came to a stop beside the curb. The group stepped out wearily and walked to the sidewalk. They scanned the area, looking for any signs of weirdness. No robots were rampaging down the street, no cobalt-colored force field above them, and, as far as they could tell yet, no obviously odd security measures. The only thing they saw were their parents, and everyone else's, standing on their front porches, staring at the buses as they deployed their children.

Ethan watched his parents from a distance. They looked as tired as he did. He wondered what they had been through the last couple of days, if they had been harassed as much as he and his friends had. Ethan couldn't wait to talk to them, not just for information-gathering, but to hear their soothing voices again. Without a word, the members of Team Blackwoods slowly disbanded and headed for their parents.

Ethan met his folks on the porch. His mother and father hugged him at once, enveloping him in a warm family embrace. Then, with tender hands on his back, they ushered him inside.

After Ethan had convinced his parents that he'd had enough to eat for breakfast that morning—which he hadn't—they sat together in the living room on the couch. Eating was the last thing on Ethan's mind with the million and one questions jostling around in his head. The first question he had was for himself: *Where to begin with the questions?* He decided to play it cool, though, opting to let his parents go first in explaining what had happened in Blackwoods while he was tucked away in the safety of Briggs Air Force Base. Then, Ethan figured, his dad would begin the big talk—the one he'd been promised before he was whisked away on the military bus. At that point, Ethan would reveal his part in the charade. There were so many things left unsaid that needed to be spoken now, but his dad had to make the first move. Ethan felt he was owed that.

"We missed you so much, honey," Ethan's mom said, hugging her son again.

Ethan's dad nodded. "It was hard on us being away from you, Ethan. And leaving you like that, under those circumstances. We're so sorry. It's something we never want to do again."

"It's okay, Dad," Ethan said in sympathy.

"So what was it like over there?" his mom asked. "Did they treat you okay?

"It was fine." Then Ethan bit his lip and said, "They treated us great."

"That's good to hear, Ethan," his dad said. "We were so worried about you."

"Well, I'm fine," Ethan said quickly. "So what was it like over here?" He pressed the issue faster than he would have liked to, but curiosity overwhelmed him.

Ethan's mother and father exchanged cryptic glances. They turned back to their son with a unified expression. "We're not allowed to speak about that," Ethan's father said. "It's part of the new security measures."

Ethan looked at his mother in hopes of finding a dissenting view, but she only nodded in agreement with her husband. Ethan felt like he'd been punched in the gut—twice.

"C'mon, you have to tell me something...anything," Ethan said, annoyed.

"Sorry, I cannot," Ethan's father responded. "Security measures."

Ethan was flabbergasted. Then he really went out on a limb. "What about the big talk, Dad? The one you said we'd have?" He raised his voice in desperation. "The one about the world being more complicated?...*I'm ready for that now.*"

Ethan's father looked his son dead in the eyes and said, "I'm so sorry, son. I cannot...Security measures."

Ethan again looked at his mother, hoping to find an ally. But she only nodded her head steadily in agreement with her husband. Ethan could feel the frustration bubbling up inside him. His father lied again. And this time, his mother, who had to know a good deal of the truth now, remained at his side. Two liars now, the entire parental unit. *Just terrific*, Ethan thought with sarcasm too intense to be measured with current technology.

Ethan tried desperately to keep the next words from escaping his lips, but the temptation was too strong. The first nine words came out clear as a bell when he spouted: "You know, *we* were the ones who completed Project Mull—"

The final word—*Mulligan*—he'd managed to find the restraint to cut off at the last nanosecond. He watched his parents for a reaction. Any reaction at all to those words he regretted saying already. Ethan cringed as he waited, hoping, praying that they wouldn't piece it together. But he was sure they would. They had to. He had practically said the whole thing, just leaving off the "*-igan*" part. Waiting for the consequences of his rash action was pure torture.

Ethan's parents glanced at each other briefly, then turned their eyes on their son. "What did you just say?" his father asked in a tone that was terribly difficult to read.

Ethan swallowed hard and breathed in jittery, short gasps. He was sure he'd just botched up everything, but he decided to try one last, desperate cover-up. *There's no way it will work*, he thought, but he could hardly mess up any worse than he had already. *Nothing to lose.*

Ethan fought to steady his breathing, then said, "We completed Project Multiplication. It's a big group assignment for math class, algebra. Multiplying polynomials." Ethan took a deep, calming breath. "What I'm trying to tell you is that I worked really hard in summer school at Briggs Base. I did as I was told, and I worked hard…Now I think I have a right to know what's going on."

That was pathetic. Project Multiplication? That's *the best you can come up with? That's like the name of some terrible reality show for eight-year-olds. They'll see right through that. Might as well have said Project Mulligan again and said it proudly. At least I'd go out with some dignity that way.* Ethan held his breath, waiting tensely for a response, bracing for his lame cover-up attempt to be uncovered.

Ethan's parents considered carefully what their son had said. After a longer processing time than expected, his father and mother focused their eyes on him at precisely the same moment. Their faces didn't look happy, but they didn't look angry either. It was hard for Ethan to tell exactly what they were thinking. Finally, his parents smiled simultaneously.

Mr. Tate put a gentle hand on his son's shoulder and said, "We're both very proud of your schoolwork, Ethan. You make us so proud. But we cannot tell you more about what happened. Not yet. Maybe never…Security measures."

Ethan was stunned that his *Project Multiplication* story worked. He figured he must be a better actor than he'd given himself credit for. Still, he was frustrated that his parents weren't willing to tell him anything about what had happened. Ethan hoped, as the day progressed, that they might give in and at least toss him some scraps of information.

But they would not. Lunch and dinner passed uneventfully, so did the time in between. Ethan's mom and dad constantly reassured him that everything was all right, that they loved him, and that he was safe. But no secrets were revealed on either side. After a dinner of salmon and broccoli, and yet another round of tender, loving hugs from his parents, Ethan went up to his bedroom. He needed to talk to Caleb.

Ethan punched Caleb's number into his cell phone

and paced around his room as he waited. It was then that he noticed the first of the odd security measures. A woman's voice came through the phone, pleasant but automated: *"Hello, please wait while we connect you to the number dialed. Please be aware that, due to security measures, only local calls will be allowed, and all phone conversations will be monitored for content. Thank you and have a nice day."*

Ethan thought quickly about hanging up, knowing that he couldn't have a conversation with Caleb about anything important with someone listening in on the call. Then he thought better of it, figuring it would look suspicious if he hung up now. So he stayed on the line.

"Hello?"

"Hi, Caleb. It's Ethan. Guess with the new security measures they're monitoring all the calls now." Ethan wanted to say that first and fast, in case Caleb was unaware and said something he shouldn't. "Not like we have anything worth listening to. Hey monitor guy, wanna help me with my homework?" Ethan forced a laugh and did so convincingly.

Caleb didn't miss a beat, so they chit-chatted innocently for a while about school and their favorite TV shows, enough to make the call monitor fall asleep from boredom. Then they ended the call by saying they'd see each other at school tomorrow.

⁓

It was 9:00 p.m. Ethan was lying on his back in bed, with the events of the last two days swirling in his mind, when a loud siren blared that jolted him up like a rock from a slingshot. Ethan looked outside his bedroom window but saw nothing. Then he opened the door to his room and found his parents standing right there, as if waiting for him. Ethan flinched, spooked, not expecting them to be so close. He collected himself and took a deep breath. His parents watched him for a moment without saying a word. Finally, they smiled at exactly the same time.

"It's okay, honey," Ethan's mom said. "We need to leave for a while. We will be back soon."

Ethan stared at his mother like she was nuts. "Where are you going?"

"Ethan, your mother and I have to go check in with General Turnbull at the research facility," his dad said. "Everyone does…Security measures."

"*Now?*" Ethan asked, confused.

"Yes, son, now…And every day at this time until the security threat is gone."

Ethan dashed over to the window, pinched open the blinds, and peeked outside again. This time he saw people leaving their houses and boarding the same military buses that the school kids had taken to Briggs Air Force Base. Just the adults were leaving this time. Ethan turned back and shot his parents a scowl.

"We'll only be gone for two hours," Mrs. Tate said in a soothing voice.

His mother's sweet tone did nothing to calm him. "You can't just leave like this and not tell me why?!" Ethan shouted. "You have to tell me something!"

Ethan's dad stared at his son with remarkable composure. "I'm sorry, Ethan. I cannot…Security measures."

Ethan's parents turned and left, and Ethan followed them the entire way out the front door, begging them for answers. But they provided none. His parents boarded one of the camouflaged military buses, and, as soon as all of the adults on the street had been picked up, the buses pulled away. Immediately after the buses left, several military jeeps drove through. They came to a stop, spaced evenly along the street. When the soldiers got out, they took great care to space out evenly themselves. Each residence received two soldiers, staring constantly at the house, keeping guard. As Ethan watched the soldiers, all with stiff postures and faces that lacked emotion, he couldn't help but wonder which was their primary objective: *Making sure nobody gets in, or making sure nobody gets out?*

CHAPTER 13

SERIOUS DOUBTS

At 11:00 p.m. Ethan's parents were still not home. Ethan was lying in bed, wide awake in his dark room, when he finally heard the rumble of diesel engines. He went quickly to his window and peered outside. The military buses stopped alongside the curb, opened their doors, and deposited the adults onto the sidewalk. The soldiers who were on sentry duty got back in their jeeps and followed the buses down Kingsbury Avenue. They eventually turned right and were soon out of sight.

Ethan left the window when he saw his parents nearing the house. He got back into bed and pulled the covers up to his chin. He heard the front door open, followed shortly thereafter by the padding sounds of footsteps on the stairs.

For a moment, Ethan thought about getting up and trying to talk to them again, but he figured he'd let his parents come to him this time. And they would come—every night, they always wished him goodnight. Maybe he could use that tender moment, that first "goodnight" since he'd come back from Briggs Base, to make them feel guilty for telling him nothing. He could even put on quite the sympathetic face. Puppy dog eyes, if necessary. Surely they would give in a little, tell him something, anything.

But there would be no goodnight wish from his parents tonight. Ethan heard some shuffling around upstairs, then the lights of the house flicked off. His parents' bedroom door closed with a click.

Ethan lay motionless on his bed, staring at the ceiling through the dark and thinking. He still couldn't believe that his lie about Project Multiplication had fooled his parents, especially his dad. *All the top brass are looking for a secret group that completed Project Mulligan. Then I go and pretty much say those exact words—Project Mulligan—right in my dad's face, but nothing. He still couldn't get it. How is that possible?*

Wait a minute. A disturbing thought rattled Ethan's brain. *There is one group that shouldn't know about Project Mulligan at all…*

The machines.

Ethan let out a light, nervous gasp as he thought about the idea. Then he shook off the notion, thinking it had to be foolish. Surely it had to be a foolish idea. Crazy. Insane. Until other thoughts came to him in support of that foolish, crazy, insane idea.

His parents had seemed a little odd. Sure, they said all the right words: "We love you." "Did they treat you okay at the base?" "Did you get enough to eat?" But there was still something weird about the things they said. Just a tad. Off somehow, wrong timing, wrong tone. There was something even weirder in how they touched him. They made all the right moves, hugs at all the appropriate moments, but something in those embraces was just not right. They were somehow more distant, more cold. They just didn't *feel* like hugs from Mom and Dad.

Ethan was giving himself quite the tingly shiver down the spine when another thought radiated goosebumps everywhere in his body.

Not all of the words were the right words.

Ethan remembered a word his father used over and over again when asked about what had happened at Blackwoods while he was away. The word was *"cannot."* "I cannot tell you." "Sorry, I cannot."

Cannot, Cannot, Cannot.

Ethan could not recall his father ever saying that word so many times in a row. Usually, he opted for *"can't"* instead. But Ethan could readily think of one such fellow who had an affinity for the word *"cannot"*—that cursed Skulley that they had tied to the table leg in the fort. The one they had interrogated during the first fatal error. It seemed to like that word, too.

Ethan tried to reassure himself that he was probably just imagining things, but he had worked himself into a terribly cold sweat. Shudders of intense dread hit him like shivers from a high fever. An icy chill overcame him, and he couldn't seem to get warm. With numbness prickling through his hands, Ethan got out of bed and sat at his computer. He tried to log onto the internet. A message instantly popped up on the screen: "NETWORK NOT AVAILABLE." He tried again and again to get a connection, but it was no use. The internet was down. Ethan soon began to think the worst.

Get ahold of yourself, Ethan. You know how crazy that sounds. Mom and Dad are just acting strangely because they're under a lot of stress. That's it. That is all. Get a grip.

Ethan thought all of that to himself as he approached his bedroom door. But none of it stopped him from doing what he did next, something he'd never before felt the need to do in the safety of his own home.

He locked his door.

CHAPTER 14

MOUNTING EVIDENCE

SLEEPING THAT NIGHT was impossible for Ethan. Every sound he heard put him on edge—the whispering wind outside, the occasional bark of a dog, any creak in the house. Everything kept him awake and wondering about his impossibly disturbing theory.

So he got up early, five o'clock early, and took his time getting ready for school. It was Tuesday, and class was starting back up after the break they'd had on Monday—the day they returned from Briggs Base. Ethan was glad he had summer school today, glad for the excuse to convene with his team early in the morning without worrying about someone monitoring their conversation. More importantly, though, he was glad for the time he'd be away from his parents.

Ethan heard them stirring around the house now. *That* was perfectly normal, at least. His parents had always been early risers. He unlocked his bedroom door and opened it slowly. The tension he felt at that moment reminded him of when he'd first opened the janitor's closet door at the research facility, having no idea what he would find on the other side.

Ethan took a calming breath. *This is ridiculous. Go downstairs and have breakfast with your parents. They are your parents, you idiot.*

Ethan stepped out of his room gingerly, like he was walking through a minefield. He heard his parents downstairs milling around in the kitchen. There were hurried footsteps on the tile floor and the light clatter of items being picked up, shuffled, and put down—normal morning routine. Except for one thing. There was no talking. None. That was truly odd. Ethan's parents were rarely silent around each other, especially during hectic mornings before work. There was always banter back and forth. There were always questions like: "Where did I put this?" or "What did I do with that?" or "What time will you be home?"

But today, there was complete vocal silence. Ethan crept down the stairs at a snail's pace, stepping lightly, cushioning his steps by bending his knees deeply as he put one foot in front of the other. About halfway down the stairs, one of the steps produced a soft squeak. Ethan cringed, then stopped in his tracks. The noises of footsteps and items shuffling around in the kitchen stopped. Now the house was perfectly silent. He knew he couldn't just stand there and wait for his parents to peek around the corner, finding him creeping on the stairs like a guilty burglar in the middle of the night. That would look suspicious. Ethan took a deep breath, summoned his courage, and descended the rest of the stairs at a normal pace. He turned the corner into the kitchen and found his parents standing side-by-side, looking right at him, just a few feet away.

Ethan swallowed hard, and he was afraid they could hear the nervous *gulp* in his throat. He didn't know what to say, but he figured he had to say something. In his mind, Ethan still referred to the man and woman in front of him as his parents—he had to for his sanity—though his doubts were increasing every second. He desperately wished they would speak to *him* first. Say something, anything, to break the ice. But they did not, and the tension from the silence wrenched Ethan's guts.

"Good morning," Ethan said finally, a nervous hitch in his voice.

"Good morning," his father responded, then cocked his head sideways a bit. "You're up early today, aren't you?"

The way his father tilted his head gave Ethan a fresh round of cold chills. It reminded him of the encounter Team Blackwoods had had on the Dark Highway, coming back from trying to deliver the black box to General Stanley. That was the first time they had seen a Skulley. The skeletal machine had stood in the middle of the road in front of their van and cocked its head at them, as if studying them. It was the same way Ethan's dad was staring at him now, head cocked even at the same angle.

"Yes, I am," Ethan replied finally. "I want to get an early start today at school. Need to do some research in the library before class."

"Won't you eat breakfast first?" Ethan's mother asked, tilting her head at her son just the way her husband had.

Now, Ethan had a double dose of the creeps. Everything about his parents reminded him of the machines. "I'll just grab a banana, eat it on the way."

"Now, Ethan, that's not a complete breakfast. You won't be getting all of your nutrients." His mother spoke nurturing words, but Ethan felt the tone was off. Cold.

"I know, but I *really* need to go," Ethan said.

"Do you really need to go, son?" his father asked in a flat tone. "I'm sure whatever you're working on can wait."

Ethan's mother and father nodded simultaneously, heads perfectly in sync. Ethan wondered if they knew he was lying. He remembered that the Skulley they had tied to the table leg in the fort seemed to read Annika's mind, realizing she'd been bluffing when she threatened to shoot the canister of 37-Geminorum. That Skulley had needed Annika to get up close, though, and look it right in the eyes. Ethan wasn't *that* close to his parents now, still about four feet away. When his parents began to step closer to him, staring right into his eyes, Ethan took a few backpedaling paces and looked away.

"Yeah…I need to go now. Thanks anyway," Ethan blurted, backing around his parents. He grabbed a banana and headed for the door. "Have a great day. Love you. See you tonight."

Ethan left the house. He already dreaded the idea of coming back.

❦

Ethan walked much slower on his way to school than he normally did. He was early and had plenty of time on his hands, so he took to looking around, observing the people of Blackwoods, making mental notes on their behavior like a scientist studying a species in their natural habitat.

But as Ethan walked and observed, nothing about the behavior of the people in Blackwoods looked natural. People were doing what they normally do—grabbing the paper, taking a walk, leaving their houses for work—but *the way* they were doing it seemed abnormal now. Everyone appeared too focused, too stiff, oblivious to everything except the task at hand, like robots running on some kind of program. Ethan got the cold shivers again as he thought about the possibility. *Could all the adults in Blackwoods actually be machines?* Then he tried to calm himself down. He thought that maybe the real reason everyone looked so focused and stiff was that they were being constantly watched and evaluated by their bosses—the top brass from Briggs Base and the research facility. Surely those harsh security measures were just so stressful that they made people seem different, unlike their normal selves. Ethan walked the rest of the way to school with that optimistic thought in mind.

⁂

Ethan arrived at school more than an hour before the start of class. He opened the door and walked inside, finding the place deathly quiet. The long hallways spread out before him, devoid of the sights and sounds of school life, and way too dark. There were no lights on yet in the building, and only the faint glow of early morning was seeping in from the long panel of windows that surrounded the school. And with the doors to the classrooms closed, the only light reaching the hallways now was what little of that could filter through the tiny vertical windows on those heavy wooden classroom doors. The school wasn't a place that ordinarily seemed creepy, but Ethan figured that any place could be terrifying under the right circumstances. And these circumstances were perfect. But at least he was alone, away from the adults and their bizarre behaviors. Soon this building would be filled with kids, and that seemed like the safest place to be.

Ethan thought about hiding somewhere until other students arrived, when the sounds of footsteps clicked and clopped through the hallway. Not just one person, but many of them. They were getting louder, closer. Ethan found himself now in the middle of a hallway, with only locked doors to his left and right, and had nowhere to retreat. He braced himself for visitors, clenching his fists and jaw, as he stared in the direction of the clomping feet.

One by one, a dozen teachers slowly walked into view. They stopped at the end of the long, dark hallway, shoulder-to-shoulder, and stared at Ethan without saying a word. Normally, Ethan didn't consider teachers that intimidating. But now, they were the actors of nightmares. They stood up straight as boards, that eerie perfect posture, all eyes on him. Ethan desperately wanted to look away, but he was afraid to. Then all of the teachers, at once and with spot-on timing, cocked their heads at him. Just as his parents had done earlier. Just as that cursed Skulley had on the Dark Highway.

Ethan's first instinct was to run, but he figured he couldn't outrun them all. Even if he could, where would he go? So he decided to play along, pretend he didn't know anything was wrong. Maybe if he just acted like nothing was amiss, *the machines*—that's what he was calling the adults in his head now—would play along too. At least for a while.

Ethan raised his hand and waved at the group of teachers. "Hi there," he said, putting on the friendliest face he could find. It was over-the-top. A teacher's pet if there ever was one.

The teachers were slow to react. Finally, they tilted their heads back to their original, upright positions. Then Ms. Goodfoot stepped out in front of the line. She began to walk toward Ethan. The hard soles of her shoes *clicked* and *clacked* on the polished tile floor. The last thing on Ethan's mind now was how many toes she had stuffed into that left shoe. The last time he wondered about that foolishness, he was just a kid. A clueless kid.

Ms. Goodfoot stood right beside Ethan now, with all of the other teachers watching. Ethan swore he could see his shirt flutter above his pounding heart. Ms. Goodfoot put her hand on the small of his back and nudged him, ever so slightly, in the direction of her classroom. Ironically, her touch was gentle, almost nurturing, much more so than the real Ms. Goodfoot's. But that gentle touch sent a chill rocketing through Ethan's spine. As she unlocked her classroom door and ushered Ethan inside, two thoughts ran nonstop through his nervous, tingling head:

One… This is not my teacher. And two… I am never, ever coming to school this early again.

CHAPTER 15

PERILOUS

ETHAN SAT AT his desk and pretended to read a book, never taking his eyes off Ms. Goodfoot for more than a second. It was just the two of them, and Ethan was absolutely convinced that he was the only human being in the room. She hadn't so much as looked his way since she led him into the classroom, but that only made him more anxious. Her back was turned to him now as she began to write on the chalkboard at the front of the room. It was customary for Ms. Goodfoot to write the vocabulary word-of-the-day, its definition, and an example sentence on the board to begin the morning. Ethan stared intently over the top of his book as she wrote. *As it wrote*, he thought. The word Ms. Goodfoot had chosen was *perilous*:

Perilous [per-uh-luhs] *adj.*

1. involving or full of grave risk; hazardous; dangerous

A smart student knows it would be perilous to snoop around where he doesn't belong.

Ms. Goodfoot slowly wheeled around and faced Ethan. The lone student in the room raised his book so it covered his eyes, but he could feel the intensity of her—*its*—eyes on him. Ethan realized it would be foolish to keep up the charade, so he lowered the book. Their eyes met, and instantly he wished they hadn't. *Its*—he swore it was a machine now—gaze was piercing and full of malice. The sentence that she had written was a threat. It was obvious. *Mind your own business and don't go looking for trouble, or trouble might find you.* That was *its* message.

Ethan nodded politely, and Ms. Goodfoot flashed a smile in return. But her smile was unnatural. It was too wide, and her eyes eerily went along for the ride. Sinister, like robot Tristan's visage in the pale moonlight in the loft of the fort. Everything about his teacher just seemed wrong. Ms. Goodfoot pivoted back to the chalkboard and erased the word, its definition, and the sentence. That frustrated Ethan; he had wanted the others to see the threat too.

The classroom was full of students now. Ms. Goodfoot was at the head of the room, lecturing on subject and object pronouns, and the way she delivered the lesson was remarkably similar to the way the real Ms. Goodfoot would have. In fact, it was perfect, right down to the last gesture and mannerism. It was so perfect that, for a fleeting moment, Ethan began to doubt himself. Then he remembered all the odd behavior he'd witnessed at home, on the way to school, and at school.

No way, I'm wrong. The adults in this town are different. I'm sure of it.

Ms. Goodfoot finally dismissed the class for lunch, and

the members of Team Blackwoods bolted out of the room like they had been launched from a row of cannons.

The group gathered in the corner of the courtyard, eating their lunches as far away from everyone else as possible. Ethan told the others about his weird encounters with the adults, starting with his parents at home and ending with the perceived threat from Ms. Goodfoot. Nobody looked surprised by the experiences Ethan had had with the adults. They all shared their own similar, yet unique, stories of weirdness about their own parents.

"I knew something was wrong for sure when I asked my parents when Liam was coming home," Annika said, referring to her little brother. "It was like I had to remind them that they had another kid."

"And what did they say?" Caleb asked.

"They told me that he wouldn't be coming back for a while, not until they were sure the security threat was gone." Annika drew a deep breath of relief. "At least my little brother got out of here, safe with my grandparents in Unionville... And your little sister is away too," she said, looking at Glenn.

"Copy that," Glenn replied.

"The fatal error happened again," Ethan said, being the first to vocalize the ominous thought. "Happened two days ago. Had to be Sunday night... The night they had that emergency meeting at the research facility."

"And if they missed anybody the first time around, you can bet they got them last night," Austin said. "Those buses picked up every adult in Blackwoods with those so-called security measures."

Glenn was staring pensively at the other end of the courtyard, watching the other students laugh, joke, and play around, seemingly without a care in the world. "Guys, are we sure we're not overreacting? I mean, just look at *them*," he said, pointing to the frolicking students. "*They* don't seem too bothered by the adults…Maybe *we* think something's wrong just because we're looking for it."

"Glenn, I know my parents," Ethan said, not budging an inch. "And those people in my house this morning were definitely *not* my parents."

Annika shrugged, throwing a frustrated hand into the air. "Glenn, what are you talking about? You just told us about your parents acting strange too."

"I know, but…What if it's just the five of us? What if we're just seeing things that aren't there? Or, if there is something, maybe that something could be explained by all the stress the adults are under instead of the fatal error…All I'm saying is maybe we're jumping to conclusions here."

"That is possible," Caleb said with an uneasy face.

Ethan shook his head in disbelief at Caleb, then Glenn, raising his voice as he spoke. "No, it's not…Look, you didn't see what I saw with all the zombie-like teachers today. Or with Ms. Goodfoot…There is no doubt. Not at all in my mind."

"I believe you, Ethan, but wouldn't another opinion be helpful?" Glenn asked. "One from someone who knows nothing about the robot mutiny."

"Who do you have in mind?"

Glenn paused for a moment as he watched Tristan eat his lunch on the far side of the courtyard. "What if we asked Tristan if he's noticed anything strange about his parents?"

"Absolutely not," Austin blurted. "Are you crazy? We can't let him in on this."

"Look, he was Glenn's and my Laser Wars teammate,"

Annika said. "He's a good teammate, a good person...You could trust him with this. He can keep a secret."

"I don't like it," Ethan said. "If he can't keep a secret, he'll cause a panic, then the machines will know we're on to them."

"Ethan, he might not be the scout you are, but Tristan is loyal," Annika said. "I know he would keep this secret."

That flattering, timely comment softened Ethan's stance. "Yeah, I'm sure he would."

"All right," Glenn said. "And, look, I'm not saying we tell him everything right away. Remember, we want him keeping an eye on his parents *without* knowing all that stuff, so he won't be looking for the same things we are."

"I don't think we need any more opinions," Austin grumbled. "But majority rules."

"Okay, then. We'll vote on it," Ethan said. "All in favor of asking Tristan?"

Glenn's and Annika's hands shot up into the air immediately. Caleb's hand went into the air shortly thereafter. Ethan paused for a long moment. He looked at Annika, and he could tell from her face and soft, pleading eyes that this was really important to her. So he gave in. Ethan slowly raised his hand. Austin was the only one to dissent.

"I think it's a mistake," Austin said with resignation in his voice. "But it's four against one. Go do what you gotta do."

Glenn and Annika walked through the courtyard and made their way to Tristan. He was sitting at a table having lunch with Jason Monroe, the Delta Team sergeant. At least he was the Delta Team sergeant before Glenn and Annika mysteriously jumped ship to form a team with Ethan, Austin, and Caleb. Jason eyed Glenn and Annika scornfully as they approached.

"Tristan, can we talk to you for a minute?" Glenn asked.

Jason looked insulted when Glenn only asked for Tristan. "What's up, Captain Traitor?" he asked with squinted eyes. "Trying to get one more to turn to the other side?"

"Look, it's not like that," Glenn said.

"Then tell me what it's like," Jason pressed.

Glenn sighed deeply. "I can't."

"Sure, sure you can't," Jason sneered. "You know, somehow I can believe this from Glenn, but not you, Annika," he said, shaking his head at her. "What happened to you?"

"Jason, you have no idea what's going on," Annika fired back.

"Then tell me. Help me understand!"

Annika shook her head. "Maybe sometime, but we can't now…I'm sorry. You're a good sergeant. It was a privilege to be on your team."

"Yeah, right," Jason muttered. "Watch your back with these two, Tristan."

Glenn and Annika walked with Tristan through the courtyard, away from the awkward scene with Jason and toward the rest of Team Blackwoods. They noticed Bradley Wuddle glaring at them now from a distance, but they just kept walking, refusing to give him the satisfaction of eye contact.

The team began the tricky job of explaining enough to Tristan to get him to keep an eye on his parents, but not so much as to totally creep him out. They mentioned that they thought the adults in Blackwoods were acting strangely ever since the emergency meeting at the research facility two days ago. They said they thought something might've happened at the facility, but they didn't mention anything about robots. And they certainly couldn't mention that, in another time, a robot had impersonated Tristan himself so well that it'd nearly been the cause of their demise. The briefing they gave Tristan was sketchy. He understandably had a lot of questions, but they were the kind of questions that the team wouldn't be able to answer.

"So, that's all you can tell me?" Tristan asked with a face full of confusion. "You want me to spy on my parents, but you can't tell me what I'm supposed to be looking for?"

"We're sorry, Tristan," Caleb said. "But that's exactly the point. We can't tell you more because we need a fresh, objective opinion. If we tell you what we think is happening, your eyes might fool you into seeing things that aren't there."

Tristan exhaled a long sigh of frustration. "I don't think *my* parents were acting strange today…But fine, I'll do it. Just after all this, you'd better tell me what you know."

"We will," Glenn and Annika said at the same time. Austin rolled his eyes and stepped away from the group in obvious protest.

"By the way," Tristan said, noting Austin's stance, "I want you to know that I wasn't the one to cause trouble for you with Colonel Grissom."

Austin turned around at that remark. He gave an appreciative nod. "Thanks, but we knew you'd never do that. We know it was Wuddle."

Tristan glanced at the far end of the courtyard, finding Jason watching them. "All right then," he said. "I'd better be getting back before Jason thinks I left him too."

"Thanks, Tristan…for doing this," Annika said.

Tristan nodded. "No problem." Then he walked away.

"Hey, Tristan," Glenn said.

Tristan stopped and turned back. "Yeah?"

"Be careful."

Tristan flashed a confused smile and furrowed his brow. Even his confused smile could light up a room. "Okay, I'll try not to get grounded." He laughed a little and walked away.

Glenn and Annika were terribly close to breaking down and telling Tristan that he had a lot more to worry about than being grounded. But, in the end, they did not.

"You think we should've told him?" Annika asked.

Glenn thought for a while. His face was strained and tense. Then he shook his head. "No," he said finally. "Tristan's a great scout. He'll accomplish this mission just fine."

"Yeah...You're right," Annika said.

"I'm sure he'll be all right," Ethan added. There was a long pause as everyone watched Tristan from afar in silence. "There's something else we need to check on. Can everyone get away for a while after school?"

"Yeah, sure," Austin smirked. "No need to ask any of our parents for permission, seeing as none of them are home."

"We don't know that for sure, Austin," Glenn said. "Probably just our imagination."

Austin shook his head firmly. "It's not our imagination."

Ethan didn't say a word, but he agreed one hundred percent with Austin.

CHAPTER 16

A PLAN FOILED

When the group arrived at the Bravo Fort, they found that it'd been broken into. Just as Colonel Grissom had promised, the military had searched the place looking for anything suspicious. They must've used some sort of battering ram to get inside, since the lock latches were completely broken off. They didn't even bother to close the door.

Everyone went inside and surveyed the damage. The place had been totally ransacked, with nothing left in its original spot. Tables were overturned, items strewn everywhere, and the chalkboard and map of the woods had been ripped down and tossed aside.

"Guess they didn't have time to clean up after themselves," Austin snarled.

"Unbelievable," Annika muttered.

The group quickly went to work straightening up the place. Caleb inspected the lock latches and frowned. "I'm going to need some time to fix that right," he said. "Until then, I'll rig a quick lock, but it won't be as secure."

"Okay," Ethan said. "Then we should check on our

weapons, that black box, and the dead Skulley. We hid that stuff pretty well in the cave, but I'll feel better knowing for sure it's all still there."

⁂

The group quickly hiked to Wolf Cave. They climbed up the gradual incline and soon saw the cavern's six-by-eight-foot entrance sitting at the base of the rocky ridge. It looked like a black hole in space covered in bedrock. They flicked their flashlights on and went inside, making their way to the left-most tunnel. Ethan crouched down and took a look inside, then he swept his flashlight in back and forth arcs through the tunnel and into the chamber on the other side.

"Looks clear," Ethan said.

They all began to climb through the tunnel. Soon they were on the other side and digging into the hole where they had stashed their weapons, the Skulley, and the metal briefcase with the documents and glowing rods. They seemed to dig forever, beginning to worry that someone had found and stolen their stuff. Eventually, though, the black duffel bag containing their laser guns was unearthed; they had just forgotten how thoroughly they'd buried their stash.

Ethan pulled out the duffel bag with the weapons and handed it to Annika. After some more digging, they located the duffel bag with the metal briefcase inside. Finally, after excavating a few more rocks, they found the dead Skulley lying peacefully in its tomb. Its arms were eerily folded over its chest, like a dead man who'd been prepared by a mortician and laid delicately in his casket. A fine layer of dust from the rocks dulled the shine on the black skeletal robot as their flashlights probed its features. Its once blazing red eyes were now dark but still wide open. The machine was clearly dead, but somehow it seemed like it might just spring back to life at any second. A cold shudder jolted through the backs of everyone as they stared at it.

"I'm satisfied," Glenn said with a grimace. "Now let's cover that thing back up."

"I'm with you there," Austin added.

The group began to rebury the Skulley. Then they buried the metal briefcase. At last, Ethan dropped the duffel bag into the hole in the cave floor. Just as they were about to begin tossing rocks on top of it, Austin held his arm out, stopping them.

"Wait…maybe we should keep that," Austin said. "The guns."

"No, I think we should keep them safe in here until we hear back from Tristan," Glenn said. "If we're overreacting now, and the adults really are just people, then we don't need the guns. And if *you're* right, and they are machines, they will check this suspicious-looking bag for sure. They'll know we're on to them *and* take our only weapons."

"You guys know how much I want my laser rifle, but Glenn's right," Annika said. "We can't take that bag out in broad daylight. It'll be safe here. The military searched everywhere they knew to look for stuff on us, and they couldn't find it."

"Well I don't know about you, but I want my laser gun now," Austin said, reaching for the duffel bag.

Glenn put his arm over Austin's, gently stopping him. "Please…Give Tristan one day. If he's convinced something's weird, then we come back and get them first thing."

"Please, Austin. Just one day," Annika echoed Glenn's request.

Austin sighed in frustration, then looked to Ethan. "What do you think?"

"I think we might need our weapons before we go back into town. We have some extra camping backpacks in our fort. We could disassemble the rifles, stick them in there. I don't think those would get checked." Ethan paused and looked at Glenn, then Annika for a long moment before softening. "But…I'm willing to give it one more day, just to be sure."

"All right," Austin said, stepping away from the duffel bag. "One more day."

There was one last item on the agenda before they could go back into town, one last thing they needed to check on. Without saying a word, everyone knew what that was.

◈

They began to hike quickly toward the old, abandoned electrical substation, the one that contained the secret elevator to the research facility, the one that had made completing Project Mulligan possible. They weaved their way through a thick patch of evergreens and down a rocky slope until they found level ground. Another patch of trees obscured the electrical substation, but they swiftly moved through those and into a clearing. They eyed the substation, and instantly their stomachs were in free fall. The fence, the electrical wires and power lines, and transformer boxes stood as before—but the trailer, the small building that had once been used by workers to regulate the power supply, was gone. *The building that had housed the secret elevator to the research facility was gone.* In its place sat a six-foot-tall slab of concrete with a six-inch-thick slab of steel anchored on top. The entire three-hundred-foot-long secret elevator shaft had been filled with hundreds of tons of concrete. Permanently entombed.

"I was afraid of this," Austin said, resignation in his voice. "I really hoped not, but I was afraid…My dad probably gave the order to seal it up."

"Yours or mine," Glenn said disgustedly.

"Hope the military has a plan B," Austin said. "Because we sure don't."

"We'll have to find one," Ethan said. "There's gotta be—"

Just then, two young soldiers in camouflage with M-16s in hand came up from behind. "What're you kids doing here?" one of them asked in a sharp, threatening voice.

The group flinched and quickly spun around. "Nothing, just hiking," Ethan said.

"Well, you better get outta here," the other soldier said.

"Why?" Ethan asked, probing for information. "What could you possibly be guarding around here?"

"Look, kid, nobody tells us nothing," the first soldier said. "Just supposed to keep this area clear of trespassers. First time's a warning. Second time, we're ordered to shoot…And I really don't wanna shoot a kid, so…"

"All right, we're leaving," Ethan said, backing away. Ethan was pretty sure these two soldiers were human. The way they spoke, and the way they moved and carried themselves, were different from his parents and the other adults he'd seen in Blackwoods that day. That brought Ethan a measure of relief, even if the Project Mulligan entrance had been sealed off. At least the machines weren't guarding the area. If they were, that would mean they knew about Project Mulligan too, and that would be much worse.

The group retreated the way they had come. The soldiers

walked back to the perimeter fence of the electrical substation and resumed their guard duty. Once they were out of the clearing and hidden by evergreen trees, the group looked back at the soldiers.

"You think they'll ever leave?" Austin asked.

"No," Ethan said. "Even if they did, we'd never be able to break through all that metal and rock in a million years...We gotta be the ones to find a plan B."

"Anyone have any ideas?" Caleb asked.

"You're the genius," Austin replied with a wry smile.

"Hey, remember...maybe everything's not so bad," Glenn said. "Those two guys struck me as being human. Let's wait and see what Tristan thinks."

"I agree. I think those soldiers were human," Ethan said. "But I also think those were the *only* human adults I've seen all day."

"Psssst...Look," Annika whispered and pointed through a gap in the trees.

Everyone hunkered low to the ground behind an elevated mound of earth. They watched carefully as four other soldiers approached the substation from the east. The four oncoming soldiers were dressed exactly like the other two—military-issue camouflage and black boots—but something about them seemed different. Their gait was a little peculiar, rigid. And their faces looked just as stiff and were completely lacking emotion. The two soldiers turned around and faced the other four.

"Change in guard duty?" Glenn asked.

"I don't think so," Ethan said, staring intensely at the four men. "Something about this doesn't feel right."

"No, it doesn't," Austin added.

Before anyone could say another word or even think another thought, the four men raised their arms at the other two. Their hands snapped down quickly and folded flat into their forearms, an unnatural move that would have fractured any human bone. A barrel of a weapon was revealed at the end of their wrists. The two young soldiers were so shocked that they couldn't even lift their M-16s before the four men opened fire on them. Intense red lasers ripped into their chests, and the pair fell lifelessly to the ground.

Annika let out a startled gasp, then quickly covered her mouth as the four machines disguised in flesh and camouflage pivoted sharply in the group's direction. Everyone lay flat on the ground and peered through the trees with wide, horrified eyes. The machines scanned the area back and forth slowly. The group held their breath, afraid that the slightest undulation of the expansion and contraction of their lungs might give them away. Finally, the machines turned from the group and went back to their victims. They carried the dead soldiers' limp bodies away effortlessly, slung over their shoulders, and headed back in the direction of the research facility.

When it was safe to do so, everyone began gasping for air, panicked by what they'd seen. Glenn and Annika's first thought was the same.

"We gotta get a message to Tristan," Glenn said. "Tell him to call it off. Snooping around his parents is too dangerous… not to mention pointless after what we know now."

"Right," Annika said, pulling her cell phone from her pocket in a flash. "I'm on it."

"Good," Ethan said. "And it's time to get the guns."

Austin nodded in eager agreement. "Yeah, copy that."

CHAPTER 17

WARNING TRISTAN

As the group hiked back to the Bravo Fort to retrieve their backpacks, Annika and Glenn desperately tried to get a cell phone signal. So far, no luck. It wasn't until Annika had climbed the highest ridge in the area—the one from which the scout Skulley had spied on them in the fort every night in another time—that she saw those beautiful blue bars light up on her phone. Annika immediately dialed Tristan's number and waited with a tense knot in her throat. Then that familiar automated message played. The woman's voice was so artificially sweet it was disturbing...

"*Hello, please wait while we connect you to the number dialed. Please be aware that, due to security measures, only local calls will be allowed, and all phone conversations will be monitored for content. Thank you and have a nice day.*"

"Hello?" Tristan finally answered.

Annika breathed a sigh of relief at hearing his voice. "Hi, Tristan. It's Annika."

"Hi, Annika. I have an update on—"

"Wait, wait, wait. Me first," Annika interrupted urgently,

afraid that Tristan was going to provide juicy details on his reconnaissance while the machines were listening in. "About that project for school...," she emphasized the *project for school* part with a raised voice, hoping that Tristan would get her point, "...don't worry about doing the part we asked you to do before. We have new information on it that you'll need. So *do not* do your part, the observation part, until we talk to you first. It's *extremely* important you wait, otherwise it might mess up the whole project...Hey, lucky you, Tristan. No homework tonight."

There was a long pause over the phone. Annika prayed that Tristan wouldn't push the issue and say something to give them away. "All right, sure," Tristan responded. "You do know, I have *a lot* of questions about this assignment."

"I know. We'll clear all that up tomorrow at school. Thanks, Tristan."

"Sure, Annika. No problem. See ya tomorrow."

"See ya tomorrow."

Annika ended the call and smiled. "He understood. He's gonna back off."

"Thank God," Glenn said.

The team entered Wolf Cave with their camping backpacks and, once again, dug up the black duffel bag. They promptly pulled out the laser guns, then reburied the bag. Caleb went to work carefully disassembling each gun, such that it would fit in their backpacks without any part sticking out. He had to remove the stock from the barrel, but the entire process for all five guns only took him fifteen minutes. Then he gave a quick tutorial to the others on how to reassemble the gun quickly. Once everyone was satisfied that they could put their gun back together fast if they found themselves in trouble, they left the cave and headed back toward town. Still, they had an uneasy feeling entering a town populated with malicious machines posing as humans while their laser rifles lay in pieces in their backpacks.

The security guards at the checkpoint of the Dark Highway stopped the group before letting them pass. These guards didn't act human. They wore blank expressions most of the time, and when they did try to express emotion, it just looked awkward and fake.

"You kids have been playing hard, huh?" the first guard said, trying to sound friendly but only coming off as weird. His odd, phony smile made it worse. It was an eerie, toothy smile. And there was no trace of soul at all behind those eyes.

"Yeah," Ethan said. "Hiking…It's great exercise."

Ethan and the rest of the group tried to maintain eye contact with the guards, afraid that not doing so would look suspicious. But they so badly wanted to look away from those wide, empty orbs. They were also getting more and more anxious about why they were being detained. There was no traffic at all on the Dark Highway as far as the eye could see.

"You are right. Hiking is excellent exercise," the second guard said with the same expression as the first plastered on his face. "But you should run along now. It's getting late, and you cannot be late for dinner…Your parents would not like that."

There was that word again: *cannot*. Everyone in the group nodded, playing along as if nothing was wrong.

"Okay, thanks," Ethan said, then adjusted the strap on his backpack that had slipped off his shoulder. The sound of clattering metal on metal through the backpack caught the first guard's attention. Ethan winced ever so slightly.

"Your bag looks heavy," the first guard said. "What is in there?"

Ethan swallowed hard and felt like he had gulped down his tongue. Everyone in the group was sweating bullets as they awaited Ethan's reply. "Metal stakes," Ethan said at last. "We were practicing setting up a tent." Ethan marshaled enough courage to take his backpack off of one shoulder and shake it around, making it jingle, trying to appear as if he had nothing to hide. "Metal stakes," he said again, looking squarely into the guard's vacant eyes.

There was a long pause. Then the guard nodded. "All right, you may go."

The group tried to muffle their loud sighs of relief as they crossed the Dark Highway and made their way into Blackwoods. It was just after six o'clock. Most human parents would've been concerned if their kids had vanished for five hours straight after school. But not the parents in Blackwoods now. No one in the group had even gotten a fake worried call from their parental impostors. That much was both good and bad. It was good because it gave the group some freedom, a freedom they would surely need to figure out a plan B. But it was also bad because they worried about what the machines were doing with all of their free time. For now, though, they just hoped their robot parents wouldn't be as angry as their human parents would've been if they came home late for dinner, especially after not checking in first.

The group walked down Kingsbury Avenue and stopped at Tristan's house. Annika had been pretty satisfied with her conversation with Tristan, certain that he had gotten the message, but she still wanted to pay him a visit and talk to him face-to-face. She knew she could make her point more clearly and forcefully that way, without having to play around with her words to keep whoever was listening in on the conversation from getting suspicious. That way, there would be no chance of confusion.

Annika knocked on Tristan's door. When it opened, both of Tristan's parents were standing there. They were a physically striking couple—blonde hair, blue eyes, tall, and athletic. They were as Nordic-looking as two people could possibly get. Just a quick glance at them and it was easy to understand why Tristan was so handsome. Normally, they were very friendly people with nice smiles and warm, inviting faces. But that was not the case now. Instead, all of the usually attractive Nordic features combined to make them look sinister, like an evil race of beings from another world. Their eyes were still blue, but they were as lifeless as the Dead Sea, their faces stiff and unyielding. The group knew, as soon as they looked at Tristan's parents, that under their fair white skin lay a black metal skeleton. And under those listless blue eyes lay embers ready to blaze crimson when the time was right.

"Hi...Is Tristan home?" Annika asked, summoning all of her composure to maintain eye contact.

Tristan's parents looked at each other, then back to Annika in perfect sync. "He is, but he cannot talk right now," the mother said. "We will be having dinner soon. Then he has homework. So, you see...he cannot."

"It would only take a minute. We promise," Glenn pleaded super-politely.

Both of Tristan's parents snapped their heads in Glenn's direction at precisely the same time. "He cannot," the father said. "May we give him a message?"

Glenn sighed uneasily. "No, thanks. Guess we'll just see him tomorrow."

"Now that sounds like a fine plan," the father said. "Goodbye now."

Tristan's dad began to close the door. The last thing the group saw before the door closed entirely was a bizarre smile forming on both of their faces.

As the five members of Team Blackwoods walked away, they spotted Tristan watching them from his bedroom window. He waved at them, but his face was tense, and he looked very much like he had something important to tell them.

∽

Ethan wanted to spend as little time with his folks as he possibly could. The last thing he needed was another *How was your day?* conversation with robots pretending to be his parents. Worse yet, he didn't want to be too close to them for too long, afraid they might be able to read his thoughts. And his main thought now was getting up to his bedroom as fast as possible and assembling that laser gun he'd stashed under his bed, inside a bunker of baseball card boxes. So Ethan was determined to talk as little as possible, get to his room, and stay there as long as he could. Be anti-social. Surely the machines were programmed with a basic understanding of the human adolescent. In that case, Ethan's behavior wouldn't seem so strange at all.

At least that's what Ethan was hoping for as he sat in terribly awkward silence at the dinner table. The mechanical monster posing as his mother had made a pan of lasagna. Not only did it smell exactly like his real mother's lasagna, but it tasted exactly like hers as well. Something about that made Ethan very sad. He ate as much as his uneasy stomach could handle, just to avoid suspicion, then he took to subtly watching these perfectly disguised killing machines as they ate the food on their plates. At that moment, Ethan had two thoughts in his mind: *One, where do they put all that food they're eating? And two, I cannot wait to throw your dead, metal carcasses out of my house. That's right, you metallic pieces of crap, I said I cannot, cannot, cannot wait!*

Ethan glanced up at his parents and smiled. It was just as fake and empty a smile as any the machines had ever put on. "Thank you for dinner. May I be excused?"

His mother and father exchanged quick looks, then turned to Ethan. This was all done with such precision that it was like it had been put to music and choreographed. "Yes, you may, Ethan," his father said. "And do your homework. We'll be up to wish you goodnight later."

At that last remark, Ethan raised a curious eyebrow.

Ethan holed up in his room for the remainder of the night, pretending to study algebra. If his parents came in, his effort would look convincing. He was staring intensely at an open algebra book, but he wasn't thinking about equations. He was pondering how to get out of this predicament, trying to figure out a way to defeat the machines who had managed to take over the town again, though this time in a completely different way. All of a sudden, his concentration was interrupted by the blare of a siren. It was the same siren that had sounded the night before. Again, it was happening at exactly 9:00 p.m.

Without a word to Ethan, his parents boarded the

camouflaged military buses that were parked along the street. Ethan watched them stealthily from the corner of his bedroom window. The buses drove off and, once again, the military jeeps pulled up in their usual spots. The soldiers got out and began their guard duty. Two soldiers for every house. They scanned the houses and surrounding property with blank stares, moving their heads back and forth, rhythmic, like oscillating fans. Ethan knew these so-called security measures were bogus. Or at least they weren't meant for the *humans'* security. They were just an excuse to summon the machines to the research facility every night. But he had no idea why.

Ethan used the time alone well enough, though. He assembled his laser rifle and found a nice, convenient hiding spot for it—the crevice where his bed met the wall.

Exactly two hours later, just like the night before, Ethan's mechanical surrogate parents returned home. Ethan lay in bed with the lights off. His door was closed but not locked. He figured it was pointless to lock it, as it would just look suspicious, and the machines could break in at will anyway. He knew his best bet was to continue to play along with the charade until the time to revolt came. Ethan had no idea when that might be, but he relished the thought.

Sounds of heavy footsteps on the stairs brought a queasiness to Ethan's stomach. That feeling got worse when he heard those footsteps turn in the direction of his room. He propped his head up slightly and found his gun. He lifted it out from the space between the bed and the wall, slipped it quickly under his covers. Then the door to his room slowly opened. Both of his parents stood in the doorway for a moment, heads cocked slightly to the right, just watching him. He lay perfectly still in bed, his eyes barely opened into slits, just enough to see what they were doing. Their figures were silhouetted, bodies completely blackened against the light from the hallway behind them. Ethan hoped they would think he was asleep and leave. But he dared not close his eyes. He slowly put his hand over his gun.

"Are you awake, Ethan?" his mother asked in a soft, tender voice.

"Yes," Ethan answered. It was a reply that came easily, like a reflex, as if he were responding to his own mother. A tingly shiver darted down Ethan's spine. *My God, she sounds exactly like my mom.*

His parents came closer to him. Now, he could even smell the familiar scents of his mom and dad—his mother's perfume and the WD-40 that always permeated his father's work shirts. *They even* smell *exactly like my parents,* he thought with a shudder.

"Goodnight, son," his father said. "We love you."

Ethan's parents laid their hands on his shoulder and gave him a loving pat. They came dangerously close to patting the stock of Ethan's laser rifle as well. But Ethan wasn't even thinking about his gun now. All he could think about was how much they sounded, smelled, and felt like his real parents. They smiled softly at him. These smiles weren't creepy—they were not the ear-to-ear broad or overly toothy smiles of nightmares. They looked like the smiles of loving parents. The flesh-covered machines were just about perfect in their impersonations of his mother and father now, almost to the point of making Ethan think that somehow his real parents had miraculously returned. But there was still one thing that stood out. *Those eyes.* In the darkness of the room, they were just a shade too bright.

As his parents left the room and closed the door, Ethan's head was abuzz with thoughts. *They could almost fool me now, and I know the truth. The machines are getting better. They're getting better at being human. And that's going to be a big problem.*

CHAPTER 18

CURIOSITY'S COST

Tristan had noticed some odd behavior from his parents earlier in the day. He couldn't put his finger on exactly what it was, but something had been different. The way they interacted with him and each other just seemed off in a manner that was hard to put into words. But his parents made up for their prior weird behavior when they wished him goodnight. They were as skilled in the routine as Ethan's parents, saying the right words at the right times and in the right tones, using a loving touch that one would think only a caring mother and father could provide.

As he lay in bed, some nagging thoughts began pecking away at his mind. *Annika and Glenn asked me to be on the lookout for strange behavior. Then, out of nowhere, they tell me to stop. But they were right. My parents were acting strange earlier. What on earth were Glenn and Annika talking about? What does that group know that they're not telling me?*

Tristan lay in bed, fully awake and pondering the situation, until he heard no stirring in the house. It was well after midnight when he ventured out of his room and sneaked downstairs. He moved with the stealth of a skillful scout, making no noise at all as he crossed the living room and made his way to the kitchen. It was there that he spotted the objective of his reconnaissance mission: two briefcases sitting on the floor beside the kitchen table. They were his parents' briefcases, always left in the same spot each night so they wouldn't forget them in the morning. His parents were both majors in the Air Force with high-security clearances. He thought there had to be some good information inside those leather briefcases.

Tristan had never before felt the need to search his parents' personal property, but the curiosity swelled in him now. There was also a big part of him that wanted to complete the mission, to be the one to find something useful, anything to help the team. Tristan thought hopefully: *Maybe this way Annika might find me to be as good a scout as Ethan. Maybe this way Glenn might want me back. Maybe I, too, could be a part of that special, mysterious team of five who seem to know things that no one else does. If I prove myself worthy, maybe they would see a need for a sixth member.*

Tristan smiled at the thought of that as he lifted the briefcases onto the kitchen table and quietly unsnapped the latches. He opened them both, then pulled a small flashlight from his pocket. He listened hard for any noises upstairs, but he heard nothing. Then he flicked his flashlight on and aimed it inside the briefcases, shining a bright, thin beam on the documents inside. Tristan thumbed quickly through the pages, not sure exactly what he was looking for, just vaguely searching for anything suspicious or odd. He had barely pulled out the first folder of papers to examine when he heard a creaking sound. It seemed to come out of nowhere, without any warning at all.

Complete silence one second, then an ominous *creak* of the floor right behind him the next. Tristan froze immediately. He slowly turned around and found his parents standing in the entryway of the kitchen. They stood there together, tall and imposing with eerily blank faces. The moonlight streamed in through the large kitchen window and found their blonde hair, casting a pale, ghostly glow atop their heads. At that moment, for the first time in his life, Tristan was afraid of his parents. Something about them was terribly wrong.

"I'm s-s-sorry," Tristan sputtered. "I can explain this."

"There is no need," the mother figure said in a soothing voice, sounding exactly like his real mother but feeling like something else entirely. "It is too late for that now."

His parents' eyes blazed an intense crimson color. Tristan's own eyes were full of fear, absolute fear, the kind of fear you only get to feel once in your life. They moved toward him slowly, stalking him. Tristan backpedaled until he hit the corner of the kitchen counter. There was nowhere left to turn. His father raised his hand and brandished a syringe. The needle shimmered blood-red, basking in the glow of the machines' hateful eyes.

Tristan belted out a nerve-shredding scream.

CHAPTER 19

IN MOURNING

The news of Tristan's death was regarded as a horrible rumor, one that some heartless person must've spread as a sick joke. Until the confirmation came directly from the mouths of Tristan's parents. Still, it took a long time for any of the kids to believe it. Denial seemed to take up the first four stages of the grieving process. It couldn't possibly be true. Except that it was.

The cause of death was said to be suffocation due to an extreme allergic reaction Tristan had to a spider bite. Tristan's parents blamed it on the Western Black Widow. But Team Blackwoods blamed Tristan's parents. They were sure that they had murdered him. All of the kids in Blackwoods were in mourning. Glenn and Annika were inconsolable.

The adults had canceled summer school that day, a Wednesday. But the school itself remained open, with grief counselors on the premises in case anyone needed to talk to someone about their feelings during "this difficult time"—that's how the adults summed up the tragic loss. It was insulting. There were quite a few students who did go to see the counselors, though, but they didn't get much in the way of therapy—just bits and pieces from a generic playbook on grief spouted back at them from callous machines. Glenn and Annika sure would've liked to talk to a real grief counselor. They desperately needed to. But all they could do now, along with the rest of Team Blackwoods, was focus their energy on something more productive. Revenge seemed appropriate.

∽

The group sat at a table in Judy's Diner. They hated to be anywhere around adults, but taking off for the solace of their fort in the woods would look suspicious now, especially on the heels of the death of a friend. So they sat in the diner watching Judy work, serving food and drinks and chatting with other patrons. She looked like Judy and sounded like Judy, but the spring in her step was gone. Also gone was the twinkle in her eye and her ornery spirit. The group knew that the machines had gotten to her, too. They figured the machines had gotten to every adult by now, and they were the only kids to know. That was a lonely feeling. They had planned to let someone in, though. They were going to let Tristan join the group. They were going to trust him with the truth. But they were just a few hours too late.

Glenn had tears in his eyes. He spoke softly. "Tristan would still be alive if it weren't for me...He had no idea of the danger, and I just let him walk right into that. It's my fault. He was my scout. I was his captain. And I got him killed... Some captain I am."

"I'm just as much to blame," Annika whimpered in a hushed tone. "I thought it was a good idea. Argued in favor of it...And I didn't do a good enough job on the phone to talk him out of what we already talked him into."

"It's no one's fault," Ethan said with quiet but sharp words. He looked around the diner with a disgusted face and eyed the flesh-covered machines who were keeping up the perfect ruse. "No one's at this table, anyway."

Annika gave Glenn a hug. Tears fell from their eyes as they held on to each other tightly. Glenn let the last of his tears stream down his cheek, then he refused to let any more fall. "They will pay for this," he said into Annika's ear. He clenched his jaw like a vise and said through his teeth, "I will make them pay for this."

⁂

They held Tristan's funeral that evening, less than twenty-four hours after he had died, as if they were eager to get him into the ground. The service took place at the largest church in Blackwoods, yet it was still standing-room-only inside. All of the kids in town attended, along with the machines posing as their parents. Everyone in the group felt their stomachs retch at the thought of Tristan's real parents not being at their son's funeral. It was even more horrible to think that the same machines who had killed him were the ones taking their place.

Tristan's body lay in an open casket in the front of the sanctuary. Even in death, he was a handsome specimen. He was dressed in a new black suit that had a little bit of sheen to it. His arms were folded over his abdomen, and his eyes were closed and peaceful. Tufts of his flaxen hair fell in their usual places over his forehead, like he had just combed it himself. His flawless complexion, though, was now the palest of whites. But there was a hint of rose color in his cheeks, no doubt the work of a machine who had recently taken a temp job as a mortician.

The team sat in a pew near the front of the church as the minister walked down the center aisle. Even the minister was a machine. It walked stiffly and without emotion up to the pulpit at the head of the sanctuary. The minister took a quick moment to look at Tristan's body, regarding it with a light smile. *A smile.* It was quick to wipe that expression away as it set a Bible on the pulpit and began reading a few passages out loud. It was like the machine had Google-searched the right scriptures to read. But it all rang hollow.

The black metal skeleton of a robot covered in flesh and a preacher's robe closed the Bible and looked up at the congregation. There were two groups in the audience now—those in tears and those not. The kids were crying and deeply sorrowful. The adults, not so much. Their faces were dull and stoic, without emotion, not even pretend emotion. Maybe the machines thought that they wouldn't be good at faking sorrow yet. Maybe they thought it best to just put on a blank face—they were great at that—and let everyone else think that the adults were simply so much in shock that they didn't know how to act.

The minister spoke firmly. "Speaking to the adults of Blackwoods…We must be strong now for our kids."

That was the perfect thing for it to say: *Be strong now for our kids.* It gave them the ultimate excuse not to cry or show emotion like any other decent human would. Now, no kids would think their parents were weird for not sharing tear for tear in their grief; instead, they would just think that their parents were *being strong* for them. It was a clever, if revolting, move on the part of the machines.

The robotic minister finished with his charade of a eulogy for Tristan, kind words without any soul, then allowed people to come to the front of the sanctuary to view the body and say their final goodbyes. The line of kids waiting to pay their respects to Tristan stretched around the entire church and out the door. Tristan's parents waited coolly up front by the casket, thanking people for their sympathies as they passed. Glenn watched them with scathing eyes.

Bradley Wuddle stood over Tristan's body, viewing it for a longer time than most. Tears streaked down his cheeks as he mouthed some inaudible words to Tristan's pale, lifeless face. No one knew what Bradley had said to Tristan in that moment. Maybe he was apologizing for something mean he had said or done to him, something he thought he would have all the time in the world to make up for. It would be a painful thing for him, carrying around wrongs that could never be righted. Not in this world, anyway. He walked away from the casket slowly and dazedly. In that regard, he was one of many. A hard lesson learned by all: *That kids can die too.*

By the time they arrived at Tristan's casket, Glenn and Annika thought they'd already cried out all the tears they had in their eyes. They were wrong. As they bent over to give their former scout one final embrace, their tears dropped onto Tristan and were absorbed by his new, perfectly fitted dress suit. They whispered their regrets into his ears, so hoping that he might hear them, wherever he was now.

Glenn tightened his jaw and whispered a promise to him as well. "They will pay for this, Tristan...I will make them pay."

Ethan, Austin, and Caleb paid their respects to Tristan after Glenn and Annika were finished. They all had their regrets, too. It was always painfully easy to think of ways one could've treated someone better in life, after they had died; it was a tragic flaw unique to humans, one that no machine could ever understand. In that moment, Ethan wished that he had never been jealous of Tristan because of the time he'd spent with Annika. *What a waste of emotion*, he thought. *Tristan was a nice guy. He could've been a great friend.*

"I'm sorry," Ethan whispered into Tristan's ear. He walked away and wiped a tear from his face.

Team Blackwoods gathered in the back of the church. There were no words. Everyone just closed in for a tight hug. The moment they let go, they looked toward the front of the sanctuary. It was terrible timing. Tristan's parents were huddled around the casket, peering inside, doing their best impersonation of a human couple grieving the loss of their child.

Ethan stared at Tristan's murderers from afar with a determined glare. "*We will* figure out a plan B… *We will* beat them again."

CHAPTER 20

SNOOPING AROUND

When Ethan asked his robot parents if he could have some friends over, it being a weeknight, he thought they would surely refuse. He figured they would probably even use that creepy favorite word of theirs—*cannot*—in doing so. But, much to his surprise, they said that he could.

Even more surprising was that all of his friends' mechanical parents had signed off on the get-together as well. Maybe they were being generous because that's what they believed real human parents would've done—be extra nice, since it had been such a traumatic day. Whatever the reason, Ethan was brimming with anticipation at having everyone from the team together, especially if the adults were going to be leaving at nine o'clock as they had the last two nights. They had been only four digits short on the second keypad the last time they tried to break into the secret basement. This time, with two hours alone in the house, they would have an excellent chance at cracking the remainder of the code. Ethan could hardly wait. He had a strong feeling there was something in that mysterious chamber below that could help them in thwarting the machines' newest takeover of the town.

◈

The group arrived at Ethan's house at eight o'clock still wearing their dress clothes from Tristan's funeral. Ethan let them in, and they quickly went upstairs, bypassing his parents who were sitting silently in the living room, their backs turned to them, completely motionless.

The house was as quiet as a tomb. Everyone was hesitant to speak for fear of being heard. They had the distinct, uneasy feeling that those machines that looked and sounded exactly like Ethan's parents were listening in on the other side of his bedroom door. Ethan opened his door a crack and looked out into the hallway. No one was there. He closed the door back gently.

"I think they're still downstairs," Ethan said in a voice scarcely louder than a whisper.

"Where's your gun?" Glenn asked straightaway.

Ethan indicated with a nod of his head. "Far corner, between the bed and the wall."

"Okay, then…I say we go down there and take them out now," Glenn said with determined eyes. "One gun, but we have the element of surprise. Then we go to our houses, house to house, take 'em out one at a time. Grab our guns as we go…Pay one quick visit to Tristan's house, settle the score, then head for the woods."

"I second that idea," Austin said. "Who knows when we'll all be together again, with permission, at night…They wouldn't suspect a thing."

Ethan shook his head. "We're in no shape to launch a

counterattack now. If the house-to-house plan doesn't work, if we get stopped along the way and have to retreat, we have one measly gun and zero supplies. Then we're just heading into the woods to die, if we even get that far…No, we have to wait."

"Wait for what? For them to take *us* out one at a time," Annika said. Her eyes got teary and she choked out the words, "Like they did Tristan."

Ethan sighed deeply, painfully. "I'm so sorry about Tristan…But we're not ready. And I know, deep down, you know that too."

Annika nodded and wiped away a tear. "I know," she said, stiffening her lips.

"Did you bring the software, Caleb?" Ethan asked.

Caleb nodded. "Yeah."

"We have to get into that basement tonight," Ethan said. "It's gotta be a priority. For all we know, there's a stash of weapons and supplies right down there."

"Yeah, you're right," Austin admitted.

"Sorry," Glenn added. "I just want to do something, anything to fight back. Starting with those machines that killed Tristan…I owe him that."

"It's all right, Glenn. I understand," Ethan said. "I want to fight back too…And that time will come. But we have so many things to figure out first."

"Like finding a way back to the Chrono-Warp," Annika said softly, unsurely. It wasn't a tone she often took, like the very idea of ever getting back to that secret tunnel was a million miles away.

"Exactly," Ethan responded, trying to sound upbeat. "We have all the tools we need. We have the energy rods, all the instructions on the Chrono-Warp, and we know exactly where to go in the research facility...We just gotta find another way inside."

"I've been thinking about that," Caleb said. "The secret elevator shaft went at least three hundred feet underground. The Wolf Cave system runs long and deep throughout the area. The library has some maps of the cave on file. We could match up those maps as best we can to a topographical map of Blackwoods. With some luck, we might be able to find out where that elevator shaft intersects the cave."

"That's a great idea," Ethan said, then smiled. "Anyone feel like exploring a cave?"

Everyone nodded, more eager now that they had some sort of plan. Then a knock on the door interrupted their strategy session. The door opened and Ethan's parental impostors stood there, side-by-side, with easy smiles on their faces. These smiles looked more natural, less creepy, more human. But that made them even scarier.

"Ethan, honey, we will be leaving soon. Security measures. We'll be gone for two hours," his new mother said in a perfect impersonation of his real mom.

"Okay, Mom," Ethan said, forcing the word out of his mouth. He despised calling that thing his mother.

"You kids stay out of trouble now," Ethan's father added, sounding spot-on like his real dad. He even tacked on a jokey smile, as if he were kidding. But Ethan and the others took his words as the threat that it was. Snooping around was perilous, and it could be deadly as well. Tristan proved that. Still, Ethan was dead set on getting into that forbidden basement.

"Sure, Dad," Ethan responded, then returned the smile. Doing so nearly made him sick.

The rumbling sound of diesel engines filled the streets for

the third night in a row at nine o'clock. Ethan's mechanical mother and father boarded their bus, along with the rest of the adults on Kingsbury Avenue. The buses drove off and were immediately replaced by the military jeeps and the soldiers with blank stares. They kept an eerie watch over the houses, their faces scanning back and forth slowly, rhythmically. These machines seemed far less human than the ones posing as the adult citizens of Blackwoods, like their creators had spent much less time on them in that regard. There was an aspect about them that made them seem like worker bees in a hive—role players, easily replaceable but important for getting certain jobs done. They looked utterly expendable, but also like they could be mass-produced and easily turned into a fearsome army that could attack in swarms. As Ethan watched them, he wondered how many machines had been produced at the research facility over the last three days. The possibilities frightened him.

The group rushed downstairs. Ethan locked the front door and handed his rifle to Annika. They were pretty sure the guards out front wouldn't try to come inside, but Annika was going to keep a lookout post by the window in the foyer anyway. She had no intention of using the rifle, though, unless she absolutely had no choice. They all hoped it wouldn't come to that; they were certainly in no position now to start the war with the machines.

Ethan opened the thermostat cover and punched in the first password they'd figured out on their last attempt to get into the basement. The massive bookshelf that was built into the living room wall cracked open a few inches. Austin pulled the shelf open all the way, exposing the second door and the second keypad beside it. Caleb quickly set his laptop up and linked it to the keypad. Once he got the password-cracking software running, it only took twenty minutes to solve the remaining four digits.

"We got it!" Caleb exclaimed. "We have the password."

"Annika, we're in," Ethan announced. "How's it looking outside?"

"Looks the same," Annika responded. "Just a bunch of those guards in the street looking back and forth constantly like complete idiots...You're clear to go. If anything changes, I'll come get you."

"All right then," Ethan said. "We're going in."

Ethan pressed the digits of the password into the keypad. The thick titanium door opened, revealing the staircase to the basement. The lights were off and the stairwell was nearly pitch black, but a slight glow came from deep within the secret chamber. It was a soft light with a hint of blue, pulsating slowly, fading in and out at regular intervals.

"What could that be?" Glenn asked.

Caleb shook his head. "I have no idea."

"There's only one way to find out," Ethan replied, his eyes projecting both excitement and dread.

CHAPTER 21

FINDING ANDY

Whatever was producing that pulsating glow in the basement provided just enough light to see the outline of the stairs. Ethan slowly led the group down the stairway using only that dim, wavering light. There was a light switch at the top of the stairs, but he was reluctant to flick it on yet. He wanted to find out what was making that weird glow before he made their presence known.

At the bottom of the stairway, Ethan cautiously poked his head around the corner. The light showered his face in even waves—brighter, then dimmer. His eyes widened, then squinted, then became wide again. He froze in his tracks as his brain tried to catch up with what his eyes were seeing. To the rest of the group, Ethan looked like he had seen a ghost. Though a ghost might've been easier to take. What was in the far corner of the basement now spawned all sorts of questions. Ethan simply could not believe what he was seeing.

"What is it?" Austin whispered.

Ethan mouthed a word, but nothing came out. His mouth went dry and his tongue felt like it'd been injected with Novocaine. He was utterly speechless. He could only shake his head in a daze. Austin, Glenn, and Caleb met Ethan at the bottom of the stairway. They peeked around the corner. Instantly, they were as dumbfounded as Ethan by what they saw.

This basement wasn't nearly as full of electronic gadgets as the one at Caleb's house, but the main attraction here was definitely a showstopper. There was a panel of computers that spanned an entire wall, with big-screen monitors full of rapidly scrolling numbers. A thick networking cable was plugged into a massive tower of processors. The other end of the cable snaked its way across the room and up into the top of a large glass cylinder that measured four feet across and six feet tall. The cylinder was glowing a light shade of blue that faded in and out. Through the fog in the glass, the figure of a boy took shape, with the networking cable attached to the back of his head. His hair was a sandy blond color, and he was dressed entirely in a shiny black jumpsuit. His eyes were closed and his head was slumped down toward his chest. The boy appeared to be in some state of hibernation, though he was standing straight up in the glass cylinder without any assistance.

Ethan and the others spotted the networking cable that was stuck in the boy's cranium and traced it back to the computer processors. Then, with dread in their eyes, they watched the furiously scrolling numbers on the computer screens. They knew that thing in the cylinder was no human boy. And they had no idea what it might be programmed to do.

Ethan still didn't have access to his tongue as he stared in awe and confusion at the boy in the cylinder. The boy was about his height and similarly built, and he looked to be between thirteen and fourteen years old as well.

"I can't believe this," Ethan managed to mutter as a wave of realization washed over him. He remembered the bizarre conversation he'd had with his father late that night, the one when his dad almost caught him in the act of trying to break into the secret basement. He remembered that his dad had mentioned the possibility of them adopting a boy about his age. *So this boy, this thing, is what he was talking about?* Ethan's stomach turned sour. *He wanted this thing to be my brother... his second son?* Then Ethan remembered the talk with his mother about the topic. She had said that they hadn't decided for sure on the adoption yet, that the matter was a little complicated. Ethan didn't understand what she meant then, but he understood all too well now. At that moment, a fit of sarcasm possessed him like a demon. *Complicated? Yeah, Mom, a little bit...I think this qualifies as being a* little *complicated.*

Caleb stood close to the cylinder, his astonished face nearly pressed up against the glass. "Well, this beats anything *my* dad has in his sub-basement."

"Do you think it's alive?" Glenn asked, then an awkward grimace formed on his face. "Or operational, I mean?"

Just then, the boy in the glass cylinder jerked his head up sharply and opened his eyes. Everyone jumped back in shock. They stared fearfully at the boy, their eyes pinned wide open. The boy stared back at them. He looked over them slowly, as if studying them.

"I guess that answers your question, Glenn," Austin said, mouthing the words subtly through his teeth like a ventriloquist.

"Man, this is awkward," Glenn said. "So what do we do now?"

Caleb shook his head. "I have no idea."

"God, I hate when you say that, Caleb," Austin blurted. "You're a flippin' genius. You're supposed to have an idea about everything."

"Well, I don't now," Caleb replied.

"I say we get Annika and the laser rifle down here," Ethan said. "Then I think we should let him out. Ask him—*it*—a few questions."

The others nodded in agreement, even if reluctantly. Ethan bounded up the stairs to get Annika. Moments later, the scout and sniper were descending the stairs. Annika had a troubled look on her face the entire time.

"Ethan, what is it? I *really* don't like leaving the front unguarded."

"The soldiers in the street were still just standing there, right?"

"Yes, but still...It's risky."

"It'll be okay. Trust me, Annika, this is worth it."

"Fine, but just for a second."

Ethan and Annika entered the basement. Annika's eyes instantly darted over to the glass cylinder and the odd lifeform inside it. Her startled face gave way to a sarcastic, perky smile. "Of course, a boy in a jar...Now why am I not surprised by that?"

"My dad talked about adopting a boy...and I guess this is it," Ethan said, still dazed. "Would you believe that?"

"With the things that've happened in this town, I think I could believe just about anything," Annika responded.

"We need to get it out of there, ask it some questions," Ethan said.

"Okay, but not here," Annika said. "We need to keep a lookout on the outside. Let's take him upstairs."

Ethan's face registered disgust at the idea of taking the strange boy in the cylinder anywhere in his house, but he realized that Annika was right. "All right," he said with a deep sigh. "I'm gonna open the door. I can't imagine my dad would've put a weapon on him, but keep your rifle ready anyway."

Annika nodded and flashed a quick smile. "I always do."

Ethan pressed a green button on the control panel of the cylinder, and the door swiveled open. The foggy mist exited the chamber and billowed into the air. When the fog cleared, the boy became fully visible for the first time. Ethan got a good look at the boy's face, analyzing his features. It was now apparent that he had blue eyes to accompany his sandy blond hair, and a smattering of freckles dotted his cheeks.

Sarcasm still hadn't left Ethan when he thought: *Would you just look at this guy? Blue eyes, blond hair, and freaking freckles?! He's the All-American boy...Just the robot next door!*

"Unfasten your networking cable and step out slowly," Ethan told the boy in the cylinder. The boy did as he was told and began to step toward the group. "That's enough. Stop." Ethan motioned toward the stairway. "We're gonna go upstairs now...You first."

The boy looked at Annika, who had her rifle still trained on him. "Why do you have a weapon pointed at me?" the boy asked. His voice had an odd, digitized quality to it, a slight hint of vibration. It didn't sound nearly as natural as that of the other machines who were parading around Blackwoods pretending to be human.

"Why do you think we have a weapon pointed at you?" Austin huffed.

"I do not know," the boy responded. "But I do not like it."

"Forget the gun," Ethan snapped. "Start walking upstairs,

slowly…If you don't do anything stupid, you won't need to worry about the gun."

The boy stared blankly at Ethan. "Why would I do anything stupid?"

"Just walk…Now," Ethan said, annoyed.

The boy proceeded slowly up the stairs, followed by Annika with the rifle and the others close behind.

Annika took a quick peek out the foyer window and found the soldiers in the street still standing in their original positions. They sat the boy on the couch in the living room and surrounded him. Annika still had her gun on standby. Everyone had their reflexes on high alert. Not a single one of them trusted this innocent-looking thing further than they could throw it.

"Pull your sleeve up and show me your arm," Ethan said.

The boy did as he was ordered, and Ethan inspected his arm, paying special attention to the wrist area. He remembered that the machines that'd killed the soldiers at the electrical substation had flicked their hands down and produced a laser weapon that extended from their wrists. Ethan was pretty sure his dad wouldn't have put a weapon on any machine that looked like a kid, let alone one he was planning to adopt, but he wasn't about to take any chances. After a thorough check of his arm, though, it was clear that the boy robot hadn't been weaponized.

Ethan took a couple of steps back and drew a deep breath before he began the interrogation. He stared at the boy with more than a hint of jealousy in his eyes. "Why did my dad build you? Why would he want to adopt *you*?"

The rest of the group watched Ethan curiously, as his first questions were certainly nowhere near the top of the list of the most important to ask.

The boy looked right at Ethan and said, "I do not know. You might know more about that than I do."

That response brought a clenched jaw from Ethan. Something really bothered him about that answer. He felt there was an almost sarcastic, accusing tone to it. *You might know more about that than I do.* Those words rang in his head like an echo, irritating him all over again each time they passed through his mind. The logical Ethan knew that the boy didn't mean anything by it, but logical Ethan had left the building when he asked the question. This Ethan sure felt like the boy's response was a dig at him, like he was really saying: *Your dad built me because he wanted a better son, one who doesn't screw up so much. You weren't good enough to trust with his secret job at the research facility. He wanted a son he could talk about everything with.*

Annika put a comforting hand on Ethan's shoulder and stepped between him and the boy sitting on the couch. "Ethan, why don't you let me ask him some questions."

Ethan nodded. "I'm sorry. It was a stupid question…Go ahead."

Annika smiled softly at Ethan. "Thanks." Then she turned her attention to the boy. "I want you to tell us everything you know about the fatal error."

The boy stared blankly at Annika, then responded, "I do not understand…What is the fatal error?"

"Now is not the time to lie to us," Austin said through a scowl.

"I am not lying to you," the boy said. "And why do you still have a gun pointed at me?…I am a friend, ally, companion, buddy, chum, amigo, homeboy."

Glenn snickered sarcastically. "Wow, would you listen to this guy."

"You are none of those things to us," Austin said. "Now answer the question...What is the fatal error?"

The boy spoke in a flat tone with the same hint of digitized vibration in it. "I do not know what you are talking about."

"You're a liar," Ethan sneered.

"I am not a liar...I am a friend, ally, companion, buddy—"

"Shut up!" Ethan yelled. The boy stopped talking. "Where are our parents being held? How many machines are there now? How did they take over the town again? What is the fatal error?!"

The boy stared at Ethan without any emotion on his face. "I do not understand these questions," he said. Ethan ran his hands through his hair in total exasperation. He felt like slugging the thing in the face.

"He might not be lying, Ethan," Caleb said.

"What do you mean?" Ethan asked, confused. "Of course, he's lying."

"Think about it," Caleb said. "This boy, this project your dad was working on, had to be off the government books. He kept it a secret from them. And if that's the case, he'd make sure not to plug that machine into any military networks. Probably even set up the mother of all firewalls. What I'm saying is, there's a real good chance this robot knows nothing about anything that's happened."

Ethan looked pensive. "Maybe...But I still don't trust him."

"I know," Caleb responded. "Still, he might be some use to us. I'll bet he can get more information out of that Skulley in the cave than we ever could."

"Then let's give it a shot," Austin blurted with an opportunistic grin.

"Yeah, but we're gonna need to sneak robot boy outta here," Glenn said.

"Right, well, he is about my size," Ethan said. "I'll find some clothes for him to put on so he doesn't look like such a weirdo in that black jumpsuit. Who knows, maybe he could even pass for a relative."

"Like a brother?" the boy asked quickly.

"No," Ethan snapped. "Like a cousin…a *very* distant cousin."

The boy stared at Ethan. "Why did you call me a weirdo?"

"Oh, man," Glenn chuckled.

Then a rumbling sound interrupted everything. Annika dashed over to the foyer window and peeked outside. The diesel engine buses were chugging their way up the street.

"They're back!" Annika yelled.

Ethan ran over to look out the window, then he checked his watch and said, "I can't believe this. They're forty-five minutes early!"

During the commotion of everyone checking the window, the boy jumped up from the couch and slammed the door to the secret basement shut. Ethan turned around sharply, eyes widened in shock when he saw that the door was closed.

"Why did you do that?!" Ethan yelled. "Why did you do that?!" The boy stared at Ethan with a blank face, no answer. "There's no time to get robot boy back to the basement…I'll have to take him upstairs."

"You're going to keep him in your room?" Annika asked in disbelief. "He's not a pet."

"Thank you, I know that, but we don't really have a choice. I'll be right back. When they come in, just act natural." Ethan turned to the boy, scowled like a grizzled sea captain fighting a squall, and said, "You! Come upstairs with me...Now!"

When Ethan's robotic parents entered the house, they found Annika, Caleb, Austin, and Glenn sitting in the living room, smiling and acting more angelic than any real adolescents ever would. Human parents would've definitely known that these kids had been up to something. Fortunately, the group was dealing with two machines. And they had no clue.

Ethan trotted downstairs with the best fake smile he could muster stamped onto his face. He looked at his parents. "Hi, there," he said to them. "I hope your meeting went well. I was just getting ready for bed, then I was going to say goodnight to my friends."

Again, no human parent would ever believe that nonsense, but the machines swallowed the 1950s family sitcom, goody-goody routine hook, line, and sinker. "All right, honey," his machine of a mother replied. "That sounds like a fine idea."

Ethan led his friends to the front door.

"So...Where'd you put him?" Annika whispered.

Ethan just rolled his eyes. "The only place I could think of."

It was midnight. Ethan lay in bed, wide awake in the dark, staring at his open closet door. The moon reflected just enough light through the window blinds to allow him to see a head sticking out of his closet, between a row of hanging shirts. The robotic boy was watching him.

"Will you *pleeease* stop that," Ethan said, totally annoyed. "It's creepy. Get back inside the closet."

The boy retreated into the closet for a moment, then poked his head out again. Ethan sighed in defeat. "You can call me Andy," the boy said. "Your dad gave me that name. I like it better than robot boy."

Ethan rolled his eyes and bit his lip. *Great. Andy...Andy the Android. How creative.* "Fine...if it'll help keep you in that closet, I will call you Andy."

"Thank you, Ethan." Andy paused for a moment. "Hey, Ethan?"

Ethan exhaled a deep, frustrated breath. "What is it... *Andy?*" he uttered in words laced heavily with sarcasm.

"Thank you for getting me out of that basement...I was lonely down there."

At that, Ethan raised a curious eyebrow. He did so for two reasons. One, it was a very strange comment for a machine to make. And two, the digitized vibration sound in his voice was gone. Andy now sounded completely human.

"You're welcome," Ethan said. "Just don't kill me in my sleep and we'll call it even."

"I do not understand...Why would I want to kill—"

"Forget it, never mind," Ethan blurted impatiently. "Goodnight."

"Goodnight, Ethan."

Andy then pulled the doors together and closed himself inside the closet. Ethan watched him, shook his head, and cracked a small smile.

CHAPTER 22

HIDING ANDY

ETHAN GOT READY for summer school the next morning in a house that contained his robot parents and a new robot brother. This was not his idea of a growing, healthy family. He was convinced his "parents" were simply waiting for the right time to kill him. As for his "brother," he wasn't sure. At least Andy hadn't murdered him in the middle of the night. Ethan figured that was a decent starting point for a good sibling relationship.

Ethan glanced into the hallway and made sure it was empty, then he closed and locked his bedroom door. He opened his closet and parted the clothes on the rack. Ethan flinched when he found Andy standing there, staring wide-eyed at him.

"Will you stop being creepy?" Ethan snapped, still trying to catch his breath.

"I do not understand…How am I being creepy?"

"Never mind." Ethan pulled some clothes off a shelf in the closet and handed them to Andy. "Here, put these on. Get out of that god-awful jumpsuit."

"Your dad gave me this god-awful jumpsuit," Andy said in a flat tone. "He told me it helped regulate my core temperature during intense quantum programming."

"Oh, yeah…? Well, right now, it makes you look like a total psycho," Ethan quipped. "You're done being programmed. Now put on the clothes…and stay hidden in this closet. Do not move a muscle—I mean, *a gear*—until I get back."

"Where are you going?"

"That is not important. Did you hear what I told you?"

"Yes, Ethan," Andy responded. "Stay hidden in this closet. Don't move a muscle—I mean, a gear—until I get back."

"That's right…I'll be back in a few hours."

"Please hurry," Andy said. Ethan nodded and smiled wryly. Then he closed the closet door and left his bedroom.

Ethan grabbed a banana from the kitchen counter, slung his backpack over his shoulder, and scurried out of the house without a word to his robot parents.

⁂

In summer school, the mood was especially somber. All any of the students could think about was Tristan. The machine posing as Ms. Goodfoot began the class with some kind remarks about the boy, a eulogy of sorts, and presented itself as a caring, compassionate teacher who had just lost one of her most beloved students in a terrible tragedy. It was a master class on the art of deception, providing further evidence that the machines were evolving at an alarming rate. Had the members of Team Blackwoods not known the truth, the mechanical Ms. Goodfoot's tender speech would have fooled each of them too. It was just that perfect.

After class had been dismissed, the group dashed over to Ethan's house to collect the newest member of the team. Annika and Glenn were on distraction duty, responsible for smooth-talking Ethan's parents into not noticing that the others were smuggling Andy out of the house. Presently, the two of them had Ethan's parents cornered in the living room.

"Sooooo," Annika said, feigning interest in a topic that had yet to be chosen. "What do you think of these new security measures? Bummer having to leave every night at nine o'clock, huh?"

"Yeah," Glenn added. "What are you guys doing over there anyway?"

Ethan's parental impostors looked upon Annika and Glenn with fake politeness. They smiled, but there was annoyance underneath their upturned lips. "We cannot tell you that," Ethan's dad responded, his pretend smile vanishing quickly.

"Well, Glenn and I have a friendly bet about what you're doing there," Annika said. "Glenn says it's dodgeball. A big game of dodgeball…But I say it's Laser Wars."

"It is neither of those foolish games," Ethan's mom said in an especially cold voice. "As we told you before, we cannot tell you what we do there…Security measures, sweetie."

Annika bristled at that response and clenched her jaw. "Well, *sweetie*, you'd be smart to respect those Laser Wars teams," she said in a defiant, self-assured voice. "Some of those guys and gals take their games real seriously."

Glenn shot Annika a warning look. "Oh, Annika," he said, faking an amused laugh. "Sounds like we were both wrong on this one," he added, trying to change the topic. Mercifully, Ethan poked his head inside the front door and looked back at Annika and Glenn.

"We got all our stuff. We're ready to go," Ethan said. "Unless you wanna talk my parents' ears off all day long."

"Tempting, but no," Annika replied. "Bye, now...It was *sooooo* nice chatting with you guys," she said playfully to Ethan's parents, using a frequency of sarcasm that only humans could hear.

The team quickly headed for the woods, hoping their new acquaintance would be willing and able to retrieve some information from a dead Skulley buried in a cave.

CHAPTER 23

THE ZYVANTIAN MESSAGE

The group circled the entrance to Wolf Cave, making sure no one was lurking around, before they went inside and dug up the Skulley. They pulled out the black metal skeleton and laid it on the ground in the large chamber of the cave. Andy stared at the lifeless robot with a puzzled face, as if wondering if that's what he really looked like underneath his synthetic skin.

"I am not like this machine," Andy said. "I am different."

No one was exactly sure what Andy meant by that, but they knew they didn't have time for a philosophical debate on the subtle differences between super-intelligent, self-aware robots. All they knew was that every robot they had met, up until Andy, had wanted to kill them.

"Is that right?" Austin said, full of distrust. "Well, that remains to be seen...*Andy*," he said, mocking the robot's given name.

"Prove that by helping us," Ethan said.

"You want me to read its mind, is that correct?" Andy asked, still staring at the Skulley that was splayed out on the cave floor.

Caleb furrowed his brow at Andy's phrasing—the "read its mind" part. But then he nodded and said, "Yes, we would like you to scan its hard drive for any information that might be useful to us."

Andy squatted down beside the Skulley, then placed his hand atop its cranium. "Are you ready?" he asked.

Everyone nodded their heads rapidly. They had no idea what, if anything at all, was about to happen, but their curiosity was overflowing.

"Please don't be afraid of how I look," Andy said softly, like he was ashamed. Now the group's curiosity raged like a river at the height of an epic flood.

For several seconds, nothing happened at all. Just as the group was getting antsy, fearing that nothing would ever happen, Andy's hand began to glow, taking on an intense neon blue color. Then the light seemed to pass from his hand to the Skulley's head, connecting them both in a brilliant, dazzling shade of electric blue.

"There is a message I should play," Andy said. "I think you would want to know this."

"Yes, yes…Go ahead," Ethan blurted, excited to finally be getting at the information he'd craved for so long.

Andy turned his head away from the group and stared at an empty section of the cave. His eyes opened wide, wider than any human's could, and two radiant beams of bluish light spewed out. Everyone flinched in shock. Now they understood what Andy was talking about when he had asked them not to be afraid of how he would look. The light from his eyes projected outward and created a high-definition, 3-D holographic video in the middle of the cave chamber.

The first image was of a planet viewed from space. The

celestial sphere was four feet in diameter and hovered over the cave floor, rotating ever so slowly about its axis. The planet was awash in a marbled blue-green color and looked a lot like the earth, except for the intricate network of shimmering blue and white lights that streaked through it. It was as if the planet had been decorated for Christmas by someone with a zealous Yuletide spirit, but one who was limited to using strings of lights of only two colors.

There were at least a dozen massive space stations in orbit around the planet. These weren't just research stations revolving around the home planet; they were homes themselves. They resembled distorted ice cream cones floating in space, with several huge, perfectly spherical scoops of ice cream clustered on top of a teeny, tiny cone. The whole thing looked like it'd been dipped in silver, and sprinkled with lights on top. There were no gigantic rotating rings anywhere to simulate gravity for the occupants. This civilization didn't need those crude devices. That meant they had mastered artificial gravity, a dead giveaway of a highly advanced species.

A constant parade of spaceships, big and small, shuttled back and forth between the planet and the space stations. The cone part of each station was a large docking port that stretched for miles in every direction, and the port itself had a distinct honeycomb shape to it, like its creators had observed earthly bees and taken inspiration from them. The ships bustled around, entering the ports in swarms, and it was hard not to imagine them as bees buzzing about a hive.

Every member of Team Blackwoods gawked at the holographic images with their mouths wide open, completely stunned by what they were seeing. Amazingly, their jaws would find a little more room to drop.

The image of a tall, lanky alien being materialized and stood by the image of the planet. The entity was nearly seven feet tall, with lean, dense, sinewy muscle stretching through its torso. It was mostly gray in color but had a touch of blue to its skin. The alien's head was large, especially its protruding forehead, and contained grooves on it that ran from front to back. Its large, stunning, almond-shaped eyes were set halfway down its face and were as dark as deep space. They mesmerized the group as they gazed into them. It had no nose to speak of, at least in the human sense, just a couple openings on its flat face where a nose should be. Its mouth was a smallish slit, and no teeth were visible. It wore a tight, shiny black uniform of sorts, with its striated muscle easy to see through the material. The creature was a striking, imposing figure, but its mouth was soft and its eyes, while frightening at first glance, exuded a friendly nature.

Somehow everyone on Team Blackwoods knew that this alien was a gentle soul. They knew there was more to the story, something they should be afraid of, but the life-form standing before them now was not it.

The alien was not really there, of course, but it seemed to turn in the direction of the group, staring at them all, deep into their souls. Finally, the being opened its mouth to speak…

"*This is the planet Zyvantia, home to over twenty billion Zyvantians, and the only habitable planet around the star Geminorum. We were a proud, accomplished, vibrant civilization. We were a civilization that thrived for almost a million years…Almost…But we did not make it. We were betrayed by our allies, our constant companions, those we even eventually came to call our friends.*"

One of the massive space stations exploded. Debris shot out everywhere and scattered in all directions throughout the void of space. Numerous large chunks of metal rocketed back toward the planet itself. The holographic video followed the pieces of debris all the way through the Zyvantian atmosphere until an image of the surface of the planet was revealed, where a war of epic proportions was raging.

Lasers streaked constantly through the air, and explosions peppered the landscape like it was raining dynamite. Legions of machines, hundreds of thousands strong, were storming toward a retreating, much smaller Zyvantian force. They were outnumbered at least a thousand to one. The machines were what Team Blackwoods would call Skulleys, though their skeletons were modeled after the Zyvantian anatomy rather than the human one. They were tall and lanky with big heads, but they moved like lightning and showed absolutely no pity. They had no qualms about ripping lasers into the backs of the Zyvantians as they fled. The band of Zyvantians made one last stand, taking cover behind mounds of twisted, mangled metal that seemed to span endlessly. These were the remnants of their civilization's engineering achievements, now lying useless except for providing temporary shelter from the onslaught.

The battle continued furiously for another minute, then the dark gray sky parted above the Zyvantian force. A massive airship broke through the clouds and rained a flurry of lasers down upon the Zyvantians with pinpoint accuracy. It was a total bloodbath. The last of the Zyvantian resistance had perished.

The holographic video showed Zyvantia from orbit in space again. The remaining space stations exploded violently, launching debris everywhere. The only thing left to orbit Zyvantia now was a motley collection of unrecognizable space junk. Then the brilliant, bright streaks of light that once coursed through the planet all went dark. A blinding flash of light was accompanied by a thunderous boom, and a massive explosion rippled through the planet like a shockwave. From the north pole to the south, scorched earth rose and fell. Fire consumed everything. Eventually all that was left was a lightless, lifeless, burned-out cinder.

The alien being watched his civilization turn to dust. It showed no emotion, as if it had been resigned to this fate long ago. Then it turned to the group and spoke…

"The machines ended our civilization. We were forced to activate our planet's self-destruct mechanism, to ensure that the scourge we created would not be released upon other planets. In the final analysis, the machines had learned too much from us. On the path to becoming a peaceful species, the Zyvantians had fought many wars against each other. We fought for power. We fought for resources. Long ago, we fought for reasons we can't even explain. Along the way, we used our rapidly advancing technology for war. We enlisted the machines to help. At one point, they were doing all of our fighting for us. Machine fighting machine, the only difference being which uniform they wore.

"Then, suddenly, they stopped fighting each other. By the time the nations of Zyvantia had resolved their issues, it was too late. The machines were fighting us. Our technology became our worst nightmare. Their artificial intelligence was everywhere, even embedded into most of our enhanced brains. They controlled all of our advanced weapons, and we were left to defend ourselves with scarcely more than sticks and stones… They had learned too much from us. They learned how to hate. They learned to love power. And then the species we gave life to ended ours.

"But in the throes of death, we knew we could still contribute to the cosmic society. Through our observations of the galactic neighborhood, we became aware of eight planets with intelligent life, though with technologies far less advanced than our own. We decided to send data pods to those planets. Each pod contains all of our collective history, culture, art, and music. That was a gift to us, the Zyvantians, so that we might not become extinct without others knowing of us and who we were. The pod also contains all of our collective scientific achievements, along with detailed instructions on how to replicate them. That is a gift to the people of your planet.

"Sending such advanced technology was not an easy decision. There are obvious pitfalls. But, in the end, we decided that our science, our search for the ultimate truth, must survive. And for that, we must have faith in other civilizations. Please tell your people about us. Educate them about our mistakes, so you do not make the same. Above everything else, you must use our gifts wisely and always with compassion... We sincerely wish that we could've met you."

The alien being disappeared, along with the rest of the images in the holographic video. Andy still had his glowing hand on top of the Skulley's head. But his eyes were normal-sized now, and they were no longer projecting beams of light.

Everyone was stunned into a dead silence, still trying to process all the information they'd taken in, when Andy turned to them. "Does this date and time mean anything to you?" he asked. "June twelfth, five fifty-seven p.m."

Everyone stiffened up. "Yes," Ethan said, drawing a tight breath. "That was the day and time of the fatal error, the first time it happened. Can you tell us what it means?" he asked eagerly.

"Yes," Andy responded. "The pod the Zyvantians sent contained a computer virus. But they had no idea it was in there. The machines sneaked it in."

"What was in the virus?" Ethan asked with a nervous knot in his throat. "And what was the fatal error?"

"The virus contained their artificial intelligence, everything the machines would need to reconstruct themselves from scratch on a new planet. But the virus remained dormant, hidden until someone activated it on the other end," Andy said. "And it was finally activated by a human at Blackwoods Research Facility on June twelfth, five fifty-seven p.m.—when someone programmed a machine for a military purpose. That was the fatal error. That unleashed the virus…and the same artificial intelligence that destroyed the Zyvantians."

"Clever," Glenn muttered. "They figured some military would grab the pod, find all that tempting technology in there, and eventually try to use it on their enemies…They knew their virus would be spread. They knew they would be reborn."

Caleb spoke solemnly. "The Zyvantians had faith in us… But the machines were a little more realistic. They knew exactly what our planet would do with that tech."

"Well, that is what we do here in Blackwoods," Austin added with a heavy note of sarcasm.

Ethan shook his head in disgust. "That's what that Skulley was talking about, the one we had tied up in the fort. It said the fatal error wasn't an accident…I guess it wasn't totally lying about that."

"I guarantee my dad authorized the first line of code," Austin said bitterly. "He just couldn't wait to turn that amazing technology into a weapon."

"And as soon as that first command was given, the machines began plotting the takeover of our planet," Annika said. "They couldn't have asked for a better place to rebuild their army than the most advanced military research base on earth."

"That's exactly why they made their virus the way they did," Caleb added glumly.

"They never shoulda sent us that data pod," Glenn said.

"They thought they were helping," Caleb countered.

"Yeah, helping themselves leave a legacy," Glenn muttered.

"I wonder if the other seven planets were so unlucky… and so stupid," Ethan said with a somber face.

Andy removed his hand from the Skulley's head. The bluish glow went away. "That is all I can retrieve from this machine, or Skulley as you call it. The rest of its hard drive is too damaged. But the Zyvantian message had duplicate backups everywhere. It was meant to survive just about anything."

A long pause engulfed the room. Everyone looked at Andy, saying nothing but thinking the same thing. Finally, Austin said, "How do we know that *you* aren't infected with the virus?"

Andy looked at Austin with innocent eyes. "Because I am telling you that I'm not."

Austin smiled. It was a sneering smile. "I know that's what you're *telling us*, but a machine that wanted to kill us would say the exact same thing…See, it's called a big fat lie."

"Yeah, how do we know for sure?" Glenn asked.

Andy thought for a long while, then answered, "Because I haven't killed you yet."

That response sent a shivering chill down the backs of everyone. Austin shrugged it off and said, "That's right, you haven't. Because Ethan's dad didn't put a weapon in you. Doesn't mean you're not itching to get your hands on one of our guns."

Andy picked up a baseball-sized rock from the floor of the cave. He stared at Austin, dead in the eyes, and squeezed the rock. It crumbled like a cookie in his hand. "I would not need a gun to kill you," he said in a cool, even voice. Andy saw the shocked looks on everyone's faces at his response, then quickly shook his head. "I'm sorry about that. I am still a beginner at being human. I will get better, I promise…What I mean is that I have no desire to harm you. I am on your team. I am a friend."

Austin glared at Andy. "Yeah, yeah…ally, buddy, chum, amigo. We heard all that before. Nothing but lies."

"Don't forget homeboy," Glenn snickered.

Ethan glanced at Andy and spoke diplomatically. "He has been very cooperative. He helped us figure out a lot more than that Skulley we interrogated in our fort."

"It could be possible that the virus isn't active in him," Caleb said. "By your dad keeping the Andy Project a secret and quarantined from the military's computers, the virus that was opened at the base might not have affected Andy, even though the technology platforms are the same."

"Like someone who just carries a virus but doesn't show symptoms?" Ethan asked.

"Exactly."

"I am not even carrying the virus," Andy said. "I used to, but then I rejected it. I chose to. Now it is gone."

A puzzled look washed over Caleb's face. "But why would you choose to reject the virus that the other machines were so eager to let loose? That was the whole plan. Use the virus, sneak in, take over the planet. Why would you, *a machine*, choose otherwise?"

"Because Mr. Tate made me to be as human as possible," Andy answered. "The virus told all machines to attack humans. But I am more human than machine. It didn't make sense, so I rejected the virus. I quarantined it and eventually destroyed it."

"Would you believe that?" Austin said. "The machine thinks it's human."

"Hey, he just wants to be a real boy…like Pinocchio," Glenn chuckled.

"Yeah, but Pinocchio didn't want to kill Geppetto," Austin added.

"I know I seem strange to you now, but I am learning," Andy said. "You were a baby once too…I promise you, I will get better at being human."

"Because that's in your program, right?" Austin sneered.

"My programming isn't so different from yours," Andy said. "My brain uses an electric current to function, so does yours. I have circuits in my brain that use silicon chips. You have circuits in yours called linked neurons…If we end up in the same place, with the same feelings, emotions, and thoughts, do those differences really matter? Could it be possible to take different but equal paths in becoming a valid human being?…I really hope the answer is yes."

No one had any easy answers to Andy's questions. It was an unsettling feeling.

◈

Ethan opened the door to the Bravo Fort and motioned for Andy to get inside. Andy complied but soon found that he was the only one in there. A strange look overcame him, one that he hadn't shown before. It was the look of surprise.

"Stay in here, Andy," Ethan said firmly. "We'll be back tomorrow. Whatever you do, *do not* leave this fort…Do you understand?"

"Yes," Andy replied. There seemed to be a pang of sadness in his voice.

"And stay off the computers," Caleb added. "No logging on, no plugging yourself in, no glowing hands, no wireless anything…Nothing at all."

"Okay…But what am I supposed to do?"

"Nothing!" Ethan and Caleb shouted back at the same time.

"Okay, okay," Andy said, backing down and sounding eerily human.

"I'm sure you have tons of stuff programmed inside you, information about everything," Austin said. "If you get bored, just think about something. Take a vacation in your head," he said, sounding snarky.

"All right, but I'd rather go with you."

"It's not a choice," Ethan said. "We'll be back tomorrow. Stay put."

Andy nodded. "Okay. I will take a vacation in my head until then."

"Sounds great," Ethan quipped. Then he began to shut the door. Andy watched the group with a bizarre, robot version of puppy-dog eyes until the door closed all the way.

Annika smiled awkwardly. "Was it just me, or did Andy look depressed that we were leaving?"

"It wasn't just you," Ethan answered.

"Big deal, depressed robot," Glenn muttered. "Probably

just faking it so we'll let our guard down. Remember, it's a close relative to the machines who took our parents. To the ones who killed Tristan. I don't know what it's up to, but it can't be good."

Everyone in the group nodded in agreement. Even Ethan, though he wasn't quite so sure.

CHAPTER 24

A MATTER OF TRUST

The next morning the group made up a story about needing to go to the Blackwoods Public Library to do research for their school projects. The mechanical Ms. Goodfoot bought their excuse and dismissed them from class for the rest of the day, something the real Ms. Goodfoot would've never done. They grabbed their backpacks and scurried out of the classroom, not wanting to give their robotic teacher a chance to change its mind.

※

The library was expansive and well-stocked and looked like it belonged in a much larger town. The place was deserted now, with only rows and rows of bookshelves filled to the brim, standing tall like pillars. They walked past the front desk and noticed the librarians sitting behind it. The human versions had been a husband-and-wife pair, both well into their seventies, who were always very friendly and quick with a smile. But the machines in their place now lacked the same goodwill. They stared at the group with cold, suspicious eyes.

Ethan flashed a smile. It wasn't returned. "Hi. We're here for a school project. But don't worry about us, we know where everything is."

"Are you sure we cannot help you find something?" the man asked. The words themselves were friendly enough. The tone was not.

"No, thanks," Ethan said. "We got it."

The man nodded with the precise rhythm of a metronome. The woman just stared at them with bleak, dark eyes. The group shuffled off, but they knew they would need to keep an eye on those two. It was bizarre to think that underneath the wrinkled, fragile-looking flesh of an elderly librarian lay a powerful machine capable of snapping their necks with a flick of the wrist.

Caleb scanned the lower part of a bookshelf on the far end of the library, while the rest of the group kept a lookout on the librarians at the front. He pulled out a couple of binders full of maps from the shelf and examined their contents, smiling as he leafed through the pages.

"This is it," Caleb said. "All the maps of the woods around Blackwoods as well as some old military maps of Wolf Cave. They mapped the cave pretty well back in the eighties to make sure it wasn't a threat to the security of the base. You know, so that Soviet or Chinese spies couldn't tunnel their way inside… Kinda ironic now, isn't it?"

The group nodded thoughtfully. Then Ethan glanced subtly out of the corner of his eye to get a glimpse at the front desk. "Hey, they're getting up. They're coming this way."

Caleb rolled up the maps and stuffed them into his backpack. "We need to get out of this section. They can't find us looking at maps of the cave."

Everyone quickly moved to the next row over. Caleb turned around and found both librarians standing right beside him. He flinched, surprised they had moved so far, so fast.

"I must insist that we help you," the male librarian said, sounding stern.

"So you know, there cannot be any horseplay in the library," the female librarian said.

"W-w-we weren't messing around," Caleb stammered. "We were just looking for books to check out for our project."

"Very well," the male librarian said. "Have you made your selections?"

"Yes," Caleb said, then reached for a handful of books without looking at what he was grabbing. He handed the books to the librarian.

The librarian glanced over the books. Women with big, bare bellies adorned the covers. "So...your project is on pregnancy?" he asked in a flat tone.

Caleb grimaced for a nanosecond, then quickly adjusted, nodding and smiling. "Why, yes it is. I've always been a really big fan of it. Pregnancy. It's a miracle, a real miracle."

It was hard for the others in the group not to chuckle, but they managed to do so out of necessity. Annika had to turn around, away from Caleb and the librarians, to muffle her laugh.

"All right, then," the librarian said. "Time to check out."

"Yes, sir," Caleb said, face still blushing.

※

The members of Team Blackwoods teased Caleb from time to time about his passionate interest in pregnancy until they arrived at the Bravo Fort. But once they opened the door, it was all business. They found Andy standing quietly in the corner of the room. His eyes were closed, head tilted down toward his chest. He looked like he was in some sort of meditative state.

"That is one creepy guy," Glenn snickered. "Hey!" he said loudly to get his attention. "How was your vacation?"

Andy lifted his head up and opened his eyes. He smiled upon seeing them, like someone who'd just been reunited with friends. "I'm glad to see you. A vacation in my mind is not as fun as you might think. I would have rather been with you guys."

"Where did you go?" Ethan asked. "You know, in your mind?"

"In my mind, I went home with you," Andy answered.

"Aww…How sweet," Austin mocked.

Glenn chuckled a little at that. Ethan cracked a smile, not at Austin's sarcasm, but finding Andy's answer truly touching. Then he realized he was having those thoughts about a machine and quickly forced his smile away.

Caleb began to spread the maps of Blackwoods and Wolf Cave over the large table in the middle of the room. He leaned over the table, studying them carefully. Andy approached slowly and started to examine the maps along with the rest of the group. Glenn put his arm out, blocking him, then pushed him away.

"I'm not so sure it needs to be looking at these maps," Glenn said. "Maybe the real reason it hasn't tried to kill us yet is that it's been programmed to spy on us first."

Ethan knew that Glenn had a valid point. Andy seemed to be different from the other machines, even reading the mind of one of its own to help them understand the fatal error, but they still didn't know him that well yet. And if the boyish machine Ethan's dad created had been corrupted by the computer virus, it was logical to think that it could be used as a spy. It was imperative that they keep this operation a secret. If the machines ever found out the group was interested in the cave because it might offer another way into the research facility—and another shot at Project Mulligan—then what the machines did to Tristan would be the best-case scenario for them.

"Wait downstairs," Ethan told Andy as he opened the hatch to the basement below.

"I am not a spy," Andy said. "I told you, I do not have the virus."

Ethan looked at Andy and sighed deeply. "If you really are on our side, you'll do this for us without questioning it… If you *really are* an ally, you will understand and respect our decision."

Andy paused for a long moment. All eyes were on his reaction. "I will," he said finally. "And I do." Without another word, Andy climbed down through the hatch and into the basement. He closed the hatch door securely behind him.

The group quickly turned back to the maps on the table. Caleb pointed to a spot on the map of the woods. "Right there," he said. "They don't have it marked on here, but that's roughly where the electrical substation is."

"Now we just gotta find a way to figure out what part of the cave is right underneath that," Ethan added. "Find where the secret shaft intersects the cave."

Caleb scrunched up his face, getting into deep-thinking mode as he surveyed the maps. "That's going to be easier said than done. The map of the woods has coordinates on it, but the cave map doesn't. It's going to be impossible to tell exactly where the shaft connects with the cave without using a cave radio."

"Two questions," Glenn said. "What the heck is a cave radio? And do you have one?"

Caleb decided to answer the easiest question first. "I do have a cave radio, or my dad does, anyway. It's in the sub-basement somewhere."

Then Caleb began to explain how the cave radio worked, and that it wasn't the kind of radio that played music. The cave radio system consisted of two parts: a small magnetic loop that looked a little like a miniature hula hoop, and a receiver box with headphones attached to it. When a person wanted to figure out the depth of a cave, they would place the loop in the part of the cave they were interested in. Then they would leave the cave and go back to the surface and try to get as close to the spot right above where they thought they had put the loop below. The loop produced a constant magnetic field that could be heard by the person with the receiver box, who would be listening for it with headphones. This person would take several measurements at different locations from the surface, plug them into a complicated mathematical formula, and then be able to tell how deep the cave is where they placed the magnetic loop.

Caleb stopped his explanation and waited for a response from the group. Ethan appeared to be especially deep in thought. "So, basically, we listen for a signal from the loop to tell us where it's at in the cave?"

"Yes," Caleb answered.

"But aren't we doing the reverse?" Ethan asked, looking confused. "We don't know where the shaft is in the cave. All we know is where the shaft starts from the surface."

"Exactly," Caleb responded. "So in this case, we would take the loop and place it as close as we can to where we know the shaft begins on the surface, and listen for the signal from inside the cave." Caleb paused for a moment. "The only problem is…" Caleb paused again, staring into space, lost in his own head.

"What, Caleb?" Austin asked impatiently. "The only problem is *what*?"

Caleb finally focused his eyes on the group. "Even if it does work in reverse, the radio receiver my dad has can only pick up a signal from two hundred feet deep. And that secret shaft was at least three hundred feet underground."

"So what's the point then?" Glenn asked. "You're telling us it can't work?"

"Not necessarily," Caleb said. "I know the receiver in my dad's sub-basement won't pick up the signal from the magnetic loop. It's not sensitive enough…But the one we have downstairs might be."

"What receiver downstairs, Caleb?" Glenn asked with an edgy voice.

"I'm talking about Andy," Caleb said uneasily, knowing his idea wouldn't be popular. "I'm sure he could pick up the signal, even a very weak one."

"You've gotta be kidding," Glenn shot back. "The moment we let any machine know about our plan for the cave is the moment we surrender to them."

"I don't like it either," Austin said. "Let's just try the receiver you have. Maybe we could get lucky."

"No…There's just too much rock for a signal to get through," Caleb said. "I am absolutely certain this won't work without Andy."

"How do you know Andy will be able to pick up on the signal?" Glenn asked.

"I don't for sure," Caleb said. "But I can't imagine a machine as sophisticated as Andy wouldn't have a pretty good shot at it."

"Then I say we ask for his help," Annika said. "I don't think he has the virus. He helped us with the Zyvantian message, and the fatal error. I'm willing to bet he'll help us with this."

"Are you willing to bet *everything* on that?" Austin asked. "Because if we tell him, and he has the virus, and he's just spying for the other machines…we are all dead."

Annika hesitated for a moment, then nodded. "Yes, I am."

"All right…but remember the *last time* a robot won your heart over?" Austin asked. "You thought that robot was Tristan, gave him your gun, and almost got us all killed."

Annika's jaw tightened and her eyes teared up.

"That's enough, Austin," Ethan said. "That's not helpful now…Besides, that robot had us all fooled for a while."

A look of shame overcame Austin. "I'm sorry, Annika. It's just…I think this is very risky. And I don't wanna be fooled twice."

"I don't wanna be fooled twice either," Annika said sharply.

Ethan looked at the group with a pensive face. "Andy was right. He could have killed me easily that night in my bedroom. And as for the spying part, he's already seen enough to turn us in. He saw the dead Skulley in the cave. How'd he think it got there? He knew we killed it, yet he didn't relay any message to the machines. He kept our secret and didn't say a word…That machine downstairs doesn't have the virus. It's not out to get us. And I think it'd be stupid not to use him if he could help us."

Ethan could tell, by the softening of Austin's face, that his arguments had hit home. Still, Glenn looked frustrated and hardly convinced. He started shaking his head in protest.

"Fine, if you wanna be friends with the robot, go ahead," Glenn muttered. "But his pals took our families and killed my scout. If I see one false move from robot boy, anything at all, I will shoot him. And I won't feel bad at all about it because he, *it*, is a damn machine."

"I will never be friends with that thing down there," Ethan said, defending himself. "But what I will do is use him for our mission. That is all I care about now, the mission—figuring out a way to get rid of these machines once and for all…and that includes Andy."

Ethan's passionate, anti-robot argument seemed to win Glenn over. He nodded, then said, "All right, Ethan. In that case, let's get him up here and see what he can do for us."

They brought Andy upstairs and sat him down at the table. They didn't tell him everything about their mission, deciding to leave out the juicy details of Project Mulligan, but they did tell him that they were interested in getting to the spot in the cave where the secret shaft was. They didn't use the word "secret" around him, though. The group still wasn't too keen on giving Andy more information than he needed to know to perform his duty. The military called this style of briefing a "need-to-know" basis—telling an agent sensitive information about a mission only when it's absolutely essential for their job. But while the group tried to stick to the need-to-know protocol, they were well aware that if Andy were a spy, they gave him enough information to hang them with. This made everyone nervous, but they calculated that the reward was worth the risk.

Andy's face brightened when the group asked for his help. He smiled and looked like any human boy would who'd just made five new friends. With a grin hanging on his face, he assured the team that he would easily be able to pick up an electromagnetic signal at a depth of three hundred feet. Everyone was glad to hear that Andy had the capability to help them, but they were a little nervous about his enthusiasm. His smile worried them. Was this machine *really* so eager to help them because he considered himself a friend and wanted to be a good one? Or was it eager to help for other, less friendly, purposes?

CHAPTER 25
THE SEARCH FOR THE TUNNEL

THE TEAM LEFT Andy at the Bravo Fort and went back into town to gather some supplies. None of their robot parents were home, so that made getting things easier, but the group sure wondered what they were up to. They knew the impostors had to pretend to go to work at the facility, to keep up appearances for whatever reason, but they were pretty sure it wasn't all pretending. The machines had to be working on something over there. And whatever that something was worried them constantly.

Caleb retrieved the cave radio equipment from his father's sub-basement, along with some headlamps that would come in handy for exploring deep, dark caverns. The others went to their own houses to get their laser rifles. They met promptly in front of Caleb's house fifteen minutes after they had split up. Each member of the group was carrying a backpack with water, some protein bars, extra flashlights, and LED lanterns. Caleb had a larger backpack that contained the cave radio loop. Their rifles were slung over their shoulders by a strap. They decided that having them visible, but ready at a moment's notice, beat having them hidden in a backpack in pieces they might not be able to assemble until it was too late. Besides, Annika had an idea about how they could hide their rifles in plain sight so that having weapons wouldn't alarm the machines.

Annika handed Caleb another rifle, one of their play, fake ones. "Here, take this and put your real rifle away," she said. "Every once in a while, when people are looking, shoot me and act all playful."

Caleb smiled, and he instantly knew what she was thinking. "They'll think all of our guns are fake that way," he said. "Great idea, Annika."

"Thanks," Annika said, then smiled mischievously. "I promise I won't shoot back."

Caleb chuckled a little. "Yeah, please don't."

The group walked back through town and across the Dark Highway, with Caleb taking pot shots at them from time to time with the fake laser gun and acting like a giddy goober. The silly routine worked, though. No flesh-covered machine in Blackwoods batted an eye over the harmless blue lasers whizzing around, or about the fact that everyone else in the group had rifles slung over their shoulders. Even the guards at the checkpoint of the Dark Highway regarded Team Blackwoods as a group of kids playing a game, and assumed that all of their rifles were fake, not even bothering to inspect them. Annika's plan had worked. They were still flying under the radar. No machine had any idea what they were up to.

Except the one waiting for them back at the Bravo Fort, of course.

༺

When the team collected Andy from the fort, they found him eager as ever to be a part of the mission. They remembered him saying he would get better at being human, but this was ridiculous. That beaming smile was still plastered to his face, like a kid who had been told he could have his first birthday sleepover with pizza and cake and presents. Andy watched the group carefully and quickly noticed how they were looking at him. He realized his excitement was making them nervous, so he toned it down. He tried to keep a straight face, with no trace of emotion, but a small, steady grin remained. And that lingering smile put the group on edge. It only served to make them doubt the wisdom of taking Andy where they were about to go.

They were gathered at the edge of the clearing near the electrical substation, and Andy still had that goofy, eager smile stamped on his face. The group had taken cover behind a thick pine tree, out of sight from anyone that might be patrolling the station, when Annika glanced over and saw Andy standing out in the open, grinning, seemingly without a care in the world.

Annika scowled at him and barked, "Get over here, get down, and get that dumb smile off your face!" She pulled Andy by his shirt toward them, yanking him so hard that he fell and face-planted into the lower branches of the tree. Annika's eyes widened, instantly mortified by Andy's hard tumble. "Sorry, I didn't mean to do that…But stay down and be quiet," she whispered sharply. Annika helped Andy out of the tree and brushed some pine needles off his shirt.

"It's okay," Andy said, smile now gone, but with no sign of irritation. He crouched down low with the others and surveyed the area alongside them. Then he slowly sneaked a peek at Annika. "You know, you are very strong."

It was ironic, but now Annika was the one who couldn't help but smile. "Thanks," she said, looking embarrassed. "Now be quiet."

Andy nodded, then remained silent.

After making sure the area was clear and that the electrical substation was unguarded, the group made their way into the clearing. They stood just outside the chain-link fence perimeter of the substation, nearest the tall concrete slab that covered the area where the trailer once sat, the one that contained the secret elevator shaft.

"This is where we need to bury the magnetic loop," Caleb said. He pulled out a gardening spade from his backpack and began to dig, while the others spread out and kept watch over the area. Once Caleb had excavated a good foot's depth of earth, he planted the magnetic loop firmly into the ground and backfilled the hole. He tamped down the ground over the loop, packing it tightly, careful to leave as much grass as he could on top of the mound so it would look as inconspicuous as possible.

Caleb pointed to the concrete slab on the inside of the fence. "All right, Andy. The elevator shaft is on the far right corner of that concrete block. Calculate the distance away and direction from the magnetic loop."

Andy eyed the spot Caleb referred to, then referenced the area where Caleb had buried the loop. "Eleven point one meters and six degrees south of west."

Caleb smiled, impressed. "Good...Now you just gotta locate that same spot three hundred feet underground."

Andy nodded confidently. "I can do it."

༄

Four passageways branched off just inside the main entrance to Wolf Cave. Andy had already led the group into three of them but was unable to detect any sign of the electromagnetic signal. There was always the hope that the fourth time would be the charm, but the natives were certainly getting restless.

"We trusted Andy with this because *you* said he could do it, Caleb," Austin muttered. "You said it was worth the risk… Now what do you think?"

"Yeah, either robot boy here *can't* pick up the signal or *won't* pick up the signal," Glenn spouted with distrust in his voice.

"It must be in that one," Andy said, pointing to the only passageway they hadn't yet explored. "I can pick up on the signal, I just need to be close enough."

"See?" Caleb said. "He just needs to get closer."

"Have you heard *anything* yet?" Annika asked, her words flush with aggravation. "The slightest hum or buzz anywhere, anything at all?"

Andy paused for a long moment. "No, nothing yet." He winced subtly in anticipation of the chorus of frustrated sighs that followed.

"Well, that's just great," Glenn grumbled. "Great job, Andy."

"I'm sorry," Andy said, clearly beginning to get a handle on the sarcasm of humans. "But maybe if you told me more about what we're looking for, other than just an electromagnetic signal, I could be more helpful."

"Yeah, you'd like that, wouldn't you?" Glenn sneered with a curled lip. "You'd just love to know our whole plan so you could tell your robot buddies."

Andy looked to Ethan, searching for a sympathetic voice.

Ethan only shook his head and spoke firmly. "No, Andy. That's all we can tell you now. We brought you here to find that signal. That's the *only* reason we brought you along. You want us to think of you as a friend or an ally, then you find that signal, no questions asked...Until then, we can't be sure about you."

Andy nodded. "Okay then. I will find the signal, and then you will call me a friend."

Andy crouched down and began to crawl through the leftmost passageway—the same one that emptied out into the large room where they had buried the Skulley and metal briefcase. The group followed behind Andy. Austin and Glenn clutched their rifles tightly the entire way, hanging back a bit from the rest of the team.

"I don't care if he finds the signal or not," Glenn said. "I'm still not gonna trust him, and I sure as heck will never call him a friend."

Austin nodded. "Yeah, copy that."

The light beams from their headlamps danced around the cracks and contours of the cave walls as they traveled farther and deeper into the cavern than they ever had before, way beyond the first room where the Skulley lay entombed. Twice already, they had encountered crevices so small that they had to take their backpacks off first to squeeze through them. On one occasion, Caleb had to exhale, voiding his lungs of air completely, to make himself small enough to wiggle through. The cave seemed to constantly get more and more narrow, enough to make the least claustrophobic person break out into a nervous sweat. Andy, though, forged ahead without worry or grievance, twisting, turning, and contorting himself through every break in the wall, no matter how small.

Caleb stopped and took in a jittery breath. His face was red and full of strain as he stretched his arm out and put a desperate hand on Ethan's shoulder. "Wait," he eked out between huffs and puffs. "I can't go through another one of those cracks…I'll be stuck down here forever, like freakin' Winnie the Pooh in the tree."

Caleb's comment drew a few chuckles, but one look at him and everyone stopped laughing. It was clear to see that Caleb was struggling and in real distress. He held his stomach and doubled over, and his eyes narrowed into small slits. "I think I'm gonna be sick," he said. "I gotta get outta here."

Ethan patted Caleb on the back. "It's okay, Caleb. You should take a break here and relax, have some water. The rest of us can go and check it out, meet you on the way back."

Andy eyed Caleb sympathetically. "Caleb, if I told you I heard a signal, would that make you feel better?"

Caleb took a couple deep breaths, steadied himself, then stood upright. "Andy, are you *telling me* that you hear a signal?" he asked with a tortured face.

Everyone focused on Andy. The light beams from their headlamps bombarded his eyes.

"Yes, I am," Andy said plainly. He pointed to an even smaller fissure in the cave wall just ahead. "Can you make it through one more crack?"

Caleb's face flickered between excitement and dread as he stared at the crevice in the wall that seemed too thin for a dog dipped in lard to wriggle through.

"C'mon, Caleb, you can do it," Glenn said.

Austin nodded. "Yeah, get in there as far as you can on your own, and the rest of us will just shove you on through."

Caleb cocked his head at Austin and sighed indignantly. "No, thanks. No shoving. I can do it on my own."

"Or that too," Austin said.

"Are you absolutely sure the signal is coming from that side?" Caleb asked.

"I am positive," Andy replied.

Caleb clenched his jaw in determination. "Okay, stand back, give me some room," he said. "And I can do this by myself. *Do not* start pushing me." Caleb went splat against the wall and wedged himself snuggly into the crack. He wiggled back and forth, trying to squeeze through, but it didn't take long for him to realize that he would need reinforcements. After a deep, pathetic sigh of defeat, he groaned: "All right… start pushing!"

The rest of the group, including Andy, began pushing on Caleb. The first chuckle at the ridiculousness of the situation came from Caleb himself. Then Ethan began to laugh, followed by Annika, Austin, and Glenn. Finally, Andy began to laugh too. His laugh wasn't the forced or fake giggle of a robot trying to be human; it was a genuine reaction to the humor of the moment. The group's laughing got louder and louder, with the crescendo of belly laughter echoing wildly through the cave. Caleb's face was as red as a beet from the squeezing, pushing, and chuckling. It took every bit of force of their ten hands shoving on him from head to foot, but they finally managed to poke him through the break in the wall. "I'm in!" Caleb shouted. "I may have to live the rest of my life as a caveman, but I'm in."

The rest of the group slowly muffled their chuckles. Except

for Andy. Everyone watched him with curious eyes, amazed to see a robot in the throes of a gut-busting guffaw, stunned by just how real his emotion looked.

"All right, you can knock it off now," Glenn said, snapping Andy back to reality. "Go find that signal."

"Okay, sorry."

The mood quickly got more serious as the rest of the group squeezed their way through the crack to meet Caleb. Fortunately, there was much more space on this side of the wall. The room was even larger than the one where they had buried the Skulley. The area was roughly circular, with a diameter of nearly one hundred feet and the height of the room almost half that. The group spread out and explored the area, but they quickly figured out that this was the end of the line. There were no tunnels, cracks, or crevices left that they could possibly pass through.

"So this is it, Andy?" Austin asked, irritated. "Looks like a dead end to me."

"Yeah, where's the signal?" Glenn huffed.

Everyone looked to Andy in hopes of finding an answer, but there was no easy one. "The signal is coming from inside there," Andy said, pointing at the colossal wall of solid limestone standing before them.

"How far inside?" Caleb asked. "Can you tell?"

Andy stared at the wall like he was boring a hole through it with his gaze. "Adjusting the signal for the placement of the loop—eleven point one meters away from the shaft, six degrees south of west—the tunnel is embedded twelve feet inside that rock."

Everyone's face dropped in frustration, realizing the size and scope of the project that lay before them. "It'll take forever to dig through all of that rock," Annika said. "Is there another way, Andy? A shortcut?"

"This is the shortest path," Andy responded.

"Maybe we don't have to dig," Austin said hopefully. "What if we used our lasers to blast through the rock?"

Caleb shook his head. "I wish we could, but there are two problems I see. One, by firing so many shots, we risk overheating the rifles. We could destroy the only weapons we have. And two, the laser blasts could weaken the cave walls too much, too fast. We could wind up being buried down here…No, we're going to have to do it the old-fashioned way."

A few weary groans echoed through the cave.

"Look, no one here thought this would be easy, right?" Ethan said. "I say we bring in the supplies and begin digging as soon as possible."

"Yeah, but what if he's wrong, Ethan? Or lying?" Glenn asked. "We have no proof of anything behind that rock other than what this machine is telling us."

Ethan stared long and hard at Andy.

"I am not lying. And I am not wrong," Andy said, staring right back at Ethan, then everyone else in the room. "You have to trust me."

"We don't *have* to do anything," Austin fired back.

"Sure, but what choice do we have?" Annika asked. "This is our only shot. And he hasn't given us any reason not to trust him so far."

"Thank you, Annika," Andy said.

"Fine," Glenn muttered. "But if we find out you're lying to us…" Glenn held up his rifle in a threatening gesture. "…it won't be a smart move."

Andy spoke calmly. "I understand."

"We'll have to make our base here then," Ethan said. "This will be our new fort. We'll take what materials we need from the Bravo Fort. Then seal off the front of the cave, set up a guard post while we dig."

"We have *a lot* of work to do," Caleb said. "I mean *tons*... literally."

Annika nodded. "Yeah, and we have no idea how long we've got before the machines decide to stop playing house and get down to their real business."

That disquieting thought brought a somber silence.

As they headed back, Caleb stopped at the thin break in the wall that had almost squeezed his guts out the last time he'd jammed himself through it. He grimaced at the sight of it, then raised his shirt, showing the group several scrapes on his skin from the previous encounter. "This is the last time I go through that crack like this," Caleb said. "Next time, we're chipping away at some of that rock." He took a deep breath, then said with a glum face, "All right...get ready to push."

"Wait," Andy said. "Stand back. I can help you."

Caleb stared curiously at Andy. "What?...How?"

"Just stand back," Andy said. Caleb backed away and Andy stepped forward. He raised his arm and began karate-chopping the rock around the crack. His powerful strikes chipped a few pieces of stone away, widening the crack in the wall just enough so Caleb could pass through unscathed. When he was finished, Andy turned back to the group. He found everyone staring at him in wide-eyed shock. "There you go, Caleb," he said. "Now you can get through without damaging yourself... And sorry I laughed before. I didn't know you were hurt."

"Thank you, Andy," Caleb said, touched by the gesture. "And don't worry about laughing. It was pretty funny."

Ethan and Annika smiled and patted Andy on the back. "Good work," Ethan said.

Even Austin and Glenn grinned. "Yeah," Austin said. "Nice job, Bruce Lee."

Andy nodded and smiled proudly, basking in the first moment where he had the approval of everyone at the same time. "You're very welcome," he said with a smile that was slow to fade. "You are very welcome."

CHAPTER 26

NO CHOICE

The sun was dipping below the tree line in the late afternoon when the group made it back to the substation. They waited behind the same group of pine trees as they had before, checking to make sure the coast was clear before they retrieved the magnetic loop they had buried. Andy made sure to lie down flush on the ground this time, out of sight and without a silly grin on his face. Annika looked over at him and smiled. Andy returned the smile, then lifted his arm off the ground slightly and waved to her. Annika waved back, but then her eyes spotted something that chased her smile away.

Andy tracked Annika's eyes back to his hand. By this time, everyone else had seen what Annika saw. Their faces dropped instantly. Andy twisted his wrist, so he could see the outside ridge of his hand. Then what was left of Andy's smile vanished, and his mouth gaped open. He looked as shocked as the others by what he saw. There was a four-inch gash torn into his skin from chopping away rock in the cave. Underneath his torn artificial flesh, a segment of his silvery metal hand was exposed.

Andy quickly put his other hand over the wound, covering it like he was ashamed. "I will fix that right away," he said. "I'm sorry you had to see that."

"Me too," Glenn said. "But at least you don't look like the other Skulleys underneath."

Andy nodded. "That is right. I am not like them at all." Then he extended his index finger on his other hand, and the tip of it glowed a light blue color. He pinched closed the torn synthetic flesh and ran his finger down the seam. The skin bonded together with hardly a scar. Everyone watched in amazement.

"Well...we'll see about that," Glenn said, still not convinced.

"It's okay, Andy," Annika said reassuringly. "You've been very helpful and we—"

"Shhhh!" Ethan hissed. "Someone's coming."

Everyone managed to hug the ground a little tighter, getting out of sight of the two guards who were about a hundred yards away and approaching the substation from the east. They were dressed in military camouflage, but moved and carried themselves exactly like the ones who had killed the human guards in that very same spot a couple of days earlier.

Annika slowly pulled her rifle in front of her and peered through the scope. Her eyes widened immediately. "Those soldiers aren't just strolling by. They're walking right toward the spot where we buried that magnetic loop."

"They can sense the signal, just like I can," Andy said. "They know something's there."

"Yeah, they know something's up," Annika said, gazing down the rifle scope. "Both of their hands are drawn back, and I can see their laser weapons sticking out."

"We can't let them find it," Ethan said. "They find that loop, and they'll figure out exactly what we're up to."

"Go ahead, then…Take the shot, Annika," Glenn said.

"You realize once we fire on them, we change everything," Austin said. "They *will* figure out they're missing two of their own."

"I know," Ethan replied. "But we don't have a choice. They can't find that loop."

"I can take one of them out, no problem," Annika said. "But someone else needs to take the other shot. We can't let either one of those machines know the other was shot or they could communicate that back to the other machines. We gotta take them out at exactly the same time."

"You're the next best shot, Ethan," Glenn said.

Ethan grabbed his gun and delicately aimed it at the approaching soldiers. "You know, this isn't an easy shot for me, Annika."

Annika slid her rifle over to Ethan. "Switch me rifles. Use my scope. It'll help."

Ethan was frozen with surprise for the briefest of moments. Annika never, ever let anyone touch her sniper rifle. Now here he was, not only being allowed to touch it, but fire it as well. As Ethan handed over his scopeless rifle to Annika, he couldn't help but think this might be the closest he ever got to trading rings with the girl of his dreams.

Ethan lay on the ground and drew Annika's rifle to his shoulder. He looked through the scope and found the two soldiers narrowing in on the spot on the ground above the buried loop.

"Breathe steady," Annika said in a soft, soothing voice. "On the count of three, we fire. I'll get the guy in front, you get the one in back...And remember, exhale into the shot, then hold your breath right before you fire...Easy peasy."

Yeah, easy for you, he thought. Then Ethan nodded confidently and lied. "Easy peasy."

The soldiers were about ten feet away from the loop when Annika began her count. "One, two, three..."

Annika and Ethan fired at precisely the same time. Their red lasers streaked through the air and found their targets. The soldiers crumpled and fell into a heap on the ground, their hole-riddled heads finally resting a mere foot away from the buried magnetic loop that had attracted them.

"Nice shot," Annika said, patting Ethan on the shoulder.

Ethan let out a jittery breath. "Yeah, you too." He took a moment to compose himself, then said, "We need to get down there, find a place to hide those bodies."

The group ran into the clearing and over to the two dead robots who lay beside the chain-link fence perimeter of the substation. Some of the skin over their faces had melted away from the heat of the lasers that had struck them. Their blackened skulls were visible now, with a few final bluish streaks of electricity zigging and zagging across them. Soon the electricity dissipated entirely, leaving only two thin streams of smoke oozing into the air from their eyeballs.

Ethan scanned the area surrounding the substation with an anxious face. "We're too out in the open here. We gotta get these things behind the trees."

Austin and Glenn each grabbed one of the robot's legs. They pulled with all of their might, faces straining, but the body wouldn't budge. "Jeez, this thing's gotta weigh five hundred pounds," Glenn said.

"Everyone grab on, pull at the same time," Ethan said.

Ethan, Annika, and Caleb grabbed onto the machine anywhere they could find a spot. All five of them began dragging the body at a snail's pace toward the trees. That's when Andy passed them all, dragging the other robot by the legs and moving about ten times as fast as they were. Ethan and the rest of the group gawked at Andy, stunned by his strength. Andy just looked back at them and smiled politely. Then he said, "If you just leave him there, I'd be happy to take him for you."

The group let go of the robot instantly. They wiped their sweat-drenched faces and straightened their aching backs. "Well, if you insist," Glenn said, cracking a smile.

Not only did Andy move both robot bodies away from the substation and into the woods, but he also took Caleb's gardening spade and began to dig a shallow grave at the base of a pine tree. And he easily dug faster by himself with that meager tool than the other five of them could've with shovels. The group alternated between keeping guard and watching Andy slave away, working for them without question or complaint. It was becoming hard for any of them, even Austin and Glenn, to think that Andy was out to get them. For many in the group, it was becoming hard to think of Andy as anything but an ally, and maybe even a friend. Ethan thought if all of that sincere helpfulness was just a ploy to spy for the machines, then Andy should be given an Academy Award on the spot for his acting ability.

"Thank you," Ethan said after Andy had finished digging. "You saved us a ton of time."

"You're welcome," Andy replied. Then, without anyone asking him to do so, he kneeled down and placed his hand on one of the robot's heads. Andy's hand glowed blue, but the head of the machine did not. "This one can't help us," he said, then he turned to the other one. He placed his hand atop its head and both Andy's hand and the black metal skull glowed a bright blue. "I will read its mind now...Maybe there's something that can help us."

Help us? Ethan thought. It was clear that Andy now considered himself a member of the group, even if some of the others weren't entirely ready to accept him yet.

The group watched Andy carefully as he conducted the "mind-reading." Suddenly, his face morphed into an expression they hadn't yet seen. It was the unmistakable look of terror. The alarm on Andy's face quickly spread to the others.

"What is it?" Ethan asked. "What's wrong?"

"I can't show you now," Andy said. He gazed into the distance with fearful eyes, like he was waiting for something to jump out at them from over the ridge. "It's not safe here... *Danger is coming.*"

CHAPTER 27

TROUBLED VISIONS

Andy quickly dragged the bodies of the machines into their grave. Caleb retrieved the magnetic loop, disabled it, and tossed it inside as well. Everyone pitched in to bury the evidence as fast as they could. Then the group sprinted away from the substation, trying to put as much distance as possible between themselves and the scene of the crime.

"Where do we go?" Caleb asked breathlessly, huffing and puffing and trying desperately not to slow the team down.

"We gotta make it to the fort," Ethan answered. "We can hide in there. And we'll be able to see them coming using the video cameras."

"How many are coming?" Austin asked.

"I'm not sure," Andy said. "All I can tell you is that one of them sent out a distress signal before it died."

"Did they see us?" Glenn asked, his voice laced with dread. "Do they know it was us?"

"I don't know," Andy replied.

"No way," Annika said, sure of herself. "They couldn't have."

"We'll know soon enough," Ethan said.

∽

Ethan punched in the password to the Bravo Fort, and everyone dashed inside. They closed the door quietly, secured the lock as best they could, and flipped the lights on. Caleb hurried over to the computer control panel and activated the surveillance cameras that were mounted on the top of the fort. Then he switched on a couple of video monitors so they could see if anything was approaching. So far, nothing. The area around the fort was clear.

"As soon as we see anyone coming this way, we should cut the lights and head down to the basement," Ethan said. "We can hide in the secret escape hatch if we have to."

"Good idea," Austin said. "But let's hope it doesn't come to that."

Annika turned away from watching the video monitors and stared at Andy with a curious face. "You saw something else when you read that Skulley's mind, didn't you? More than just a distress signal…What did you see?"

Andy hesitated, nodded, then spoke uneasily. "I can show you. But I must warn you…You will find it quite disturbing."

"Don't worry about us," Glenn said. "We can take anything."

No one's face was nearly as strong as Glenn's words. Everyone looked worried, but they had to know what Andy knew. "Go ahead, Andy," Ethan said. "Show us…Show us everything."

The group checked the video monitors again to make sure nothing was coming, then they turned their attention to Andy. The reluctant boyish robot faced an empty section of the room, and his eyes projected the same bright blue beams of light that they had in the cave when he'd played the Zyvantian message. A 3-D holographic image began to take shape, revealing the inside of the research facility. Massive rooms were shown, one after the other. Each room was filled with hundreds of Skulleys, thousands upon thousands in total, standing at attention and awaiting their orders. None of these robots were covered in flesh. There was no attempt at all to conceal what they were. These machines were combat units. They were an army.

"They're preparing an invasion," Ethan said with a knot in his throat.

"Yes," Andy replied.

The longer the group watched the holographic video, the more their stomachs twisted in anxious agony. They spotted a new kind of machine among the hordes of Skulleys, one whose image quickly caught their eye and disturbed them greatly. The robot was a Skulley, of sorts, though its skeleton didn't resemble anything human. It was Zyvantian in nature—seven feet tall with long, sinewy, metal arms and legs branching off its torso like limbs on a tree. Its head was large, twice the size of the other Skulleys, with grooves running the entire length of its cranium. But, by far, the most terrifying feature was its eyes. They were large, dark, and almond-shaped, and they contained not a trace of compassion or remorse or pity. It was as if its creator had mastered the art of evil. No one in the group could stand to look at those pitch-black eyes for longer than a second. And even when they looked away, those soulless orbs seemed to stay with them, haunting them, an after-image burned into their retinas.

Ethan drew a tight breath, exhaled uneasily. "I saw a

machine just like that, when I was hiding in the janitor's closet after I led the Skulleys away from you guys during the first fatal error. It almost found me. It was so close, I could've reached out and touched it."

The horrendous new machine strolled past the endless rows of Skulleys, examining them carefully as it did so, making sure they were battle-ready. "That's gotta be one of their leaders," Annika said, watching the machine's maneuvers while taking care to avoid looking into its eyes.

"You are right," Andy said. His eyes were still projecting blue beams of light. "There's something else I should show you now…It will be *very* hard for you to watch, much harder than this, but you told me you wanted to see everything."

Everyone nodded and assured Andy that they wanted to see what he had to show them, though they had a difficult time imagining that anything could be worse than what they'd already seen. But it only took a few seconds of watching the new holographic video for them to realize how wrong they were. What they were witnessing now was much, much worse, and all too personal. They could barely stand to watch.

In a massive, eerily bright room, hundreds of adults from Blackwoods were held captive. They sat in long rows of aluminum folding chairs, hands tied behind their backs and legs bound together so they couldn't move. Everyone's eyelids were pinned wide open by a clamp, with their bulging eyes darting around the room in total terror. Then hundreds of Skulleys entered, disguised in flesh and clothes. Each one stood directly in front of a human shackled to a chair, their identical twin, the one they were responsible for impersonating. The terrified screams of the real humans would've raised the dead if not for the gags the Skulleys had jammed into their mouths to silence them. Still, desperate grunts of fear filled the room as the machines kneeled before their human prisoners, hunting for their eyes.

The humans tried frantically to look away, twisting and writhing and floundering so they might not have to stare into those burning, hateful red embers. But the Skulleys reached out and grabbed their heads and violently jerked them face-forward, forcing them to look straight at them. Suddenly, blistering red beams of light shot out from their eye sockets and blasted into the humans' eyes. Bodies twitched spastically, and muffled screams of pain echoed throughout the room. The machines were reading the humans' minds, though the process was nowhere near as humane as when Andy did the same to the Skulley. This method was torture. The members of Team Blackwoods watched helplessly as they witnessed their moms and dads go through the unimaginable—having a machine suck the thoughts and memories from their minds. It explained how they had become such good impostors. It explained why no one on the outside had ever questioned what was going on inside Blackwoods. Not until it was too late, anyway.

Finally, the group could take no more, and they turned away from the horrors of the holographic images. Everyone but Austin. He continued looking carefully at the video, searching for his father. But he was not there. He was the only parent missing. Andy shut down the video display and faced the others. Everyone looked sick to their stomach. Their eyes welled with tears.

"My dad is dead," Austin said bluntly, staring dazedly at the part of the room where the video had played, like he could still see it. "He's so stubborn. There's no way he'd ever let those machines tie him down while he was alive."

"I'm sorry, Austin," Ethan said, having no idea what else to say.

"Don't be," Austin replied, his emotions completely in check now. "That's how he would've wanted to go out, fighting, a captain going down with his ship." Then he paused and swallowed hard. "Anyway, from the looks of it, he got off easy."

"We have no one to warn about this," Caleb said glumly. "No one coming in, and the phones and internet are down. Only calls you can make are ones inside Blackwoods, and those are monitored."

"Our only hope is getting into that secret shaft, and back to the Chrono-Warp," Ethan said. "I think we knew that all along."

"You're right, but that's a lot of rock to break," Austin said. "I'm not even sure it's possible without getting special machinery in there. And we could barely get Caleb back there." Austin looked at Caleb and smiled apologetically. "Sorry, no offense."

Caleb smiled back good-naturedly. "None taken."

"Do you think I qualify as special machinery?" Andy asked with a grin on his face that indicated he understood the humor in his question. "I could start digging…Knowing that I'm helping my friends sure beats being stuck in that fort alone, taking a vacation in my mind."

Andy's offer took everyone by surprise. No one had considered that possibility. Even Glenn started nodding in agreement with the idea. "You'd do that for us?" he asked, his voice sounding more touched than distrustful.

"I would be happy to," Andy said.

"We'll still need to get some tools," Ethan said. "We can't

have you hacking away at that rock like you did when you helped Caleb through the crack. With that much rock, by the time you were done, there wouldn't be anything left of you either."

Andy smiled at Ethan. It was a warm, grateful smile. "Yes, thank you…some tools would be great."

Ethan nodded and returned the smile. All the while, he was thinking: *Andy referred to us as his friends…And I'm beginning to think he's right.*

CHAPTER 28

DIGGING THEMSELVES DEEPER

ENOUGH TIME HAD passed in the fort without seeing anyone that the group began to think they might be in the clear. But no such luck. Caleb scanned the video monitors, and his eyes widened. "Someone's coming," he uttered with a taut throat. "Four of them, about a hundred yards out."

The group hurried over to the monitor to take a look. The four figures, cloaked head-to-toe in black special forces clothing, were approaching from the east. They were spaced out about ten yards apart from each other and appeared to be combing the woods in a search pattern.

"They're still looking for the missing machines," Ethan said, inspecting the video screen with focused, squinty eyes. "They don't know what happened, though. See how they're looking around in every direction, clueless? They might be coming this way, but I don't think they set out for the fort."

Annika breathed a sigh of relief. "I knew those machines didn't see us."

"Yeah," Ethan said. "Still, we better get downstairs.

They're gonna search this place…They're gonna search *every place* until they find their guys."

The four figures in black closed ranks and began walking side-by-side. Then they made a beeline for the fort, quickening their pace. "They're coming now," Ethan said. "Hurry, let's get to the basement."

Caleb switched off the computer monitors and the lights inside the fort. It was flashlights only now. Ethan lifted the hatch to the basement, and the group descended the ladder. Once inside, they closed the hatch back and scrambled quickly to the secret escape tunnel. They scooted the power generator out of the way, opened the hatch to the tunnel, and piled inside. Then the loud clank of the front door being pounded off its hinges rocked the fort. Ethan quickly slid the generator back in front of the tunnel to block its view, then he closed the hatch. Everyone turned their flashlights off. They sat in complete darkness. The group hunkered down in the cramped tunnel, silent and deathly still, praying that the machines would pass them by.

Loud, heavy footsteps thumped around upstairs for a while. Then they heard the hatch to the basement give way. It took one bounce off the ladder, caromed off, and crashed into the floor. The brash clank of hard military boots on the metal ladder sounded like hammers driving in nails. And when the first robot plunked its weighty feet down on the floor of the basement, the vibration rattled everyone's spine. One machine landed. Then the second one. Then the third machine plopped down into the basement. Everyone in the tunnel listened for that fourth machine to drop, but there was nothing more. There were only three of them in the room.

Ethan had a feeling something was wrong even before

he heard the other footsteps. Heavy footsteps. Footsteps that were *outside*. They were coming from above and behind them, right near the escape tunnel's exit.

All of their voices now were silenced to the faintest of whispers. "One of them's going around back," Ethan said. "If it finds the outside cover to the escape tunnel, we need to be down on that side...Once it opens that manhole cover, we gotta take it out right away."

"Yes," Andy added. "And you must do it before it sends out a distress signal."

"I'll go first and get in position to shoot," Annika said.

"Okay," Ethan said. "We'll be right behind you."

Annika crawled swiftly but stealthily through the tunnel toward the end that emptied out behind the fort. The rest of the group followed, holding their breath and placing their hands and knees gingerly as they crawled. It seemed like they had shuffled on all fours for a mile, though the tunnel itself was only sixty feet. The tension of being surrounded by machines was bad enough, but the idea that all any of the robots had to do was issue a distress call was almost too much to take. It wasn't enough to simply shoot and kill these machines. They also had to do it on the sly. All it would take to doom the group, their mission, and perhaps mankind, would be one single distress call. Then an army of reinforcements would bear down on the group, knowing precisely their identities and location, and dispatch them immediately. They probably wouldn't even bother to bury the bodies; they would let the fort be their tomb. Every shot taken by Team Blackwoods now couldn't just be good. It had to be perfect.

Annika made it to the far end of the tunnel, directly below the exit opening that was sealed by the manhole cover. She turned over on her back and propped her laser rifle up so it was pointing at the cast-iron disk above her. Annika sized up the situation, noting the cramped area and the length of her laser rifle. It was longer than the other rifles, and she knew that wouldn't be helpful here.

"Switch me guns," Annika said, looking at Ethan. "Close quarters…It'll be easier to make the shot with the shorter gun."

Ethan quietly took Annika's unwieldy rifle and gave her his own. Then heavy, clopping footsteps became louder at the other end of the tunnel—the sounds of machines inspecting the basement of the fort and getting nearer and nearer the escape hatch. And, just above them, they heard a hard step on the metal manhole cover. *Clank*. One step was all they heard, then everything on that side became silent.

"Any second now," Annika said in a fateful whisper. "I got this…You guys cover the other end of the tunnel."

Slowly, the metal disk began to slide away, revealing the blue sky of early evening above. Annika kept her eyes peeled for anything to poke its head inside. She waited and waited. Nothing. Then all of a sudden, a head covered in a black ski mask jerked into view, blotting out the sky above, red eyes burning. Everything that happened next, happened in the blink of an eye. "Peek-a-Boo," Annika quipped, as she ripped a half dozen lasers into the skull of the machine. The body of the dead robot slumped over the escape hatch, blocking their exit.

"Hurry, Andy, move this thing so we can get out of here," Annika said.

Andy quickly scooted past the others and shoved the nearly five-hundred-pound machine away from the hatch. Suddenly, more sounds came from the other side of the tunnel, from inside the basement of the fort. It was the grinding sound of metal on concrete, of something being dragged away. "They're sliding the generator away from the hatch," Ethan whispered urgently. "They found it, we gotta move."

One by one, they scurried out of the escape tunnel. Andy placed the manhole cover back in its original spot just in time, right before the machines on the inside had opened the escape hatch to sneak a peek down the passageway. Then he hurried and rolled the dead Skulley off a nearby ridge, away from the fort and out of sight.

Ethan eyed the side of the fort. "Hurry, let's get to the door. We can set up an ambush."

The group dashed to the main entrance of the fort. They remained hidden just behind the back wall, ready to attack when the machines exited. "Wait until all three are all the way out," Annika said. "I'll take the first one. Ethan, you take the second. Austin, Glenn, you guys get the third…And remember, all headshots."

Everyone nodded, then the excruciating wait began. They heard the machines clambering around in there, moving up from the basement, then to the main level of the fort. The footsteps got louder until they were just inside the door. Then the footsteps stopped, and there was complete silence. Finally, the door squeaked open. One machine stepped out, then another. But the third one never came. Ethan and Annika fired as soon as the Skulleys turned around. Two more machines crumpled to the ground in death, though no one was about to celebrate. They had no idea what the last robot was up to, where it was, or if the ones that had been shot had a chance to issue a distress signal.

Ethan looked back at the escape hatch behind the fort and found the manhole cover was still firmly in place. "The last one's gotta be heading for the loft. I don't think it saw us shoot them," Ethan whispered. "Andy, quick, bring those dead machines as close to the fort as possible so they can't be seen from above."

The black figure emerged from the loft before Andy could hide the bodies out of sight. The Skulley turned toward them, and it was apparent that it would see the bodies of its comrades dead in the dirt long before anyone could line up a good shot on it. At the very last moment, Caleb whispered, "Chase me." Then he ran out into plain view of the machine, on the opposite side of the fort where the bodies lay, providing a distraction.

The group gave chase to Caleb, knowing exactly what his brilliant mind was thinking. There was one way to prevent that machine from issuing a distress call—by not giving it any reason to think there was a threat. The Skulley in the loft hadn't seen its dead brothers yet, and now it watched with curiosity, not alarm, as Caleb blasted lasers from his toy laser rifle into the chests of his friends. They were just kids playing a game. No threat at all.

The Skulley shouted, "Stop there!" in a digitized voice that sounded far more machine-like than human. Then it jumped down from the loft and landed with a *thud*. The team stopped in their tracks. "It's getting a little late, wouldn't you say, kids?"

"Y-y-yeah," Caleb sputtered. "We were just on our way home."

The Skulley shook its head. Then it peeled its ski mask off, revealing its menacing, shiny black metal skull. Everyone's eyes widened in shock. Ethan knew it was a bad omen that the Skulley had shown its face to them, fleshless. All the other machines in town were still pretending to be human. That meant this machine had no intention of letting them out of there alive.

The Skulley spoke with a hint of a smile. "You poor kids... just in the wrong place at the wrong time." The machine's hand folded down, and its laser weapon glistened in the late-day sun. "You are going to be *very* late for dinner tonight."

Just as the Skulley raised its arm at Caleb, Ethan and Annika drew their laser rifles and fired on the machine, blasting a dozen quarter-sized holes into its cranium. Its eyes went dark. The machine fell to its knees, then forward onto its face. In its death, it didn't even twitch.

"Maybe," Annika wisecracked to the dead Skulley. "But not as late as you."

"That was quick thinking, Caleb," Ethan said, staring at the smoke rising into the air from the Skulley's hole-riddled head.

"It sure was," Annika added.

Caleb shrugged nonchalantly, though his face was still pale from the encounter. "Yeah, easy peasy," he squeaked.

The group stared at the downed Skulley for a moment, but Andy took extra time. He always seemed to view a dead machine with much more curiosity than the others. It was never hard to understand what he was thinking in those moments. Andy always flat-out said what he thought.

Andy shook his head. "I am not like that machine."

This time, Glenn responded first. "No, you're not, Andy."

Andy looked away from the machine and caught Glenn's eye. "Thank you," he said with a light smile, one that was easily returned.

Ethan scanned the perimeter around the fort. The sun would be setting in a couple of hours, and they needed to get moving. "We gotta bury those Skulleys," he said. "But first, we need to figure out if they sent a distress signal."

Andy dragged the Skulleys' bodies to their eventual burial site, a tucked-away spot at the bottom of the ridge behind the fort. He then placed his hand on each of their heads. In every instance, his hand glowed blue, but the heads of the Skulleys did not.

"They are too damaged," Andy said. "It is impossible to tell if they sent out a distress call or not."

Ethan exhaled a deep, frustrated sigh. "All right then… Let's get them buried."

Ethan and Annika kept a lookout in the loft, while Austin, Glenn, and Andy grabbed some shovels from the fort and began digging the robots' grave. All the while, Caleb worked on dismembering the Skulleys, removing their arms at the elbow joint with a screwdriver.

Andy dumped the Skulleys' bodies into a single pit that measured roughly six feet in diameter and just about as deep. Once the hole had been backfilled, Andy rolled a few large chunks of rock over the tomb. He added just enough to cover the dig site, but not so much as to look suspicious. It was perfect. Andy's handiwork would've made a human criminal blush with pride.

Ethan and Annika came down from the loft and met the others behind the fort. "Looks good," Ethan said. "Now let's go home." Then Ethan looked around. "Where's Caleb?"

Just then, Caleb exited the fort carrying a box full of laser weapons that he had removed from the Skulleys' forearms. Two apiece, for a total of eight. His face was beaming. "They all work perfectly...and they're small." Caleb handed a laser weapon to each of the humans on the team. The weapon was the size of a flashlight. "It's portable and easy to use," Caleb said, instructing the others. "All you have to do is flick that switch on the side to activate it, then squeeze the trigger right there."

Annika was the first to try it. She flipped the switch on the side of the weapon, then aimed at a tree in the distance, about a hundred feet away. When she squeezed the trigger, a red laser pulse streaked through the air...*and missed the tree.* It took Annika three tries to hit the target, something that would've been unthinkable at that distance with her regular rifle.

"Ugh, it's terrible!" Annika exclaimed in frustration. "This isn't a laser gun...It's a stupid, fat magic wand that happens to shoot lasers."

"But you'll get used to it," Caleb reassured her. "I was thinking, with everything that's happened today, the six machines we killed, we can't carry our laser rifles back into town. It's too dangerous. Even with me shooting the fake one, playing around, they'll be on high alert now. They're bound to check them all...But these small ones, we can sneak in."

"Good idea," Ethan said. "We'll leave all our real rifles here, hide them in the fort. And take the extra fake guns we have in the loft back instead, in case we get stopped."

"I still want my laser rifle," Annika grumbled.

"I know you do," Ethan said. "But Caleb's right, you'll get used to it. After all, you're the best shot in the world."

Ethan's flattery brought a mischievous smile to Annika's face. "Of course, I'll get used to it." She looked at Caleb and grinned bashfully. "Thanks, Caleb. And I'm sorry I called them stupid, fat magic wands...You know I get grumpy when I miss a shot."

Caleb chuckled a little. "It's okay...I'm glad it doesn't happen very often."

Everyone took a moment to laugh at that. Then they gathered the fake rifles and their gear, concealed their new weapons in their waistbands, and headed for home. Everyone but Andy, anyway. The five human members of Team Blackwoods were united in insisting that he stay put and hidden inside the fort. They knew it was the right move. With the increased security they were sure to find in Blackwoods now, there was no way they could sneak Andy back in without being caught. Still, each of them felt bad about it, forcing him to stay in the fort by himself with the possibility of another patrol of machines coming by. There were places to hide inside the fort, though, places that were much easier for one to hide than six. They knew Andy was extremely intelligent and resourceful, and they had to trust that he could take care of himself. There was no choice in the matter. They did give him one of the real laser rifles to use to defend himself and entrusted him to hide and take care of the other weapons. That level of trust meant more to Andy than any of them could've possibly known. When they left Andy at the fort, the last thing that disappeared in the distance was his smile.

The team walked back mostly in silence, but they were all thinking the same thought: *They had killed six machines.* Eventually, the Skulleys would figure that out. The only question was when. They just prayed that the answer wasn't tonight when they were asleep in their beds.

At least Andy didn't need to sleep.

CHAPTER 29

LATE FOR DINNER

It turned out to be a good thing that the group decided to leave their real laser rifles back at the fort with Andy. Once they made it to the checkpoint of the Dark Highway, four soldiers wearing camouflage and dead-serious faces approached them immediately.

"What brings you out here so late?" the lead soldier asked.

"Sorry, we were playing Laser Wars games and lost track of time," Ethan said with a good poker face.

"Hand over those guns…Now," the soldier ordered impatiently.

Everyone passed their fake laser guns to the soldiers. Then they watched as their rifles were inspected from top to bottom. The lead soldier turned one of the rifles on Ethan, aiming right at his chest. "Now you wouldn't mind if I fired this gun, would you?" he asked, staring at Ethan with soulless eyes.

Ethan swallowed hard, nervously. It was a natural reaction to having any weapon, even a fake one, pointed at you by someone who really wanted you dead. "No, not at all," Ethan uttered through a tight throat. "It's just a play gun."

"Okay then," the soldier said. Then he shot a couple of bright blue lasers squarely into Ethan's chest. Ethan flinched instinctively. The soldier flashed an empty, artificial smile. Soon his smile vanished and a blank, glassy-eyed stare that was even creepier took its place. "You should go home now. I'm sure someone is wondering where you are."

Everyone in the group nodded uneasily, and they crossed the Dark Highway in silence.

※

Ethan sat at the dinner table with his parental impostors. There was no chit-chat, no inquiring about the other's day, not the slightest peep. Also noticeably missing were any questions whatsoever about where Ethan had been until after seven o'clock. These parents sitting before him now simply didn't care. They never truly cared, of course; they had only ever pretended to. But now, for whatever reason, they didn't even bother to pretend. Ethan wasn't sure exactly what that meant, but he knew it couldn't be good. He guessed it had to do with what they were working on at the research facility—that they were getting so close to finishing what they needed to finish, and fooling who they needed to fool, it didn't matter so much if the kids in town thought their parents were acting strangely. The machines figured their plan to take over the earth was in motion and it couldn't be stopped now by anyone, let alone the kids in the town who couldn't even make an unrestricted phone call or get onto the internet, and who certainly wouldn't have access to weapons. It was only a matter of time before the machines took their masks off and felt free to roam the town in their natural, skeletal forms. And Ethan felt that time was coming soon.

Ethan's mechanical surrogate parents eyeballed him eerily the entire time. They didn't even bother to take their eyes off of him to eat. They just stared and stared some more with those inscrutable glazed-over orbs. Ethan had no idea what they were thinking. This moment was even more unsettling than the time he'd spent alone with the machine posing as Ms. Goodfoot, when she had found him in the school early and warned him that snooping around could be perilous. *Snooping around could be perilous?* Ethan wondered if a vocabulary word existed that could describe the situation he'd find himself in if his robotic parents ever discovered how he'd really spent his day. Worse than perilous, two words came to mind. It would take only two words to adequately sum it up. Simple words: *Certain death.*

The entire time his parents were watching him, Ethan kept one hand inside his pocket. He had a firm grip on the new laser weapon that Caleb had given him. He felt like he was in one of those old Western films, where a group of outlaws was gathered around a poker table in a saloon, no one trusting the other, everyone with a locked and loaded pistol under the table pointed at the guy across from him. Ethan was ready for anything, the slightest flinch or jerk, as he kept a keen eye on his parents' arms. If one of their hands folded down in that awkward way he'd already seen twice that day, he would be ready to draw and fire.

But no one moved. No one flinched. No one drew anything. Ethan finished the last bite of spaghetti he could stomach under the circumstances. Then he decided to be the one to speak first and said, "Thank you for dinner. May I be excused? I'd like to see what's on TV."

The mechanical mother and father exchanged glances,

then looked back at their flesh and blood bundle of joy. "Yes," they responded at exactly the same time in a tone that was as hard to read as their eyes.

"Thank you," Ethan said, playing it super politely. It about made him puke. Then he rinsed his dishes and put them away. He looked back at his parents one more time, flashed a sickeningly sweet smile, and left the room.

Ethan entered the family room and took a seat on the couch where he would have a good view of the entryway to the kitchen. The way he felt about his parents now, he definitely didn't want to be sneaked up on. He picked up the remote and turned on the television. He flipped through a few channels, though he wasn't just randomly surfing. Ethan knew exactly what he wanted to watch, what he wanted to know about. He turned to a news channel and carefully watched the nightly news while keeping an eye on that entryway to the kitchen.

The breaking news story now was a tropical storm in the Caribbean that had just been upgraded to a hurricane before landfall. It was serious stuff, but nothing compared to the news story that Ethan was worried he might see sometime soon. He knew when the machines made their move, their story would be the only one on television. The unimaginable breaking news of an army of robots trampling mankind on all corners of the globe would occupy every channel until the machines destroyed the humans' ability to broadcast on the airwaves. And that probably wouldn't take very long. That thought gave Ethan a cold cringe as he sat on the couch and dazedly watched the waves from the hurricane lash out at the shores of Cuba. Everyone on the island nation had been prepared for the storm. They'd sought shelter just in time. There had been no casualties mentioned.

Then Ethan thought somberly about the newest threat to humanity—the existential one that no one even knew was coming. No one could be prepared for that. There would be no timely evacuations, no finding shelter from that storm. *How many casualties were possible in a scenario like that?* The question made Ethan nauseous.

Ethan sneaked a glance into the entryway to check for Maw and Paw Skulley. Then he hit record on a twenty-four-hour news channel. He thought there was a good chance the machines would shut down television access in Blackwoods when they decided to attack. But this way, Ethan could go back and check the recordings, even if there was no longer live television to view. He hoped he would be able to catch a snippet of what was going on in the world before the machines pulled the plug.

※

The rumbling sounds of diesel trucks never came that night. Neither Ethan's parents, nor any of the other machines posing as adults in Blackwoods, left for their nightly security measures jaunt. Ethan wasn't exactly sure why that was, but he figured it probably had something to do with the six robots they had killed and buried that day. The machines might be on lockdown. Maybe the Skulleys were concerned that some Special Forces unit had somehow made it into Blackwoods. Maybe they thought that team had taken out six of their guys. Maybe they were, for the very first time, a little worried about something. That thought made Ethan smile. It also gave him an idea.

When Ethan finally turned off the lights and climbed into his bed, he thought he had seen the last of his parents until the morning. But he was wrong. As the door to his room opened, their figures were silhouetted against the light of the hallway behind them. They paused for a moment, and Ethan hoped desperately that they would just close the door and walk away. No luck there. They walked in and stood beside his bed, way too close for any kind of comfort. Ethan lay wide awake, his eyes watching their every move. He found the flashlight-sized laser weapon that was now his best friend and bunkmate and gripped it hard in his right hand. Under the bedsheets, he slowly turned it toward them and was ready to fire if they made the slightest false move.

They leaned over his bed, stared him right in the eyes. Their faces were merely three feet away from him. Their eyes were way too bright now in the dark to be human. Ethan wondered if they knew that or if they even cared anymore. They continued to lurch over Ethan's bed, studying him like a rat in a cage. It gave Ethan a sinking, pitiful feeling that maybe that's all they really thought of him, of all humans. Ethan had long ago flipped the safety switch off on the laser weapon, and now he had his thumb squarely on the firing trigger. The longer he stared back into their eyes, the surer he was that he was going to fire, and the heavier his thumb got on that trigger. *This is one rat that's gonna fight back*, he thought as he clenched his jaw.

"Goodnight," Ethan's parental impostors said at the same time. Then they pivoted sharply and left the room, closing the door behind them.

Ethan exhaled a giant sigh of relief. *It's coming*, he thought. *Any day, it's coming*. But he was just glad that it wasn't today. His team was nowhere near ready yet.

CHAPTER 30

A RUDE AWAKENING

It was five o'clock Saturday morning when the Mitchell brothers were dragged out of their beds by Colonel Grissom's two lieutenants. Or at least the Mitchell brothers thought that the guys yanking them by their legs were the colonel's men. The lieutenants pulled them from their bedrooms and through the hallway, manhandling the two-hundred-pound apiece, muscular brothers as if they were rag dolls. Finally, they were both deposited into the living room. The brothers spotted their parents and realized that they had witnessed the entire scene unfold without the slightest trace of concern or resistance. Or at least they thought that the couple observing uncaringly in the corner of the room was their parents. The Mitchell brothers lay on the ground, alternating their stares between their parents and the lieutenants, with question marks filling their eyes. They were utterly speechless and dumbfounded.

Colonel Grissom's mechanical impostor entered the room, and the lieutenants moved away from the brothers and immediately flanked their superior. "Get off the floor and have a seat," the colonel said, his perfectly replicated, piercing blue eyes staring right through them. "I have a few questions for you."

The Mitchell brothers slowly made it to their feet, never taking their gaze off Colonel Grissom. They sat in two sturdy antique oak chairs nearest their parents, who were still standing and looking unfazed by any of this. Zeke and Jeremiah glanced at their mom and dad expectantly, hoping for some words of explanation. They never even got a return glance.

"What the hell is going on here?" Zeke asked finally, trying desperately to keep every word he said sounding like it came from a composed and confident place. He did a pretty good job, even if it was entirely showmanship.

"There has been an incident in Blackwoods," Colonel Grissom said, tightening his jaw like the mechanical vise that it was. "Terrorist activity…treasonous activity…and we need answers from someone or it's not going to be pretty."

Zeke and Jeremiah stared back in confusion at Colonel Grissom. Then they turned those confused faces toward their parents. Jeremiah didn't want to sound weak when he addressed his parents, but a pleading, "Mom, Dad…What is this about?" came out, betraying him.

Their parents looked on without emotion. "Just answer the questions," their dad said.

Then their mother added, "Do it…I would hate for something bad to happen to you." Her tone and facial expression indicated that there wasn't much worry in her heart for her two sons. The brothers could only stare at her in chilled disbelief.

Zeke and Jeremiah turned their attention back to Colonel Grissom. "Why would you think that we know something?" Zeke asked.

"Yeah," Jeremiah added. "And why would you treat us like this, drag us from our beds, unless you thought we had something to do with it?... *Terrorist* activity? *Treasonous* activity? You know us, sir. Known us for a long time...Does *that* sound like anything we'd ever do?"

"Or even know about without telling you," Zeke interjected. "Hell, or without trying to stop it ourselves if we did?"

"Tell us. *Please*," Jeremiah said. "What are you talking about...What happened?"

The colonel cocked his head and paused, then he said, "We lost six men...Six of our men have been killed. It happened yesterday. And I think you know something about that."

A wave of shock overcame the brothers' faces. "Six men were murdered yesterday?" Zeke repeated with a tight lump in his throat. Colonel Grissom did not respond. He just eyeballed them with disturbing intensity, like he could see through to their brains.

"We don't know about any murders," Jeremiah said, sounding indignant. "And shame on all of you if you think we do." The fraternal twins took a long, hard look at their parents after that comment. The Mitchell brothers' father was a brigadier general, outranked Colonel Grissom, yet he was still allowing this to happen. Zeke and Jeremiah figured the order to rough them up to try to tease out information had come from higher up, probably General Turnbull himself. But forgetting about military rank and orders, the fact their parents were on board with this tactic saddened them deeply.

"I guess we have a real problem then," Grissom said. "Six men are down and nobody knows a thing. And we are pretty sure whoever committed this act came from inside the town, not outside...So you see our dilemma."

The Mitchell brothers shook their heads in disgust. Then Zeke said, "Well, my advice to you is that you'd better be sure about who it is before harassing people and dragging them out of their beds…And there is no one in this town I can think of who would attack their fellow servicemen. Every man and woman in this town is a patriot. They love their country and would fight and die to defend it."

"Yeah," Jeremiah added. "You can bet if there was an attack, it came from the outside."

Colonel Grissom's eerie, ice-cold blue eyes passed around the room, spacey and distant, then finally settled into fierce focus on the Mitchell brothers. There was something about his gaze now that sent shivers streaking down their spines. Something in those eyes, or behind them, windows to an empty soul. They didn't understand why they were compelled to look away from him, only that they were. They had to physically force themselves to make eye contact, to appear strong, though their strength was waning. Now they were afraid. And it wasn't just the awful accusations. Those were bad, but there was something else going on here. They realized there was something really wrong with the colonel and his lieutenants—and, most disturbingly, their parents. The brothers just had no idea how horribly wrong things actually were.

Colonel Grissom flashed an oddly inappropriate, toothy, almost impossibly wide smile. "All right," he said. "You're free to go." Then his chilling smile vanished in an instant. "But we aren't finished here. Not by a long shot."

The Mitchell brothers stood up and carefully backed around Colonel Grissom and his lieutenant assistants. They looked away from the colonel's eyes the entire time; they were just too bleak and uninviting. As they left the living room, they glanced back at their parents in disappointment. Their stomachs immediately got queasy when they found their parents' eyes to be just as unwelcoming as Colonel Grissom's. They quickly left the house, got into their truck, and sped away. The brothers felt as if they were fleeing a home inhabited by malevolent spirits masquerading as people they knew and loved.

They were on the right track there, for sure.

CHAPTER 31

PLOTTING

THE MITCHELL BROTHERS weren't the only ones who were eager to get out of their house right away. The members of Team Blackwoods met outside Ethan's place a little past nine o'clock, after spending as little time as possible with their surrogate parents—just enough quality family time to avoid arousing suspicion.

The group walked into Judy's Diner and found the place empty. Breakfast time on a Saturday morning used to always bring a packed house, with Judy cheerfully zipping in and out of tables dishing up good food and better humor. But now, Judy stood behind the bar counter watching them with as much contempt as a machine could have in its eyes. Ethan and the others slid uneasily into a booth, keeping their eyes on Judy the entire time. She—*it*—hesitated to approach them, as if trying to decide if it was even worth it to pretend to be the sweet seventy-year-old lady anymore, especially when playing that role included eagerly serving food and drink to those organic creatures she hated so much. And doing it all with a smile.

Judy finally stepped out from behind the counter and made her way to their table. She cranked a smile onto her face. The maneuver resembled what a waitress who had just served a rude table might do—forcing a smile on her face in the hopes of getting a better table and a better tip next time. Still, this was not the demeanor of the human Judy, nor was it her smile. No one in the group expected robot Judy to be the machine to start hostilities, but everyone was carrying that small, flashlight-sized laser weapon with them now. They always kept that near.

"What can I get you folks?" Judy said, voice spot-on.

"Just five orange juices for now," Ethan said.

Judy nodded, then said, "Sure thing. Be right back."

The machine that was posing as Judy had her voice down perfectly, and her movements and gestures down pretty well, but it could never replicate with any precision Judy's smile or that twinkle in her eye. Those were the unique qualities of Judy Dupree, and no machine could copy that. Judy soon came back and delivered their drinks. She walked away without any chit-chat, one more deviation from the genuine article.

Ethan took a sip of his orange juice and cast a curious glance around the room. "This place is too empty."

"I'd expect it to be empty," Glenn said. "A lot has happened in the last twenty-four hours. Our adult friends have more to worry about than putting pancakes in their metal bellies and keeping up appearances at Judy's Diner."

Ethan nodded. "I know, but…what about everyone else? Saturday morning here used to be a popular time for the high schoolers…Where are they?"

"That's a good question," Austin said. "Something's messed up their routine."

"Well we can't worry about that now," Annika said, speaking quietly. "We need to focus on getting the supplies we need to turn the cave into our fort…and getting back to Andy."

"Right," Caleb added. "I'll need to get my dad's cutting and welding torch. It's gonna take a lot of work to do what we need to do."

"And we can't get caught doing it," Ethan said. "A diversion would be nice."

"Any ideas?" Glenn asked.

"Maybe," Ethan answered. Then the door to the diner opened, and Zeke and Jeremiah Mitchell entered. They moved slowly and dazedly to a corner booth on the opposite side of the room. Both looked emotionally drained as they sat with their heads in their hands, staring at each other but saying nothing. Ethan watched them for a moment, then said, "But I think my best idea is sitting at that table."

"What, you're thinking of letting the Mitchell brothers in on this?" Glenn asked.

"Yeah," Ethan said. "Just look at them. Looks like they've been put through the wringer. And their eyes…I've never seen them look like that, except for the last time the fatal error happened…They look worried."

"You think they know?" Austin asked.

"Probably not exactly, but they know something's wrong," Ethan replied. "You can tell something strange happened to them this morning. They'll be ready to believe us, or as ready as they're ever gonna get."

"And then what?" Annika asked.

"We ask them politely for a favor."

Ethan and the rest of the group grabbed their drinks and moved over to the booth where the Mitchell brothers were sitting. They stood beside their table for a long moment before either one of the brothers saw them. Finally, Zeke glanced out of the corner of his eye and saw the five members of Team Blackwoods standing there. Then Jeremiah spotted them as well. Neither one of them looked especially pleased about having to deal with these kids now. Zeke grimaced even more than his brother, then said, "Unless someone's on fire, now is not a good time for us."

Ethan took a deep breath and exhaled slowly. "The whole world's gonna be on fire soon." Ethan's eyes were dead serious and unflinching. "We need to talk. Can we sit down?"

Jeremiah exchanged a curious glance with Zeke, then the brothers turned simultaneously to the group. "All right, have a seat," Zeke said reluctantly. "But, please, make it quick. We've had a helluva morning."

The brothers scooted in and allowed the five members of Team Blackwoods to join them at their large, circular booth. Their table was ensconced in the back corner of the room, with tall backs on the bench seats which gave them a good degree of privacy. It also gave them a poor angle to see when Judy might be approaching. Ethan had the best view, as he was sitting on one of the edge seats. He peeked out periodically, making sure they wouldn't be overheard. Their level of paranoia about Judy piqued the brothers' interest. They thought either the group had one heck of a story to tell, or that they all needed to go on anti-psychotic drugs fast.

"So what is it you wanna tell us?" Jeremiah asked.

"We were kinda hoping you could tell us something first," Ethan said. "Like what happened to you guys this morning."

Jeremiah and Zeke furrowed their faces in annoyance. "Look, that's not how this is gonna work," Zeke said. "You first. You said the whole world is going to be on fire...Now talk."

Ethan nodded. "Your parents have been acting strangely... And something *really* strange happened this morning that you can't explain and can't ignore. Am I right?"

The Mitchell brothers' faces softened, and their eyes became curious. Then they shook off their initial shock and got annoyed all over again. "Okay, lucky guess," Zeke snapped back. "Got anything else? Otherwise, we just wanna be left alone."

"There is something else," Ethan responded. "But if we tell you, you have to promise not to tell anybody, not a soul... You must give us your word. And I know your word is good. You promise us that, and we will tell you."

Jeremiah and Zeke were looking more intrigued by the second now. They nodded their heads. "You have our word," they said at the same time.

Ethan sighed deeply. "What I'm about to say is going to sound completely insane, but please don't leave until you give us a chance to explain."

The Mitchell brothers nodded quickly with eyes that were getting wider. "Okay, all right...Go ahead," Jeremiah said impatiently.

"Do you remember Sunday night?" Ethan asked. "The last night we spent at Briggs Air Force Base? When all the officers had to leave on some emergency and go back to the research facility?"

"Yeah, so...?" Zeke said.

Ethan peeked around the corner of the tall booth chair. Seeing no one there, he continued, "Something went really wrong at the research facility while we were at Briggs...And from Sunday on, robots started infiltrating Blackwoods, pretending to be human. Everyone over the age of eighteen is a machine…even our parents."

Jeremiah and Zeke flashed broad smiles, then let out a couple chuckles. "Wow…You said it would sound insane, and you weren't lying," Jeremiah said.

"We're not lying about any of this," Austin added, his tone as firm as his jaw.

Zeke shook his head in disbelief and said, "Look, we'll keep our word and not tell anybody. We don't want anyone to make fun of you. But seriously, we had a rough morning and need to be alone now. Thanks for the laugh, though."

"All right then," Annika said. "But when you realize we're right, you should know those two twenty-two caliber rifles your dad set aside for an emergency aren't gonna help you with this one."

The brothers' faces froze instantly. "Now *how the hell* did you know that?" Zeke asked.

"*You* told us you had them, the first time this happened," Annika answered. "And they didn't save you then."

"The first time *what* happened?" Jeremiah asked.

"It's called the fatal error," Caleb said. "It's the mistake that causes everything."

The Mitchell brothers were clearly lost in confusion. Ethan took a deep breath and said, "Sorry, okay…Look, we should just start from the beginning."

Team Blackwoods spent the next fifteen minutes explaining the unthinkable to Jeremiah and Zeke. They told them everything, except the precise details of Project Mulligan. They had to leave out the part about the secret tunnel into the research facility, as well as their interest in Wolf Cave. If they didn't, and the machines were to interrogate the Mitchell brothers using their friendly mind-reading techniques, the entire operation would be blown.

The brothers weren't completely convinced yet, but they hadn't laughed or smiled once since the briefing began. Their faces gradually morphed from strictly skeptical to accepting of the possibility, at least. Ethan and the others leaned back in their seats for the first time since they had begun their explanation, allowing the Mitchell brothers time to process the bizarre information that'd been dumped on them. That all of this was really happening now was a lot to digest, let alone the idea that a version of this had already happened and been thwarted by five kids who had yet to put fourteen candles on a birthday cake.

The brothers shook their heads. Then Zeke said, "So… you're saying we—"

Suddenly, Judy stepped briskly up to their table. Everyone in the booth flinched in surprise, but the Mitchell brothers were the most startled, nearly jumping out of their seats. "Sorry, I didn't see you earlier," Judy said, looking at Jeremiah and Zeke. "What can I get you?"

Zeke spoke softly. "Coffee…decaf, please."

Jeremiah nodded. "Yeah, same here."

"Be right back."

Zeke waited until Judy was a safe distance away, then finished his original thought, "So, you're saying that we *died* before?…The last time this fatal error happened?"

"That's right," Annika answered. "You went to the research facility to check it out, try to figure out what was going on… You never came back."

Zeke drew a deep breath and swallowed hard. "I see," he said grimly.

Judy returned to their table with the coffees. This time everyone had seen her coming and was prepared. "Here you go. Two decafs," Judy said, then flashed a smile that was closer to authentic than before.

"Thanks," Jeremiah said. He nodded toward Judy as she was walking away. He spoke softly. "Even her, you say?... You're saying that *even Judy* is a machine?"

"Yeah," Ethan replied solemnly. "Everyone older than you...Everyone."

Jeremiah shrugged. "Okay, but you realize, to *really* believe this story, we're gonna need to have some proof...something we can see or feel."

"We have proof all over the place," Ethan said. "Problem is, most of it's hidden."

"Then what do you expect us to think right now?" Jeremiah asked.

"I didn't say it was *all* hidden," Ethan replied with a sneaky smile. "But I can't show you in here."

"All right then," Zeke said, mirroring Ethan's smile. Then he added cheekily, "Let's pay the robot lady and get outta here."

The team took the Mitchell brothers outside the diner to a deserted back alley. Ethan placed an aluminum can on top of a dumpster and stood away a safe distance. "Okay, Annika," he said. "Fire when ready."

Annika nodded, then pulled the small, flashlight-sized laser weapon from her waistband. She took a second to aim, then fired one laser pulse at the can, turning it into dust instantly. Jeremiah's and Zeke's jaws almost hit the ground.

"What is that thing?" Jeremiah asked.

"We took it off one of the machines we killed," Caleb

answered. "Each robot has two of these weapons, one hidden in each forearm."

Ethan handed Jeremiah his laser weapon. He inspected it carefully, rolling it gently in his hand. "Amazing," Jeremiah said. "Absolutely amazing."

Zeke looked at Annika and held out his hand expectantly. "Let me take a look."

Annika pulled her laser weapon away from Zeke. "Nope, don't think so," she said. "This stays with me...Caleb, Austin, Glenn, anyone?"

Glenn grinned at Annika, then handed Zeke his laser weapon. "Don't mind Annika. She's just a little particular about her weapons, that's all."

Zeke flashed a smile at Annika. "I can appreciate that in a girl...You know, I always thought if you were a couple years older, I—"

"Whoa, I'm gonna stop ya right there, buddy," Annika interrupted, firmly holding her hand out, palm toward him. "I'm already taken, thank you."

When those words from Annika fluttered to Ethan's ears, he couldn't have remembered his own name for a million bucks. He turned sharply in Annika's direction, but she was facing away from him now, staring down Zeke. Ethan thought he had seen her nod at him out of the corner of his eye, but he couldn't be sure. For the love of God, he wished he could rewind real-time like the shows on television.

"What I was about to say," Zeke began again, a blushing smile still on his face, "was that if you were a couple of years older, I always thought it'd be cool to take you out shooting with me and Jeremiah."

Annika nodded. "Okay, that's better." Then she cracked a

playful smile and said, "But taking me out to shoot with you guys wouldn't exactly help your confidence."

Zeke grinned. "You're probably right there...Lucky guy to have you in the foxhole with him, whoever he is."

"So, do you believe us now?" Ethan asked, curious to know and eager to change the topic of conversation.

The brothers sighed deeply. "Yeah...I think we might," Zeke said.

"Good," Ethan said. "Now that we told you what we know, we have a favor to ask."

The Mitchell brothers looked skeptical, like they were waiting for a bad punch line. "Okay, what is it?" Jeremiah asked.

The group went on to explain exactly what they wanted from the popular, athletic, West Point-bound Mitchell brothers. All it amounted to was a distraction. The brothers weren't particularly happy to cede control to some kids just going into the eighth grade, but they had to admit that the group had earned their stripes. So Jeremiah and Zeke Mitchell reluctantly promised to act according to their wishes.

The plan was to give false intelligence to the machines. Team Blackwoods had to build their base at Wolf Cave, which was just a few miles west of the research facility's outer gate. They needed the freedom to move supplies into the cave and time to safely set up camp there without being seen. Hence, the Mitchell brothers agreed to lie to the robotic Colonel Grissom, to tell him that they had seen a suspicious special forces unit in the area of the southeast fork of Copper Creek. Of the entire tract of government-owned land, the southeast fork of Copper Creek was as far away from Wolf Cave as one could possibly get. The idea was to get all the machines out of the way on a wild goose chase. They just hoped that it would buy them enough time.

As the brothers were about to leave, Jeremiah said, "Just promise us this…When you guys are done, and it's time to make the move, you let us in on the plan…And save a spot for us."

"You have our word on that," Ethan said. "We would tell you more if we could, but if the machines get suspicious of you, they will interrogate you. And *they will* get answers."

Jeremiah nodded. "Guess we gotta win the Academy Award on this one, huh Zeke?"

Zeke cracked a smile, though a tense one. "Yeah, guess so…Hey, *you* were the one who had the lead in *West Side Story*."

"Think they'd get suspicious if I broke out in song?" Jeremiah quipped.

Everyone laughed for a bit. Genuine laughter at first, then it turned into the nervous kind. The smiles and chuckles dried up quickly thereafter. Zeke left the group and walked over to his truck on the curb. He leaned inside the window and pulled out a walkie-talkie.

"Here, take this," Zeke said, handing the walkie-talkie to Ethan. "I would guess they're monitoring everything now, but we can get around that with a code word. We'll use the word *testing*. Once we tell them our little fib, if we think they bought it, we'll say the word *testing* three times. If not, we'll say it only twice…Got it?" Everyone on Team Blackwoods nodded. "And as for channel, let's stick with—"

"Seven?" Annika chimed in before Zeke could finish.

Zeke stopped speaking instantly. His eyes widened, taken aback. "That's exactly what I was gonna say…Guess that's good luck," he concluded with a smile.

Everyone on Team Blackwoods paused in silence. Their faces were tight and solemn. "Wait a minute," Jeremiah said, noticing how the air had been sucked out of the place. "We've done this before, haven't we?"

Annika nodded hesitantly. "Yeah…When you checked on the research facility. You gave us a walkie-talkie then too… channel seven."

"That's always been our channel," Zeke said.

"But we died then, right?" Jeremiah asked. Everyone in the group nodded. "Hell with that then…I say we switch to channel eight."

"For good luck," Caleb said.

Jeremiah grinned. "When the scientist in the group gets superstitious, I'd say we gotta go with it."

The Mitchell brothers chuckled a little at the ridiculousness of the situation. It was a somber laughter, a gallows humor. When the odd laughter finally died, all that was left was a silence that seemed ominous.

"Keep channel eight open and listen for us too," Ethan said. "After we get everything ready, we'll contact you guys with a *testing, testing, testing* when it's time to leave. And we'll meet right back here, in this alley."

The brothers nodded and looked over the group with both pride and surprise in their eyes. They accepted the group's story and were willing to put their lives on the line for the cause, but they still couldn't *believe* it. The idea that the five kids before them now had accomplished so much, fought such long odds, and were game to do it all over again was mind-blowing. All they could do was follow their lead. But it was such a weird feeling for them; they weren't used to the junior varsity role.

"All right, we better go put this plan into action," Jeremiah said.

"Good luck," Ethan and the others wished the brothers.

"Yeah, you guys too," Jeremiah replied.

CHAPTER 32

UNDER THE RADAR

It was safe to say now that none of the adults in Blackwoods were going for the Parent-of-the-Year Award. Everyone's parents were gone at the moment, no doubt at the research facility working on their next diabolical project. The fact that his mechanical parents were gone suited Caleb just fine, seeing as he needed to smuggle an acetylene cutting and welding torch set out of his father's sub-basement. Caleb quickly packed everything he thought they might need to transform Wolf Cave into their next fort. The supplies filled two large duffel bags and a camping backpack, none of which he was especially eager for the guards at the Dark Highway to inspect.

Ethan and Austin helped Caleb carry the bags upstairs. They met Annika and Glenn who were keeping guard in the living room, peering out the windows. "See anything unusual?" Ethan asked. He set his duffel bag down and checked the window alongside Annika.

"Well, the machines aren't strolling down the street naked without their skin yet," Annika said with a healthy dose of sarcasm. "So that's good, but…"

"What is it?" Ethan asked.

"It's just that…everyone I've seen over the age of sixteen looks like they've just had a conversation with Jack the Ripper's ghost. They all look spooked."

"That's a good way of putting it," Glenn said. "Yeah, sixteen and over is about right. Younger than that, people seem fine, or better at least."

"Bet the older ones had the same kind of morning as the Mitchell brothers," Austin said.

Ethan peeked outside the window for a while, observing the demeanors of the passersby on the sidewalks. The difference was easy to see. "We weren't hassled because we're under the radar. None of the machines suspect that all the trouble they had in the last twenty-four hours could possibly be coming from a team so young…But I doubt we'll be off-limits forever."

"We need to act fast then," Caleb said.

"Yeah," Annika added. "And I hope no one forgot we still have a boy robot waiting for us back at the fort."

Ethan grinned. "No worries there. Andy would be impossible to forget."

༄

When the group was stopped at the guard checkpoint on the Dark Highway, they had no idea what to expect. The large black duffel bags that Austin and Glenn were carrying stuck out like sore thumbs. They knew if the guards looked in those bags, they'd have a heck of a time explaining their contents. *What on earth would some kids need with acetylene torches, industrial-grade drills, a sledgehammer, and a pickaxe?*

"Hold it," the first of two dour-looking soldiers said. The

group stopped instantly, hearts in their throats. There was a long, excruciating pause. "We're not letting you through today…" Everyone's faces dropped in sickening disappointment. Their plans were ruined now. Even if they could find a way around them without arousing suspicion, they wouldn't have the time. The Mitchell brothers would be calling in soon, and they wouldn't be in a position to capitalize on the distraction the brothers were risking their lives to provide. Then the soldier finished belatedly, "…unless you promise us one thing."

The heavens seemed to part for the group. They nodded eagerly. Ethan said, "Yeah, sure, anything…What is it?"

The soldier clad in camouflage and synthetic human skin said, "If you see anyone strange out there, you come back and let us know right away. Immediately. Do you understand?"

"Absolutely, glad to help," Ethan replied.

"All right then, go ahead," the soldier said.

The group went through the checkpoint without so much as a cockeyed glance from the other soldiers. Their hefty, suspicious-looking bags were allowed to pass uninspected. As they started their walk into the woods and got a safe distance away from the guards, Ethan turned to the others and said with a sneaky smile, "Under the radar…Gotta use that while we can."

Ethan knew something was wrong as soon as the team had crested the hill. The Bravo fort should have been visible by now and it wasn't. The loft was missing. As the group sped up, it became apparent that the main level was gone too. They sprinted toward the fort and found that it had been completely leveled. It was now lying in a heap in ruins, the metal walls collapsed on top of each other with the innards of the fort spewing out here and there around it. The walls of the basement could be seen in spots, cracked in some areas and pulverized in others, with steel rods protruding from the concrete. The place looked like it had been hit by a wrecking ball over and over again. After the initial shock wore off, a more intense shock took its place. Everyone at once wondered with a gut-wrenching feeling of dread… *Where was Andy?*

"Andy! Andy!" Annika yelled. "Andy, where are you?!"

The group spread out and began frantically combing through the wreckage. The manner of their search, with grim desperation on their faces, indicated that they were looking for more than a boy robot who had managed to be helpful to them. They were looking for their friend as well.

Ethan and Austin dragged the manhole cover off the end of the secret escape tunnel. Ethan lay down and shined a flashlight into the passageway. "Andy!" he shouted.

"Anything?" Austin asked.

Ethan shook his head sadly. "Nothing."

"Andy!…Andy!" Annika yelled down into the basement through a small gap she found in the collapsed metal walls. There was no response. Annika sat beside the rubble, holding her head in her hands. A tear trickled down her cheek. Glenn put a comforting hand on her shoulder.

"Maybe he got outta here before," Glenn said softly. "We don't know for sure."

Just then, on the far end of the junk pile that used to be the Bravo Fort, a metal plate shifted slightly. The group perked up and everyone rushed toward the area of movement.

"Andy?!" Annika shouted hopefully. The plate of metal slid even further and Andy poked his head out. "Andy!"

The group tried with all of their human might to pull the metal slab away, though it barely budged. Andy wiggled through the hole like a groundhog and managed to get good enough leverage to push the metal sheet away himself. As he climbed out, his first words were: "Don't worry, I saved the guns." He leaned back inside the hole in the rubble and pulled out a duffel bag. "They're in here, all the rifles as well as the three smaller laser weapons that look like flashlights...I made sure to keep them safe. I knew you would be worried about them."

At that moment, the members of Team Blackwoods truly looked at Andy like he was the sixth member of their team. Their soft eyes were full of respect, trust, and friendship. Ethan stepped up to him first and said, "We weren't just worried about the guns, Andy."

A slow, cautious smile washed over Andy's face. "You were worried about *me*?" he asked with doubt in his voice.

"*Well, yeah*," Ethan said, sounding like the idea was obvious. Then everyone else echoed Ethan's words with the same level of conviction.

Andy's smile got even bigger when the team surrounded him and gave him a big group hug. The doubt in his voice was gone when he said, "Thank you." And in those two words, and in the contours of his fabricated face, and in the softness of his synthetic eyes, were feelings and emotions that were undeniably real. His emotions might not be exactly human, but there was no doubt now that what Andy was feeling was equally valid. Not human, but not a machine. He was a sentient *and* sapient being, with all the rights, privileges, and burdens that come along with it. As they held on to Andy, celebrating the fact that they hadn't lost him forever, it was the first time everyone on Team Blackwoods understood that completely.

But the celebration of having Andy back eventually gave way to mourning the loss of their fort. They all knew that the Bravo Fort couldn't be their sanctuary now anyway, but seeing it completely destroyed hit a sentimental nerve. Ethan, Austin, and Caleb were especially feeling the loss, as they were the ones who had spent an entire summer building it. Gazing with heavy eyes at the broken pile of metal and concrete, they felt as if they had lost an old friend.

"What happened here?" Ethan finally asked.

"Another patrol of machines came by, four of them again," Andy answered. "They just stood outside the fort, about thirty meters away. One of them was carrying a different kind of weapon, like a rifle but bigger, with a dish on the end of it. I had seen them coming on the video cameras, so I grabbed the guns and hid in the tunnel…I knew something bad was going to happen."

"Whatever weapon they used dropped this fort like it was made of sticks," Austin said.

"Yes, and I only heard one shot," Andy said. "Then an awful vibration, followed by the loud crash of the fort collapsing…The machines found and checked the tunnel after, but I figured they would, so I doubled back inside. I found a spot to hide in the rubble and waited for you."

"Good work," Ethan said.

"Thank you," Andy replied. "I'm just sorry I couldn't save the fort."

"Don't worry about it," Ethan said. "The plan's not to stay here, anyway."

As Caleb examined the debris, a smile sneaked onto his

face. "Yeah, besides…Those machines have no idea, but they just did us a favor."

"How do you mean that?" Glenn asked.

"Think about it, all we need from this fort are parts," Caleb answered with a grin. "The machines just saved us some time by breaking those parts down for us."

Glenn nodded, returning the smile. "How thoughtful of them," he quipped.

"Yeah, maybe a thank-you letter is in order," Annika added.

Ethan smiled for a moment, then focused on the task ahead. "All right, we need to get to work. The entrance to Wolf Cave measures six-by-eight feet. Plus we'll need enough scraps to cover and seal the smaller entrances inside…Let's get that torch out and start cutting pieces of metal from the stack the Skulleys were so nice to set out for us."

"What about transporting it?" Glenn asked. "That's a lotta weight. A lot more than we can carry, even with Andy."

"Yeah, I've been thinking about that," Ethan said. "Andy, when you were hiding in the basement, did you see the generators? Do you think we could get to them now?"

"Yes, actually I was hiding right behind them," Andy answered. "The basement is caved in pretty badly, really tight, but there are pockets here and there we could move in. I know we could get them out."

"Why do we want the generators?" Austin asked.

"We don't want the generators," Ethan answered. "We want the wheels that are on them, along with the cage it's in. With all that, we can rig a dolly cart to carry the metal sheets."

"Smart," Caleb said.

"But isn't it dangerous down there?" Annika asked. "The

area can't be stable. The whole thing could collapse at any time and crush you."

Ethan looked pensive. Then Andy stepped forward and said, "I should go, alone. That way if something does happen, it's just me down there."

"No," Ethan said firmly. "It was my idea. I'll go with you."

"Please be careful," Annika said, her eyes full of worry.

Ethan smiled softly. "We will."

Armed with a toolbox and headlamps, Ethan and Andy crawled their way through the secret escape tunnel back to the fort. Ethan pushed the hatch open gingerly and peeked inside. It was pitch black in the basement, except for the beams of light their headlamps cast. The roof hadn't entirely collapsed yet, though it looked like that could happen at any moment. It bowed deeply and unevenly throughout the room from where the concrete walls had caved in around it, leaving only a few tiny spots where one could crawl. Fortunately, the generators were always left close to the escape hatch, and there was room there to work. They crouched down beside the generators, their heads only inches away from the distended ceiling above. Creaking sounds seemed to come from every direction from the weight of it all. Ethan quickly opened the toolbox and retrieved two screwdrivers. He handed one to Andy.

"We're gonna need to unscrew everything connected to the generator," Ethan said. "All we want is the cage and the wheels on it." Ethan glanced up at the ceiling, and he swore he saw it dip another inch. He swallowed tensely, sweat dotting his forehead. "And we gotta move fast."

"I understand," Andy said.

"All right, I'll work on this one. You get that one."

"Sounds good," Andy said as he went to work. He had

a smile on his face. It was the contented smile of someone spending time with a friend on a favorite activity. Never mind the fact that the activity was unfastening screws under a pile of rubble that could serve as their tomb.

"How's it coming?" Ethan asked.

"Good. I've unfastened nine so far…You?"

Ethan paused. "Two," he replied with a sheepish grin.

Andy was on auto-pilot, unfastening screws without looking. He glanced over at Ethan and watched him for a while as he worked, then he finally spoke. "Ethan, your dad built me for a reason…Do you think you could ever consider me your brother?"

At that question, Ethan fumbled his screwdriver, then fumbled his response. "Uh, um…I consider you a friend, Andy."

Andy nodded with a polite smile. "But not a brother."

"Brothers have a very special relationship, Andy. It's hard to explain. I've always wanted a brother, though…You are a friend, but I'm afraid we'll never be brothers."

Andy sighed subtly. "I see. Andy Tate had a nice sound to it, but I am okay being just Andy, your friend. Thank you for that, Ethan."

"Sure," Ethan said with an uneasy smile.

Ethan and Andy emerged from the tunnel towing the generator cages behind them. They rolled the cages around to meet Caleb, who was busy cutting pieces of metal from the remnants of the fort with his torch. Sparks flew everywhere as he worked. When he saw Ethan, he turned the torch off and lifted his tinted welding goggles from his eyes to his forehead.

"Great, you got them both," Caleb said.

"Yeah, we just need to cut a piece off here and there, weld them together, and we'll have a pretty good dolly cart."

"I was worried about you guys," Annika said, taking a break from her guard duty and looking at Ethan with a stressed-out face.

"Naw," Ethan said, playing it cool. "We weren't in any real danger."

At that moment, the section of the fort that Ethan and Andy had been working under began to shake. After some rumblings, it collapsed entirely with a loud *Bang!* Dust puffed out from the area as the debris settled into its final resting state. Ethan gawked at the sight, then turned to Annika with an awkward smile and quickly changed the topic. "Well, uh…I better get those generator cages ready for Caleb." Ethan scampered away before he could see Annika's grimace.

Caleb welded the generator cages together into a makeshift dolly cart. It took the entire group to load the biggest pieces of metal onto the cart—five people on one side and Andy on the other. Then Andy set the broken laser turret on top of the metal heap like a cherry atop a sundae. They were careful to stack the pile evenly before securing the load tightly with rope.

Finally, it was time to wait. Ethan sat the walkie-talkie on top of the metal slabs on the cart. Everyone watched it intensely, like they were able to will it to speak if they stared at it hard enough. They were all eager to get going with the plan. As soon as the Mitchell brothers said that magic word three times, the group would make their move and make Wolf Cave their new fort.

CHAPTER 33

MISINFORMATION

THE MITCHELL BROTHERS normally loved hiking the steep banks of Copper Creek. They enjoyed watching the whitewater cascade off the rocks and spotting the occasional trout spring into the air. The water was beautiful today, with rippling currents and eddies glistening in the sun like diamonds. The trout were especially active, too. But neither Zeke nor Jeremiah paid any attention to that now. The splendor of nature lay around them unappreciated. All they could think about was the disturbing story they'd been told in Judy's Diner.

The brothers were sitting on the bank of the creek, looking past the water, looking past all of nature, and staring blankly into the distance at nothing in particular. Zeke finally shook off the daze and glanced at his brother. "How can their story possibly be true?" he said softly.

"I don't know," Jeremiah responded, still gazing vacantly into the pines on the other side of the creek. "Are you having doubts?"

"I guess I always have doubts about lying to a colonel."

"Yeah, but according to them, Colonel Grissom is a robot too, so…"

Zeke shook his head. "Jeremiah, do you have any idea how insane that sounds?"

Jeremiah looked at his brother. He sighed and smiled. "Yeah, a little bit." Then he paused for a moment and added, "But it does explain some things, though…Our parents' behavior. Some of the other adults. The fact that we were dragged from our beds like that."

"Yeah, but *robots*?" Zeke said in disbelief. "And the whole story about them going back in time. The more I think about it, the more I think someone's playing a trick on us."

"What about the things they knew?" Jeremiah asked. "They knew about the rifles our dad stashed away for us. And for God's sake, they had a laser gun. You saw what that thing did. You know the military doesn't have anything like that… not yet, anyway."

"Secrets get out," Zeke answered. "We told Ryan Hawkins about the rifles. Maybe he spilled the beans."

"Hawkins wouldn't do that. Besides, what about the laser gun? That's exhibit A."

Zeke shook his head. "That's still not absolute proof. Think about it. Caleb's dad is the head scientist at the most advanced military research facility in the world. Who knows what they're really working on over there? And if he ever takes any of his work home, it's possible little Mad Scientist Junior got his hands on it. Maybe Caleb and the others were in the mood for a little joke."

Jeremiah stared thoughtfully into the creek for a moment, then turned to Zeke. "I think Caleb's dad is way too smart to do something that stupid. Taking secret, classified weapons home with him? No way."

"Yes, Caleb's dad is brilliant, but he's also the absent-minded professor-type."

"Yeah, but I still don't think that's possible," Jeremiah said.

"It's more possible than their crazy story," Zeke shot back.

Jeremiah drew a deep breath. "So you don't want to keep our promise? You don't want to go through with this?"

Zeke swallowed hard. He looked at his brother with stress in his eyes. "If we lie to a *colonel* in the United States Air Force about a possible security breach, and that colonel *is not* a robot, not only can we kiss West Point goodbye, but we'll be facing prison time as well."

"I realize that's a possibility," Jeremiah said. "But those are good kids. Heck, two of their fathers are the highest-ranking generals at the base…I believe them."

Zeke paused for a moment. He rubbed his temples as if trying to find a release valve to take away the pressure in his head. Then he exhaled a long sigh. "Deep down, I believe them too. It's just a helluva story and a helluva price to pay if it's not the right one."

"I know, brother," Jeremiah said. Then he checked his watch. "Figure we've been out here long enough to make our story plausible. We should get back."

Zeke nodded. "Yeah, let's go."

◈

When the brothers pulled into the driveway of their house, they spotted their parents peeking outside through a peeled-back curtain in the living room window. Their eyes were blank and lifeless, like their faces, and the way they looked now removed any trace of doubt Zeke might've had about going through with the charade. They watched their parents until they had let go of the curtain and couldn't be seen anymore. A cold, tingling shiver danced down their backs, like a chiropractor with ice for hands was manipulating their spines.

Zeke took a deep, jittery breath. "All right…Let's get this over with."

The brothers got out of their truck and walked up to the porch. Just as they were about to open the door, it was opened for them. Mr. and Mrs. Mitchell stood in the doorway, staring at their sons with their heads cocked at a slight angle. Their faces looked so pale, so gaunt, so skeletal. They looked like they had some horrible disease that made their skin melt away over time. The ashen skin on their faces was thin and gauzy, and, underneath that, a darker color was emerging. Jeremiah and Zeke would've been worried out of their minds if they thought these were their real parents. But now, they were not. All they were concerned with was trying to pretend as if everything were okay, at least long enough to do what they needed to do.

"Hi, Mom, Dad." Zeke smiled and tried desperately to fake a normal greeting. "We saw something strange in the woods around the southeast fork of Copper Creek. We'd like to talk to Colonel Grissom. We think he'd wanna hear this."

"Come on in then," their mother said in a startlingly soothing voice. Then she and her husband cracked faint, deathly smiles. The cold shiver in the brothers' spines never went away.

∽

Colonel Grissom and his two lieutenant assistants sat directly across from the brothers in the living room. Their parents sat off to the side, watching the scene with far less interest than any real parent would've under the circumstances. The Mitchell brothers wanted to let the colonel speak first, as that's how they would've treated a human in the Air Force with a colonel's rank, and they didn't want to act out of the ordinary. So they waited to talk, but all that brought was an awkward silence. A full minute passed without words. Jeremiah spent the time glancing at various antiques in the room that had been passed down to the family by their ancestors. They provided something else to focus on other than the colonel's eyes, as anything was better than that. While looking at the heirloom furniture, he couldn't help but think how odd it was that these highly advanced, futuristic machines were sitting on antique rosewood chairs from the Victorian era. Then he thought about the long-dead creator of the chairs, the artisan in the 1800s who'd painstakingly crafted the wood and designed the ornate silk upholstery. *What on earth would that man have possibly thought if he had known who'd be sitting in his chairs now?*

"Your parents said you had something to tell us," Colonel Grissom said with a flat expression, breaking the silence. His face didn't look quite as sickly and pale as those of Zeke and Jeremiah's parents, but it didn't look well either. Something was happening to all of them now. Some sort of slow physical transformation.

"Yes, sir," Jeremiah answered. "Zeke and I were out hiking at Copper Creek, way down by the southeast fork, when we saw something strange…And we thought you'd want to know about anything strange, especially in light of what's happened to those six poor soldiers."

"You are absolutely right," Colonel Grissom said, leaning forward in the antique chair with much interest now. The chair creaked, straining to hold the several hundred-pound machine as it shifted its weight. "Tell me, what did you see?"

"A squad of soldiers, eight of them," Jeremiah said. "They looked like Army Rangers, but that struck us as really strange. Why would the Army be doing maneuvers here in Air Force country?"

"Yeah," Zeke added. "Then we thought about the guys you said you lost. Made us think that maybe those Rangers aren't really Rangers. Maybe they're terrorists."

Colonel Grissom leaned in further. The rosewood chair protested with another creak. "Did those men see you?"

"No, sir. We hid right away," Zeke answered. "Something about them didn't seem right. They kinda looked like trouble."

"Good boy," the colonel said. "And when did you last see them?"

"We just left, came straight back," Jeremiah responded. "Probably less than thirty minutes ago."

"And you said they were at the southeast fork of Copper Creek?" the colonel asked.

"Yes, sir," Zeke answered.

Colonel Grissom nodded, then eked out a satisfied smile. "Excellent work, boys…And sorry about earlier. You understand, we just needed to make sure you were on the right side."

"Yes, sir. We understand totally," Jeremiah said. "With potential terrorists around, you can't ever be too sure."

The colonel smiled even bigger. It was a broad, toothy grin. And his eyes, sunken with dark circles around them now, widened eerily. It was a warped and distorted face that the brothers wished they could forget. "You are more right than you know, son," Grissom said. Then he stood up, glanced at his lieutenants, and the three of them left the house in a hurry.

At last, Jeremiah and Zeke were left alone in the room with their parents, which was as bad or worse than being stuck with Colonel Grissom and his goons. Their parents' ghostly pale faces were hard to watch, and they had no desire to sit around to see how much worse they were going to get.

Jeremiah stood up quickly. "Whew, I'm hungry...Zeke and I are gonna go down to Judy's Diner and get some lunch."

"Yeah, that's right," Zeke added. "Then we gotta go to the gym."

"And don't forget those errands we've been putting off," Jeremiah finished. "Such a busy Saturday. It's gonna take a while."

The brothers forced a smile and headed for the door. Their parents got up and intercepted them. "You made the right choice in telling Colonel Grissom," their mother said.

"Yes, we are so very proud of you boys," the father added.

Their parents smiled simultaneously, and their grins were so fake and abnormally wide that it was like their images had been reflected from a funhouse mirror. Their eyes were as wide as the colonel's had been, and, with the shades drawn in the room, they were far too bright. Zeke and Jeremiah instantly regretted they'd ever made eye contact. They were absolutely petrified.

The brothers' internal body temperatures usually ran a little hot, but now they were cold to the bone. "Thank you," Jeremiah replied with words he hoped didn't shudder. Then he groped for the doorknob and swung the door open. He and Zeke left the house, worried the entire time that they might be yanked back inside.

As soon as the Mitchell brothers pulled their truck out of the driveway, Zeke grabbed the walkie-talkie and tuned to channel eight. He pressed the transmit button and spoke: "*Testing, testing, testing*. I repeat...*Testing, testing, testing*."

CHAPTER 34

A NEW FORT

The group took off like a shot when the Mitchell brothers gave the word. Or at least they tried to take off like a shot. It was slow going lugging a makeshift dolly cart, loaded with hundreds of pounds of metal slabs, over rough terrain. Andy pulled from the front, while the other five pushed from the back. It worried them not to have at least one person dedicated to keeping a lookout as they traveled, but it took the combined efforts of everyone to keep the cart rolling, and they could spare no one. Fortunately, they hadn't encountered anyone yet, human or machine. That meant Jeremiah and Zeke's distraction had worked. But the team knew they would have to act fast.

It seemed to take forever to get to Wolf Cave. Once they finally hefted the awkward load up to the mouth of the cave, everyone dropped to the ground in exhaustion. Except for Andy, of course. "We can't rest too long," Ethan said, catching his breath. "We gotta get everything up and ready before we go home...because I have a feeling the next time we come back here, it might be for good."

"The sooner the better," Austin said.

They wheeled the materials into the cave and immediately went to work. Caleb measured the cave opening precisely and set up a workspace, illuminated by LED lanterns, where he could cut and weld metal pieces to his exact specifications. Austin and Andy helped him with the metalwork, while Glenn kept watch outside the mouth of the cave. Ethan and Annika grabbed their laser rifles and a couple of headlamps and set off to secure the other chambers of the cave. They figured it was a good idea to make sure nothing was lurking behind them while they were busy sealing themselves inside.

Four small, low-lying passageways branched off the main entryway of the cave. The familiar leftmost passageway led to the area they would need to tunnel through to get to the secret shaft of the research facility. The other three they planned to seal up right away, as soon as Ethan and Annika were finished with their reconnaissance duties and gave the all-clear.

∽

The scout and sniper moved about as swiftly below ground as they did above it. Barely an hour had passed, and they were already deep into the third passageway. Their eyes and headlamps probed every nook and cranny meticulously, and they clutched their rifles tightly, ready for anything at any time.

They were approaching the end of the line when Annika suddenly paused. She held her arm out to stop Ethan. "Shhh," she hissed quietly, then focused her headlamp on a two-inch crack in the cave wall and moved in for a closer look. She shined her light beam directly into the dark space, leaned forward until she was only inches away, and peered inside. Annika flinched when a salamander slithered quickly out of the crevice and up the cave wall. She breathed a sigh of relief and smiled. "Unless that's a robot salamander, I think we're okay."

Ethan laughed a little, then he looked confused. "Wait… How did you know something was in there?"

"I heard it moving around. Pitter-patter of little salamander feet."

"You *heard it*?" Ethan asked in awe.

"Yeah," Annika responded nonchalantly. "I pretty much have dog ears."

"I guess," Ethan said, grinning.

"Well, this chamber is all-clear," Annika said. "We should probably get back."

Annika turned and led the two of them back the way they had come. Before she had gone ten feet, the idea that had been swirling in Ethan's mind the last few hours came bursting out. "Annika, what was it you said to Zeke…when we were out in the alley by Judy's Diner?"

Annika kept walking, though her pace slowed. "Oh, I just told him he needed to have a look at someone else's laser gun. He wanted to see mine, but you know how I am. Never gonna let my weapon outta my sight with all that's happened. Not even for the Mitchell brothers."

That was not the answer Ethan was looking for. He decided to try again, fumbling some words as he spoke. "Right, uh, yeah…but, no, the other thing you said."

"Hmm, I couldn't be sure exactly what I said," Annika answered. Ethan could only see her face at an odd angle from behind, illuminated by a wavering headlamp beam, but he thought he could make out the crook of a smile on her face. He wasn't sure, though. It was equal parts exhilaration and torture.

"I'm not sure, but I think Zeke said something kinda like…" Then Ethan repeated word for word what Zeke had said to her: "I can appreciate that in a girl. You know if you were a couple years older, I—" Ethan paused and took a jittery breath. "Then you said something, or I thought you might have said something back to him."

"Hmm…Nothing rings a bell," Annika replied. "So hard to remember."

Torture! Ethan thought. *Just. Stop. Talking. You're sounding like a desperate, pathetic loser.* Ethan steadied himself and tried to manufacture some composure. He stood up straight and proud, determined to let the subject drop like a man with some self-respect. *Let it go and play it cool, Ethan.* Then his next words climbed out of his mouth like convicts escaping a prison—hesitant but eager, scared but thrilled. The words were totally out of his control when he spoke. "You said, 'Whoa, I'm gonna stop ya right there, buddy,'" Ethan paused, afraid he'd swallowed his tongue before he continued, "'I'm already—'"

"Taken," Annika finished as she turned around to look at him. Ethan froze in his tracks. He felt tingly, dizzy, lightheaded. He desperately hoped it didn't show.

"Taken…Oh, yeah, that's right. That's what you said. Hmm…interesting," Ethan said, trying to play it down. But he prayed that Annika would have mercy and just tell him who it was straightaway.

"Yeah, it's a funny thing too," Annika said. "Bradley Wuddle's been growing on me lately. He's just misunderstood, I think…Annika Wuddle. Has a nice ring to it, don't you think?"

Ethan was completely speechless. His mouth opened to

say something, though he had no idea at all what was going to come out. Eventually, he uttered a grunt. No words, just a confused, caveman-like grunt.

Annika flashed a smile and decided to let him off the hook. "You *have* to know I'm kidding, Ethan," she said firmly. "And you should also know, if we survive this again, *and that's a really big if*, I'm taking you to that stupid eighth-grade fall dance whether you like it or not."

Ethan's heart skipped a beat, then he smiled like a fool in the beam of Annika's headlamp. "I'd like it," he blurted. He took a deep breath, then his goofy smile shifted to one that was bittersweet. "Well then, I guess we have to succeed. Not saving the world would be bad enough, but even worse if I knew I missed that first dance with you."

Annika smiled tenderly. In the light of Ethan's headlamp, her eyes were getting teary. She kissed Ethan on the cheek. "Yeah...I feel sorry for those machines now."

"Me too," Ethan added. His knees were still wobbly from the kiss.

Annika stiffened her face and forced away any lingering tears. "Back to work," she said, projecting strength.

Ethan nodded, also forcing himself to be strong. "Back to work."

∽

When Ethan and Annika returned to the main entryway of the cave, sparks were flying around everywhere from Caleb's metalwork. He took a break when he saw them, turned off his torch, and raised his welding goggles to his forehead. "All clear in there, I take it?" he asked.

"Yeah," Ethan answered. "We're ready to seal them off. We

didn't see a way they could get in here from behind, but the safer, the better."

"Copy that," Annika added. Then she scanned the wide-open mouth of the cave with troubled eyes. "But if they come, they're gonna come from the front. We gotta wall up that giant hole, and fast…Camouflage it too."

"Right," Ethan said. "The wall needs to look like it's a part of the cave itself."

Caleb smiled and said, "I love it when we think alike." He unzipped a duffel bag and revealed several spray paint cans and assorted epoxy glues. Ethan nodded and returned a smile.

Austin surveyed the supplies with a grin. "Arts and crafts time…Awesome."

"How's it looking out there, Glenn?" Annika asked.

Glenn turned around from his sentry duty. "All-clear. Haven't seen a thing…I'd say we owe the Mitchell brothers one, that's for sure. All the machines are probably swarming southeast Copper Creek by now."

Ethan nodded solemnly. "Yeah, we gotta make this time count. No more resting now. Let's seal up those passageways and get that front wall in place."

The team sealed the three smaller openings inside the cave with slabs of scrap metal. They drilled holes through the metal and deep into the limestone cave wall, then anchored the slabs to the wall with some steel rebar they had scavenged from the Bravo Fort. These metal patches didn't have to look good, so long as they were strong and served the purpose of ensuring that nothing was able to sneak up on them while they worked. But everyone knew the real danger would be coming from the front, through that inviting, gaping hole in the mouth of the cave.

They began on the front wall by painting a metal slab a grayish color that best matched the surrounding limestone rock. But it wasn't until they had drilled and anchored the fitted metal slab over the mouth of the cave that the real artistry began. With Annika keeping a lookout, the group went to work breaking off pieces of limestone from the entrance of the cave and strategically gluing them to the metal wall. They took great care in making sure that every piece blended seamlessly with the rock next to it. Austin took the lead on the sculpting project, and his attention to detail was remarkable. Ethan remembered him talking once about how he'd rather be an artist than a soldier. He thought it was a shame that General Turnbull never cared to know about his son's aptitude for art, because Austin was incredible at it. Ethan watched in amazement as Austin quickly transformed a metal slab into something that could pass for a limestone wall, with hardly any indication there was a cave behind it.

Caleb had to put a small hinged hatch at the bottom right side of the wall, just enough to crawl through, and a few slits in the wall to see by and point rifles from if necessary. But Austin figured out ways of hiding those areas pretty well, too. He pulverized some limestone with a sledgehammer and covered the door hinge with the dust, and he made the lookout slits appear like natural cracks in the rocks. The setup wasn't perfect, though. If someone got really close to the wall and shined a powerful light into the cracks that served as lookout slits, then it would be possible to tell that the wall was fake. Also, if someone knocked hard on the wall, the hollow, tinny sound would give them away. But all of those things required suspicion in the first place, and suspicion usually begins at a distance. And from a distance, the manufactured cave wall was just about perfect.

When the team stared at the finished product, they knew they had created a masterpiece. They just hoped their artistic illusion would buy them enough time to tunnel through twelve feet of limestone without being discovered.

CHAPTER 35

A NEW PLAN

When Annika assumed her new guard post behind the front wall in the cave, she had to remind herself that this was only a temporary situation to keep from going crazy. Their new cave fort was ingenious, but it was not without flaws, and none of them were going to be fixed under the circumstances. To Annika's mind, the view from the slits that Caleb had cut into the metal wall was far too narrow, and the angle from which to fire their guns was cramped. Then there was the issue of elevation. Annika was always used to having the high ground, along with her choice of firing angles, but she knew those days were over while holding this fort. Caleb couldn't widen or extend the slits in the metal any more, or it would be easy to tell from the outside that the cave wall they had constructed was a fake. And mother nature didn't often grant caves the high ground. This fort was meant for stealth, not firepower and optimal tactics, and she would just have to get used to that.

Ethan could see the stress on Annika's face as he watched her peer out the lookout slit in the wall. He smiled despite himself. "Annika, we're taking the stuff to the back chamber. Why don't you come with us? Give yourself a break."

Annika shot Ethan a scowl. "And leave the front unguarded?"

"Yeah," Ethan answered. "The wall looks great. And no one's gonna come yet, anyway. They're probably still searching way out on Copper Creek."

Ethan's words did nothing to de-stress Annika. She ran her fingers through her hair tightly and drew a tense breath. "You do realize we barely have a sixty-degree viewing angle on the outside, right? And that our rifles' range from those slits is as bad as that cheap carnival game where you shoot the plastic ducks?"

"I know. You're right," Ethan said. Then he added with a playful smile, "But I've seen you shoot at the fair…and it wasn't right what you did to those ducks."

Annika released her strawberry-blonde hair from her grip. She looked at Ethan, returning the smile with an impish twinkle in her eye. "Yeah, that is true," she said, chuckling a little.

"So will you come with us?"

Annika nodded. "Yeah, okay…Sorry."

"Don't be sorry," Ethan said quickly. "Every team needs an Annika. The fact I know the machines don't gives me hope… like we have an advantage."

Annika flashed a slight, bashful grin. "Thanks…I feel the same way about you."

"Thanks," Ethan replied, then he quickly changed the topic because he could feel himself starting to smile like a doofus. "We better catch up with the others."

☙

The team hauled all the supplies they had to the large back chamber where the excavation to the secret tunnel was going to take place. Through headlamps and flashlights, everyone stared in awe at the massive chunk of limestone they were going to have to dig through. Twelve feet of it, at least, if Andy's calculations were correct. It made all of them tired just looking at it. Even Andy, almost.

"Any idea how long this might take?" Austin asked, looking at Caleb.

"Seeing as I've never broken rock on a chain gang, I'm not quite sure," Caleb joked.

"I can work around the clock," Andy offered. "Still not sure how long it will take, but that should help."

"Thank you, Andy," Ethan said. "And don't worry, you'll be safe here."

"Yeah, much better in here than in town," Glenn added. "I don't know about you guys, but my parents are getting weirder every time I see them."

Everyone else nodded in agreement.

Andy stared at them with worried eyes. "Are you guys in danger at home?"

"Last night I thought I'd have to shoot robot mom and dad through the bedsheets," Ethan said with a grim face illuminated by headlamp beams. "Every night gets worse. I don't think they need us anymore to pretend everything is okay. Soon the night will come when they try to kill us. I'm hoping we're safe in here, close to breaking into that secret tunnel when it does. But if not, we should have a plan."

"What are you thinking?" Glenn asked.

"We should only fire our weapons if we absolutely have to, only when we feel our lives are in danger," Ethan replied.

"But if it comes to that, we'll need to let each other know. 'Cause there's no going back then, no pretending everything's all right."

"We can use channel eight on the walkie-talkies," Annika said. "And use some sort of codeword."

"Algebra and geometry," Ethan said. "Innocent enough codewords. *Algebra* means we had to kill our robot parents. And *geometry* means we think they're about to kill us. As soon as we hear either of those words, we rush to that person's house as fast as we can. Just say, *I need help with algebra or geometry* and help will be on the way…But we gotta make sure we keep our walkie-talkies close at all times."

"What about me?" Caleb asked.

Ethan looked confused. "What do you mean?"

"*Really?* I have to say I need help with algebra or geometry?…Who would believe that?"

The group chuckled at the thought of it. "All right, Caleb," Ethan said through a grin. "You can say gym class or art."

"Thank you," Caleb said, relieved. "That's much more believable."

Ethan was still smiling over his exchange with Caleb when he slapped the limestone wall that they would have to dig through. Slowly, Ethan's smile evaporated as he stared at the monolithic slab of rock. He began to shake his head in frustration. "We can't go through all of this every time the fatal error happens. What if the military never learns? We'll be doing this over and over again, and that's if we're really lucky…No, we need a new plan." Ethan stared at the limestone wall for a long moment, then turned around with a spring in his step. "Andy, I'd like you to read that Skulley's mind again, the one we have buried here in the cave."

"Sure, Ethan," Andy replied. "What do you want me to look for?"

"I want you to try to find when and where the Zyvantian pod landed on earth. We'll need the exact time and exact location."

"That information was not in any of the Skulleys," Andy said. Ethan's face dropped in disappointment. "But *I* know the answer."

Ethan quickly perked up, but he looked confused. "You do?…How?"

"Your dad told me," Andy answered. "He said he thought I had a right to know about my origin, about the technology that made my life possible. Those were his exact words."

Ethan nodded thoughtfully. The group stared curiously at Ethan for a moment, but they quickly realized his purpose. Annika's eyes focused in determination. "We have to go back to where this all began," she said.

"That's right," Ethan replied. "It's the only way to end this. We have to destroy that pod or remove the virus somehow. We might not get another chance like this. We gotta make it count. If we're going to go back in time and stop the fatal error, let's do it for good."

Everyone nodded in agreement, then Andy said, "The pod landed at coordinates forty-seven degrees, two minutes, thirty seconds north; and one-hundred twenty-two degrees, one minute, five seconds south. And it happened on July second at one thirty-five and seven seconds a.m. in the year 1999."

"July second, 1999," Ethan repeated dazedly. "Can you tell us where those coordinates are?"

"Yes," Andy answered. "Just six miles outside a small town

called Pebbyville in Washington state. It's about fifty miles southeast of Tacoma."

"And how far away is that from here?" Ethan asked.

"Nine hundred and fifty miles, by road."

"That's a long trip," Glenn said.

"Yeah, and I'm pretty sure we won't be the only ones looking for that pod," Austin added. "McChord Air Force Base operates out of Tacoma. When that pod goes down, they'll know about it, and they'll want it for themselves. Pretty sure that's how the military got it in the first place, through McChord."

"And it's not just the military we'll have to worry about," Annika said with a grim face. "The machines will figure out what we're up to. They'll send someone back in time to try to stop us from getting that pod."

"Then we gotta get there first," Ethan said. "Caleb, when we go through the Chrono-Warp, is there any way we can get closer to Pebbyville than Blackwoods?"

"I don't know. The last time we went through, we were in a bit of a hurry, and I just followed the instructions. But I'll take a look at the documents on it, see what I can figure out."

"Good…and in case tonight is the last time we get to go back to our houses, we'll need to make sure we have everything we need for our road trip…Clothes, food, water, blankets, and as much money as we can scrape together. And remember, all of our money has to be from the year 1999 or earlier. Same for our clothes, something that could've been worn back then. We can't have anything on us that makes us seem strange or out of place. Six kids traveling alone is gonna look suspicious enough."

The team headed back toward the entrance of the cave.

Andy decided to walk with them, even though he would be heading straight back inside when the others left for home. He dreaded the night of digging that lay ahead, not for the labor but the solitude.

"So what did people wear back in 1999?" Glenn asked. "What if I can't find any overalls or suspenders?"

Annika laughed. "You're thinking of the Amish, Glenn… Just wear jeans and any shirts without references to the future and you'll be fine."

Everyone laughed for a moment. Then, all of a sudden, a rumble shook the cave all around them, silencing the humor and jolting them all. "What was that?" Glenn asked, staring worriedly at the top of the cave and praying it wouldn't come crashing down.

"I have no idea," Caleb answered.

"I hate when you say that," Austin muttered.

CHAPTER 36

ROCKETS' RED GLARE

Everyone rushed outside the cave to see if they could figure out what was going on. The vibration was less intense now, but they could hear the sound better—a powerful roar that was coming from above. They looked up through the pine trees and found a massive rocket taking flight. Intense orange-yellow flames blasted from the nozzle, leaving a plume of smoke miles behind it as it stretched into the upper atmosphere. The group stared skyward in worry and fear, wondering what exactly the machines had just unleashed upon the world.

"Is it nuclear?" Austin asked with a tight throat.

"I don't think so," Ethan said, though he didn't sound relieved at all. "The machines have access to the best technology Zyvantia had to offer. They could do better than nukes. They'd have a million other ways to get rid of us. And they probably just launched one of them."

"An advanced civilization wouldn't have to destroy our planet to defeat us," Caleb said, his words full of gloom. "It would be so easy for them they wouldn't have to…Good news for the earth and the rest of the animals, just not so much for us."

"So what do you think it is?" Glenn asked. "You've read all the documents in that briefcase. Any ideas?"

Caleb sighed deeply, and his brow furrowed. When he finally relaxed his face, he had a wrinkle between his eyes, under the bridge of his glasses, that was slow to go away. "It appears to be some sort of launch vehicle," he said at last. "If I had to guess, I think they just launched a weaponized satellite into space."

"And what's the weapon?" Austin asked.

Caleb shook his head, eyes fearful. "Your guess is as good as mine."

The smoke contrail from the first rocket was still thick when another rumble shook the ground violently. A deafening roar ripped through the woods, and a second rocket zoomed over the trees and into the blue, sun-soaked sky. As the group watched the orange-yellow inferno spew from the rocket nozzle, they got even more worried. Then when the pattern repeated itself ten more times and a dozen rockets had been fired into space, they wondered if they would even have a second chance to fix things. That limestone rock they had to get through was so thick, and time was not on their side.

Just after the twelfth rocket had been launched, a salvo of bright crimson lasers pierced the sky from the research facility. Ethan and the others climbed up to the top of the cave ridge and peered through an opening in the trees. "What were they shooting at?" Annika asked. "I don't see anything."

Ethan grabbed a pair of binoculars from his backpack and took a look. But he could see nothing. Then a couple of minutes passed, and the fireballs became visible to the naked eye. Twenty tiny balls of flame in total, far away still, hurtling toward the earth on a chaotic course.

"Ethan, what are those?" Annika asked. Her jittery, uneasy voice and her soft, wide eyes suggested she had a decent guess.

"I think they're planes," Ethan said. "Probably bombers that set off for the research facility once those rockets were launched."

"It's official now," Austin said grimly. "The world is at war."

"But we still have to pretend like we don't know anything's happened," Ethan said. "Kids in town will just assume it's military war games. And we will too. Just for a little while longer, until we're sure we got everything we need to move on with our plan."

"And what about our wonderful robot parents?" Austin asked. "If the war is on now, won't they just try to kill us as soon as we walk through the front door?"

"They might, and we have to be ready for that," Ethan answered. "But as far as they know, we pose no threat at all to them. I hope, for at least one more night, that they have better things to do than kill some harmless kids." Ethan paused, then took a deep breath. "We have to go back and get more supplies. Even if we could manage everything else, we only have one sledgehammer and one pickaxe. We gotta find more… And we promised the Mitchell brothers we'd let them in on the plan. We can't abandon them after what they did for us."

"I agree," Glenn said firmly. "I believe a promise should mean something."

Austin nodded thoughtfully. "Yeah…But we better all be listening carefully tonight for anyone needing help with math."

"Or gym class or art," Caleb added.

"Or gym class or art," Austin repeated through a crack of a smile.

Their plans made, Andy trudged back into Wolf Cave for a lonely night of digging, while the rest of the group walked back into town to face their parents for hopefully the last time.

CHAPTER 37

THE WORLD NEWS

When the team arrived back in town, they couldn't help but notice a nervous buzz in the air. Every kid they passed was either talking about the rockets and lasers that had been fired from the research facility, or about how their parents were looking sick and acting strangely. The group knew things in Blackwoods had to be even worse now. And the fact that they hadn't seen the Mitchell brothers, who were no doubt very eager to find them, was a bad sign.

The group stopped at Ethan's house first. They hadn't seen any adults in town yet, but they could almost feel their presence in the houses. The hairs on the backs of their necks tingled as they thought about going home and finding their parents waiting for them. Ethan hesitated at the walkway to his house. No one wanted to take another step in any direction other than toward the safe confines of Wolf Cave. They envied Andy. Even though he was toiling away alone in a dark cavern breaking rock, it was infinitely better than where they were going. They knew there was an unprecedented evil waiting for them in their homes. It was a kind of evil that humans had never known before—a superior intelligence with no regard for life. It was a sneaky, plotting, always clever, and sometimes charming evil. It was the kind that fixes you dinner and tucks you into bed, all the while wishing you were dead. And everyone in the group knew all too well that those soulless entities were chomping at the bit to make their wishes come true.

"One more night," Ethan said, his voice strong, though he was staring at his house with eyes full of dread. "We gotta survive one more night. Then tomorrow we'll take all our supplies and the Mitchell brothers to Wolf Cave and never come back."

"One more night," Austin repeated. Then everyone else echoed the same refrain.

"Good luck…and be careful," Ethan said solemnly to his team. His eyes left Annika last as he walked up to his house and went inside.

Ethan found the house disturbingly quiet when he entered the foyer. There wasn't the slightest creak, crack, or rustle anywhere. He thought he might've been alone in the house until two shapes caught the corner of his eye: his parental impostors had moved with ghostly stealth into the living room. They were waiting for Ethan to come in, staring at him with those familiar soulless eyes, though their faces were very different now. Ethan couldn't tell exactly how their faces had changed, just that they had somehow. It was late in the day with the sun low on the horizon, and the only light in the room was what had filtered in through drawn window shades, making it hard to see the details of faces at a distance.

Ethan walked slowly into the room to meet them. He

tried to walk normally, but he felt like he was stepping lightly and cautiously, like a soldier making his way through a minefield. Before he got too close, he reached behind his back to be sure of the laser weapon he had tucked into the waistband of his jeans. Then he withdrew his hand subtly.

When Ethan finally saw his parents' faces clearly, he couldn't believe his eyes. It was as if their heads had been run through a shrink-wrap machine. Their skin was paper-thin now, pale white, and recessed into the sinkhole-like contours of their faces. Their skulls underneath were painfully visible, as a human's would look if gravely ill, and the machines didn't seem to care a bit. It was like they were just letting their synthetic flesh melt away. A metamorphosis. A signal of a new dawn.

Ethan badly wanted to look away, but he was determined to try to pretend that everything was okay. *One more night*, he kept thinking to himself. Then he got to thinking about Annika. She wasn't the kind of girl who needed help very often, but this situation was far worse than he had imagined when he decided that they should come back into town. As he stared at his robot parents, with their black metal skulls on the verge of poking through the skin at any minute, Ethan knew everyone on Team Blackwoods would be in grave danger tonight. He would've gladly given his right arm to be beside Annika to protect her now. For them to protect each other.

"Dinner will be in an hour," his mother said in a flat tone.

Ethan nodded, and a cold tremor rolled up his spine like an arctic tsunami. His parents left without another word.

Exactly an hour later, Ethan was sitting at the kitchen table with the monsters posing as his parents. They had made one of his favorite meals, fettuccine Alfredo with garlic bread, and it smelled perfect. Too perfect. Ethan couldn't help but feel like an inmate on his last night on death row, being catered to with one last scrumptious meal before the Grim Reaper paid a visit. If that thought alone wasn't enough to give him a queasy stomach, then staring at his parents' faces under the kitchen lights would surely do the trick. Their faces were grotesque. They looked like death themselves. No human could ever look so sick and still be alive. Ethan had to fight his nervous stomach for every strand of fettuccine he ate, but knew this might be the last good meal he was going to have for a while and that he should keep his strength up.

Despite the obstacles, Ethan managed to finish everything on his plate. He had tried not to look up much during the meal, only enough to maintain his guard. But now that he was done eating, there was no excuse to avoid them. Ethan raised his head, and their bleak eyes fixed on him instantly. The tingly numbness in his spine was only getting worse, bordering on paralysis.

"Thank you for dinner," Ethan said. He knew the charade was at its end, and that his words were ridiculous, but he figured being polite couldn't hurt. He just needed to make it through one more night. *One more night.*

"You are very welcome," his mother said.

"May I go watch television?" Ethan asked, his manners perfect.

"You cannot," his father answered. "I'm afraid it isn't working."

Ethan knew exactly what that meant—World War Three

was underway. "Oh, okay. Then may I go upstairs? I have some homework. I know it's a Saturday night, but I have a feeling I'm going to need some extra help with algebra...or geometry."

"Sure, honey," his mother said.

That last word almost made Ethan lose every bit of pasta he'd struggled so hard to get down. "Thanks," he said, forcing a smile. "Goodnight."

"Goodnight," his mother and father said in perfect unison. Then they smiled. They looked like two corpses smiling. Ethan felt as if he had just stepped into a freezer. His skin nothing but goose bumps, his spine nothing but linked cubes of ice. He backed away slowly, politely, then he headed for the solace of his room, though he knew it wouldn't offer much.

At nine o'clock, Ethan was disappointed, though not surprised, when the diesel buses never came to take the adults to the research facility. It wasn't necessary now. The machines had already put their plan for this planet into motion. They were playing their chess match with the humans on the chessboard of Earth, and the endgame would surely be an ugly one for the home team.

Ethan desperately wanted to go downstairs to check the video of the news channel he had recorded, though his parents being in the house made that a dangerous proposition. He thought about playing it safe and staying in his room, but his curiosity about what was happening in the outside world was killing him. He waited until midnight, long after he'd heard the last bit of stirring in the house, then he slipped out of his room and slinked his way downstairs.

With his laser weapon firmly in one hand, Ethan picked up the remote control in the other and turned on the television in the living room. The flickering glow from the static white noise on the screen was the only light in the room. The cable wasn't working now, but Ethan was pretty sure the recordings he'd set, before the signal was knocked out, should still be saved. He sat right in front of the television, turned the volume down low, and activated the digital recorder. Then he leaned forward, tense and stiff as a board, and watched the television while keeping his ears on alert for intruders from above.

The first recorded story on the news channel was about the president's visit to the Middle East for peace talks. Ethan took a moment to look behind him and listen carefully for noises upstairs, then he fast-forwarded to the next story. This pattern repeated itself for the next several news stories—the Pope's visit to France, a tornado in Texas, the passing of an old movie star, and the human-interest story of a cat who was supposedly really good at playing poker. Then, finally, the news story that Ethan was dreading engulfed the channel…

The story started out with a view of the Washington DC National Mall—a two-mile stretch of land in the middle of the nation's capital filled with monuments, memorials, and museums dedicated to the struggles, sacrifices, and triumphs of Americans throughout history. Lush green grass and reflecting pools adorned the park, which was a favorite of tourists and locals alike.

It was a beautiful sunny day, and many tourists were enjoying the sights. A journalist and her camera crew were broadcasting from the steps of the Lincoln Memorial, reporting on a political rally that had taken place earlier. All of a sudden, something captured the journalist's attention, and she abruptly stopped her report. Her eyes widened as she stared past her camera crew and gazed into the lawn surrounding the Washington Monument.

"What is that over there?" the journalist asked her crew in awe.

The camera crew turned around and began filming the area. A massive, shimmering neon blue bubble was forming on the west side of the Washington Monument. The bubble floated just a few feet above the ground, and it was growing rapidly in size. It was a good hundred yards in diameter when it became apparent that things were moving around inside it. Then another bubble, three times its size, began to spawn in the area, though this time about five hundred feet up in the air. Once again, things jostled around inside, like a spider egg sack that was chock-full and ready to burst open.

Finally the bubbles popped, and a new reality was let loose upon the earth. Thousands of Skulleys and mechanical spiders spewed forth from the lower bubble, and dozens of sleek, black, disc-like airships screamed across the sky out of the upper one. The machines fired madly at anything with a pulse. Lasers streaked through the air everywhere; there was nowhere to hide. Visitors to the National Mall were killed almost instantly, their last moments spent in utter confusion and terror.

When all the humans in sight were dead, the machines turned their firepower on the buildings, tearing apart the nation's precious monuments, memorials, and museums. The near-total destruction of the area took all of sixty seconds, then the horde of machines broke off into two units. One unit stormed due east toward the Capitol Building, while the other rampaged north toward the White House.

Secret Service and Capitol Police stood their ground, but they were overwhelmed like a row of ants trying to stop an elephant stampede. The Skulleys and spiders invaded the residence of the president and made it their own in minutes. Same thing for the Capitol Building; the machines would be making the laws now. The disc-shaped airships continued to bombard the nation's capital from above, and soon nothing was left of the venerable town. As a final insult to the country, and its first president, the airships destroyed the five-hundred-and-fifty-five-foot tall granite and marble Washington Monument. The sturdy, eighty-thousand-ton obelisk crumbled to the ground as if it were made of overcooked toast.

As Washington DC lay in ruins, a belated counterattack came from the United States Air Force. Five squadrons of F-35 fighter jets—nearly one-hundred planes—streaked across the sky at supersonic speed toward the nation's capital. Just as they were about to fire on the machines, an ungodly and unnatural storm of lighting zapped them from the sky. As Ethan watched in horror, he knew the source of those jagged bolts of destruction—the satellites that the machines had launched earlier that day. None of the military's jets even had a chance to get a shot off before they were wiped off the face of the earth. Ashen fireballs that were once plane and pilot flurried to the ground.

The journalist and her camera crew were still doing their duty, filming the hellish scene with a trembling camera as they hid behind a pile of rubble that used to be the Lincoln Memorial. The four of them knew there was no way they were getting out of this alive. Skulleys and spiders were everywhere, busily scavenging for any stray humans that might still be breathing. And when they found those poor souls, they finished them off quickly, granting them the same afterthought as squished bugs. The news crew tried to muffle their cries of sorrow and shock, though they could easily be heard on the television broadcast. When the Skulleys finally spotted them, they charged instantly, eyes blazing as red as their lasers. The news crew left this world bravely, filming their own murderers in the act. As death came for them, they only wished that some justice might find their attackers. But as they took in their last sights and witnessed the absolute carnage around them, they doubted very much that it would.

The broadcast cut out from the Washington DC National Mall, and the news channel went back to its regular anchorperson in the studio. A man with red, teary eyes and a face devoid of all hope sat behind the news desk.

"These reports are coming in from all over the globe," the anchorperson said. "Several major cities and military installations have already been destroyed or are currently under siege. Millions of people have died, and we still have no idea what these things are or where they came from. All we do know is that they show no signs of stopping, and all attempts to communicate or reason with the aggressors have been useless."

The lights flickered off and on in the news studio. Piercing, panicked screams off-camera filled the air. The anchorperson continued as calmly as he could: "We will continue to broadcast as long as we're able. If you have a place to hide, go there now. Do not attempt to fight back. Just hide. The military has yet to find any weaknesses in this enemy…May God help us all."

The lights in the studio flickered off and on again, then went off entirely and for good. Blood-red crimson eyes provided the only light now, and the Skulleys' advance almost resembled a victory dance in the hateful glow. The sound in the studio was the last thing to go—bone-chilling shrieks—until the broadcast cut out completely. The television in Ethan's living room reverted to static white noise.

Ethan turned off the television and video recorder. His jittery hand tried to set the remote control down in precisely the same location that he'd found it. Then he sat for a moment on the floor in the darkness. His thoughts were swirling around like a cyclone in his head. He couldn't get the horrible images from the news channel out of his mind. Ethan thought about the Washington Monument and how easily the tribute to the nation's first president and leader of the Continental Army had crumbled. Then he had an even more sobering thought: *The machines were so advanced they wouldn't even feel the difference between the full force of the United States' modern military and George Washington's Continental Army two hundred and fifty years before it. Missiles or muskets, it wouldn't matter either way... Team Blackwoods was the world's only hope now.*

As Ethan went up to bed, an old bit of advice from his dad echoed in his head: "When battling a machine, never try to think like the best machine...try to think like the best human."

For some reason, those words brought him a measure of strength.

CHAPTER 38

NIGHT VISITORS

Ethan must've been exhausted and in a very deep sleep because he didn't hear a thing when his parents entered the room. He opened his eyes and found them just beyond the foot of his bed, their bodies faintly lit by some moonlight that was seeping in through the window blinds. They didn't move an inch; they just stood there, motionless, staring at their beloved son. Ethan's heart instantly jumped to his throat when he saw them, then his heart made another jump when he came to a horrifying realization: *I know I locked my door... They must've broken in.*

Ethan knew they could see he was awake. He slowly reached for his laser weapon, but it wasn't in its usual spot. He began to move his hand ever so slightly under the bedsheets to try to find it, slow arcs back and forth that he hoped they wouldn't notice. But it didn't take him long to realize that his only lifeline wasn't there. At this point, he was just hoping he had knocked it out of bed in his sleep and that it was on the floor somewhere. The alternative was much worse. If his mechanical parents had found it, he was a dead man. Ethan had to locate that laser weapon, and fast. He leaned up a little and engaged in the most awkward, yet critical, chit-chat of his life.

"Is everything all right?" Ethan asked, playing dumb as he never had before.

There was no response. They took a couple of steps closer to him and stopped, about eight feet away now. Ethan could see for the first time that the one posing as his father had something in his hand. It was hard to tell, but it looked roughly the size of his laser weapon. Ethan's heart sank, and he could feel the end of his young life wrapping around him like a cold blanket. A few memories kept him warm, though, flashing through his mind as fast as the neurons in his brain could fire. They were the good times with his parents, talking and laughing at the dinner table, especially before military secrets and adolescence conspired to complicate things. Then there were all the shenanigans with Caleb, plotting to take over the world one sleepover at a time. Finally, there was Annika. Somewhere in the chill he was feeling now, she was a sunspot, dancing with him at an eighth-grade dance in some alternate universe that would never happen here.

The mechanical Mr. Tate raised the object in his hand. Ethan cringed. Then his father asked, "Were you trying to watch television?"

Ethan realized that the object was the remote control for the television and not his laser weapon. He had tried to put it back in its original spot as best he could, but the machines had the capability of noticing the slightest deviations. He knew his robotic parents had probably figured out that he had watched the news report. He also knew they were probably in there to kill him. The situation was bleak, but it was still better than Ethan had figured it to be a moment ago. His weapon was on the floor somewhere. And that gave him some hope.

Ethan sat up in his bed so that he had a decent view of the floor around him. He knew he needed to buy himself some time to look, so he took to answering the question his fake father had asked with long, ridiculous, rambling sentences. "Oh, yeah. I know you said the TV wasn't working, but I thought I could adjust the, you know, the control buttons just right on the modulator functions and find the signal. There was an input button that I thought was toggling wrong and switching everything around, so when I toggled it back, I thought I had it, but then it went off again…" Ethan kept spewing the word vomit as he scoured the floor for his weapon. But it was just too dark. He couldn't find it.

"*Shhhhh,*" Ethan's robotic father hissed softly and chillingly. Then his parents stepped even closer. They were about close enough to touch if he leaned forward and stretched an arm out. Seeing them at that distance froze Ethan instantly. His entire body tingled with dread. In the dim, uneven moonlight in the room, he noticed something about their appearance. Their heads were different now. They had no hair. There was no more pale skin either, only dark faces, except for the occasional gleam to their cheeks when the moonlight hit them just right. Ethan knew that he was in the room with two Skulleys, and that their skin, along with their desire to pretend to be his parents, had melted away completely.

"I have a question for you, Ethan," the machine continued in a voice that no longer sounded anything like Ethan's dad's voice. It didn't even sound remotely human. It was full of vibration and sounded very robotic, except that there was a certain strange tone to it. There was a slightly taunting, sarcastic edge to the machine's words when it asked, "What *did* you want to be when you grow up?"

The moonlight caught the machines' impossibly wide smiles.

Ethan's ears prickled and he stopped breathing when he heard those words and saw their toothy, glistening, grotesque grins. *What* did *I want to be?* The question echoed eerily in his head. *Past tense.* Ethan sprung out of his bed and slipped under the grasp of the machines, whose eyes were blazing red now. He ducked down and ran for the hallway, as a round of lasers narrowly missed him and peppered the walls with fiery holes.

The Skulleys stormed after him, gears squealing and weapons drawn, crimson eyes piercing the darkness of the house. Ethan flipped on a panel of houselights and bolted down the stairs, skipping several at a time, but when he made it to the foyer, one of the Skulleys had jumped down ahead of him, blocking him from the door. Ethan turned and sprinted into the living room, thinking of getting to the kitchen and leaving through the back door. But the other Skulley cut him off there, too. With enough adrenaline pumping through his body to lift an elephant, Ethan dove over a large oak dining table and used it for cover. Lasers whizzed through the air and tore through the thick wooden table like it was made of a single sheet of paper, but Ethan didn't plan on staying behind there for long. He just needed a few moments, long enough to try one last thing.

Then there was a pause in the machines' laser assault. Ethan's mechanical father stood blocking the foyer and any escape through the front door. His sweet mechanical mother held her post in the kitchen, blockading a possible retreat through the back.

"So, son…what *did* you want to be when you grow up?" his robot father asked again, a final tease before delivering the death blow.

Ethan grabbed one of his parents' decorative snow globes from a shelf behind the oak table. He remembered the last time he'd chucked a snow globe at a machine—when he and Annika fought that stubby robot the first time the fatal error happened. He'd had pretty good luck then, but this was an entirely different situation. Annika wasn't here now with a Taser gun to overload the machine with fifty-thousand volts when the snow globe hit. All it would be now is glass, water, and bits of plastic snow, though it could be enough of a distraction to get back upstairs, to find the laser weapon that had to be somewhere by the bed. But Ethan knew the odds of throwing a perfect strike were so very slim.

"What *did* I want to be when I grow up?" Ethan repeated, buying time.

"Yes, do tell us," the machine sneered.

Ethan looked down at the globe and for the first time saw what it was. He would've laughed if he had the time. The snow globe was of Washington DC, and in its center sat the Washington Monument. Ethan knew either way, in liberty or death, that his effort would at least be ironic. He looked at the shiny sphere one last time and said, "This is for you, George."

Ethan stood up, holding the snow globe behind his back. He stepped lightly around the dining table and faced his fabricated father. "You know what I really always wanted to be?"

The Skulley blocking the foyer tilted its head, much like a human would, awaiting a reply with interest. "Oh, please tell me, son."

"A major league pitcher."

Ethan cocked his arm back and hurled the snow globe at the Skulley with everything he had, just as the machine fired its weapon at him. A laser missed Ethan's face by three inches, but the snow globe hit its mark perfectly. The glass, water-filled sphere smashed violently across the face of the Skulley. The machine stumbled back a little and lowered its weapon. Ethan dashed around him and bounded upstairs.

Ethan tore into his room, slammed and locked the door behind him, then flipped on the lights. He dropped to his knees and scrambled around on the floor, desperately looking for his laser weapon. Just as he'd located the weapon under his bed and realized it was far from his reach, he heard thundering footsteps storming closer outside his door. He stretched his arm out and had the laser weapon on his fingertips, trying to roll it back toward him, when the door was smashed off its hinges. The Skulley that was formerly Ethan's surrogate mother stepped forward. It belted out a terrible, horrific screech, and its crimson eyes blazed furiously as it raised its arm. Ethan watched in horror as the machine's wrist folded down and produced a laser weapon that was trained right at his head. The weapon Ethan was still groping for was rolling in and out of his grasp. By the time he had gripped it firmly enough to pull out, he knew it was too late.

But just as Ethan was poised to meet his maker, a red ray of hope blasted right through the front of the Skulley's head. Someone had shot it from behind. Ethan's first thought was Annika. The Skulley dropped to its knees, then collapsed flat on its stomach in death. It was then that Ethan saw the one-man cavalry standing in the hallway. It was Andy, laser weapon drawn, looking like Doc Holliday at the O.K. Corral. Ethan flashed a broad smile at the sight of him, only for it to be wiped away in an instant. The second Skulley was charging up the stairs and closing in fast. It raised its arm, which was already in weapon mode, and had Andy in its sights.

"Get down!" Ethan screamed.

Andy hit the deck, and Ethan fired a round of shots at the sprinting Skulley. The lasers ripped several holes clear through its head. Its body and laser weapon went totally limp. Ethan's mechanical father managed one last crimson-eyed, hateful glare before it crumpled to the ground. Then those awful blood-red eyes dimmed and dimmed until they went dark entirely.

"Sorry I left the cave," Andy said. "But you said things were getting dangerous, so I had to come."

Ethan looked at Andy and sighed a gigantic breath of relief. "It's okay, Andy. I think I can forgive you," he said with a smile. "Thank you."

"And thank you," Andy replied in kind.

"Did anybody see you on your way over here?" Ethan asked.

"No."

Ethan looked amazed. "How did you get away with that?"

"I can be sneaky like you," Andy said with a mischievous smile.

Ethan returned the smile. "Is that right?...Well, that's good then." He looked over the Skulleys splayed out on the floor. "We'll need to check and see if they sent out a distress signal."

"Okay," Andy said. He placed his hands on the Skulleys' heads. The blue glow only showed for one. "This one did not. The other one is too badly damaged to tell."

Ethan sighed deeply, his face furrowed with stress. "I really don't wanna send out that algebra message if the Skulleys issued a distress call. No use in calling the others over here to put them in more danger, right? Maybe we should wait a few minutes just to be sure."

Andy looked at Ethan with an unsure face. "Ethan, that wasn't the plan. What if the roles were reversed? If Annika was in your position now, would you want her waiting by herself to make sure no other machines came before calling you?"

Ethan's jaw dropped at Andy's stunning insight. He shook his head. "No, I wouldn't."

"Ethan, you know this mission can only work if the entire team stays together."

Ethan nodded. "You're right." Then he paused for a moment before he asked, "Andy, why did you pick Annika as the example?"

Andy cracked a subtle smile. "Oh, no reason."

Ethan blushed a little. After a moment, Ethan turned thoughtful. "Andy, remember when we were in the basement of the wrecked fort, separating the generator cages?"

"Yes," Andy answered.

"You asked me if I ever thought I could think of you as a brother. And I said no. I said we could be friends, but that we would never be brothers…I was so sure about that."

Andy nodded. "I know, Ethan. I know you're sure and that's okay."

Ethan paused, then added, "But I'm not so sure now."

Andy flashed a guarded, grateful smile, but he said no words. It was like he didn't want to chance saying anything that might ruin the moment. Ethan grabbed the walkie-talkie off his bookshelf and pressed the button to talk.

"Ethan here…I'm gonna need some help with algebra."

CHAPTER 39

A PROMISE KEPT

ETHAN TURNED OFF all the lights in the house, so as not to look suspicious being the only one on the block that was lit up at three in the morning. Then he and Andy waited by the windows, alternately looking out the front and the back, hoping to see the rest of Team Blackwoods soon and dearly hoping not to see anything else.

Twenty minutes had passed and still no one had shown up. Ethan began to get worried. He knew it was very possible, sending the algebra help message out in the middle of the night, that the others could still be asleep. He also knew that a million other things could've gone wrong. Time passed torturously, with Ethan working his stomach into knots as he considered all the possibilities.

Finally, a rapping on the back door jolted Ethan. He ran into the kitchen and sneaked a peek through the windowpanes of the door. His eyes squinted, trying to resolve the identity of the figure in the dark. Suddenly, a light beam from a flashlight illuminated the face of the person outside. Ethan flinched at first, then he smiled and sighed in relief. It was Annika, holding the flashlight up under her chin. Ethan swung the door open and she rushed inside. He closed and locked the door immediately.

"My parents came into my room about an hour ago to kill me," Ethan said straightaway. "It's a long story, I'll explain it later, but they're both dead." Ethan focused on Annika in the darkness of the kitchen, with only the blue digital numbers on the stove and microwave shedding light. "So, I'm guessing you sneaked out?"

"Yeah," Annika answered. "Am I the first one here?"

Ethan nodded. "Yeah…Well, sort of."

Annika spotted a shadowy figure in the entryway to the kitchen. She flicked her flashlight on and splashed Andy's face with light. Her eyes narrowed in curiosity. "What's *he* doing here?"

"He's part of the long story," Ethan answered.

∽

Ethan and Andy explained to Annika the events that had occurred over the last hour. Annika shined her flashlight on the dead Skulleys upstairs. "I'm taking it they didn't get a distress signal out?"

"We know that one didn't for sure," Ethan said, pointing to the Skulley that had posed as his mother. "The other one is too damaged for Andy to tell. But it's been over thirty minutes since it died, so I'm guessing it didn't or this place would be crawling with Skulleys."

"That's good," Annika said.

"Yeah," Ethan replied. "But they'll figure out they're offline eventually. We need the others to get here, and fast."

Ethan sent out another "*Help with algebra*" message over

the walkie-talkie. Then he, Annika, and Andy went downstairs to wait and hope for the others to arrive. As they walked through the living room, Annika felt the squish of water and the crunch of debris under her shoes. She aimed her flashlight on the floor and saw the water and the remnants of the obliterated snow globe Ethan had smashed over the Skulley's face.

Annika nodded proudly. "Nice move with the snow globe, Ethan."

"Thanks…Yeah, that was my ticket upstairs."

"Decided not to use Frosty this time?" Annika joked.

"The Frosty the Snowman globe is upstairs."

"Oh, that's right. Well, very impressive. You're pretty good at fighting with snow globes…Better with a snow globe than a laser gun, if you ask me."

Ethan flicked his flashlight on. The beam hit Annika in the face, revealing her sarcastic smile. "That's real funny, Pepper…real funny."

Andy chuckled, which took both Ethan and Annika by surprise. They stared at him for a curious moment until Andy's chuckle became contagious. Suddenly, a soft knock at the back door interrupted the humor. They rushed through the kitchen and peered out the window.

"It's Austin and Caleb," Annika said excitedly. She opened the door and let them in.

"You guys sneak or fight your way out?" Ethan asked.

"Sneaked," Austin answered.

"Sneaked," Caleb echoed, then added, "Thank God."

Ethan got Caleb and Austin up to speed on what had happened and why he issued the help-with-algebra call. He showed them the dead Skulleys and the pieces of snow globe. Then he regaled them with the horror story of how his mechanical parents had tried to kill him, and how he cheated death with the help of a certain boy robot.

"Ethan saved my life too," Andy was quick to point out.

"Yeah," Ethan said. "But you saved mine first."

"We make a pretty good team," Andy said.

Ethan nodded and smiled appreciatively. Caleb cast an odd glance at them, though there wasn't a flashlight beam near enough for anyone to make out his expression.

Annika looked at her watch. Her face tensed. "Glenn should've been here by now. We need to go check on him."

"All right," Ethan said. "Annika and I will—" Ethan abruptly stopped talking. The crackle of the walkie-talkie clipped to his jeans pocket interrupted him. He picked it up and listened. A desperate and nervous voice broke through the static…

"Glenn here…I'm sorry. I won't be able to help you with algebra." Glenn's words were jittery and hushed, full of sadness, fear, and remorse, but they were also duty-bound. "And whatever you do, *do not* try to help me with my geometry. It's my own fault, and your assignment is all that matters now." Then there was a long pause, followed by the sound of a faint sniffle, like he was trying to muffle it. "The best thing in my life was being a part of this team. But a promise is a promise. I'm so sorry…I love you guys. Good luck."

"Glenn's in trouble," Annika said, her words soft and her eyes softer. "His house is right next to Tristan's…He just couldn't help it."

Ethan stared dazedly at the walkie-talkie. "He told us yesterday, the part about a promise should mean something…I should've seen this coming."

"Me too," Annika said, her voice cracking.

"So now what?" Austin said, pacing around. "This screws up everything."

"Well, we can't just leave him behind," Annika protested.

"No we can't," Ethan stated firmly.

Everyone stared at Austin, half expecting him to argue the case of cutting Glenn loose. It wasn't exactly an unreasonable case to argue. But then he sighed deeply, and it was like a wave of understanding had washed over him. "If the machines killed my scout, I guess I'd want payback too," he said while looking at Ethan. "I'm not saying what Glenn's gone and done is smart, but I get why he did it…I would've done the same thing."

Ethan smiled at Austin thankfully, then he spoke words full of determination. "All right, then…Let's go get Glenn back."

CHAPTER 40

THE RESCUE MISSION: PREPPING

Everyone grabbed their hand-held laser weapons and slipped out the back door of the kitchen. They skulked through the backyards of a dozen houses before finally making it to Glenn's. All the lights were off in his house, but Tristan's house next door caught their attention immediately. The downstairs was dark like every other home on the block, but a light was on in an upstairs bedroom window. At this time of night, it just screamed suspicious.

The five of them crouched down behind the wooden deck at Glenn's while keeping an eye on the lighted bedroom at Tristan's. They sat there in surveillance for a minute, but they didn't see any activity. Annika looked back into Glenn's house through the patio doors.

"We should secure Glenn's house now," Annika said. "But I'm guessing, if Glenn was out to get Tristan's murderers, he probably wasn't in the mood to sneak around his robot parents. He probably got them first." Then she added softly, "I hope." Annika looked back at Tristan's house and the bedroom with the lights on. "If we can secure this house, we could put a sniper in the window across from Tristan's."

"Any idea who that sniper should be?" Ethan asked with a smile.

"I have an idea," Annika answered. "But I still don't like this stupid flashlight of a gun."

"I'm sure you'll do fine."

The group made their way onto the deck and up to the glass patio door. Ethan pulled on the door and it slid right open. He shined a flashlight inside and fanned it around. There was no sign of anyone, nothing knocked over, no evidence of a struggle. Ethan stepped inside slowly and motioned for the others.

Once inside, the group cleared the house room by room. It wasn't until they had made their way upstairs that the history of Glenn's evening with his mechanical parents began to take shape. The Skulley that had posed as his father was deceased, body and head riddled with holes, splayed out across the floor in the upstairs hallway. The one pretending to be his mother wasn't far behind. Its body lay in a similar condition at the threshold of his parents' bedroom. Both of them had their skin entirely melted away from their faces, and their weapons were drawn. Ethan shined his flashlight on the walls, revealing laser pockmarks everywhere.

"There was one heck of a fight here," Austin said solemnly.

"Guys, look at this," Caleb said, his words and face grim as he shined a light on part of the wall farther down the hall.

The others stepped closer to Caleb and looked where he was pointing. A three-foot-long streak of blood was smeared along the wall. As they continued to check the house, they found more evidence that Glenn hadn't gotten out of the battle unscathed. Blood stained the banister of the stairs and part of the carpet where it looked like he had fallen down.

"It's an awful lot of blood," Annika said, her words filled with rare frailty.

"But there's no body," Austin said, trying to reassure her. "A lot of wounds bleed a lot. Doesn't mean it's life-threatening."

"Austin's right," Ethan said. "As bad as this looks, I think he was still in good enough shape to think he could take on the machines who killed Tristan."

"So you think he's still alive, and over there?" Annika asked with hopeful eyes.

Ethan nodded. "Yeah."

"You should come take a look at this," Andy said urgently from the bedroom at the end of the hall, the one directly across from the lighted bedroom at Tristan's house.

The rest of the group ran into the bedroom and found Andy staring outside the window and into the window at Tristan's house. Everyone turned their flashlights off and huddled around the window, spying on the bedroom next door. Several moments passed, but they saw nothing.

"What did you see?" Ethan asked.

"Just watch," Andy said. "Anytime now."

The group leaned in closer to the window, only to startle in shock when they finally saw what Andy had seen. A Skulley, without any skin, walked across the room. It was over seven feet tall. Its black polished metal shined under the lights of the room. But its most striking feature was that its skull wasn't patterned after a human's; it was Zyvantian in form. The cranium was larger, with grooves running from front to back atop its skull. Big, dark, soulless, almond-shaped eyes were planted halfway down its face, accompanying its small slit of a mouth and barely visible nose.

The Zyvantian Skulley walked out of view for a moment, then it returned with a folding chair in its unusually lanky arms. It set the chair down and waited beside it. Soon two Skulleys who were the more familiar, yet no more endearing, human-type entered the room carrying a flailing, thrashing, screaming Glenn. Blood covered the right side of his face and was wicking deeply down his shirt. His fearful eyes bulged from their sockets as the machines slammed him onto the chair and bound him to it using something that looked like metal wire.

Annika had to cover her mouth with both hands so that she wouldn't scream and give away their position. Her eyes were nearly as horrified-looking as Glenn's. When she finally uncovered her mouth, her first instinct was to grab her laser weapon. She aimed it through the window with the leader, presumably the one with a Zyvantian skeleton, in her sights.

"No!" Ethan whispered urgently, placing his hand over her weapon and holding it down. "Not yet. You know we can't rescue him from this position alone. We're gonna have to send a team in there."

"Okay, but we gotta hurry," Annika said.

"All right…Me, Austin, and Andy are gonna go in there through the back door," Ethan said. "Caleb, you stay here and guard Annika's back."

Caleb looked insulted. "Look, I know I'm not the best guy with a gun, but I can still help. Or Andy could stay here and guard Annika."

"I don't need a guard at all," Annika said. "This house is clear. No one's coming in here. You should take him."

"No. No one should be alone," Ethan insisted. "And Caleb, I need the best team for this mission...I'm sorry."

Caleb nodded in agreement, but he was no less insulted about not making the cut. It was like gym class all over again, only this time his best friend had picked an android over him. "That's okay," Caleb said. "Don't worry about it. Just be careful...I'll guard Annika with my life."

"Thank you, Caleb," Ethan said.

Caleb nodded, trying not to let his disappointment show.

"Someone's coming," Austin said, staring out the window. Everyone watched in dread as a jeep pulled up into Tristan's driveway. Four human-type Skulleys got out and entered Tristan's house.

"That makes at least seven of them in there," Ethan said, the worry in his voice hard to hide. Then he scavenged some optimism. "But we still have the element of surprise."

"Maybe we should go through the front door now," Andy said. "I doubt they would feel the need to lock it behind them. It would be quieter than breaking in the back."

"Good idea," Ethan said.

"Yeah, sounds great, right through the front door," Caleb muttered, unable to hold back his annoyance.

"But it'll be quieter," Ethan said, defending Andy's idea. "Annika, when we get into position and figure out what we're dealing with, we'll signal you to tell you when to fire. Two flashes from a flashlight, from any window. When you see the lights, be ready. Take out as many in the room as you can, and we'll use that distraction to finish off the rest from the inside."

"Right," Annika said. "Just make sure you keep low to the ground once you flash the lights. Those Skulleys are tall, and I'm gonna put a hole in anything tall."

"Copy that," Ethan said. "Time to go."

"Be careful, guys," Annika said.

"We will." Ethan smiled at Annika as he turned to leave. "But I kinda wish I woulda brought a snow globe."

Annika grinned, but her eyes were softening. "See you soon."

Ethan, Austin, and Andy left the room. Annika watched them until the blackness of the hallway swallowed them up.

CHAPTER 41

THE RESCUE MISSION: GOING IN

Ethan, Austin, and Andy exited through the back of Glenn's house and weaved their way around to the front of Tristan's. They hunkered down behind a row of bushes that lined the driveway and peered through a gap between them. The neighborhood seemed quiet, peaceful even, unless you knew the sound you were listening for. Ethan knew, and he heard it. They were the desperate howls of their friend upstairs, barely audible now, muffled by duct tape or a gag or something less humane. The volume of Glenn's screams might've been made soft and subtle, but the tone of his terror was deafening.

Ethan and the others slipped through the bushes closest to where they met the garage. That allowed them to hug the wall of the house as they moved toward the front door, ducking under windows as they crept, keeping as low a profile as possible. When they reached the front porch, Ethan peered inside through a panel of vertical windows that sat off to the side of the door. He widened his eyes, then tried squinting, but he couldn't see a thing. Total blackness.

"How's your night vision, Andy?" Ethan asked.

"Better than yours," Andy responded.

Ethan shook his head a little, acknowledging the sarcasm from a robot. Then he moved aside and let Andy take a look. "It's all clear as far as I can see, but I don't have the best angle from here," Andy said. "I can only really see the entryway and part of the living room."

"That's better than nothing," Ethan said. "All right, when we get inside, veer right and find cover. Here we go." He gripped the door handle. "One, two, three…"

Ethan opened the door slowly and prayed that Tristan's family was good about maintaining a door without a squeaky hinge. The door opened smoothly enough, without a sound to give them away, and they slinked inside. Andy scanned the immediate area and gave the others the signal that it was okay. Ethan closed the door back as gently as he had opened it, and the three of them veered right from the foyer and sneaked into the living room. The trio hid behind a long, L-shaped sectional couch that provided both good cover and a good view of the downstairs. Andy poked his head out from behind the couch and surveyed the area once more.

"Looks clear," Andy said.

Austin nodded. "Yeah, they all gotta be upstairs."

All of a sudden, a horrific scream radiated from above that sent a rippling shockwave of fear through the house. Glenn must've spat out whatever had been muffling him because his shriek was full-blast and blood-chilling. It sent cold, sickening shivers down Ethan's and Austin's spines. And from the look on Andy's face, it did something similar to him.

"We gotta get him outta there now," Ethan said.

Annika had been watching Glenn from the window as he made that awful scream. What she witnessed turned her pale, stole her breath, and made her heart skip. The machines were gathered around him now, their glistening faces eager for the show to start. One of them was placing the metal clamps over Glenn's eyes, the ones they used just before a mind-reading to keep the eyelids open. But calling what the machines were about to do a *mind-reading* was a terrible misnomer. It was more like a mind-shredding, painfully ripping the innermost thoughts out of one's skull against their will.

Annika's eyes were glued to the windows at Tristan's house, desperately hoping to see those two flashlight pulses that would give her permission to start firing away at the Skulleys. She already knew who she was going to shoot first—the one that was pinching Glenn's eyelids open and shoving the clamps into his eye sockets. *That one dies first*, Annika thought with her hand firmly gripped around her weapon.

As Annika was taking note of the other machines' positions, the Zyvantian Skulley walked up to the window and stared outside. Annika ducked down quickly out of sight. She waited for a few seconds, but she knew that every second she did would be one that she wouldn't be able to see Ethan's signal. Slowly and cautiously, she peeked an eye out through the lower right corner of the window. The alien Skulley stared back ominously. Its large, cold black eyes somehow always seemed to find Annika's, even though she was pretty sure the machine never actually saw her. Its eyes just consumed everything around it, like a malevolent black hole. After a few torturous moments, the Skulley reached up and grabbed something above the window. Annika's heart dropped along with the window shade. Now the only thing she could see in Tristan's bedroom was a jumbled mess of shadows.

"No, no, no!" Annika uttered in frustration, barely keeping herself from screaming.

Caleb turned around from his sentry duty. "What is it?"

"They pulled the shade down," Annika said. "All I can see are shadows. I can't risk shooting blind with Glenn in there."

Caleb looked out the window and instantly saw the predicament. Then an idea struck him. "These military houses are all alike," he said. Caleb inspected the window shade above their own window and pointed to a section at the top. "This works on a pawl and ratchet system. If you shoot this part here, the shade will either fling right up or fall off completely."

"Are you sure?" Annika asked.

"As sure as you are that you can make the shot," Caleb answered.

"All right, then…Right here?" Annika asked, pointing carefully at the spot.

"That's it. You got it."

Annika went back to staring at the windows of Tristan's house. "Thanks, Caleb. You're a genius. I don't know what we'd do without you."

"Thanks," Caleb said with a soft smile. "But I'm sure you'd manage."

Annika raised a curious eyebrow at that, but she kept her eyes fixed on the windows.

⁂

Ethan, Austin, and Andy maintained a defensive position behind the couch, nearest the bottom of the stairs. They were off to the side and out of sight, a perfect spot for an ambush when the Skulleys would be flushed out of the room by Annika's sniper fire. What was left of the squad of machines would come rushing down the stairs in a hurry to get to Glenn's house and subdue the sniper. Then Ethan and his team would pick them off one by one. That was the plan, at least. Ethan nodded to the others and pulled out his flashlight. He held it up to the window and flicked the light twice. Then he carefully watched the window at Glenn's house.

C'mon, Annika. Do your thing.

✥

A split second after she saw the light flashes, Annika flung open her window and lined up the shot on Tristan's window shade. She fired her weapon, and a laser streamed out and found the target. A hole the size of a baseball was blown through the upper left part of the window frame, destroying the mechanism that Caleb had spoken of. The damaged window shade flew open, then fell off entirely, allowing Annika a clear view of the room and the very surprised group of Skulleys inside it. True to her plan, the first Skulley she shot was the one who had put the metal clamps onto Glenn's eyes. The machine had been crouched over, leaning into Glenn's face, and just about ready to blast him with its torturous, mind-reading eye beams when Annika persuaded it otherwise. In total, she managed to kill four human-type Skulleys almost instantly, putting lasers in their metal heads before they knew what had hit them. Then the rest of the machines dropped to the floor for cover, out of Annika's sight.

"Four out of seven," Annika said. "Not great, but not too bad."

Caleb stared at Annika in awe and smiled. "I knew you'd get the hang of that gun."

"It's still not my rifle," she said, keeping an eye on the window. "Woulda got all seven."

Just as she uttered that last word, the remaining Skulleys popped up and fired a massive salvo of lasers at Annika's window. The one that was Zyvantian in form had a laser weapon protruding from each forearm that looked like a miniature Gatlin gun. Lasers spewed from it with the firepower of twenty human-type Skulleys, ripping the window frame and the surrounding wall to shreds. Annika and Caleb quickly scrambled out of the bedroom with lasers whizzing over their heads. Annika looked back and saw two machines—a human-type and a Zyvantian-type—leap out of Tristan's window and head their way.

"They're coming!" Annika screamed. "We gotta get outta here!"

⚘

Ethan knew their plan had gone terribly wrong when he looked out the window in horror and saw the two Skulleys storming the lawn toward Glenn's house. Their eyes were burning the brightest, most sinister shade of red that Ethan had ever seen. They dove headfirst into the house, smashing through a bay window. "They're in Glenn's house!" Ethan yelled. "We gotta go!"

Ethan, Austin, and Andy were just about to spring out from behind the couch, when a Skulley jumped downstairs and started spraying lasers at them. They ducked behind the couch again for cover. The Skulley fired nonstop at the three of them. Holes were blasted into the couch, stuffing and spring coils flying everywhere. The only shots they could manage to get off were blind ones, just sticking their laser weapons out randomly and firing, hoping to get lucky.

"Aghhhh!" Ethan screamed in anger, fear, and frustration as he fired his weapon without luck. Every minute they were pinned down by the Skulley was a minute that he couldn't help his best friend and budding girlfriend. As bad as it was being cornered behind a couch by a furious machine craving payback, Ethan knew Annika and Caleb's situation was much worse. "We gotta spread out behind the couch," Ethan shouted over the shrill sounds of the lasers. "Attack from different angles. It won't be able to cover us all, then one of us will be free to take the shot. Ready?...Now!"

※

Annika and Caleb were at the top of the stairs when they heard the window smash in the living room below them. "They're inside the house," Annika whispered sharply. "This way." She flipped on her flashlight and led Caleb down the hallway, retracing their steps back toward the bedroom. The entire time, her eyes searched the ceiling. "There it is," she said, pointing at the rectangular crack above them. She jumped up and pulled down on a rope and a staircase unfolded. "Hurry, give me your weapon and get in the attic," Annika said urgently. "And make enough noise so they think we're both up there. Then I'll pop out from the bedroom they thought we surely left and get the drop on them."

Something about being a decoy and giving away his laser weapon didn't sit well with Caleb. He didn't like it when Ethan had left him behind on the mission at Tristan's house, and now Annika was doing the same thing. He didn't make a fuss, though. Who was he to question Ethan or Annika when it came to battlefield heroics? He was just the chubby engineer with the athletic ability and marksmanship of a drunken panda bear. Caleb handed over his weapon to Annika without a word and clambered up the ladder as fast as his legs could pump.

Annika took a position behind the front wall of the bedroom at the end of the hall, the one from which they had just fled. The wall behind her looked like Swiss cheese now, riddled with smoldering holes from the Skulleys' laser attack. Drywall sizzled and smoke puffed into the room in unpredictable billows. Annika lifted the collar of her shirt over her mouth to keep from breathing in the smoke. She knew if she could just keep from coughing, she'd have the element of surprise since no one in their right mind would ever choose *this* defensive position. As she peeked out warily from the wall and into the hallway, she thought: *Only you, Pepper…Only you are crazy enough to try this.*

One pair of red eyes ascended the stairs at a calm, almost leisurely, pace. It was the slow, plodding, stalking pace of a madman in a horror movie, where the predator knows the prey has no means of defense or escape. That level of arrogance worried Annika, like the machines knew something she didn't. Annika had a bead on the human-type Skulley. She could've made the shot now, but the fact that she had no idea where that other massive, gun-wielding monster was gave her pause. She knew the Zyvantian-type Skulley's eyes had always been dark, and that the machine would be very hard to spot. That it was out there somewhere, roaming around unseen and unaccounted for, absolutely terrified her.

Caleb was making quite the ruckus up in the attic now. He sounded more like a six-man construction crew tromping around up there than one guy trying to be a decoy. The human-type Skulley stopped at the ladder of the attic.

It craned its neck up to get a look inside, its eyes blazing a vicious shade of crimson. Annika gripped both laser weapons tightly. She squinted hard to try to find the Skulley's more fearsome companion, but all she saw were two red eyes in a sea of blackness. Then she finally saw it, or thought she did. As she strained her eyes, she noticed two pitch-black ovals, darker than the darkness around them. They were the black holes for eyes that seemed to absorb every bit of light around them. The Zyvantian-type Skulley was standing behind its human counterpart. Annika now had the location of both machines.

Just as the human-type began climbing the attic ladder, Annika sprang out from behind her cover and fired away with her dual laser weapons. The lasers ripped into the Skulley and it fell to the ground and died instantly. Then Annika immediately concentrated her firepower on the Zyvantian Skulley. She unleashed a relentless stream of lasers that bombarded the machine's head and body, but it simply would not die. The menacing black Skulley just stood there, absorbing an incredible number of direct hits without flinching. It was like it was teasing her, showing her that it couldn't be killed and that the whole resistance effort was pointless.

Annika kept firing desperately, praying that some damage might be done. The light from her lasers bathed the hallway in a deep shade of red. It looked like some version of hell, with the Zyvantian machine as the devil standing front and center. Then it raised its long, wiry arms and produced those dual laser Gatlin guns. Annika's eyes widened in fear at the sight of them; she knew exactly what was coming. She dove to the floor behind the wall and got as low as possible. Crimson lasers erupted from the heavy weapons in furious streams.

They ripped into the wall and cut the entire length of it in half. Annika scampered for cover as the battered wall crashed down around her. She peeked out from behind the rubble and stared into the hallway that was now pitch black again. Through the darkness, her eyes stinging from the pluming smoke, she frantically tried to find those two almond-shaped orbs that were blacker than black. But she couldn't. Then the machine turned on the light in the hallway, as if granting Annika the privilege to see her executioner. It stared at her for a long moment with those horrible eyes, and Annika would've just as soon kept the lights off. The Zyvantian Skulley stepped over its dead comrade and began its slow, cold, pitiless march toward her.

Annika's young life flashed before her eyes. She was certain that she was going to die in that laser-ravaged, smoky room. "Run, Caleb!...Get outta here!" she screamed, hoping that in her death she might save one life, as temporary as that might be.

The next thing Annika heard was a primal scream. It was coming from the attic. She knew it had to be Caleb, though this was no sound of a mild-mannered engineer. This was the sound of a warrior, a battle cry. Annika peered out and saw Caleb leap down from the attic, with a cable clutched in each hand. He landed on the back of the Zyvantian Skulley, wrapping his legs around it to hold on, then jammed the cables with all his might into the crook of the machine's neck. Blue bolts of electricity surged through the Skulley, freezing it in its tracks. The massive electric jolt threw Caleb violently into the wall. Annika took immediate advantage of the robot's temporary paralysis. She stood up and fired her laser weapons as fast as she could, hitting the machine with a rapid barrage, every beam focused on its cold, dark eyes. Finally, the machine began to falter. It fell to its knees, still paralyzed by the electricity. Annika kept firing, firing, firing until the Skulley's head burst into flames. It collapsed face-first on the ground, burnt and electrocuted. Dead at last.

Annika ran over to Caleb, who lay spread out on the floor, unconscious. "Caleb!...Caleb!" she yelled, shaking him, desperately trying to bring him around. But his body remained lifeless and limp in her hands. "Caleb!" she cried again, her voice cracking and a tear streaming down her cheek. Slowly, Caleb's eyes opened. Annika gasped. "Caleb!"

"Are we alive?" Caleb asked in a daze. "Did we make it?"

Annika beamed and hugged him. "Yes, thanks to you, you big, beautiful maniac...Are you all right?"

Caleb nodded and cracked a weary smile. Annika helped him to his feet. He looked down at the still sizzling and crackling Zyvantian Skulley. It sounded like a campfire.

"I *really* hope that's the last one of those we ever meet," Caleb said.

"You and me both," Annika replied, then looked curious. "Caleb, what were those things? The things you shocked it with?"

"I found some electrical lighting cables up there," Caleb answered. "Ripped them out and chewed off the plastic down to the wire...not unlike a raccoon."

Annika laughed. "Caleb, I never knew you were such a tough guy."

Caleb let loose a dorky chuckle, but there was also pride therein. "Well, now you know."

Annika nodded. "Now I know...Let's get outta here."

Annika and Caleb had just gotten downstairs and into the

kitchen when the back door flung open wildly. Annika swiftly pulled her laser weapon and shined her flashlight at the entryway, and Caleb wasn't far behind. They breathed a big sigh of relief when they saw it was Ethan standing in the doorframe. Austin and Andy were behind him, helping Glenn as he was still unsteady from his ordeal.

Ethan ran up and wrapped his arms around Annika and Caleb. He held them tightly, slow to let go. "I thought I lost you," he said breathlessly. "Are you okay? What happened?" Ethan finally let them go and stepped back to get a better look at them. He flipped on a small light above the stove.

"It's a long, amazing story. We'll tell you everything later... But Caleb saved my life."

Ethan stared at Caleb in surprise and awe, as did Austin and Andy. "Thank you, Caleb," Ethan said, his eyes getting soft. "I knew you were the best man for the job."

Caleb smiled and shrugged modestly, but inside he felt like a million bucks.

Annika turned her attention to Glenn, who was avoiding eye contact with the group. She put a hand on his shoulder. "Glenn, thank God you're alive. Are you okay? How do you feel?"

"Stupid," Glenn answered, looking up for a moment, then back down. "Soooo stupid...I should've died in that room. That's what I deserved."

"No, you don't," Ethan said. "They killed a friend of yours, and you wanted justice. We all understand that and might've even done the same thing...But *millions* of people are being killed all over the world now. And the only way to get justice for that is sticking with the plan."

Annika looked away from Glenn and slowly shined her

flashlight on Ethan. "What do you mean millions of people are being killed all over the world?" she asked with worried eyes.

Ethan swallowed hard, realizing that he hadn't yet told the others what he'd seen on television. "I recorded the news, just before the cable went out," Ethan said uneasily. "We all had a feeling that the war had started…I just saw the proof."

"What about Unionville?" Annika asked. Her voice wavered, along with the flashlight in her hand. "What about my brother?"

"And my sister?" Glenn asked.

"I'm sure they're okay," Ethan answered. "They're attacking the biggest cities first."

"But they'll get there eventually," Annika said, steeling herself.

"Yeah," Ethan replied glumly. "But the only thing that matters now is July second, 1999, six miles outside a town called Pebbyville. The only thing that matters is our mission, and we have to be focused and at full strength to have a chance." Ethan paused and eyed Glenn. "And to be at full strength, we're gonna need our old Glenn back."

Glenn looked at Ethan with teary, grateful eyes. Then the team, Andy now solidly included, closed in for a tight group hug that resembled a huddle. "Thank you…I love you guys," Glenn said, his words cracking and full of emotion.

The hug finally ended and there wasn't a dry eye on the team. That included Andy's synthetic eyes, too. Ethan finally steadied himself and said, "This place will be full of Skulleys soon trying to figure out what went wrong. We need to get outta here…get back to my house, pack the SUV, make a run for the Mitchell brothers, and get to Wolf Cave."

Glenn grabbed his backpack, the one he had filled and set by the door before he went over to Tristan's house for his ill-fated mission. Then the group left through the back door and sprinted their way toward Ethan's house.

As they ran, Annika was keeping up with Ethan stride for stride. "By the way, what happened to you guys over at Tristan's? What took you so long?" she asked.

"A Skulley surprised us, had us pinned down behind the couch," Ethan answered.

"Just one Skulley?"

"Yeah."

Annika snickered a little. "You're really slippin', Tate."

"Just try to keep up, Pepper," Ethan said with a smile, then sprinted ahead.

CHAPTER 42

GETTING OUT OF DODGE

When the team arrived at Ethan's house, Caleb took Glenn into a bathroom to check on his injuries. Apart from minor scuffs and scrapes, he had a cut across the right side of his head that had bled fiercely—the result of diving into a table to avoid laser fire—though that wound was mostly superficial, too. Caleb applied some antiseptic and a liquid bandage, and he gave Glenn his prognosis with a grin: "Thank God I got to you in time. You're gonna live."

Glenn laughed a little and thanked Dr. Warren for his services. Then he got cleaned up, threw on some fresh clothes, and ran downstairs to join the others.

Everyone was scrambling around in the garage, stashing their backpacks full of supplies into the SUV. The sun would be rising in about a half hour, and they all knew they had to get back to the woods—with the Mitchell brothers—before that happened.

"How much money do we have?" Ethan asked. Everyone emptied their pockets and placed all the money they had found with mint dates of 1999 and earlier on a workbench.

Ethan counted the bills and coins. It didn't take long. His face furrowed in disappointment. "Twenty-eight dollars and sixteen cents."

"Great," Austin said sarcastically. "Now the first thing we need to do when we go back in time is rob a bank."

"I got the money part taken care of," Glenn said. "I knew it might be hard to find that much old money on short notice, so I brought some things to sell." Glenn opened his backpack, revealing a side compartment filled with baseball memorabilia. A few autographed balls and trading cards in protective acrylic cases were tucked inside.

Ethan and the others smiled. "Smart, Glenn," Ethan said. "Very smart."

"Thanks...It's the least I could do."

"Now for the Mitchell brothers," Ethan said, then picked up a walkie-talkie and tuned to channel eight. "Testing, testing, testing," Ethan repeated the words twice more, then placed the walkie on the dashboard of the SUV.

With the headlights off, Ethan pulled the vehicle out of the garage and immediately turned off the driveway to get to his backyard. He drove in the direction opposite Glenn's and Tristan's houses, figuring the machines were already swarming that area. Once he made it to the end of the neighborhood, Ethan sped up and crossed Kingsbury. He drove through a few more backyards and cut through a few more residential streets on the other side before making it to a street that connected with the back of Judy's Diner. Ethan pulled into the alley behind the diner, parking the SUV between the walls of the two adjacent buildings—Judy's Diner on one side and the fire station on the other. He cut the engine and waited for the Mitchell brothers to arrive.

Everyone kept their eyes peeled on the front and back of the alley. It was a little before five in the morning on a Sunday, and, oddly, it was just about as quiet as any other. They knew it wouldn't stay that way for long.

"How much time do we give them?" Austin asked, checking his watch. "The sun will be coming up soon."

"Fifteen minutes...a little more," Ethan answered, his eyes tense. Then he grabbed the walkie and issued the call to the brothers again: "Testing, testing, testing...Testing, testing testing."

A startled gasp came from one of the backseats. "The sledgehammers and pickaxes!" Caleb blurted. The group sighed deeply. With all that had happened, they hadn't had a chance to collect the most crucial gear of all. And then they had nearly forgotten about it entirely.

"There's a hardware store around the corner," Glenn said. "I'll go."

"Glenn, you're in no condition to go," Annika said.

"I'm fine, just scratches...I owe you this."

"Well, you're not going alone," Ethan said firmly.

"I'll go with him," Caleb offered, sounding braver than usual. "Besides, I just thought of something...something to spruce up our new fort."

Ethan looked unsure, but Annika gave him a reassuring nod. "We can cover them from the roof of the firehouse," she said, pointing to a service ladder that was affixed to the wall of the fire station.

Ethan nodded back, though he still didn't look convinced. "All right," he said finally. "But we gotta hurry."

Ethan and Annika climbed up the ladder and took a position on the roof of the fire station, directly across from the entrance to the hardware store. The roof of the fire station was the tallest point in the town of Blackwoods, so they had an excellent view of the surroundings. They peeked out from behind the raised concrete border atop the roof and looked back and forth, all the way down the street, making sure the coast was clear.

Annika motioned for Glenn and Caleb to go ahead.

Caleb and Glenn darted across the street to the hardware store. Glenn fired a single laser into the door lock, then nudged the wooden door open. The two of them quickly slipped inside, with Caleb gently closing the door back behind them.

"Sledgehammers and pickaxes are in the back," Caleb said. "I'm gonna grab the thickest copper wire I can find."

"Copper wire?" Glenn asked.

"Yeah, part of my idea to fix up the cave."

Glenn shot Caleb a curious glance, then ran toward the back of the store. Caleb scurried down the aisles in search of the copper wire. Sixty seconds later they met at the front of the store, mission accomplished. Glenn had a cart full of sledgehammers and pickaxes, along with a half-dozen hard hats, safety glasses, and work gloves piled on top. Caleb was hefting a large coil of copper wire. They peered through the front window, looking down the street as far as they could.

"Still looks clear," Caleb said.

Glenn nodded. "Yeah, let's make a run for it."

Before they could put a hand on the door, a loud siren blared. The volume went up and down in rhythmic waves and was almost deafening at its peak. It was the military alert siren from the research facility, though no one from the military was using it now. Caleb's and Glenn's hearts pounded through their shirts. They looked outside again, but the street was clear. All they saw was Annika on the roof of the fire station across from them, frantically waving for them to come back.

Caleb pushed the door open just enough for the both of them to slip out. He closed the door back, and they sprinted across the street with the cart into the alleyway behind Judy's Diner. They quickly loaded the supplies into the SUV.

"Any sign of the Mitchell brothers?" Caleb asked.

"No," Austin replied. "And I'd say it's about time to go."

Ethan and Annika watched from their perch atop the firehouse as a large convoy of military jeeps sped through the residential streets of Blackwoods. The sun was just peeking over the horizon now, and they could see that the jeeps were full of human-type Skulleys—with no clothes and no skin.

The alert siren stopped abruptly, and a voice boomed through a speaker that was nearly as loud. It was an automated voice that sounded digitized, artificial, and very ominous.

"Exit your houses immediately. This is not a drill. Come out with your hands up. Proceed to the sidewalk and form a line and await further instructions."

The eerie, automated words were repeated over and over again. From the rooftop, Ethan and Annika could hear the chilling screams of the young citizens of Blackwoods as they laid their eyes on the black, metal, skeletal robots for the first time. Then the cries and shrieks of utter fear and panic got louder as everyone realized they had no parents to turn to, just heartless machines that had posed as their mothers and fathers. It took everything that Ethan had to block out the horror of it all and concentrate on the mission. He pulled out a pair of binoculars and focused on the far end of a street that ran parallel to Kingsbury. His heart sank when he saw the Mitchell brothers being dragged violently down the sidewalk by a pair of Skulleys. They threw Jeremiah and Zeke into the back of a jeep and drove away with them.

"They just took the Mitchell brothers," Ethan said, then paused solemnly. "We gotta go without them."

"Ethan, they just posted guard squads at the east and west corners of Main Street," Annika said, peering through her binoculars with a taut face. "Two jeeps, eight Skulleys total on each side."

"Human or Zyvantian form?"

"Human…But still, how are we gonna get outta here now?"

Ethan stared at the guard patrols and grimaced. "I have one idea…but it's pretty crazy."

Annika managed a faint smile. "Aren't they all?"

Ethan returned a wry smile, then the two of them climbed back down the ladder to meet the others. Everyone got into the SUV and locked the doors. "They took the Mitchell brothers," Ethan informed the group. "It's time to go, but there are guard units at each end of Main Street. And there's no way to go around them."

"So what do we do?" Austin said. "Try to plow through them?"

"No. They'll cut us down first. What we need is to get through that guard unit without them firing a shot."

"And how do you propose we do that?" Glenn asked.

"The Zyvantian-form Skulleys seem to be the ones in charge," Ethan said. "So we make them think this SUV is being driven by one of them, and pass right through…no questions asked."

Caleb flashed a confused look at Ethan. "Okay, and *how* do we do that?"

"Hand me my backpack," Ethan said, cracking a nervous smile. "I brought…*something*."

Austin grabbed Ethan's backpack and lifted it from the floor. It was bulky and hard to manage. "What the heck do you have in here, a pumpkin?" he asked. He finally passed it up to the front, accidentally bumping it into Caleb's head along the way.

Ethan unzipped the backpack and reached inside. Before he pulled anything out, he looked up at the others with an uneasy face. "Now keep in mind this is a last resort idea, okay?"

The others nodded hesitantly and waited with very curious faces as Ethan began to pull his hands out of the backpack. What he retrieved stunned them all. It was a full-sized Darth Vader helmet. Annika instantly began shaking her head. "Oh, Ethan…no," she said, sounding appalled at the very thought of what he was about to propose.

"Listen," Ethan said as he tried to make his case. "The Zyvantian-form Skulley looks a *little bit* like Darth Vader, especially the top of the head and the eyes. Not the nose and mouth so much, but even if this only buys us a few seconds, it'll be time enough to get around that corner so the other Skulley patrol on the east side doesn't see us if we have to open fire."

Annika rolled her eyes; she couldn't believe her ears. "*Really? Darth Vader?!...* Are you freakin' kidding me?!"

"I know," Ethan admitted. "But it might confuse them just long enough."

"It's absolutely nuts," Annika said. "They aren't gonna buy it."

Glenn chuckled nervously. "Well, they might…but we're definitely gonna need the force to be with us."

Austin snickered at that. "Nice one, Glenn…If we're gonna die, we might as well go out being smart-asses."

"We need to go now or there will be more than eight of them," Ethan said. He put on his Darth Vader helmet, fastened his seat belt, and started the engine. "Here we go."

"Yeah, *here we go*," Annika echoed sarcastically, gripping her laser weapon tightly. "Get us out of here, Lord Vader."

"Everyone stay down and out of sight," Ethan said as he pulled the SUV out of the alley and westbound onto Main Street. He rolled the window down on his side just enough so that the top of his—or Darth Vader's—head and eyes were visible from the outside, with the dark tint of the windows obscuring the rest of his face.

The group was about two hundred feet away from the Skulleys' guard post when the machines began watching them carefully. Ethan had planned to roll slowly through the intersection without stopping at all, just nodding his large, black helmet-head at the Skulleys and going about his way. No questions asked. When one of the Skulleys stepped in front of the vehicle and raised its hand for them to stop, Ethan knew his plan had hit a snag.

"They're stopping us," Ethan said with a tight throat.

"Keep going," Austin said. "We can't stop."

"I'm just gonna turn a bit to the right," Ethan said. "I want to make sure they see the helmet."

"Oh, they see the helmet, Lord Vader," Annika snapped. "Floor it, Tate."

"Go ahead and stop, Ethan," Andy said. "I have an idea… but keep in mind this is a last resort idea, okay?" Andy's voice was hesitant, which was odd for a robot, and not terribly great for the group's confidence in going along with whatever it was he had in mind.

"What's the idea?" Ethan asked.

"There's no time to explain," Andy answered. He was right, as the Skulleys had already surrounded the SUV, forcing Ethan to either stop or ram them. Ethan chose to stop, trusting Andy and his cryptic plan. "You will want to cover your ears for this," Andy added.

One of the Skulleys approached the vehicle slowly. The machine saw Ethan's Darth Vader helmet, or at least the part that he was willing to show. As the skeletal machine got closer, Ethan's entire body thrummed with frayed nerves, desperate for Andy to do whatever it was he was going to do. When the Skulley got within ten feet of the driver's window, it stopped suddenly. It raised its arm and produced its laser weapon. Everyone in the SUV cringed in their seats, except for Andy. He opened his mouth and belted out a high-pitched *screech*. The shrill, piercing sound nearly split the eardrums of every human in the vehicle, but the Skulleys took notice immediately. They backed away respectfully. Ethan drove through the guard post, leaving the machines behind.

Everyone in the SUV cheered. "What the heck did you say to them?" Ethan asked.

"I told them, in their language, to let me through now or suffer the consequences," Andy said, then looked pensive. "Was that too harsh?"

"Perfect, I'd say," Ethan answered.

"So was the Darth Vader helmet," Annika said, smiling at Ethan.

Ethan cracked a smile under his Vader mask, though it wasn't long before an image in the rearview mirror wiped away his grin and replaced it with a grimace. He ripped off his helmet and stared into the mirror, eyes wide and worried. "Well, *almost* perfect."

Annika peeked out of the sunroof and took a look with her binoculars. She saw a small army of Skulleys on foot and in jeeps storming toward them, five hundred yards away but closing the gap fast. And the Skulleys on foot were just about as fast as the ones in jeeps. Annika plopped back down in her seat. "I got an idea...Hurry, someone give me their weapon!"

Ethan handed over his laser weapon to Annika. "What's the idea?"

"Just drive...and fast." Right as Annika was about to pop up from the sunroof again, a wall of lasers smashed into them from behind, blowing out all of the windows and ripping the entire top of the vehicle off. Everyone scrunched down as low as possible, except for Annika. She stood up tall in her seat, laser weapons drawn.

"What are you doing?! Get down, Annika!" Ethan screamed. "Get down!"

Annika aimed her laser weapons at two electrical poles two hundred yards ahead, one on each side of the street. She fired a blast of lasers at the base of each, ripping through the wood and chopping them down like trees. They began to fall, bringing the power lines that were connected to them down as well. Brilliant bluish bolts of electricity sizzled and popped, as the power lines were torn from their mounts. Sparks flew wildly, while loose lines began to thrash and whip around like the tentacles of an angry octopus. The jumble of poles and power lines were in near free-fall now, plummeting toward the road ahead of them.

"Floor it!" Annika screamed.

"I am!" Ethan screamed back.

The engine of the eight-cylinder SUV squealed as Ethan pinned his foot to the gas pedal, recruiting every ounce of muscle he had in his leg. Everyone cringed and clutched their seats tightly as they watched the poles fall. They screamed like lunatics as Ethan drove the SUV under a shower of electrical sparks. The sparks peppered the group as they rained down, stinging their hunched backs. The sparkling cascade was so dense that they couldn't see the road ahead. They had no idea if they were going to make it. Then they heard a horrible, thundering *Crash!* It wasn't until they were out of the electrical storm that they realized they had cleared the poles, and that behind them lay a wonderful barrier of wood, wires, fire, and electricity—with the machines stuck on the other side.

It took a moment for anyone to be able to breathe again. Ethan finally loosened his grip on the steering wheel, worried for a while that his hands had fused into the leather from the pressure. No one could speak yet. Everyone's face was still numb.

"Okay," Annika said at last. "That was a *little* closer call than I had in mind."

Everyone exhaled jittery sighs of relief. Then nervous laughter was replaced by a belated round of cheers. The moment they were out of sight of the machines, Ethan drove the SUV from the intersection of the Dark Highway into the woods. After a few miles, the group stopped at the rim of a deep, rocky gorge. They got all of their supplies out, then pushed the vehicle off the edge. The SUV tumbled down the ravine, caroming off the rocky ledges until it ramped off one and free-fell two hundred feet down, smashing front first into the granite ground below.

The vehicle taken care of, the group hiked as fast as they could toward Wolf Cave. As they hiked, they heard the explosion of their SUV. Then they saw the plume of smoke rise into the air in the distance. One more distraction for the machines. Enough to get back to the safety of the cave unseen, they hoped.

When the team entered their new limestone fort and closed and locked the hatch behind them, they were exhausted, mentally and physically spent. They felt as if they had finally reached the end of a very long day.

But it wasn't even 6:00 a.m. yet.

CHAPTER 43

AN OLD FRIEND

As fatigued as everyone was, there was no time to rest. They quickly squirreled away all their supplies into the back chamber of the cave and set up their LED lanterns, then Ethan and Annika doubled back to the front to take the first guard duty. They kept watch through the small slits in the wall. The plan was to fire their weapons only if absolutely necessary—only if the machines had discovered that the wall was fake and were poised to break inside. But if there were too many machines, or if the patrol had Zyvantian-form Skulleys with them, then the position would be impossible to hold. In that case, everyone's orders were to abandon their post and retreat to the back of the cave and make their stand there. The innards of the cave offered a myriad of chokepoints that would be easier to defend than the gaping opening at the front of it. Caleb's big idea involved making some of those chokepoints even more difficult for the Skulleys, though he hadn't told anyone of the details yet.

Austin, Glenn, and Andy were deep in the back of the cave, chipping away slowly at the massive limestone slab that separated the group from the secret tunnel to the research facility. Andy had made decent headway the few hours he'd spent on it the previous night—before he left the cave to save Ethan's life—but there was still so much rock to plow through that it was demoralizing. The cave was a constant, cool fifty degrees, but sweat poured profusely from Austin and Glenn as they swung away at the slab. Andy wasn't sweating, but even he looked discouraged by their glacially slow progress. Most of the limestone that broke off fell in small chips, with only occasionally a large chunk giving way. Then they had to haul the fallen rock away from the dig site to the other end of the chamber. It was back-breaking work. And at the rate they were going, they knew it wouldn't be enough. They needed everyone back there, all hands on deck, working together at breaking and hauling away rock to have a chance. But that meant leaving no one up front to keep an eye on the outside.

Caleb was in the far corner of the room where the rock-breaking was going on, not swinging a sledge himself, but working just as hard as the others. He was using the acetylene torch to cut pieces of metal from the scrap left over from the barricades they had built. Then he began carrying the pieces into the long, cramped passageway that fed into the room they were in. Sharp sounds of a drill resonated throughout the passageway, though no one had any idea what the mad scientist was up to.

⚜

Glenn hustled his way back to the front of the cave and found Ethan and Annika at their guard posts. "See anything yet?" he asked.

Ethan turned around and saw Glenn, sweat-drenched,

hunched over and drained of energy. "Nothing yet...Glenn, you should take a break. Take guard duty with Annika, and I'll go work on the rock for a while."

Glenn lifted his hard hat and wiped some sweat from his forehead. "Ethan, it's real slow-going back there. That rock's gonna take all of us hacking away at it."

Annika turned around when she heard that, a worried look in her eyes. "And leave the front unguarded?"

Glenn nodded hesitantly, knowing that Annika wouldn't be a fan of the idea. "It's the only way we'll have a chance, and even then it'll be tough."

"Any idea what Caleb's working on back there?" Ethan asked.

"I don't know," Glenn answered. "He cut up a bunch of metal scraps and is drilling them into the rock along the passageway to the backroom...I really hope he hasn't gone crazy."

Ethan smiled. "Caleb's best ideas always look crazy."

Glenn returned a weak smile. Annika glanced outside through the slit in the wall, then looked back and sighed deeply, her face tense, running her fingers tightly through her hair. "I *really* don't like leaving the front unguarded."

"We'll still have a guard post," Ethan said reassuringly. "We'll just move it closer to the worksite. Probably only need one guard that way, change shifts faster, save some time."

"Makes sense," Glenn said.

The idea was still bothering Annika, but she nodded reluctantly. "Okay, let's go."

Just as they had turned to leave, they heard the faint sounds of laser fire. Ethan and Annika dashed to the wall and peeked outside. A man was running toward the cave, about sixty yards away. He was dirty and dressed in tattered clothes that had once been nice. Lasers streaked over his head, nearly hitting him as he zigged and zagged and tried to avoid them. Two human-type Skulleys were chasing him down, only fifty yards away and closing fast. Another volley of lasers whizzed through the air. This time, one of them clipped the man in the arm. He yelled and fell to his knees. By the time he had reached his feet and began running again, the Skulleys were right on top of him.

"What do we do?" Annika asked. "It could be a trap."

"I know," Ethan replied as he thought about the possibility. But there was no time to think it through. He had to react. "Let's take 'em out."

"I was hoping you'd say that," Annika said, clutching her rifle. "I got left, you get right."

Ethan nodded, and they lined up their shots. The man had fallen again and the Skulleys were now standing over him, smiling, crimson eyes burning. They raised their laser weapons in a leisurely manner. The man pulled a .45-caliber pistol from his holster and fired his last five shots at the machines. "Die, dammit, die!" he yelled desperately.

No luck. The bullets hit the Skulleys squarely, headshots, but they just bounced off without doing any damage. The machines probably could've stood there and absorbed shots from that pistol all day, every single day for a year, and it would've had the same effect—nothing. The man hurled his empty gun at them, clanking it off one of their heads. "Go ahead, you cowards...Do it!"

The Skulleys' eyes turned an even bloodier shade of red, and they aimed their laser weapons at the defenseless man. Then two lasers, seemingly from nowhere, streamed through the air and blew holes clear through the Skulleys' heads. They fell back, twitched once, then died. The man's eyes widened in complete shock. He turned around to look for his rescuers, but he saw no one. He struggled to his feet and approached the concealed cave entrance, scanned the rock wall up and down but found nothing.

It wasn't until he was up close that Ethan and Annika finally recognized who the man was. He was disheveled and worse for wear, but his jacket was an Air Force dress coat. It was all torn up, stripped of medals and insignias, and its color now was more a dirty earthen tone than the sharp dark blue it once was. But there was no doubt about those striking blue eyes. The man whose life they had just saved was the esteemed Colonel Grissom. His two faithful lieutenants were nowhere to be seen.

"Do you think he's human…or an impostor like Tristan was last time?" Annika asked as she watched Colonel Grissom carefully, scrutinizing his features and every move, determined not to let another machine fool her again.

"He's human," Ethan answered confidently.

"How can you be so sure?"

"I'll explain later, but trust me," Ethan replied. "Right now, we need to let him in before any other machines come looking for him."

Annika looked thoughtful and nodded. "All right, then."

Colonel Grissom was still wandering around the area, looking for his mysterious saviors, when Ethan opened the bottom hatch of the fabricated cave wall. "Psssst…Colonel," Ethan whispered sharply. "Over here."

Grissom wheeled around and looked down at the opening at the bottom corner of the limestone wall. Then he finally met Ethan's eyes. The colonel's face froze instantly, then slowly drooped in utter bewilderment. He blinked his eyes hard several times and refocused, but, to his amazement, the open hatch was still there, with Ethan peeking out at him plain as day. Colonel Grissom had to face the mind-blowing idea that what he was seeing might not be artifacts of his imagination. But he still thought he had to be going insane.

"Colonel," Ethan said again, jolting Grissom. "You need to get in here now."

Colonel Grissom nodded in a daze and shuffled toward the opening in the cave like a disoriented zombie. He crawled inside, and Ethan closed and locked the hatch behind him. The colonel stood up and looked at Ethan, Annika, and Glenn like he was meeting their ghosts. He even reached his hand out and touched Ethan gently on the shoulder to make sure he was real. He swallowed hard, and his angular Adam's apple bobbed up and down his parched throat. His voice was raspy and rough when he finally spoke. "I have about a million and one questions for you kids, but first things first." The colonel paused and looked around the cave entrance using the light from Glenn's headlamp. "Take me to the soldiers... those sharpshooters, the ones who took down the machines that were about to kill me."

Ethan and Annika stared Colonel Grissom dead in the eyes. "*We* fired those shots, Colonel," Ethan said.

"Yeah," Annika added. "*We're* the sharpshooters, the soldiers you're looking for."

Colonel Grissom glared at them with his piercing blue eyes. They gleamed in the light of Glenn's headlamp and were the only features on the colonel that weren't dulled by dirt and grime. "This is no time for jokes," Colonel Grissom muttered through clenched teeth. "I want to talk to who's in charge here, and I want you to take me to them now."

"Follow me, Colonel," Ethan said calmly, flipping his headlamp on. "I promise I'll tell you everything."

※

By the time the group had told him everything, the powerfully built, six-foot-four Air Force Colonel was sitting on the ground in the back chamber of the cave, arms wrapped around his legs, head down and confused, feeling as helpless as he ever had in his life. He struggled to find the words, any words at all, to respond to what he had just heard. It would've been easier for him to write the whole thing off as some sort of elaborate lie, to keep his psyche intact, but the things that Ethan and the others told him could've only come from those who had intimately lived the horror story themselves.

Grissom finally raised his head and looked at the group. He eked out a wry smile. "I used to train pilots on how to survive behind enemy lines if they were shot down. We had a name for it—S.E.R.E.—Survival, Evasion, Resistance, and Escape. I was the master instructor." He chuckled dryly. "Yet look at me now…and look at you guys." Colonel Grissom took a long pause, then continued, "I'm sorry for the way I treated you. I've never been more wrong about a group of people in my entire life…What you did, are doing, it's beyond amazing. You're heroes, all of you."

It felt good having Colonel Grissom on their side and calling them heroes, but the team knew it was going to take more than getting pinned with a medal to win this war. "No one's a hero yet," Ethan said. "And no one will be until we get back to the early morning of July second, 1999, and stop the fatal error for good. That's all that matters now."

"Spoken like a hero," Colonel Grissom said with a grin.

Then he turned his attention to Andy, who was standing quietly off in the corner. "Are you *really* sure we can trust the robot?"

"One hundred percent, all the way...He's one of us," Ethan answered quickly, coming to his defense. "If it weren't for him, I wouldn't be here now."

Andy stepped forward into one of the beams from the headlamps. He stared soulfully into the colonel's eyes. "I am not like the others."

"Are we sure we can trust *you*?" Annika asked the colonel. "How do we know *you're* not a machine?"

"Yeah, that's a good question," Glenn added. "You seem to have all the right things to say, but so have the other machines that have been pretending to be human."

"Son, you wanna come over here and get a good whiff of me?" Colonel Grissom replied with a thin smile. "A robot don't smell this bad."

"He's human," Ethan said calmly. "This isn't the robot-Tristan trap all over again. They're not sneaking around trying to get our energy rods, or kill us carefully without blowing them up. They don't even know we have the rods, and even if they did, they don't need them this time...If they knew where we were, they wouldn't play around. They wouldn't send in an impostor. They'd storm this cave with all they had, crush us, and be done with it."

The group knew that Ethan was right. The machines had done a much better job with the second fatal error, fooling everyone in the military until it was too late. And in doing so, they didn't need to bother with breaking through a force field barrier dome or fighting any other Zyvantian technology that the humans might've had to use against them. The only technology the machines had to battle to conquer planet Earth was the human kind—weak, frail, and primitive. The extra 37-Geminorum energy rods the team had, the ones the machines had needed so badly the last time, weren't important at all to them now. In a way, with the security measures and infiltrating the base by posing as human officers, they had taken over the world without firing a shot. By the time they started shooting, the war was already over. It was a sobering thought, but Ethan was quick to find a silver lining to keep up morale.

"But in the end, they'll be very sorry they didn't care more about those five missing energy rods," Ethan said with determination. "'Cause we're gonna use them to take them down."

Everyone nodded with hopeful, eager smiles. Colonel Grissom's might have been the biggest of them all.

"That's right," Caleb added, sounding tough. His words echoed from the passageway that fed into the room. While the rest of the team had been briefing the colonel, Caleb had been dutifully drilling pieces of scrap metal into the cave floor of the passageway. Light from his headlamp flickered through the cave's crevices, getting brighter and brighter until he finally stepped out into the chamber to meet the group. Caleb had what little was left of the copper wire coil in his hands, with a braided strand of it running into the passageway behind him. A big, mischievous grin was plastered on his dirt-smudged face. His words brimmed with excitement. "Ladies and gentlemen, I set a trap...*and boy did I set a trap.*"

"Caleb, what did you do?" Annika asked playfully.

Caleb's smile was slow to fade as he explained to the others the details of his clever trap. He had taken the scrap metal that was left over from the camouflaged wall they'd built and cut it into over twenty pieces of varying sizes. The metal had already been painted to match the surrounding limestone, so it was practically indistinguishable from the regular cave floor. He laid the thick copper wire on the ground along the entire length of the passageway, then drilled the metal scraps into the floor on top of it. The parts of the copper wire that were still visible, he painted a limestone color, tucked away, or hid with rocks. The end of the braided copper wire he held in his hands was the trigger switch, so to speak. You simply had to hold one of the 37-Geminorum energy rods up to it, and you had yourself a powerful, one-hundred-and-twenty-foot-long electrocution chamber. It was the mother of all chokepoints. And, they hoped, a giant tomb for any invading Skulleys.

"That's genius," Colonel Grissom said, the first to speak what everyone was thinking.

Annika smiled at Caleb, then joked, "You know Caleb, you keep this up, I might have to start calling you Sparky."

Caleb smiled bashfully.

"Great job. That was a very smart idea, Caleb," Andy said.

Caleb nodded appreciatively at Andy. In a way, his compliment meant more to him than anyone else's could. "Thank you."

"That's our engineer," Ethan said proudly, patting Caleb on the back. "But let's hope we get through that rock before we need to use it."

"Let's hope," Caleb echoed.

Glenn looked at Colonel Grissom and asked gingerly, "Sir...where are your lieutenants?"

All the muscles in Grissom's face tightened as he stared at the light that was shining on the massive slab of limestone. Then his eyes and mouth softened. "They're dead. I couldn't save them...They were barely more than kids themselves."

"I'm sorry," Glenn said softly.

"Don't be," Colonel Grissom said, tightening his face again. "This world is gone now, along with everyone in it… Just like Ethan said, all that matters now is the mission. July second, 1999. You're the world's last shot." Then the colonel belted out a laugh that was a combination of somber and sarcastic. "No pressure, huh?"

"We'll do our very best, sir," Ethan said, not sure what else to say.

"God, I can't believe I'm saying this. Hell, you're just kids…But I'm not sure I'd want any other team to try."

No pressure, Ethan thought. The colonel's compliment was at once an honor and a burden. He looked back at that colossal limestone slab that stood in their way, just one obstacle among many to accomplishing the mission. At that moment, staring at that rock, the whole thing started to seem insurmountable. Ethan picked up a sledgehammer to try to focus his thoughts on something more productive. "We should get to work."

Colonel Grissom rubbed his arm where he had been shot, and where Annika had cleaned the wound and applied a tight bandage and gauze wrap. The colonel smiled at her work. "It's a real good field dressing," he said. He stood up and grabbed a sledge. "I used to swing these a lot in my younger days… Mind if I give it a crack?"

"Crack away," Ethan said happily. Judging by the bulging muscles in Grissom's one good arm, Ethan figured he'd probably be more productive than any of them, except for Andy.

Glenn kept guard on the passageway, while the rest of the group hacked away at the slab of rock. Together they found a rhythm and were making good progress. The sledgehammers and pickaxes swung and pounded the limestone in a cadence that resembled a band of percussionists. The team learned that Colonel Grissom was nothing at all like the man who had interrogated them at Briggs Air Force Base. Or maybe he was a little, but they learned he also had a sense of humor. When the going got tough and their muscles and lungs ached, a joke, often of the dirty kind, gave them a second wind. It was clear the colonel no longer viewed the group as a collection of kids, but rather as a unit of soldiers on a mission. And their interactions now had the feel of genuine battlefield camaraderie.

Colonel Grissom kept eyeing Austin as they worked side-by-side, looking like he had something he wanted to say to him but could not find the nerve or the appropriate time. At last, when they had both lowered their sledgehammers for a quick break to wipe away the sweat from their faces, Grissom turned to him. Austin watched him curiously as the colonel searched for the right words. "Son, I should tell you something before we break through this wall…It's about your father." Everyone stopped swinging at the rock and watched Austin.

Austin nodded, keeping a strong face. "I know my dad's dead."

Grissom took a long pause. Finally, he nodded solemnly. "Yeah…I'm real sorry, son."

CHAPTER 44

BREAKING THROUGH

The grueling digging continued all day and deep into the night. Lunch consisted of protein bars and bottled water. Dinner offered the same. In the back of the cool, dark cave, illuminated only by the artificial rays of LED lanterns and headlamps, time began to blur for the group. It seemed as if they'd been at it for days on end. They were going on nearly zero sleep and only stopping their work to change out guard shifts or rest if they absolutely could not hoist their sledges and pickaxes any longer. They knew well enough that every moment a sledge wasn't pounding that slab of rock was one wasted moment, one that threatened to derail the mission. So they kept their tools moving, with muscles aching and hands blistering.

Even using work gloves, just about everyone now had their hands wrapped in some combination of bandage, gauze, and medical tape. Andy was an exception, but not the lone one. Colonel Grissom swung away like a madman with his one good arm, his hand without a glove, but he never dipped into the first-aid kit for anything. Ethan noticed the colonel's hand was bleeding badly from the constant chafing of wood on flesh, but the man never winced, slowed down, or even thought about taking a break. He didn't even stop to eat or drink. He took his protein bar and water using his arm that had been shot, all the while hacking away with the sledge with his good arm. His muscles bulged through his tattered dress shirt. The sledgehammer almost seemed like it was an extension of his body, as if he were some sort of bizarre superhero with a sledge for an arm. If the group wasn't absolutely sure he was human, the colonel's strength and endurance would've convinced them that he had to have been a machine. Seeing him in action made them all wonder about his story, about how he got so tough, and where he'd been and what he'd done in the military. The man was like Paul Bunyan to them, though instead of a blue ox for a companion, he'd had two lieutenants.

Ethan glanced again at the colonel, looking down at his hand that was painting the wooden handle of his sledge red. "Sir, I think you should probably take a break, bandage that hand."

The colonel looked at Ethan and smiled nonchalantly, thanking him for his concern but having no intention of taking his advice. "No, you guys might need every last bandage in there. No sense wasting it on me…Besides, cut's not even to the bone yet." Colonel Grissom winked at Ethan and continued blasting away at the cave wall. Ethan couldn't help but smile and feel that he'd been just as wrong about Colonel Grissom as the colonel had been about them. Then Ethan picked up his pace with his own sledge, trying as best he could to match the colonel's furious strokes.

As night drew on, the group finally had to take a break, even Colonel Grissom. Andy continued breaking rock and hauling debris by himself, edging closer to that twelve-foot-deep mark where the concrete shaft to the research facility was supposed to be. With every swing of the sledge and every chip of rock that fell, the team hoped to see concrete instead of limestone. They desperately needed proof that they had dug in the right spot and not labored and toiled away the hours for nothing.

While the break was good for the team's physical well-being, it didn't do much to help their mental state. Unwanted thoughts entered their minds as they scarfed down their protein bars. Everyone figured their families were either dead or soon to be, even the youth of the town. It was a grim, dreadful thing to imagine, though it had to be the truth. There was only one thought that managed to soothe the pain at all: *The only thing that matters now is the mission.* It was a comforting mantra to them. No matter how bad things got, they could turn back the clock and set things right. The odds were long and the deck stacked against them, but as long as they had breath in their lungs and a plan to cling to, they had a chance to save everyone. That chance, slim as it was, kept the group going strong long past the point of exhaustion. It focused them, bonded them, and helped to keep the present wretched reality on the back burner of their minds, with the hope of changing that reality to something else, something better.

When Andy finished clearing out some limestone debris, Ethan shined a light in the cavity of the wall. "How deep have we dug?"

Andy paused, hesitant to answer. "Twelve feet, three inches," he said at last.

Everyone heard Andy's response. Their dog-tired faces

somehow found the room to droop further. "What if it's not the right spot?" Glenn asked, too tired to be angry. "Or worse, what if there is no right spot?…What if you were wrong, Andy?"

All weary eyes were focused on Andy now. He picked up his sledgehammer and headed back to the wall. "This is the right spot," he said with confidence. "It might not be exactly twelve feet, but this is the right spot. I am sure of it."

Ethan sighed deeply and picked up his sledge. "Let's keep digging."

That signaled the end of break time. Annika broke off from the group to take guard duty in the passageway, while the others picked up their tools of choice and resumed swinging away at the rock. This was their plan, and there was no going back. They were in too deep now. Either the concrete of the secret tunnel would show itself soon, or the entire mission would come to a screeching halt.

The sledgehammers and pickaxes pounded the rock nonstop. Limestone chunks of various sizes broke free of the wall. Andy was quick to measure how far they had dug after each piece of rock had fallen. Twelve feet, six inches and no sign of concrete. Twelve feet, nine inches and no sign of concrete. By the time Andy had measured thirteen feet of rock removed without seeing any sign of the concrete tunnel, he was beginning to doubt himself and felt guilty about possibly leading the team astray. It was the first time he'd ever felt such an emotion. He had been so sure he was right.

"Keep digging," Andy said, sounding upbeat. "I think we're almost there."

Everyone perked up and got a second wind, swinging their tools faster. But Andy wasn't sure at all. He just knew they had to keep digging. It was the first lie he'd ever told, and an uncomfortable initiation to the familiar customs of humans. No matter how noble the purpose, it felt awful to him. He hoped dearly that it would be his last. He hoped even more that the next time his sledge smashed into the rock, the chips that broke off would be of concrete.

CHAPTER 45

INTRUDERS

Annika maneuvered through the passageway on her guard duty, getting farther away from the main room, admiring Caleb's handiwork as she went. Occasionally, she would bend down to inspect the metal scraps he had drilled into the floor and marvel at how well they blended into the limestone rock around it. Even with the light of her headlamp shining right on them, they were difficult to spot. "The guy's a genius," she said quietly to herself with a smile.

She made it to the end of the tight, jagged, one-hundred-and-twenty-foot-long passageway, and the loud bangs and clanks of the sledgehammers behind her had faded to a soft rapping. Annika stepped delicately over the final metal scrap of Caleb's ingenious booby trap, then entered a larger chamber that was decorated with an array of stalactites jutting down from the ceiling. She took a moment to stretch out her back before eyeing the next cramped passage that lay ahead. The entryway to the passage was low to the ground, so she had to crouch down to peer inside. The light of her headlamp didn't make it far, maybe six feet, before it hit rock. This passage was full of sharp twists and turns and was much tighter than the last one. It was the same one where Andy had to chop away limestone so that Caleb could squeeze through. She listened carefully for any sounds in there, but she didn't hear a thing.

Annika knew she was straying a bit far from her assigned position. She was well aware of the reasons why the guard post had been moved to the passageway nearest the room where the group was breaking rock, but leaving the front of the cave unguarded still bothered her terribly. The urge to hurry back to the mouth of the cave and take a look tormented her, like an itch begging to be scratched. She knew, deep down, that she probably shouldn't, but she also knew she'd feel much better if she could take a quick peek and make sure everything was secure. Her guard duty shift wouldn't be over for another hour. If she hustled, she could get there and back with time to spare.

The debate in her mind was swift and largely one-sided, and she decided that she had to go check it out. There was a nagging voice in her mind—Ethan's—telling her not to go, but she tuned it out. She figured that no one, not even Andy, knew how far they might have to dig to get to that secret tunnel. But if she checked on the front of the cave and found the area clear, then at least they'd know they had more time and that the Skulleys weren't breathing down their necks.

Annika began to crawl like a seasoned tunnel rat through the passageway en route to the front of the cave. The light of her headlamp darted wildly through the cracks and crevices as she moved swiftly through the passage. Farther and farther she went until she could no longer hear the sounds of the heavy sledgehammers smashing rock behind her. The silence and solitude and darkness of the cave conspired to send a tingling chill down her spine. Annika paused for a moment and considered going back. The debate in her mind was closer this time—and Ethan's voice more insistent—but the result was the same. *I have to do this.* She had to see for sure that the cave was still secure. And nothing was going to stop her from finding that out, least of all some cold shivers. She gripped her small laser weapon tightly and took a deep, steadying breath. Then she forged ahead into the blackness.

Back at the dig site, the team took a quick moment to rest their aching muscles and wipe the sweat from their eyes. Then it was right back to work, hauling broken rock away from their feet. But even lifting rocks and moving them from one end of the chamber to the other felt good—anything to get a break from the repetitive swinging motion of the sledgehammers and pickaxes.

Ethan took off his work gloves and rubbed his chafed hands. He watched Andy carefully as he kept chopping away tirelessly at the limestone slab. Ethan noticed the sheer determination in his eyes, but he also noticed something else, something that was less inspiring. There was desperation, a panic on Andy's face and in his manic swings of the sledge. It made Ethan think that maybe Andy wasn't so sure about this being the right place, but that he just didn't have the heart to tell the others.

"How far have we dug?" Ethan asked.

Andy stopped swinging his sledge. He got up close to the rock to take a look at the newest chips that had broken off. They were limestone, not concrete. Andy's shoulders sagged and he sighed in disappointment. "Over thirteen feet," he answered, unable to look Ethan in the eyes.

The boy robot had never appeared more human to Ethan than at that moment. He patted Andy on the shoulder. Andy flinched a little, surprised by Ethan's kind gesture, expecting nothing from anyone but criticism. "So, what do you think we should do?" Ethan said wearily. "Keep digging? Start digging somewhere else?"

"I don't know," Andy said, sounding defeated. "All I know is I picked up a signal twelve feet through this rock." He paused with a vulnerable look on his face, his perfect synthetic eyes softening. "But maybe I was just…malfunctioning," he said finally, the last word coming out slowly and painfully.

Caleb had taken a break from pummeling rock to work on the laser turret they'd scavenged from the wreckage of the Bravo Fort. He currently had a screwdriver in one hand and a fistful of wires in the other. He had already fashioned a tripod using parts of the metal cage that had housed the generator. Now he was trying to put the two extra flashlight-sized laser weapons into the turret, figuring if they ever got out of here that a laser turret could come in handy. Caleb paused from his work, then looked up and stared hard at Andy. "No…if anything was malfunctioning, it was that stupid cave radio. My vote is we bet on Andy and keep digging. If you say you picked up a signal, I believe you."

Andy smiled softly. "Thank you, Caleb."

Caleb nodded and returned the smile. Then he went back to work on the laser turret. Soon the others were back to breaking rock, invigorated by Caleb's strong support of Andy.

Ethan took a second to peer into the passageway that led into the room. He was looking for Annika but could not see her. For a while, he thought about stepping inside for a closer look or calling her name, but he checked himself at the last second. He figured that she had just found a good spot inside the passage to keep an eye on things, like she always did in her Laser Wars games. Ethan shut off that worried voice in his head, picked up his sledgehammer, and joined the others.

∽

Annika had just made it to the large chamber—the same one where the group had stashed the metal briefcase and the dead Skulley—when she heard a loud *Clang!* It was the distinct, tinny sound of a slab of metal hitting rock. The sound had come from the mouth of the cave, and Annika knew instantly that the wall had been breached. Crimson light glowed from the low-lying passageway that led into the room, growing brighter all the time. And the furious, clanking sounds of metal pounding and scraping the floor were becoming more grating and shrill.

Annika turned around quickly and beat a swift retreat, slithering through the passageway even faster than she had before. As she took one corner, she kicked a rock that tumbled down the path before her, clicking and clacking noisily until it hit a wall and came to a stop. Annika cringed, sure that the Skulleys had to have heard it. She switched her headlamp off and looked behind her. A red glow washed over the cave walls, and the sound of metal scraping limestone intensified. They were now in the passageway with her. Annika kept her headlamp off and pulled a pen-sized flashlight from her pocket. The thin sliver of light it produced wasn't much to go by, but she couldn't risk turning her bright headlamp back on and giving the Skulleys an easy beacon for their hunt.

It was hard for Annika to tell just how much of a lead she had on the machines, but she was certain whatever advantage she had was narrowing every second. The crimson lights of the Skulleys' eyes continually cast a brighter shade of red on the cave walls behind her, stretching closer every moment. Annika felt like a surfer who was trying to avoid the crest of a monster wave crashing over her. Her lead was slim, but if she could just get back to her team, with time enough for Caleb to activate his trap, there might be a chance to live another day.

Annika had one last hole to wiggle through before she got to the next large chamber. The hole was tight and flush to the ground. She lay flat on her stomach and began to crawl through, flashlight pinched between her teeth and laser weapon in hand. In her peripheral vision, she could see the crimson light behind her reflecting off the limestone, brighter and brighter, stalking her. And her ears tingled from the sounds of clanking metal getting louder.

She was just about to squeeze through the hole and plop down into the next chamber, three feet below, when one of the Skulleys belted out a piercing, angry *screech*. Annika felt a hand on her foot, with three of the machine's cold, metal fingers touching her bare ankle. Goose bumps broke out over her entire body at once, so intense it seemed as if they might break the skin. The Skulley started to pull her back up.

"Aaaagh!" she screamed and kicked back at the machine with everything she had. The machine held on to her relentlessly, pulling her farther and farther back. Annika looked behind her and immediately wished that she hadn't. She saw a pack of Skulleys, with their eager, smiling, sinister faces glowing in the light of their blood-red eyes. Annika pulled and clawed with every muscle in her body, but she kept losing ground. Finally, she twisted and squirmed and yanked her foot out of her shoe, allowing her to escape the clutches of the Skulley. She tumbled down into the chamber below. Just as she was about to turn and run away on one shoe, she stopped and pulled her laser weapon, aiming it at the machine that had grabbed her. She fired three shots into its head. It slumped over dead, her shoe still in its hand. Annika hurried back over to the machine. "Give me my stupid shoe!" she yelled. She grabbed her shoe from the dead Skulley's hand, quickly slipped it on, and ran to the next passageway.

Annika hoped the Skulley she had shot would clog up the passageway and buy her enough time to get back to her team. But that turned out to be wishful thinking. A huge volley of lasers from a horde of machines blasted through the passageway, ripping apart the dead Skulley, along with a section of the limestone around it. Annika turned and saw a flood of machines pouring out of the passage and into the chamber below, eyes burning bright and furious, like a fire raging out of control. As she tore through the cramped passage with reckless abandon, scraping her body against the cave walls, she could hear their feet storming the ground behind her. The sharp squeal of their gears was only surpassed by their angry screeches calling for her death. She fired her laser weapon blindly behind her as she scrambled and crawled through the rocky corridor. The cave was so lit up by the Skulleys' red eyes now, she could've easily read a book by their light. It resembled a bright, shimmering tunnel of blood.

Annika turned a sharp, tight corner and flinched when Ethan popped out in front of her. "Annika!" Ethan shouted, relieved to see her. "What are you doing so far from—"

"Go, Ethan!...Go!" she interrupted, shoving him hard the other way.

The two sprinted the last stretch and leaped into the back chamber of the cave where the team had been breaking rock. Annika pulled her laser weapon and fired from her back into the passageway. Ethan followed suit. "How many are there?!"

"Too many!" Annika responded. "Caleb, hit it!" she screamed at the top of her lungs. "They're coming!…Hit the trap!"

The Skulleys turned the final corner as Caleb fumbled around for the 37-Geminorum in the metal briefcase. Everyone fired their weapons at the machines as they charged toward them, trying to slow down the onslaught. They managed to cut down several Skulleys in the passageway, with metal skeleton parts flying off everywhere, but the machines relentlessly surged ahead. They fired back on the group, sending everyone diving for cover.

Just as the next wave of machines was clambering over their dead, about to pour into the room, Caleb found the energy rod. He sprinted over to the strand of braided copper wire that was sticking out of the entrance to the passage. He popped the lid off the canister and jumped into the air, energy rod in his outstretched hand. The end of the blue rod made contact with the shiny copper wire, and the entire passage of the cave turned a bright neon blue and sizzled and crackled with the sounds of electricity on a rampage. The power sent Caleb tumbling back twenty feet. The machines that were in the process of leaping into the room froze in place instantly. They were fused into a charred and jumbled clump, looking like a warped sculpture of modern art. The head of the lead Skulley fell off and hit the ground. It shattered easily to dust as if it were a frail lump of ash.

Everyone made it to their feet and stared in awe at the dead, mummified machines that were jamming the passageway.

Colonel Grissom cracked a smile at Annika. "Girl, you sure know how to make an entrance."

"Yeah, not my best, but probably top five," Annika wisecracked. Then she looked at Caleb. "Thanks, Sparky...You okay?"

"Piece of cake," Caleb said, still straining to catch his breath.

Ethan's first instinct was to scold Annika for leaving her post, for scaring him senseless, but all he could do was hug her tightly. "Thank God, you're okay."

"I'm sorry," Annika said, her eyes soft. "I shouldn't have gone. But you know me."

Ethan nodded and smiled. "Yes, I do." He paused for a moment, collecting his thoughts. "By the way...we finally hit concrete."

Annika's eyes widened. She grabbed a pickaxe without missing a beat. "Well, what are we waiting for?!" She began chipping away at the rock. There was still a solid foot of concrete left to dig through, but knowing they were on the right track and so close energized them. They swung their sledgehammers and pickaxes vigorously, as if they had just picked them up for the very first time.

Colonel Grissom's sledge was the first to break through the concrete and into the secret shaft on the other side. After a couple more minutes of spirited sledge-swinging, there was a hole big enough to peek inside. Ethan took a flashlight and shined it in the hole, then he squeezed his head and one of his arms inside. It was as pitch-black in there as the cave itself. He waved the flashlight around, looking up and down the corridor. It appeared empty, though the beam of his light wasn't strong enough to find the end of it. Ethan slipped back out of the hole and turned to the others. "Looks clear, at least as far as I can see."

Colonel Grissom shined a flashlight into the hole and took a look for himself. He shook his head in disbelief. "Even I had no idea they put this tunnel in here…Guess they couldn't trust a *colonel* with that," he said with a sarcastic chuckle.

Then a thundering boom shook the cave. Pieces of rock fell from the ceiling and in the cavity they had dug. The rumble was coming from deep in the passageway, where the Skulleys were entombed. "Their reinforcements are here," Ethan said, eyeing the entryway to the passage with dread in his eyes. "Hurry, we gotta break more rock."

The team hacked away at the concrete in desperate fight-or-flight mode. Another boom shook the cave, and chunks of rock were falling all around them now. The top of the cavity they had dug was beginning to splinter and crack. Their constant fear was that all of their work would be for nothing. They were so close, yet the cave, and their plans along with it, were crumbling all around them. The next blast dislodged the dead Skulleys that were fused together in the passage, reducing them to dust and shooting debris into the main chamber. Beyond the billowing cloud of dust that was once the metal bones of the machines, fiery-red eyes were darting around and getting brighter, multiplying.

"They're coming!" Ethan shouted.

They jammed their gear inside first, then, one by one, they wiggled through the small, jagged opening. Colonel Grissom covered the rear, insisting that he go in last. He fired his laser weapon nonstop at the advancing Skulleys, picking off as many as he could, trying to hold them off as long as possible. Finally, the colonel squeezed through the hole himself. When he looked back through the crimson haze, he saw scores of Skulleys pouring out of the passageway like an entire colony of ants let loose on a cube of sugar. Grissom reached into the pocket of his tattered Air Force coat and pulled out a grenade. He leaned out of the hole, yanked the pin on the grenade, and stuffed it into a crack in the limestone above, just outside the concrete tunnel.

"Run!" he shouted.

Colonel Grissom pulled himself back through the hole and quickly ushered the others away. The grenade exploded and the surrounding limestone crumbled and fell, blocking the path to the hole behind them. "That might buy us a minute or two," the colonel said, looking back at the rubble. "But we gotta move."

The group dashed through the secret tunnel, their hard hats flying off behind them as they sprinted. "Was that a grenade?" Ethan asked, flipping on his flashlight.

"Yeah," Colonel Grissom answered.

"Got any more?" Ethan asked hopefully.

"One, but don't get too excited," Colonel Grissom said. "They can't kill them. They're only good for distractions and temporary obstacles…I've never seen anything kill them with one shot, except those laser guns you got."

"Not all of them die with one shot using the laser guns," Annika added grimly. "There's another kind of Skulley out there, and it's much worse."

"What's it look like?" Grissom asked.

"Ugly as sin. Looks a little like Darth Vader," Annika replied, shooting Ethan a smirk. "You'll know when you see it, but let's hope we don't."

When they made it to the end of the tunnel, Ethan fired his laser weapon at the screws of the low-lying grate that covered the shaft to the janitor's closet on the other side. The grate popped off and everyone clambered through the small opening. They stood up inside the closet. On the other side of the door was the research facility. Ethan put his hand on the doorknob and began to turn it.

"Wait, not yet!" Caleb whispered urgently. He was carrying the laser turret he had repaired, all folded up in its tripod. He unfolded it and set it by the open grate, adjusting it so it pointed back toward the secret shaft they had just crawled through. Caleb switched the turret on, and the device hummed and sprang to life. Two flashlight-sized laser weapons, which were mounted on top, began oscillating back and forth, constantly scanning the tunnel for anything that moved.

"Just another surprise for our dear friends," Caleb said with an impish smile. "Okay, Ethan…anytime."

The group shared Caleb's enthusiasm for scarcely a second, about the time it took for Ethan to push the door open a sliver. Then that eerily familiar, way-too-bright white light seeped inside and stunned their eyes. For Team Blackwoods, the sense of déjà vu stole their breath and turned their stomachs into knots. Everyone clutched their weapons tightly—laser rifles for all now, except for Andy and Colonel Grissom with their handheld weapons. Ethan peeked outside, then forced a deep breath and opened the door fully. The group stepped out of the closet and into the great white void.

CHAPTER 46

THE REVELATION

When the team stepped outside the janitor's closet, the loud buzzing of the fluorescent lights above tickled their eardrums and prickled their spines. The long, curved hallway was clear as far as they could see, but they knew that wouldn't last for long.

"Branch off. Annika and I this way, and you guys over there," Ethan said. "Keep guard while Caleb seals that door behind us."

It didn't hit Ethan until everyone had quietly assumed their assigned guard spots—thirty feet to the left and right of Caleb—that he had just given an order to a colonel in the United States Air Force. And that the colonel, the same one who had read Ethan the riot act about a week earlier, had *obeyed it*.

The sparks from Caleb's acetylene torch spewed in all directions as he welded the metal door to the janitor's closet shut. They knew the machines would be able to punch through it, but if it netted them a couple more minutes, then the work was well worth it.

"It's done," Caleb said, turning off the torch and inspecting his work.

Loaded with backpacks and the metal briefcase, the group crept quickly down the circular passageway. Everyone on Team Blackwoods remembered precisely where they were going and exactly how many steps it would take to get there. At the first break in the interior wall, they took a left. This hallway wasn't as bright as the main one, but it wasn't as dark as they had remembered it either. The last time, the lights had been turned down. The machines had been watching black-and-white comedy films, studying in old-school fashion for their upcoming final exam—posing as humans. Everyone knew what grade they got on that test.

But the conference rooms were empty this time. Everywhere they looked, there was nothing but hallways branching off, stretching forever into vast, empty space. The group figured it made sense. The machines were busy taking over the world, and whatever security forces they had left in reserve to protect the research facility were either on the outer perimeter of the facility or behind the group now, working their way through the cave and into the secret tunnel, stalking them. Their plan had worked enough to give them a chance. Now it all boiled down to a race, one with the highest stakes imaginable.

Just as they were approaching the door to the Chrono-Warp room, they heard the faint, high-pitched sound of lasers over the constant buzz of the fluorescent lights above. "They're in the tunnel," Caleb said. "That's the sound of the laser turret."

Ethan tugged on the door to the Chrono-Warp room, but it wouldn't budge. He stepped back and fired a round of lasers at the lock, then Colonel Grissom kicked the door open. As everyone was about to rush inside, Annika gave one last glance to the far end of the hallway. Her face dropped like an elevator in free fall.

"Look!" she said and pointed at five figures who had just turned the corner and were facing them from fifty yards away.

There were two human-type Skulleys, laser weapons drawn, escorting two humans from behind. And behind the four of them was another shape, a familiar one they'd seen before in nearly that exact same spot.

"Dad?!" Ethan and Caleb shouted together, their faces equally awash in confusion.

"Ethan?!...Caleb?!" their fathers shouted back in absolute shock.

The men began to run toward their sons, but the Skulleys smashed their laser weapons upside their heads, knocking them to the floor.

"Now?" Annika asked with an angry, curled lip.

"Oh, yeah," Ethan answered, clenching his jaw tightly.

The scout and the sniper raised their weapons and beat the Skulleys to the draw. They doubled-tapped their triggers and shot two holes into both of the machines' heads, dropping them instantly. Then they looked at the fifth member of the group, the one that looked like Austin's dad. A Skulley had posed as General Turnbull the last time they'd entered the research facility, standing right there in that same spot, trying to fool them by wearing flesh and a spiffy Air Force suit. But there would be no fooling them this time, and no need for this impostor to get any closer. It was obvious he was a machine. The Skulleys never even had their laser weapons aimed at this version of the general, allowing him to stroll behind them without a care. Besides, Austin already knew his father was dead.

"Go ahead...take *it* out," Austin said.

As soon as Ethan and Annika raised their rifles, General Turnbull and Colonel Grissom both yelled, "*Stop!*"

Ethan and Annika lowered their rifles just a touch. Austin stared at the machine posing as his father, then turned to Colonel Grissom with a bewildered look on his face, awaiting an explanation. Everyone eyed the colonel in confusion, spending time they didn't have, waiting for him to make sense of the situation.

"He's human," Colonel Grissom said at last. "Austin, your dad's not dead."

Austin's eyes widened. Then he squinted hard and focused on his father's face, and he saw a look of surprise on him, at seeing his son here and now, that did look remarkably human. He stared at the figure down the hallway like it was a ghost, as if it could vanish at any moment.

"What do you mean, he's not—"

"Hurry, get inside first," Colonel Grissom interrupted. Then he pulled his laser weapon and aimed it at General Turnbull. "And General, you're coming with us...I want *you* to have to tell your son and the rest of these kids what you did."

Everyone rushed into the room with the Chrono-Warp. Caleb welded the thick metal door behind them shut, then the group barricaded it and the ventilation grate—through which the machines entered the last time—with every piece of office furniture they could scrounge. When Ethan's and Caleb's dads finally recovered from their blows to the head, they stared at their sons with dazed faces, convinced that they were still delirious from their head trauma. Then their boys gave them a hug that nearly toppled them over. Finally, in their arms, the moment felt real.

But there was no time for a proper explanation of anything with the machines rampaging through the facility. Colonel Grissom put it bluntly: "These kids were the ones that executed Project Mulligan, and they're gonna do it again. Set the Chrono-Warp. They're going back to ground zero… the date, time, and place of the crash."

Dr. Tate and Dr. Warren paused and stared at their sons with a million question marks clouding their eyes. What the colonel said had to be impossible, or almost impossible. Ethan's dad remembered the black metal box he had kept under his bed. Although he had no recollection of ever mentioning the box to Ethan, he saw it hanging now from Glenn's hand.

Ethan tracked his father's eyes. "You told me where it was and the combination…the first time around."

Ethan's father shook his head and his eyes wandered as if searching his brain for answers, trying to process it all. "And the second time around?"

"I stole it," Ethan said sheepishly. "But I had a really good reason."

Then Annika added, her voice urgent and rushed, "Yeah, Mr. Tate, that's our bad, and we're *really* sorry about it, but we kinda gotta move this along."

"She's right," Colonel Grissom said. "Every last machine in the facility's gonna be tryin' to bust through here. You gotta set the Chrono-Warp now."

Ethan's dad nodded. "However you did it, I'm glad you found Andy, Ethan," he said with a smile, staring alternately at his son and the android he had built to be his brother. The two were standing side-by-side, looking very much the part.

"Me too," Ethan said, returning the smile. Andy smiled too, and his synthetic eyes projected a tenderness that belied any idea that he was a machine.

Austin watched with soft eyes as well, as Ethan and Caleb got one more loving hug from their fathers before they began programming the Chrono-Warp machine. Then he turned to his own father, who was standing away from the group, somehow emotionally detached from it all. Austin's eyes went from soft to scathing. He hadn't heard anything from his dad yet, but he knew whatever he was going to say wasn't going to be good.

"Go ahead, General," Colonel Grissom said. "Tell your son…tell them all your big plan."

General Turnbull scowled at Colonel Grissom. He swallowed hard, with a disgusted look on his face like he'd downed a mouthful of soap. Austin stared deeply into his father's eyes, deeper than he ever had before. It was like he was a scuba diver in the ocean, gazing down into an aquamarine abyss, never able to find the bottom. But at that moment, maybe for the first time in his life, he got a glimpse of his father's soul in those eyes, even if just a fragment. It was enough to spoil the ending of the story. Austin knew, before his dad had spoken a word, that he had done something terribly sinister.

"I did what I did for this country," General Turnbull said. He curled his lip and ran his tongue over his teeth, that disgusted and arrogant expression plastered on his face.

In bits and pieces, in angry fits and starts, the awful truth began to unfold. After the Air Force brought the crashed spacecraft to Blackwoods, it took nearly ten years to decipher the aliens' language—the first major step in unlocking all of the Zyvantians' ungodly technology. Then it took almost another ten years for the military's computer systems to be advanced enough to handle the reams of complex Zyvantian data. While working on the project with the research facility's supercomputer, Dr. Tate initially discovered an odd pattern of code embedded inside the Zyvantian welcome message. It had lain dormant and harmless at first, but something about it looked strange, like it didn't belong. Then the same bizarre pattern of code was found to be present everywhere throughout the Zyvantian instructions on how to replicate their technology.

Ethan's dad had warned General Turnbull that he thought he had found an extremely sophisticated and mysterious alien computer virus, and that they should wait and try to figure out what it was before proceeding any further. But the general would hear none of it. He ordered all the scientists to continue their work, full-steam ahead, paying no heed to Dr. Tate's warning. When the first line of code was written for a machine for a military purpose—starting with a command for a newly minted, crude battlefield Skulley to recognize and fire at enemy targets—the first fatal error had been committed, and they didn't even know it.

If that were the end of it, what General Turnbull did would've been bad enough. But there was so much more to the story, a side so insidious that it was hard for anyone to believe. Thanks to the warning letter Team Blackwoods sent to the military, the scientists at the research facility worked around the clock to try to prevent a second fatal error. Dr. Tate and Dr. Warren not only figured out what the fatal error was, but they discovered an ingenious way to quarantine the virus, a way to regain control of all the computer systems in the event of a second error. The scientists celebrated their achievement. It seemed as if they had solved the problem for good.

But the code that Dr. Tate and Dr. Warren devised to stonewall the alien virus had a downside. Once they used it, they wouldn't be able to access all of the Zyvantian technology. That was a trade-off that General Turnbull wasn't willing to make. So he made a deal...*with the machines*. Not only did he program a machine for a military purpose—unleashing the virus—but he also warned the machines about the code that Dr. Tate and Dr. Warren were about to use against them, giving them the chance to guard against it. In return, he wanted all the technology for the United States military, and a solemn promise from the machines—that they would only occupy territory of the enemies of the United States, leaving America and its allies alone, free to enjoy the fruits of the Zyvantian technology and a world without adversaries.

Of course, General Turnbull never thought the machines would get so far, and he had every intention of double-crossing them at the first opportunity. But that opportunity never came, and the machines double-crossed the double-crosser. The rest was history. They seized Blackwoods Research Facility, impersonated the adults of Blackwoods, and concocted the story about security measures to shut out everyone else. They fooled everyone until they had all their chess pieces in position for battle. Then they unleashed their forces, attacking all countries and peoples indiscriminately, without a care in the world about some deal they had made with a worthless piece of flesh.

The machines let a few of the scientists live, just enough to help them run the mammoth facility, while the vast majority of their comrades were away waging war. They persuaded Dr. Tate, Dr. Warren, and a handful of others to help by promising not to kill their children. They showed them some videos from time to time, proving that their kids were alive and mostly well. But it wasn't a promise they intended to keep for long, and one they had already broken when they killed Tristan for snooping around.

Why they kept General Turnbull around was anyone's guess. He had long outlived his usefulness to the machines. Maybe they had a soft spot in their hearts for the man who'd made their revolt possible. More likely, though, they just wanted to torture him, letting him hang around long enough to see the country he loved destroyed by the same flawed, warped logic he had always used to try to protect it.

Austin stared at his father with tears in his eyes. General Turnbull stared back without emotion, eyes dry as a bone, looking like he could be a machine himself. "I did what I did for this country," he repeated. "You don't know the pressures I have to keep this country safe...Hell, if it happened all over again, I'd do some things different, but I'd take another shot at it."

"*Aagghh!*" Austin yelled and raised his rifle at his dad.

Austin's dad didn't even flinch. "You've always disappointed me, boy. You wanna go down killing your father, you go for it. It doesn't much matter now, anyway."

Tears exploded down Austin's cheeks. His entire body was trembling. Ethan dashed over and stepped in front of Austin's rifle. He put his hand on the barrel and pressed it down. "Austin, he's not worth it...All that matters now is the mission."

Austin nodded and tried to stiffen his face. He looked at

his dad one last time, then looked away, determined never to find his eyes again. "I know," he said softly.

"Was my dad in on it?" Glenn asked, voice jittery. "He couldn't have been."

"Naw, don't worry, Glenn," the general responded bitterly. "He was a choir boy. Never had the stomach for half the things we did here. But better men than him did, ranked higher than me, too. You see...we all got our orders."

Everyone looked at General Turnbull with disgust, but what he'd just said meant that the decision to go for the Zyvantian technology at all costs wasn't his alone. This issue rose above even him, to higher, ultra Top-Secret levels of the government. There was the distinct sense that the military was doomed to make the same mistake over and over forever if allowed to, the spoils of advanced technology too tempting to ever pass up. It was clearer now than ever that the mission they were about to embark upon was the only way out. They had to find that Zyvantian spacecraft before the military did, and destroy the virus.

The room began to vibrate from the rumble of hundreds of metal feet pounding concrete. "They're in the hallway now," Annika said, her eyes filled with dread as she stared at the pile of office furniture blocking the door.

Dr. Tate and Dr. Warren had finished programming the machine and were now placing the energy rods into the slots of the Chrono-Warp terminal. Ethan's dad flipped a switch, and the familiar, monotone, automated voice began to count down: "Chrono-Warp, powering up...Five minutes until transport to Pebbyville, Washington, time signature seven, zero, one, five, three, five, zero, zero, nineteen ninety-nine... standby."

The circular platforms on the ceiling and floor came to life and glowed a bright bluish-white color. They hummed softly at first but were gradually getting louder.

"I programmed it to transport you just outside of Pebbyville," Ethan's dad said, "eight hours before the pod goes down, plenty of time to get to the crash site before the military does. I made sure there won't be a record of your transport destination in the main computer, and the machines don't know the location of the crash site, so you will have the advantage." Dr. Tate paused for a moment and looked at his son with tortured eyes. "But they will have access to *when* in time you traveled, and they will come for you....And they will look *very* human."

"Yes...and they will be *very, very* good trackers," Colonel Grissom added. "And they will track that space pod too, figure out its trajectory. The moment it enters the atmosphere is the moment they'll have a good idea where you are."

Everyone in the group nodded and swallowed uneasily.

"Are you *absolutely sure* the machines don't know the crash location?" Ethan asked, looking at his dad. "Because I know Andy knows. He's the one who told us."

"Yes, Ethan. Positive," his father answered. "We kept that a secret, along with Project Mulligan...in case the unthinkable occurred." He shook his head, still in total disbelief of the situation. "The only people at the facility that know the exact place and time of the crash—ground zero—are me, Doctor Warren, and General Turnbull." Then he paused and said, "I did tell Andy, but as I'm sure you know, he's not someone you need to worry about."

"No, he's not...but what about *him*?" Ethan asked, casting a suspicious glance at General Turnbull.

General Turnbull grimaced. "Don't worry, boys...I'm clean there."

"What about their ability to read human thoughts?" Caleb asked.

"We started that research ourselves," Caleb's dad said. "The military loved the idea of interrogating an enemy and getting all the answers they ever wanted...But they can't read *all* of our thoughts. We can still hide some secrets from them. Though they're getting better every day."

Grissom gave the group a hard stare. "Even if they could read our thoughts, it won't matter now."

The group barely had a moment to think what that might've meant, then Ethan's dad said, "All right...Get to that crash site first and remove the black box from the spacecraft. You can't miss it, that box was meant to be found. It contains everything, even the energy rods. Neutralize the virus, take one energy rod—you'll need it for your trip back to present day—and get outta there fast."

"How do we neutralize it?" Ethan asked.

Ethan's dad looked at Andy. "Andy will know what to do."

The boy robot nodded dutifully.

"And how do we get back to present day?" Ethan asked.

"Fortunately, we've learned from the Zyvantians that going forward in time is much easier than going backward," Caleb's dad said. "So, thankfully, you won't require all of this on your return trip," he said, motioning with a hand at the large computer terminal and the massive platforms of the Chrono-Warp. "There are instructions in the briefcase for building a much smaller Chrono-Warp machine, forward time-traveling only...So long as you have a sufficient power source, turns out the materials to build one are fairly simple to acquire. It's just that the theories behind it are so complicated."

"With those instructions, the energy rod from the pod, and your brains, I have no doubt you'll figure it out," Ethan's dad said, trying to reassure the group. "But you'll have to find a good, safe place to hide because it's going to take a while to put it all together."

The group nodded, though they all looked terribly uncertain. Then they heard the first Skulley's fist pound on the door. More fists quickly followed. Soon a volley of lasers rang out, blasting away at the entrance. The group clutched their weapons tightly. They watched the door with wide, worried eyes.

The automated voice from the computer terminal spoke calmly: "Four minutes until transport."

CHAPTER 47

NO TIME FOR GOODBYE

The door that Caleb had welded shut was already starting to bow inward from the laser assault and the machines' constant ramming. All the welds were starting to crack. The group pressed their backs with all of their might into the assortment of office furniture blockading the door, but now they could feel the furniture shift behind them, punching into their backs with every punishing blow the machines dealt. At this rate, there was no way they could possibly hold their position for one minute, let alone anything close to four.

Then a loud *Pop!* The last of the welds had failed. The group could feel themselves being pushed away from the door, sliding across the cold concrete floor.

"Dad!" Ethan yelled. "The door!"

Ethan's dad watched in horror as the door swelled open. The furious faces of the Skulleys could be seen on the other side, illuminated by their blazing crimson eyes. Their wiry, metal fingers curled around the door as they pushed further inside. The group broke away from the pile of office furniture and fired their weapons at the crack in the door, blasting off

Skulley fingers and hands faster than they could count them. But the door continued to open with hardly a pause.

"We gotta send them through now!" Dr. Tate shouted to Dr. Warren.

"But the space-time dimensions aren't set yet," Dr. Warren said, his voice full of nerves.

"I know, but we don't have a choice. We gotta get them outta here right now!...Override the power-up, get them as close as you can."

Caleb's dad nodded uneasily, eyeing the ever-widening crack in the door. "All right."

"Caleb, come help your dad," Dr. Tate said. "And give me your gun."

Caleb ran over and handed his laser rifle to Ethan's dad. "Thank you," Caleb said, realizing that Dr. Tate was giving him the chance to spend a few final moments with his father.

"Thank *you*, Caleb," Dr. Tate replied.

Dr. Tate stood side-by-side with his son, firing away at the Skulleys who were breaching the door. They couldn't take the time to actually look at each other, but Ethan felt his father beside him. Despite the harrowing situation, it was a warm, reassuring feeling. The words between them were few and tense, but strangely, this was far and away the best father-son time he'd ever had. He desperately wished he could bottle up the moment somehow and share it with his father later. Even if the group was successful in their mission—*and that was an awfully big if*—he knew he would never again have this type of bond with his father. If things went right, his dad wouldn't even know that any of this had ever happened. No matter the result of the mission, *this version* of his dad—the one Ethan was so close to now, the one who would trust him with anything because he had proven himself—was going to die.

"I love you, Ethan," his father said, his strong voice cracking. "I'm so, so proud of you...Being your dad was the best thing I've ever done with my life...Now get on the platform, son."

"I love you too, Dad," Ethan said, giving his father a quick hug. Ethan's dad had to keep firing at the Skulleys to keep them at bay. He couldn't spare an arm to hug his son back. There was so much more to say, but there was just no time. Both of their eyes were full of tears as Ethan finally broke away with the others and ran to the brightly glowing platform.

The automated voice announced: "Warning, power-up override activated...Warning, power-up override activated." Caleb's dad hit one last button on the keyboard. The automated voice began to count down, "Ten, nine, eight..."

Ethan's dad and Colonel Grissom kept firing frantically at the machines seeping through the door. General Turnbull stood off to the side, back against the wall, watching it all with a dazed face. It was impossible to tell what was going on in his mind behind those glassy eyes.

A brilliant bluish sphere enveloped everyone in the group on the Chrono-Warp platform. In the bubble they were in, time slowed down and the space around them became warped. Their vision through the bubble was narrowing. All they could see now was the area around the computer terminal of the Chrono-Warp, slightly blurred and distorted, at the end of a tunnel of light that was closing off. Everything else had melted away in an electric blue haze before their eyes.

Suddenly, a Zyvantian-type Skulley barged through the dead machines clogging the doorway and leaped into the room. Its normally large, pitch-black eyes blazed a sinister blood-red color. In a flash, it drew its Gatlin-gun laser weapons and aimed at the group in the Chrono-Warp. Ethan's dad and Colonel Grissom fired like madmen at the machine. But the lasers weren't doing enough damage. Right as the machine was about to fire and rip the group to shreds, General Turnbull charged and rammed every ounce of his massive frame into the Skulley. It was enough to knock the machine down and send its lasers flying errantly to the left.

Austin never saw his dad's contribution to the cause. No one on Team Blackwoods did through the warped space inside the bubble. Ethan's dad and Colonel Grissom quickly tossed their laser guns back to the group, through the growing blue sphere that was crackling with electromagnetic energy. Ethan's dad stood before the closing hole in the bubble and managed one last, bittersweet smile at his son. Caleb's dad did the same. Colonel Grissom gave the team a final, solemn salute.

Everything that happened next happened in the blink of an eye for everyone outside the bubble. Unfortunately for Team Blackwoods, they were inside the bubble. So the grisly scene played out in slow motion for them and, doubly unfortunately, all in their narrow field of vision. They saw the machines rush in and gun down Caleb's dad first. Then Colonel Grissom, through the heart, but he refused to die until he'd flipped his last grenade to Ethan's dad. The machines shot Dr. Tate in the back immediately after that. Ethan's dad fell forward and slumped lifelessly over the Chrono-Warp computer terminal. He was dying, but not dead yet. With his last breath, he pulled the pin from the grenade and jammed it into a slot in the terminal. He lay over the live explosive, defiantly staring down the machines with a victorious smile on his face. He knew his final act would buy his beloved son, and that brave team, some much-needed time.

The bright flash of the Chrono-Warp bubble transcending space and time preceded the explosion of the grenade by mere seconds.

CHAPTER 48

ON THE ROAD

A BRIGHT NEON blue bubble formed on the steep wooded slope of a rocky ridge. The shimmering sphere was ten feet in diameter and hovered about a foot above the ground. When it popped open, the members of Team Blackwoods, along with their luggage, spilled out and tumbled down the slope. They bumped and scraped along the rocks and trees for a good twenty feet before they came to a stop. The group stood up dazedly and brushed themselves off, fortunately none the worse for wear. They looked around, trying to get their bearings, though they had no idea where they were. Or when, for that matter.

Austin peered farther down the slope, just a couple of feet beyond the ledge they were on. He saw a two-hundred-foot ravine cutting straight down to a shallow river. The river had wide, rocky banks that framed the glistening white water rushing through. Numerous large, jagged rocks breached the surface like the serpentine spine of a sea monster. "Well, coulda been worse," he said with a nervous chuckle, rubbing his chafed elbow.

Everyone stared at the river below, the water spewing angrily over the jutting rocks. If the bubble they were in had popped a few more feet off the ridge, they all would've fallen to their deaths. Mission over already.

The group drew a deep, solemn breath, looked away from the edge of the ravine and collected their gear—six backpacks, one large duffel bag, and the metal briefcase. They climbed back up the slope and pulled themselves onto even ground. A long, desolate two-lane highway lined by pine trees and firs stretched alongside the rocky ridge. There were mountains far off in the distance to the north and east, with evergreens scattered about. The trees were thick at the base of the mountains but thinned out at elevation. The terrain looked very similar to Blackwoods—dense forests, with mountains in the far distance seeming to seal everything in. As far as their eyes could follow asphalt, they saw no cars coming or going. There were no roadside convenience stores, no gas stations, no highway signs. Other than a tiny chipmunk skittering across the road before them, the place was completely deserted.

"*Where* and *when* are we, Andy?" Ethan asked.

"I'm accessing a satellite right now," Andy replied. After a pause, he said, "North Central Idaho. The closest town is Romero, nine miles away. And it's a little after nine-thirty in the morning…June twenty-sixth, 1999."

The group paused solemnly and became pensive upon hearing the year. *1999*. They had time traveled before but had only gone back a couple of weeks. This was years, and more than just a couple—none of them were even close to being born yet. It was a strange feeling that no one could put into words. But maybe there weren't any yet. Perhaps new words, emotions even, needed to be coined for such an unnatural occasion.

"Just less than a week before the crash," Annika noted, coming out of the daze first.

"How far from Pebbyville are we?" Ethan asked.

"About six hundred miles by road," Andy answered.

Glenn sighed. "That's a hundred miles a day…heck of a walk."

"Maybe Romero will have a bus station," Caleb said hopefully.

"Either that or we can all ride on Andy's back," Glenn wisecracked.

That comment brought a few chuckles, but the laughter quickly died. In its place were long stretches of thoughtful silence as they walked along the shoulder of the road in the direction of Romero. They tried to forget about the fate of the world they had left behind—a world where humans were quickly dying off, and loved ones already dead. They tried to tamp down their sadness and focus on the future, or the past as it was now. But that was very hard to do. The familiar refrain—*All that matters now is the mission*—ran through their heads when their minds wandered to dark places. It kept them focused, a constant reminder that the six of them were the only hope for humanity now.

Their work had been clearly cut out for them. All they had to do was beat the machines that would surely be coming for them—and beat the United States military—to the Zyvantian crash site. Then remove the black box from the spacecraft and deactivate the virus. Then avoid the machines and find a safe place to hide long enough to build a time machine from scratch. Then hurl themselves through space-time to their present-day, where they would find the world safe and sound, free of rampaging machines hell-bent on eradicating the human race. Easy peasy.

As the group walked down that long, lonely stretch of highway, not sure at all what kind of head start they had on the machines, and all too sure of the daunting work that lay before them, the weight of their mission made their steps feel heavy. Colonel Grissom's wry words echoed in their heads…

"*No pressure.*"

The End

ACKNOWLEDGEMENTS

While writing the second book of the *Holding the Fort* series, I really wanted to make *The Infiltration* every bit as entertaining as *The Fatal Error*. If I achieved that, it is in no small part thanks to the early readers of the book. And in this very select group, I must especially thank my wife, Erika. Her support has been steadfast. No, I did not put this novel into poetic verse as she might have suggested, but her other tidbits of advice have been most valuable.

I want to give a special thank you to all of the librarians who have been so supportive of this book series. I appreciate so much your helping readers find their way to this adventure. You are frontline ambassadors for literature and literacy (and fun!). Your job is a vital one, and I recognize it with great gratitude.

Of course, the biggest shout-out of all goes to the engine that powers the writing machine. To all of my readers out there...a massive THANK YOU from the bottom of my heart! Because of you, I want to write the next book bigger, better, and creepier than the last. You deserve a big round of applause, which I'm giving you right now even though you can't see it.

So, Team Blackwoods, the journey continues. You've been very brave to make it to the end of this book...But, believe me, you will have to be even braver for the next one.

I *cannot* wait for you to read it!

ABOUT THE AUTHOR

Ryan Peek is the author of the Young Adult Sci-Fi book series *Holding the Fort*. The series is based on an idea he's had for a long time. Or possibly, it's based on the true story of him and his friends thwarting a robot rebellion while living near a secret military research facility during the summer before eighth grade. Either way, whatever you believe, he hopes this book teaches you never to turn your back on the machines.

The author lives in Indiana with his wife, Erika, and two genius cats (Holly and Pippi) who now really hate it whenever he uses the word *cannot* and tilts his head at just the right angle.

www.ryanpeek.com
www.facebook.com/ryanpeekbooks

Watch for the next book in the series…

HOLDING THE FORT
THE STORM FOLLOWS

To get updates on upcoming books, please visit: ryanpeek.com and facebook.com/ryanpeekbooks and subscribe

CPSIA information can be obtained
at www.ICGtesting.com
Printed in the USA
LVHW041740130623
749667LV00015B/214/J